Crossing the Crazy Woman

Rod McFain

2021 White Bird Publications, LLC

Copyright © 2021 by Rod McFain

Published in the United States
by White Bird Publications, LLC, Austin, Texas
www.whitebirdpublications.com

Paperback ISBN 978-1-63363-552-4
eBook ISBN 978-1-63363-553-1
Library of Congress Control Number: 2021948244

PRINTED IN THE UNITED STATES OF AMERICA

Dedication

For Linda—My Annie Laurie
Her face, it is the fairest,
That e'er the sun shone on.

In Remembrance of Mikalena.
A magnificent horse and best friend.

Crossing the Crazy Woman

**White Bird
Publications**

We are all a bit broken in some way, but
remember...even broken crayons can fill
a page with glorious color...

—*Author Unknown*

Chapter One

1868

Going home was like holding a woman—something he didn't do often enough. Graham Wehr, Gray to everyone except his mother, wouldn't trade ten acres of the Bighorn Mountains for the entire Great Plains. For four days, he rode through nothing but dry rolling hills and bluffs. Only April and the tall grass was turning brown from hot weather and little rain. The golden plains, for Gray's part, the Indians could keep 'em.

Sweat stung Gray's eyes; his mare smelled of it. Flies swarmed around them, a few of them horseflies drawing blood every time they bit. Gray only half expected to see the Platte River from the top of this new bluff. When he brought the bay up the crown of the hill, he didn't. The ache in his knees and back deepened. "Lena," he sighed at the sight of more endless vista, "next time I pull a stunt like this, you oughta throw me and kick me in the head."

Well past mid-afternoon, the sun cast long shadows, but the heat refused to ease up. The day, like the whole trip home, drug on long and tedious. Of course, the only likely relief from the boredom on this prairie would be having Sioux or Cheyenne shooting arrows at him.

The Teton Lakota living in the valleys and mountains close to Wehr's home lived peacefully with the whites. Early settlers came to the valley before 1830 and worked hard at making friends with the Lakota before building the little town they named High Meadows. The last real trouble with any Indians had been a Blackfoot raid in 1834. In March and April of 1865, when the Lakota and Cheyenne gathered their forces for attacks against every white settlement from the Powder River area through the Bighorns and Bozeman Trail, High Meadows remained safe.

Now, the Lakota nations: the Ogallala, Hunkpapa, Brule, Miniconjou, as well as the Northern Cheyenne, were dying of cholera, smallpox, and measles, all gifts from the white man. Stumble across bitter Indians outside the sanctuary of High Meadows, and Wehr faced two choices; outrun them or fight.

A lazy breeze drifted out of the west—barely disturbing the grass, but enough to provide a welcome break to the absolute stillness. Four or five miles further on, Lena started to snort and tug at her bit. Wehr gave the horse her head. Fifteen minutes later, the bay stood knee-deep, splashing her head in the Platte River.

After the mare drank her fill, Wehr nudged her back up on the bank. He stepped down and untied his bedroll. He decided not to bother with building a campfire, sometimes an invitation for unwanted guests. His aching back made stretching out on the cool grass along the river more appealing than a hot meal. Gray would eat jerky for dinner, build a fire in the morning.

At forty, Wehr stood a raw-boned six feet, his flashing green eyes framed by heavy sideburns trimmed neatly at the bottom of his ears. His wavy blonde hair surrendering to a few streaks of gray when the sun hit it right gave him a bit of a roguish appearance, and women considered him a dashing figure.

His mother came from a wealthy Boston family, and she educated him herself, even teaching him French. As a young boy, his father, also Boston raised, listened to fur traders describe the majestic Bighorns. Andrew Wehr recognized the mountains calling. Ten months after he and Rebecca married, they headed west. They named their first son, born on the trip, Graham.

Once dark settled, slumber came fast and deep. Gray didn't stir until heavy dew and a crisp morning chilled him awake. The sun still on the rise, he thought about curling up and going back to sleep. But, instead, Wehr cooked breakfast and put the fire out before anyone else in the area woke up.

While the smell of bacon cooking wafted through the camp, the fifteen-hand bay started to whinny and dance at the end of her tether. Her long mane glistened shiny black; her black tail touched the ground. Well balanced, with a nice slope to her shoulders, Lena possessed an innate ability to anticipate a cow's moves. She could stop and turn instantaneously to cut a cow out of a herd.

"What's the matter with you? You don't eat bacon." As Wehr spoke, the little mare's ears perked up, and her eyes flashed. "There's plenty of grass. What do you want, a drink? Come on. We'll go down to the river," Wehr stroked her face and untied her lead rope.

After the mare drank, Wehr finished his breakfast, kicked dirt on his fire, and rolled up his blanket. The Platte ran deep enough Lena would swim across, which meant starting the day wet, cold, and miserable. Still, better than sleeping last night damp, chilled, and miserable.

"Why don't I learn to stay home with a bed and people to cook my meals?" He knew why. He liked being alone, and he enjoyed talking to his horse, which he did often. "If we run across anybody out here, they'll most likely be Indians. I'm mentioning this so you'll be ready. I'll be wanting you to outrun those Indian ponies. You can—can't you?"

The river turned out to be colder than he expected. On the

other bank, the mare gave herself a vigorous shake. Wehr hated a horse shuddering underneath him. Riders looked foolish when their horse shook. He once saw a fella fall off a shaking horse. Of course, the man was drunk at the time.

Wehr urged the horse northwest across the prairie. Another cloudless day, two hours after sunrise, and already hot. At least drying out from the river crossing would only take a short time.

Around mid-morning, something, a sound or a movement, scared the bay. Lena whirled to the right and reached top speed by her second stride. Wehr, half-asleep from the heat, did not spin with her. Instead, he bounced on the ground. A few strides away, the mare stopped and turned around. After looking around, she decided whatever spooked her left. She relaxed her muscles and began grazing.

"Are you loco?" Sitting up, Wehr gingerly tried to move. The mare walked back over to him and grazed at his feet. He got hold of one of her reins and laid back flat. "Kick my butt, and call me Charlotte. I'm too old for that, Lena. Are you trying to kill me?"

Wehr, a little sore, got up. Little stunts she pulled didn't bother him. On the contrary, they made him fonder of her. He admired her spirit. She did not intend to throw him; she overestimated his riding skills. About a quarter-mile off, a stream meandered down a small coolie. A clump of oaks made it a proper place to take a rest and eat some jerky. Wehr started to climb on the horse but decided a pleasant walk would exercise his aching muscles.

Some live oaks offered ample shade for lunch. Wehr pulled Lena's saddle, and she rolled in the grass before starting to munch at the tender young shoots along the bank.

Deer Tracks covered the mud around the stream. Wehr imagined fresh meat for dinner. Instead of hunting, Wehr let himself slip into a mid-day nap, something that disgusted him. He did not believe in sleeping in the middle of the day.

Shortly after noon, Wehr struggled with being half-asleep, half-awake. He wanted to be on the trail, but he couldn't shake off the sleep. His horse snorting down by the water and flies buzzing around his face woke him.

He saddled and headed northwest along the North Platte. A few hours from where the river forked, Yellow Bird meant a bed and a meal. He thought about making Lena lope all the way, a little payback, but he didn't. They loped awhile and walked awhile. Somewhere ahead, the Platte would bend and slip under a high bluff. After three hours of riding, Yellow Bird would be the perfect place to stop.

The shot split the still air. Pop! Pop! A second and third rang out. *Go to the sound of the shooting.* The war ingrained that—it repulsed him. Still, he kicked the bay mare, and she leaped forward into a canter and a full gallop cutting through the clumps of sage and along a group of willows. The ground flew past as they charged up the river—*to the sound of the shooting.*

Minutes later, Wehr swung his horse down under the bluff while reaching for the Navy Colt strapped to his belt. A horse and man stood at the edge of the water, only strides ahead. Wehr jerked back on the mare, sliding her to a stop. The man backed into the shade of the cutback, so the shadows hid his face.

Friend or enemy? Gray cocked his weapon and pointed at the shadowy figure. Friend or Enemy?

"Hello, Gray. I didn't expect you out here."

Gray's muscles relaxed. He eased the pistol hammer down. "What were you shooting at?"

"Water moccasins, three of them."

"Well, how are you, Jimmy?" Gray asked, holstering the revolver and stepping down off his horse. "I thought you were in Kansas."

"I'm on the way back to Kansas now. I'm a deputy marshal in Hayes. And hell, I wish you'd stop calling me Jimmy."

Wehr looked his friend over, picturing "Wild Bill" Hickok wearing a marshal's badge. "I pity the poor people of Hayes."

Hickok chuckled, "You won't need to pity them long. I'm

thinking of hiring on as a scout for the Tenth Cavalry." Hickok spat some tobacco. "You aimin' on makin' Yellow Bird tonight? I shot some stinking old buffalo hunter back there."

"What did he do to need killin'?"

"He stunk."

Gray thought a man's odor an odd reason to shoot a man but did not respond. "I didn't kill him. Plugged him in the shoulder." Hickok paused. "Never seen an uglier devil. I should have shot him in the face, improved his appearance."

Hickok having such a light attitude about shooting a man always perplexed Gray. Gray shot some himself, but never with the enthusiasm of Jimmy Hickok. Gray's shootings were in self-defense or at the other man's initiation unless he counted Indians. They had been enemies on the battlefield, a different issue.

"You know why I'm here. What are you doing out here?" Hickok asked while studying Gray's bay mare.

"You remember Ben Green?" Gray asked. "Some gun hand killed his son down in Boulder; over some woman, a whore, I suppose. Ben took the boy's death hard, and the guy getting away near killed him. He wanted me to go after him. He wouldn't leave me any room to refuse."

Hickok sat and took off his broad-brimmed hat. Wehr sat alongside him. "Did you catch him?" Hickok asked, wiping the hat's sweatband with his neckerchief.

Gray nodded his head, "Across the Colorado border into Kansas."

Hickok lay back on the grass. "Take him back for trial?"

"Nope."

Hickok chuckled. "I guess he lacked enthusiasm about the trip?"

Wehr laughed. "Not enthusiastic at all. I hollered his name and told him I meant to take him back to Colorado. He yanked his gun." Wehr shook his head. "Stupid of me, the way I handled the situation. If I walked in with my mouth shut and busted his head, I could have tied him up and drug him back without shooting him." For some reason, Gray mentioned it being unseasonably hot the day he shot the man, a Tuesday.

"He was a fool to pull a gun on you; hell, you're a famous gunman," Hickok mused. "I wouldn't let it trouble me, though. A court would have hung him, making him just as dead." Hickok rolled a cigarette. "Ben still married to the German woman?"

"She died," Gray said. "Less than a month before the boy got killed. She passed in her sleep right next to ol' Ben. It's been a challenging year for him," Grey said.

Hickok sat up. "Well, I guess life gives no guarantees."

"I suppose not. But some people get a heavy burden to bear."

Hickock, not one to dwell on tragedy, changed topics. "How is Ally doing?"

Ally Hart, there was quite a woman. Gray tossed a rock in the river. "Did you know she was near forty when we helped her fight that damn Dierden Kane? I thought she was closer to my age. She was near ten years older."

"She was a feisty gal," Hickok laughed. "I bet she still is. I'd like to see her again."

"She's dead."

"Dead? Well, I'll swear. That is a surprise."

"The doc said she had a cancer. She just sort of withered away, died with a lot of pain. By the end, she was on so much laudanum she was never really conscious." Gray stared across the river. "Damn, it was hard to watch. She married Quint Swain. I believe she was happy with him. You know Jimmy; I think she missed Elijah Yancy right to the end. That old man was good to her. She was always grateful."

After another thirty minutes of talk about Hickok's adventures and growing reputation, Gray stood and tried to stretch out his stiff back, which creaked or cracked once or twice for every mile he covered over the last few days. "I better climb back on that horse. It'll be well after dark when I make Yellow Bird."

Hickok gave the mare another thorough look. "You're riding a mighty fine horse. You interested in a swap? I might throw in a dollar or two 'cause you're an old friend."

"You need more than a dollar or two. I wouldn't trade Lena for a dozen horses."

"I swear, Gray, I'm tempted to head back with you for the companionship. If I did, I'd probably end up killin' the foul-smelling buffalo hunter and his two friends."

"Yeah, I suppose you better head on down to Kansas. You got a gang waiting for you." Both men saddled up.

"Well, give my regards to the buffalo hunter, Gray. Ask him if he's taken a bath yet. And say hello to your sister. She's a handsome woman."

Chapter Two

Annie ran her hand through the Indian paintbrush, dotting the landscape where she led a yellow mare and playful weanling. The morning sun glistened off the river's ripples and stony bottom. Lush dew-covered spring grass wet her boots. As she walked through the waist-high flowers, a slight breeze riffled the newly leaved aspens. These little pleasures brought Annie back here almost every day.

She remembered the first time she danced and ran through this meadow as a child weaving her dreams about a home in this beautiful spot. She never regretted building.

Annie Laurie escaped the world in this private refuge, hidden down among its trees, river, and sky. She took the halter off the mare and let her go. The golden palomino's snow-white flaxen tail and mane caught the sun. Sweet and gentle, she took only a step or two away, over to the edge of the water to drink.

Annie pushed the spring filly away. "Get back, Little Bit. Go rub on your mother. I'm not your scratching post." The little horse ignored her protests. "Quit."

Annie sat down in the soft grass along the bank and closed

her eyes. The tranquility of the meadow drew her here. Oddly, it created a balance in her life, as the turmoil of the man attracted her to him. "Please keep him safe. Bring him home again."

Chapter Three

In 1868, two hundred thirty-two people called High Meadows in the Montana Territory home. Located in a green valley in the Bighorn Mountains, the town boasted two churches, a schoolhouse, a dry goods store, and a restaurant. There was no talk of building a saloon. The women wouldn't hear of one.

Forty years earlier, four families established High Meadows. The Clarks packed all their belongings and went back to St. Louis in 1834 after their two daughters died of fever. The Lauries built a dry goods store and raised three children. Two who were killed. The Josephs were farmers with five sons. A baby girl succumbed to smallpox, and a Blackfoot raiding party killed a three-year-old daughter and a five-year-old son.

Rebecca and Andrew Wehr and their infant son, Graham, came in 1829. She and Andrew had a daughter, Jean, and a second boy, Paxton. Rebecca Wehr convinced the men in High Meadows to build a school. She taught there six months out of the year. A painting of her still hangs, memorializing her as the school's first teacher.

In 1831, Andrew Wehr speculated cattle would one day be an essential part of the new territory and talked George Joseph into being his partner in twenty-five head. The idea grew into a moneymaker, and thirty-eight years later, the Wehr/Joseph Ranch raised most of the beef sold in Montana. Except for Gray, the Wehr and Joseph children stayed in the valley, dedicating their lives to the cattle business and its hard work.

Gray Wehr wandered in and out of High Meadows. Paxton, his brother, four years his junior, burned with feelings of resentment toward Gray, who might ride off for three months, half a year, or more on any given day. Jean loved her two-year-older sibling. No one dared say the slightest thing about him, not in her presence.

The Joseph boys ignored Gray's absences. They paid him the same rate they shared in the profits themselves when he was on the ranch. Gray never asked for anything when he was gone.

The other residents of High Meadows liked Gray Wehr. As a young man, he gained a reputation for being capable with a gun, which made High Meadows, in their view, a place safe from outlaws. Annie Laurie hated the gun notoriety. Nevertheless, she loved Gray Wehr.

Adrian Cain, a quarrelsome old man of seventy who lost his wife and daughters to the same fever that killed the Clark children, spent most of his time sitting in a straight-back chair in front of Nellie's Restaurant. A skinny fellow who always, somehow, had a three-day beard sat there now, spitting tobacco juice all over his shirt, his feet, and the porch as Gray Wehr, worn out from the two-week ride home, tied his mare to the hitching post.

"Where you been the last couple of months?" the old man growled.

The old man's tobacco-stained shirt almost made Gray laugh out loud. "Down in Colorado. I went after the man who killed Ben Green's boy."

Cain cut loose a spit of tobacco, landing in his lap. "I never did like his kid. He was too lazy to work and deserved killing."

The old man sat up in his chair. "And you ain't much better. Your sister and brother bust their hind-ends day and night, and you take off whenever the mood strikes. They oughta throw you off the place."

As Wehr stepped up on the porch, he shook his head at the grumpy old devil. "I'm getting something to eat, Adrian. Why don't you go find yourself an old dog to kick?" The old man stammered back at him, but Wehr stopped listening.

Gray liked Nellie Bascomb, a small brown-haired woman in her late thirties. One waitress, a sassy girl about seventeen, and an old Mexican cook Wehr brought to High Meadows about sixteen years back after saving the Mex from a Kansas lynching worked in her restaurant. Nellie, Jean Wehr, and Annie Laurie became inseparable friends after Nellie's family came to High Meadows when Nellie was four. Nellie gave Graham his nickname, so displeasing to his mother. "Well, hello, stranger. Are you here as a customer or to give me somebody new to talk to?"

"I suppose if I don't spend money, you'll throw me out. What can you fix without too much trouble and won't cost me much?"

Nellie kept wiping off tables with great enthusiasm, given the job's mundaneness. Each one covered by a green oilcloth purchased the past winter to replace the old red and white ones was spotless. The floor and the walls of the restaurant were pine. The walls shined from a heavy coat of varnish and constant dusting. "Sanchez won't be in until four," she said, glancing up from her work. "But I suppose I can still cook a steak. Why don't you go upstairs and wash off some dirt while you're waiting? You look like you've been sleeping in a horse stall. Smell like it, too."

Gray seldom thought much about his appearance. But Nellie always made him self-conscious. "There's not a lot of places to bathe out on the trail."

The little woman turned, squinting her eyes. "Did all the rivers and streams run dry?" She went back to washing tables. "Go on upstairs. Fresh water is in the pitcher, and soap is in the dish. You don't have to take a full bath; wash your hands and face. I want to see you while I'm talking to you."

"Don't you want to see me in a bath?"

Nellie winked at him as he headed up the stairs. The room, a pleasant place with blue and yellow floral wallpaper, sported a washbasin, tub, pitcher, soap, and fresh towels.

Wehr tucked his collar down in his shirt and rolled up his sleeves. He poured some water over his head and washed his hair and face leaving a bowlful of dirt.

He dried with one of the hand towels and brushed his blonde hair straight back with a brush Nellie kept in one of the dresser drawers. The washbowl, now full of dirty soapy water, needed to be emptied. Not wanting to leave a mess for Nellie to clean, he walked over and opened the window. He stuck his head outside, making sure the old man still sat on the porch. Wehr took the bowl and dumped water on the old man's head.

Some people said Adrian Cain was forgetful in his old age. Either it wasn't true, or he suddenly recalled every swear word in the English language. "Sorry, Adrian, I forgot you were on the porch," Gray pushed the window closed and laughed as he straightened his collar.

Nellie stepped away from the cafe door as he came back down the stairs. "I hope the Lord doesn't strike you down. You might have sent him into some kind of seizure."

"Just trying to wash some tobacco spit off your porch. It's unappealing. Tobacco juice is unappetizing for people coming in here."

Chapter Four

At forty, Annie Laurie was, by anyone's standards, a gorgeous woman. Tall and thin, her dark brown hair showed slight highlights of auburn when the sun hit it right. Her eyes, a soft brown, contributed to every eligible bachelor for two hundred miles wanting to court her.

Annie inherited the dry goods store when her parents grew too old to work before selling the place six years later to a new family from Virginia. Now she lived outside of town and spent her time raising horses. Annie beamed over the two-year-old stallion she delivered to Jean, a liver chestnut with a white sock on his right rear foot and a little white ring around a front foot. Jean would make him a birthday gift to Gray.

As Annie rode on the Wehr/Joseph Ranch, Jean sat on the fence watching Paxton and three Joseph boys brand steers. She stopped by the corral as the steer Paxton was trying to hold down jerked free, kicking Ethan Joseph in the process. Before the animal escaped, Paxton threw him down again, and Ethan pressed the branding iron hard into its red hide.

"For heaven's sake, Ethan, you're supposed to brand him,

not set its hind end on fire." When Annie spoke, Ethan looked up at her, a mistake the animal took advantage of, kicking him as he ran off.

"You want to come down here and singe some of these? I'll be happy to sit and watch," Ethan said to her.

Annie stepped down off her horse. "Well, I sure wouldn't let myself be kicked twice by the same steer."

Zach Joseph considered Annie's arrival reason enough to take a break from work. "This the one Jean's giving Gray?"

Annie scratched the colt with pride all over her face. "He's a looker, isn't he? I think Gray will like him. If he shows up in time for his birthday," she said with frustration and perhaps concern coming through in her voice.

Jean hopped down. "I've never seen a prettier colt. Gray's going to love him."

Zach slapped at the colt's nose when the little stud tried to bite him. "He's got a handsome head, looks like his old man. Why don't you sell him to me instead of Jean?"

Paxton and the other Josephs joined the conversation. Paxton gave Zach a shove. "To you? She wouldn't sell him to Jean except she's giving him to Gray."

"True enough. I want him to go to somebody who can ride him. And none of you could stay on him. He's tried to bite you twice. If I gave him to you, he'd chew both your arms off in a week."

Paxton and the Josephs all liked Annie, and they laughed at her insults. Jean took the lead rope. "If you're done in time, you can come up and eat with us."

"Done? Hellfire, we won't be done before noon tomorrow. I'm not waiting that long for a meal. You plan on all of us for supper. And make a pie for dessert."

"We'll run straight to the house and bake you up a mincemeat pie!"

"Mincemeat is about what you would bake us," Zach called back.

As Annie and Jean walked away, Annie's demeanor changed. "Rumors are swirling about the government trying to make the Indians sign a new treaty."

"I doubt the Lakota will agree to any peace," Jean said, referring to them as Lakota, not Sioux, a term the Lakota did not like. "But I guess the army can talk to them."

"They say the Indians get everything north of the North Platte and east of the Bighorns."

Jean stopped walking. Her eyes tightened. "Including the Bighorns?"

Annie shrugged. "They say everything east of the summits of the Bighorns. I'm not sure if that includes our valley or not."

Jean stopped; her body stiffened. "Well, we've been here for a long time. I doubt the Lakota would object to our staying. How many chiefs signed the treaty?"

"The information is only trickling in," Annie said, "so I'm not sure. Red Cloud, Spotted Tail, Sitting Bull, and Gall are supposed to be there. They say Crazy Horse is refusing to sign. I don't know if he came in."

Jean turned the chestnut colt into a stall in the barn. "Where's all this taking place," she asked as she closed the stall door.

"Fort Laramie, I think. I can't say if it's true or not" Annie paused for a moment. "But I'm worried. I don't want some treaty putting us out of our homes."

Chapter Five

Gray finished his meal as Sanchez and Nellie's waitress came in. "Señor Wehr, did you kill the man who shot Ben Green's boy," the old Mexican asked

"I did. He pulled his gun," Wehr said, offended over Sanchez taking for granted he killed the man.

Sanchez headed to the kitchen without looking at Wehr again. "Señor Green will be happy now."

"Hi Pop," Millie said, kissing Gray on the side of his face and offering him another cup of coffee. Wehr smiled at the girl and complimented her on her calico dress, but anxious to go home, he declined her offer. Millie flopped down on his lap with an arm around his shoulder and demanded some details about his journey, something she was always jealous over.

Wehr stopped by the Green house to tell Ben about his son's killer. A little less than an hour after leaving Nellie's restaurant, he rode on the Wehr/Joseph Ranch. The sun was all but down when Gray put Lena in the barn. He overlooked Annie Laurie's palomino in the last stall. He would be surprised at the house.

Gray's dad built the Wehr home in 1840. Rebecca insisted on two stories. "Because our only neighbors are Indians doesn't mean we're going to live in a teepee." The house had been re-roofed twice. Most recently, six years ago, when Paxton fell off and broke his left leg, leaving him with a slight limp in his walk and an intense gripe in his disposition.

Gray smelled the apple pie before he went up the porch steps. He took off his hat and used it to beat the dust off his clothes. Nuisance, their old black dog, was pacing at the door, whining about being let in. The dog trotted over and sat in front of him. "Move, you blame pest; you're not goin' in with me. Now go away." He opened the door, pushing Nuisance away with his foot. "Jean, you home?"

The two women winked at each other but didn't go to the door. Annie spoke first. "Well, looky here, Jean, you bake a pie, and guess who drags home."

Gray came into the sitting room smiling. "Annie Laurie, you're a sight for sore eyes." Gray Wehr couldn't remember a time not loving this woman. Bending over, he gave her an affectionate but Victorian kiss.

No one in High Meadows understood why they weren't married. But the reason was simple. At least in Gray's mind. At nineteen years old, in a Kansas saloon, Gray shot a man with a gun reputation. The man's reputation passed to Wehr. For years, he became the prey of every malcontent with a gun. Over the last twenty years, gunslingers and drunks who thought themselves gunslingers challenged him.

Some shot at him from behind, and one fired while he slept in bed. The drunken Kansas cowpuncher, looking for a reputation, first missed high, then wide to the right. Wehr's gun lay on a table on the opposite side of the room, but he used a clay pitcher full of water sitting next to his bed to knock the man unconscious.

Gray left home so often because he feared outlaws and killers with reputations to embellish would come searching for him, bringing unnecessary danger to High Meadows—at least he claimed that. And since Gray hated the idea of widowing

Annie, it stopped the trip to the alter.

Jean, a beautiful woman with flashing blue eyes, got up to hug her brother. As Jean hugged, she pinched him in the small of his back, making him jerk away. "You catch the killer?"

"I did," Neither of the women said anything else.

"You're still wearing that ugly brown hat." Annie stuck her foot out and gave her beau a light kick, a push, really.

"Hats and boots, Annie, hats, and boots. The uglier they are, the more comfortable they are."

Annie stood, "I'll go check your pie. Your brother needs a bath."

"Well, there ain't too many hotels with bathtubs out on those plains."

Annie, in the kitchen, when Gray answered, ignored him. Jean, wearing brown pants and a cream-colored shirt, sat back down and pulled her feet up under her on the couch. Her blonde hair hung down to her shoulders. "Did you go by the green place?" she asked, almost whispering.

"I did. The first thing Ben said was, 'did ya find him?' I told him, 'he's burning in hell.' He went out on the porch and left me standing alone. Never said another word to me."

"He's an old man Gray. You got him some justice," Jean said.

Wehr sat down on the oversized couch, sinking into its deep seat. "Who made justice my job?"

Annie came back in, juggling three pieces of hot apple pie. Hearing the conversation from the kitchen, she changed to a lighter subject. "I thought you were going to take a bath?"

"Well, you ought to confine your thinking to your business." Gray smiled as he reached for the pie. "It's my house, and if I want to sit here dusty and dirty, filthy and stinking, I guess I can. I don't remember asking you over here anyway."

"If I waited on you to be around to ask me someplace, I'd never go anywhere." She sat next to Jean, putting her feet on the couch, proving herself as at home as the man of the house. With both women now comfortable, Annie brought up the

Indian treaty.

Because any treaty would impact everyone in the valley, Gray explained what he knew. "The army called the Sioux to Fort Laramie. Red Cloud and Spotted Tail are supposed to be there. First, I heard Sitting Bull came in, but a gambler at Yellow Bird said he didn't."

Jean and Annie were concerned about the treaty talks, especially his sister. "What about Crazy Horse?"

Crazy Horse, a Sioux shirt wearer, found notoriety among the whites because of his part in the so-called Fetterman Massacre two years earlier. Eighty cavalry troops from Fort Kearny, under Captain William J. Fetterman, had been lured into chasing a handful of Indians. Under Red Cloud's leadership, with Crazy Horse leading a decoy party, the Sioux wiped out Fetterman and the whole force. Ironically, Fetterman bragged earlier, with eighty men, he could wipe out the entire Sioux nation.

Gray was not surprised Jean asked about Crazy Horse. She carried an illogical fear of the Ogallala warrior. Gray blew on a fork full of pie. "Word is he wouldn't come in. I can't tell you which chiefs signed. The gambler said Spotted Tail did, but Red Cloud and some of the others want the forts closed first."

Jean sat her saucer on the floor. "What are the terms supposed to be? Was this gambler at Fort Laramie?"

"The treaty gives the Lakota the Black Hills. No white men are allowed in. Lakota, Cheyenne, and Arapaho have hunting rights on everything north of the North Platte and east of the Bighorn Territory."

Annie frowned and shifted her feet off the couch. "What about us? It sounds like they are giving our valley to the Lakota."

Gray didn't want to upset the women. "I doubt if anybody mentioned High Meadows," he said as he started to pull off his boots. "Red Cloud is mad about the forts. We've never been a threat. We've always been friendly. I don't think the Indians are concerned about us."

Gray watched Annie shift uncomfortably. "I hope they don't blame us for more whites coming out here. The Lakota might consider it a reason to attack us."

That brought out Jean's defiant side. "My mother and father built what's in this valley. I've lived my whole life here. I won't give my home up to some treaty I took no part in making."

Gray stretched out and pushed down on his aching knees. "Well, I doubt we'll be under attack by the Lakota tonight...or the government either. I'm headin' for a bath and bed. I'll see you ladies in the morning." He gave Annie another kiss and brushed his hand along the side of Jean's face before heading up the oak stairs.

Jean picked up the pie plates and headed into the kitchen. Annie let her eyes follow Gray up the steps before going to help Jean clean up. A few minutes later, the women walked arm in arm up the stairs. Jean paused at her brother's door to say goodnight. Annie Laurie opened the door to the guest room.

Chapter Six

Gunfire shattered the early morning. Blue-shirted men were screaming and dying. Terrified horses charged through the bedrolls, some stepping on still sleeping or dead soldiers. Wehr lunged for the Springfield propped against his saddle, but before he reached the rifle, the nightmare ended.

The morning was crisp, the sky bright blue. Horses whinnied in the pasture, and the hands knocked around down at the barn. Gray leaned out his open window and told himself, again, he would never leave this valley—nightmares or no nightmares—gunmen or no gunmen.

Annie yelled up to him. "Breakfast is on! If you want any, you best hurry." Wehr pulled on his boots and headed down the stairs toward the smell of bacon.

Paxton and Zach Joseph were sitting down. Jean slid eggs on their plates. Zach, the middle Joseph child, started talking when Gray came into the kitchen. "Well, what time did you drag in? Musta been after dark."

Gray sat down and laid his napkin in his lap as Annie gave his shoulder a little squeeze. "At dusk, it was dark by the time

I cared for Lena and got up to the house."

Paxton blew on his coffee and took a quick drink. He spoke without looking up. "Did you shoot the guy who killed the Green kid?"

Gray dropped his fork on his plate. It clinked and bounced onto the floor. More irritated, Gray rubbed the back of his hand, put both forearms on the table. "You ever think of saying 'hello?'"

Jean frowned at Paxton, interceded. "He figures if he's in a sour mood, he may as well make everybody else mad." She punctuated her remarks with a stern glare at her younger brother. Paxton did not want to initiate a fight with his sister. There was no reason to start the day with a bowl full of gravy running down his face.

"What's he in a grouch about this morning?" Gray asked Jean, ignoring Paxton.

"Maybe he stepped on a goat head," Jean said as she finished putting the breakfast on.

Zach Joseph loved talking. And the sibling tiff gave him his opening. "Gray, you missed a lot by being gone. I'll tell you; life in this valley is exciting. The grass in the north pasture grew six, eight inches. The Baptists and Presbyterians got together for a box social. Can you imagine?"

After half an hour, Jean put a stop to his constant babbling. "Paxton, bless this food." Zach feigned surprise at being told to shut up as Paxton bowed his head, aware Jean expected him to repent over his rudeness to his brother. He did not. After eating and a spirited argument between Jean and Paxton, the women cleaned up the kitchen while the three men went out to work.

Paxton asked about the Indian treaty. Gray gave an abbreviated version, knowing he'd repeat the whole thing in a few minutes with the other Joseph boys and the rest of the men.

Gray delivered a message from Jean to the youngest Joseph boy to saddle Annie's palomino and Jean's gray. Gray handed the women their reins and asked Jean if she was going over to Annie's or into town. "I'm going to order supplies.

Remind Alan he'll need to send a wagon in to pick them up tomorrow. I doubt if I'll be back for lunch, so you boys are on your own." Annie and Jean kicked their horses into a lope.

Paxton, Zach, and Gray found Alan and the rest of the hands at the south pasture's far end. Alan, the oldest Joseph boy, was five years the senior of Gray Wehr. His father died in the spring of 1862, his mother three months later. Gray's dad died almost seven years ago, his mother two. Before she passed away, Rebecca Wehr insisted the families elect one person head of the ranch. They chose Alan, and he proved himself more than capable. Except for Zach, no one questioned or argued with Alan. Zach delighted in asking for explanations about every decision made.

One of the hands asked Gray about a peace accord at Fort Laramie. Before Gray answered, Alan interrupted. "Before we start into the treaty, we need to deal with these missing cattle. I think we've still got about thirty head unaccounted for." Alan shifted toward Gray. "Ethan and I camped up here last night and were up searching at first light. Unfortunately, we couldn't find those blame cows."

Zach stiffened, slapped his reins on his knee, and shook his head. "They've been rustled; can't you get that through your thick skull?"

Gray still struggled with the idea. Nothing had ever been stolen off the ranch or anywhere in the valley. "Who'd rustle our cattle?"

The question chafed Zach. "Well, if I knew, I'd go hang 'em."

Gray scratched the back of his neck. "I can't remember any theft around here, not ever, especially livestock. The Sioux don't steal from us. When they need food, they come and ask. We've never turned them down."

Zach spat a wad of tobacco, glared at Gray. "Are you

deaf? I didn't say Indians stole 'em. Hell, don't you think white men can steal?"

Ethan, like Gray, didn't accept the idea of cattle thieves. "If somebody is rustling 'em, where are they taking them?" he asked. "You can't drive cattle out of this area without being seen."

Paxton, James, and the two hired hands sat silent. This conversation wasn't going to produce any new ideas. So Alan gave everyone an area to search. "Gray and I will head up into the mountains and see if we can find any sign. Paxton, you, and Zach track down by the river. The rest of you head back up to the upper meadows." Then, with Zach grumbling about wasting time, they all started.

Alan Joseph considered Gray to be the most skilled of all his partners. Whenever he needed advice or wanted to discuss business, he always singled him out for a private talk if Gray was around.

So, when they turned their horses west and started for the Bighorns, Gray figured his partner was interested in more than looking for cattle. "I need to talk about something." Gray assumed he meant the Indian negotiations since everyone in High Meadows exaggerated the rumors, and concern escalated. What Alan said made Wehr stop his horse. "I think Zach's right. I think someone took those cows. We didn't lose ten head last month, closer to forty. Paxton knows how many. Zach, Ethan, and John don't."

"Did you tell James how many?"

Alan climbed off his horse. "Paxton's convinced James is responsible."

James Joseph and Paxton Wehr never liked each other, not as kids, not as men. But this was too much. Gray also dismounted. "Paxton can think up some foolish ideas and convince himself they're true, despite having no evidence. But I can't believe he thinks James is stealing from us." Wehr paused. "Paxton told you, James is taking our cattle?"

"He was a little more diplomatic."

"Well, it's a ridiculous notion. James would never rustle

from us. I'll say something to my brother."

Alan shook his head. "Don't. Paxton's right. Or at least I think he is. I thought so before Paxton came to me, but I can't figure out what to do. I can't lynch my own blood."

Gray still didn't believe any of this. He forced a laugh at the idea of hanging James. "Nobody's gonna hang, James."

Alan managed a slight grin of his own, "Well, you better tell Zach."

"You think James is rustling our cattle?"

"I think Cal Bowden and his boys are helping him. My guess is they slip out at night, cut a bunch out, move them over on his place, and up the Bozeman Trail. Bowden raises cows. No one is gonna question him moving beef. I didn't say anything before, but I think over a hundred head disappeared in the past eighteen months or so, a few at a time, eight, ten, a dozen. At first, I thought we were losing them to wolves or a cougar. I started to wonder if the Lakota took them. I thought about riding out to try and find Paints His Horse. 'Course, I didn't think too long."

"So you're branding."

Alan laughed again. "Your sister is convinced I've lost my mind. She keeps telling me we haven't branded in years and have plenty of work to do around here without inventing any. But a rustler will have a hard time selling cattle with a W Bar J burnt on their hind-ends."

Gray didn't relish thinking someone he grew up with would steal from the families. "One hundred head, lots of cows, even over a year-and-a-half. What do you want to do?"

"I can only think of two things to do. Confront James, or try to catch him. I prefer catching him. That way, if we're wrong, well, I won't cause trouble by accusing him."

Gray didn't want to call a lifelong friend, someone as close as a brother, a cattle thief.

"We're more than half done branding," Alan continued. "So, if they intend to take anymore, they'll have to be quick. I thought you and I might tell the others we're going down to Fort Laramie to find out about the treaty situation. Which somebody's going to have to do, I suppose. But I want to handle this first. You and I can set up camp over by the Bowden place and see what happens. If nothing, we'll come back as soon as the branding is done."

It was a sensible idea. "Do you think Bowden might be doing this on his own?" Gray sensed Alan wanted to say yes, but Paxton had convinced him otherwise.

Chapter Seven

Annie let herself be convinced to ride into town with her friend. They dropped off Jean's supply list at Keller's General Store. Mrs. Keller, on the far side of sixty, kept them talking for the better part of an hour. They discussed everything from the weather to the arrival of the Swain baby. She assured Jean her supplies would be ready early the following day.

Jean and Annie headed toward Nellie's restaurant. They gingerly picked their way across the porch covered with Adrian Cain's tobacco spit. Annie gave him a dirty scowl as she tiptoed past him. In the kitchen with Sanchez, talking about the Friday night menu, Nellie shouted she'd be right out. Friday nights were something in High Meadows; almost everyone came into town, ate at Nellie's, and caught up on all the week's activities. People showed up with everything from checkerboards to fiddles.

Jean and Annie sat, and Jean yelled back to Nellie. "That old man's spitting tobacco all over your porch again."

Nellie called back, asking if Millie was out in the café. "I'm back here straightening up the storage room." Millie dreaded what was coming.

"Go out and clean up old man Cain's tobacco spit." Millie hated cleaning up the tobacco spit, but she grabbed a broom and headed for the front door, stepping out like she was walking across a plowed field.

"There goes a girl on a mission," Annie chuckled.

"Look at this mess you're making out here. Why don't you go sit somewhere else? We're trying to run a café here."

Old man Cain didn't take sass from some kid who waits tables. "I'll put my ass wherever I want to, and don't you be sassing me." Adrian cut loose a stream of tobacco landing on Millie's calico dress. Right on the front—a nasty, awful brown blotch.

"You old goat." The broom crashed down across the skinny old man's head and shoulders.

"You little witch!" Bam—a second blow, fiercer than the first, scratched his face and started blood flowing. Adrian Cain lit into cussing, hobbled across the boardwalk, and attempted to make an escape. Millie landed two more solid blows across his back, one on his skinny hind-end before the old man got off the porch. She got in three or four more brutal ones as he ran and limped his way down the street, calling the girl names she never heard before.

Two people came out of the blacksmith shop to witness the commotion. Millie followed Adrian down the dusty street and laid down some more licks. The old man turned and tried to kick her. His long leg and foot flying through the air made the scene almost laughable. On his third attempt, he lost balance and flopped on his back, still kicking at the girl.

Mrs. Keller came out of the general store narrow-eyed, nostrils flaring, and arms wildly waving at nothing. "Quit hitting him! Stop that right now! You can't be hitting him with a broom. You stop right now."

"The old goat spit tobacco all over the front of me. I'm

gonna beat him to death."

"You'll do no such thing. You leave that poor man alone."

"I'll break his neck the next time!" Millie flushed red, gave the old man one more swat, turned around, and, covering four feet with every stride, headed back to the restaurant.

"I'll be speaking to Nellie about your behavior, young lady."

Millie whirled around, "Maybe I'll give you a whack! Speak to her about!"

Nellie, Jean, and Annie failed to regain their composure before Millie came back in the front door. They were howling too hard. Annie spoke first, "Did you spruce up the porch?"

"It's not funny." Mad and crying, snot and spit spewing from her nose and mouth, Millie threw the broom on the floor before stomping her way to the kitchen and out the back door. Annie, Jean, and Nellie pitied the girl but didn't stop their laughing.

Mrs. Keller came huffing through the front door. Nellie stood and went to meet her while waving her away with her hand. "I know. I'll take care of everything, Mrs. Keller. I'll be correcting her. Don't you worry." Mrs. Keller wagged her finger, got in the last word, and headed back to her store so mad she peed herself.

Jean caught her breath enough to tell Nellie she better check on her daughter.

Five minutes passed before Nellie collected herself enough to find Millie. She found her sitting on the back porch sobbing like she'd had a sound whipping. After a lot of coaxing, Millie came back inside. They sat at the table with Jean and Annie. Millie, now pouting, blubbered again; it wasn't amusing.

Annie put her arm around the girl. Millie stuck her tongue out at Annie. At first, there was a snicker or two from Jean. Nellie couldn't hold herself together. Discipline was lost, Discipline never worked on Millie anyway.

Chapter Eight

James Joseph, bald with a sandy-colored beard, stood over six feet and weighed 240 pounds. Once lighthearted, James deteriorated into a cold man who didn't think life dealt him a fair hand. He never married, being afraid to propose to the only woman he ever wanted, and now James blamed everyone else whenever things didn't go his way.

Though the same age, people would guess white-haired, leather-faced Cal Bowden, older than James Joseph. He had three sons: ages twenty-two, nineteen, and seventeen—all shiftless. All four were in the corral when James Joseph rode up.

Bowden climbed over the fence. "I hear Wehr is back."

James, not intending to stay long, didn't step off his horse. "He was. But he and Alan left this morning for Fort Laramie. They want to find out what's going on between the Army and the Indians. I want to move some cattle tonight. Zach's pitchin' a fit about rustling. Alan's branding everything. If we want anymore, we'll have to take 'em now."

"Suits me," Bowden said. James wanted to take seventy-five to a hundred more head. "They think they're being stolen, so we may as well take as many as we can." They agreed to meet on the upper range of the Wehr/Joseph ranch right after midnight. James Joseph turned his horse and started for home.

Gray Wehr and Alan Joseph figured that since their still unbranded cattle grazed in the north pasture, anyone driving them to the Bowden place would run them through a ravine about a mile up the river. They made their camp and set up their lookout.

For early spring, the day had been hot and sultry. The night smelled of a coming storm. Lightning flashed, and thunder rolled. Around 11:30, the air turned cold, and slow chilling rain made the night dismal.

Nasty weather makes cattle jumpy; cutting them from the herd proved quite a task for five cowboys, three lazy. Complicating things, the youngest Bowden boy rode a skittish green-broke horse that kept trying to throw him.

By 2:00 a.m., they only had thirty-five head. James Joseph wondered how he got tied up with such an inept bunch as the Bowden's. Fed up, he decided they would settle for the cattle they had. "We'll come back tomorrow night and steal another thirty or forty head."

With the storm pouring down in sheets, they herded the bawling animals into the draw and up toward the Bowden place. A deaf man would have heard them coming for the last fifteen minutes. Dripping wet Gray and Alan sat on their horses about twenty-five feet apart. Most of the cattle moved through before James Joseph, and the Bowden's came along. Soaked, miserable, and careless, they wouldn't have noticed an entire cavalry waiting for them.

When a lightning bolt lit up the sky, one of the Bowden boys caught a glimpse of the two men. He went for his pistol. Gray Wehr's voice cracked through the howling wind splitting the air like a shot. "Don't do it, boy!" The other riders, heads jerked up. Alan Joseph wearing a soggy black hat, water pouring from the brim, aimed his rifle right at Cal Bowden. The downpour and black night made it impossible to tell if Gray had his gun drawn.

James Joseph glared at his brother. Alan wanted to say something but struggled for words. Gray didn't. "Sit easy, boys. You got guns on?"

Seventeen-year-old Clint Bowden couldn't keep his mouth shut. "I ain't armed. Please don't shoot; I ain't packin'."

James stiffened in his saddle, defiant eyes screaming at his brother. "Well, what now? You going to string us up?"

Why didn't Alan think more before acting? Why didn't he and Gray make up a definite plan?

James's angry voice split the night again. "You gonna hang your kin?"

Rain dripped from Alan's enormous mustache, dropping off his chin. He couldn't speak. Hell, he couldn't move. He sat with his rifle pointed at the center of Cal Bowden's chest. James screamed again. "Well, what are you going to do, you self-righteous ass?"

Gray sounded as calm as if he lay in a meadow getting ready for a nap. "I believe we'll start by having you fellas toss your guns away. But let's be careful about handling them."

None of the cattle thieves made any moves. Gray spoke again. "Cal, I want you to listen to me. First, you tell your boys to shed their pistols. Then you tell James to drop his. And this is the part where you want to pay real close attention. If they don't, I'm going to put a bullet in your gut. I want them dropped now." Alan glanced over at Gray, back to the cattle rustlers.

The oldest boy grabbed his pistol, destroying any chance of a peaceful solution. Before the boy even aimed, Gray shot. Whether the boy was young and dumb enough to think he would win a gunfight or didn't want his pa threatened, no one would ever know. He flipped off the back of his horse, landing with a thud knocking out any air left in him.

Cursing like the devil himself, Cal Bowden yanked his pistol. Someone was going to die. Alan Joseph pulled the trigger of his rifle, a reflex action. The hunk of lead slammed through Bowden's lung and heart, tumbled downward and out his lower back, killing him long before he hit the ground.

James got his revolver out and pointed at his brother. Before he pulled the trigger, Gray squeezed his. The bullet ripped through James' arm, below the elbow. One Bowden boy jumped from his horse, crying and begging the men not to shoot him. Marcus Bowden's horse tore into a bucking rampage at the sound of the first shot. He threw the boy, breaking his collarbone. Alan Joseph's horse reacted no better to the shooting and pitched Alan with his first lunge.

Lena planted her feet, didn't move a muscle. Wehr swung off her back, trying to locate James Joseph, the only one who might still be a threat. Lightning flashed again; a lump, dark and unnatural, caught his eye. James, face down and cussing, kept kicking his foot back and forth, trying to ignore the throbbing in his right arm.

Wehr was far too experienced in this sort of thing to relax until the situation was controlled. "Sit up, James. Sit up! Show me your hands."

The man wallowed in the mud. "You shot me, damn you. Go ahead and finish me."

Wehr's unruffled demeanor disappeared, his muscles tensed, anger took over. "If I don't see your hands, I will. I'll not fret about it, either." Wehr's voice cut like a knife through cold skin, convincing James, Wehr meant what he said. He tried to roll off his bloody arm. The effort caused him to vomit, not that it mattered in all the rain.

"Alan, are you all right?"

"I'm not hit. Are you?"

"No. Keep an eye on your brother while I check these boys." Gray found the oldest boy with a bullet in his belly. He turned to the other two Bowdens. "You two, get over by James." The younger boy, Clint, still whimpering, almost ran to where Gray motioned. Marcus struggled to his knees. Gray pulled him to his feet.

"How's my pa? Is he all right?"

"He's dead," Watching the boy's hands, he barked orders. "I want you over here where I can see you. You still have your gun?"

"No, I must of lost it when my horse throwed me."

"Show me your hands!" Once satisfied the boy was unarmed, Gray helped him, not very gently, over where James and Clint sat, beaten down in the rain like soggy hounds. The younger boy asked Alan if they plan to hang him.

"No, boy, we ain't. But we'd be justified too."

Wehr glared at James. "It's a poor excuse for a man, stealing from his own family." He waved his weapon at the other Bowdens. "Now, two men are dead. What the hell got into you?"

Before James answered, Marcus interrupted. "My brother's dead?"

Gray showed no compassion. "Your brother's gutshot. Nothing can be done for him. You can sit with him if you want. He might experience some peace if he dies in your arms. I doubt it, though." The boy stumbled over and put Brad's head in his lap. The mortally wounded boy's breaths were shallow, raspy with long lapses. Marcus held his unconscious brother, rocking him with his one useable arm.

Alan stood, staring at James. "I'm thankful the folks are gone. I'm truly glad. Climb on your horse, and get out of this valley. If you come back, I'll kill you myself."

James hurt from the tips of his fingers to the middle of his back. He thought he might pass out. But he would not give his brother the satisfaction. "How am I supposed to mount a horse with a road apple size hole in my arm?"

"I don't care a damn bit how. But if you don't, I'll kill you right now."

Somehow, James Joseph did struggle up on his horse and wandered off into the dark and the rain. Brad Bowden was dead. Alan told Marcus they would send someone out to do the burying at first light. They pushed the two boys on their horses and headed toward the house. They wouldn't wake Alan's wife or children. Jean Wehr would deal with all of this.

The rising sun was turning the sky red when Alan, Gray, and the two surviving Bowdens got back to the house. Waking his sister would be a mean-spirited act. So, while he tried to wrap Marcus' shoulder to make his collarbone more comfortable, Alan got the stove going and the coffee brewing.

Deciding which Bowden boy was in the sorrier shape was quite a task. Marcus ached from a broken bone, but Clint kept sobbing about his pa and brother. He started begging Alan not to string him up. Disgusted, Marcus cuffed his brother with the back of his hand, and Clint regained some of his composure. But not before he woke Jean.

She rushed down the stairs. Gray cut her off in front of the kitchen. "What's wrong in there, Gray? And I thought you went to Fort Laramie."

Gray sat on the couch and pulled Jean down next to him. He always broke bad news looking people straight in the eyes. This conversation was not going to be happy.

"James has been stealing our cattle. We caught him last night and ended up killing Cal Bowden and one of his boys. The other two boys are in the kitchen with Alan." He said it, now; for some ridiculous reason, he started thinking how sparkling his sister's blue eyes were.

Jean sat without saying anything. Gray gazed off at the stone fireplace across the room. Jean slid her stockinged feet across the red and black Persian rug their father gave their mother as an anniversary present two years before his death. After collecting herself, she asked about James.

"He's shot in the arm. Alan told him to leave the valley. I think he told him he'd kill him if he came back, but I'm not sure."

Jean leaned back into the couch. "Who shot him? How

bad is he?"

The whole thing now started settling down on Gray. His eyes glazed, his mind slowed down. He tried to reconnect with his sister. "What?"

"I asked who shot James. How bad?"

Wehr closed his eyes to pull his thoughts together. "I did. He meant to shoot Alan." Wehr lay back. "I think the bullet struck him under the elbow. Probably blew his arm half off."

She wanted so much to ask if James would die, she didn't. She cared too much for her brother to ask unanswerable questions. "What about the two boys in the kitchen?"

"One's got a busted collarbone. His horse pitched him when the shooting started. The younger one, I think he's lost his mind. He keeps bawling like a little kid, asking us not to hang him."

Jean got up. "I'll try to help them. You sit here for a minute." Jean said, rubbing his shoulder before going to the kitchen.

Twenty minutes later, Alan came into the sitting room. "Jean said Paxton will be in for breakfast in a little while," Gray said. "We're gonna take these boys upstairs. I thought you and I would tell Paxton what's happened. We'll let him tell the others."

Gray managed enough strength to stand up. "I'll go hitch a team. Let's you and me fetch the bodies. Nobody else needs to see them."

By the time Gray had the wagon ready to go, Alan had told Paxton, who at least had the decency to keep quiet. He met Gray outside the barn, and they started back to the draw leading to the Bowden place. Alan spoke first. "I didn't expect what happened. I guess it was a weak plan." Gray sighed, didn't say anything.

Chapter Nine

Noon passed before the men got the two bodies over to Ben Wright. Wright wasn't an actual undertaker, but he did all the burying, and the town paid him five dollars a body out of their treasury. Gray and Alan gave an abbreviated and brisk version of the events, which killed the Bowdens. Afterward, both men, numb and too tired to head home, went to Nellie's.

"You two look rode hard."

"Button it up, Nellie," Alan growled.

"Millie, bring some coffee in here before I slap these old grumps." Nellie went back to work wiping off tables, looking up as Wehr walked by on his way to the kitchen. "Where are you going?"

"To see your cook." Gray went through the swinging doors into the kitchen. "Listen, Sanchez, I need a favor."

"If I can, Señor."

Wehr told the old Mexican what happened the night before. "I want you to go looking for James. I'm afraid he'll bleed to death if he doesn't get help."

"It could take much time to find him. Nellie will be mad

if I leave. Can you not go yourself?"

Wehr was in no mood to argue with Nellie's cook or to offer explanations. "I'll handle Nellie. James can't have gotten too far. If you don't find him in three days, come back. "Wehr grabbed the old man's sombrero from the hook next to the window. "And go out the back door. Alan's out front, and I don't want him to know about this."

"This is inconvenient for me," the old man mumbled as Gray pushed him through the door.

"Yeah, well, saving your neck from stretching was inconvenient for me. So quit your bellyaching and go." Gray got the old man out the door with little more protest.

He went back out front and sat at a table with Nellie. Alan fell asleep at another table, but Gray still kept his conversation with Nellie to a whisper. "I sent Sanchez off on an errand for me. He may be gone a few days."

Nellie set her palms down flat on the table, her eyes narrowed. When she started to speak, Wehr put his finger over her lips. "I'll send Annie and Jean over to help you. Jean will explain everything."

Gray and Alan were back home by mid-afternoon. Alan saddled his horse and headed home. Gray unhitched the team and went to the house; the ranch work could wait another day. He was going to bed.

Chapter Ten

If he tried to ride out of the valley, he would bleed to death, so James headed to the Bowden homestead. He left his horse in a barn stall still saddled and bridled and wobbled to the house.

The Bowden house was no more than a rough log cabin. The men living there didn't worry much about housekeeping. He found some clean towels and tore them into strips for bandages. He cut the sleeve of his shirt open with his knife. Joseph thought he'd find his forearm hanging on by a few shreds of skin. The area was black and dark purple around the hole, which turned out to be only about his thumb's size, evil but not as ghastly as he feared. No stripes ran up and down his arm, a hopeful sign. He cleaned up the wound and wrapped the torn strips around it in a makeshift tourniquet.

He found some biscuits and honey in a cupboard. He coated the biscuits with the honey, ate two, and eased himself into one of the beds. Despite his tearing pain, sleep came almost immediately.

Chapter Eleven

When Gray got home, he told Jean about sending Sanchez out hunting for James and his promise to Nellie. Jean offered to fix her brother something to eat before she headed into Nellie's, and he went to bed.

"Something easy. I'm not too hungry. I'll saddle your horse."

Gray found Jack, Jean's gray gelding, out in the pasture instead of the barn. The horse walked right over to Gray, and Wehr quickly had him saddled.

When he got back to the house, Jean gave him a sandwich and poured a glass of milk. "If Nellie's busy tonight, I'll stay in town with her. And our supplies are ready, so send someone in with a wagon in the morning."

Jean sat down across from her brother. "Do you think James will leave High Meadows?"

The question dumbfounded Gray. "Hell yes, he'll leave." His brusqueness was uncalled for, and he knew it. "I'm sorry, Jeanie. James and Alan tore into each other, yelling and screaming. I mean before the shooting started. James showed no remorse. I don't think the Josephs would accept him back."

"How bad do you think he's hurt?"

Gray, quite aware Jean wanted a detailed answer, looked at his sister. She wore a red flannel shirt buttoned up to the collar. Her face was pale and tired-looking. Gray took a swallow of the milk. "There was a lot of blood. If you're asking me if he's gonna die, I can't say. If he does, I suppose it'll be because he bleeds to death. But I didn't exactly examine his arm." Gray paused from taking another bite of the sandwich. "Aren't you hot in a flannel shirt?"

Jean didn't want to start a fight with her brother, so she let the shooting drop. She did want to ask why they didn't bring James back to the doctor. They could have patched him up before throwing him off the ranch. Apparently, abandoning him had been Alan's doing, so pushing Gray on the topic was pointless.

"How are those two boys acting?"

Jean sighed. The sadness in her eyes spread over the rest of her face.

"They slept most of the day. I took them some lunch. They ate and went back to sleep. The little time they were awake, they've been sheepish. But who knows what they'll do when they perk up." Jean stood and took the saucer and empty glass to the sink. "Dick is the only hand, not doing something. When I go to town, I'll send him in to sit guard over them. That can't hurt anything."

Jean led her gelding out of the barn, sent their hired hand to the house, and rode off. She headed toward High Meadows until she was out of sight of the house. Then she turned Jack and loped toward the Bowden cabin.

James' horse stood in a stall, the saddle covered in blood. A trail of blood led to the house. She opened the door slowly and called James's name. After no response, she went inside, where she found him asleep on one of the beds. He still had his gun in its holster. She thought the wisest thing would be to remove the revolver. After all, she couldn't be sure how this man she had known all her life would react.

She laid the pistol on the floor and started to unwrap the bloody bandages. James lurched, took a few seconds to focus his eyes, and looked startled to see Jean. "How'd you find me?"

"From what Gray said about last night, you couldn't have gone too far. I figured you might come here."

James tried to sit up, but the whole right side of his body ached, and he gave up on the effort. "Are you alone?"

"You're not overly popular. Not a lot of people clamored to come along. Lay still and let me look at this."

James took a deep breath, fell back on the bed, and tried to hold his arm up for Jean to remove the makeshift bandage. When she pulled the last towel back, she couldn't stop herself from shutting her eyes and turning away. Her reaction sent a chill through the wounded man. "How bad?"

"It's not pretty, but I guess I've seen worse things. I'll wash the blood off. Where's the liquor in this house?" James told her to open the cupboard above the pump. She'd find whiskey.

Jean ripped up some more towels and a couple of shirts to use for bandages. She came back with some soapy water and the whiskey. James almost flew off the bed when she poured some of the water onto the wound. Jean laughed for the first time all day. "If you think water's bad, wait 'til I pour whiskey on you."

James Joseph lived a rancher's life; he did not shrink from pain. He didn't scare. But his voice shuddered when he again asked about his arm.

"I'm not a doctor, but it's not good. At least there are no stripes. I think that's a positive sign as blood poisoning goes." Jean scratched his hand and fingers. James didn't react.

He felt nothing in his hand and fingers, but he sure felt his elbow and forearm. "Can you wiggle your fingers?" The man tried, only a twitch, which may have been involuntary. "Lay your arm out off the side of the bed, and bite down on this rag. I'm going to pour some of this whiskey over the wound." James Joseph thought the woman set him on fire. He bit down on the old shirt so hard a decaying tooth crumbled. His arm shook violently for almost a full minute after she stopped pouring the liquor.

Jean didn't say anything until James relaxed his bite on the rag. "I found this salve in the other room. I'll put some on the wound and wrap you back up." Whatever the greasy ointment was, it soothed the pain. "Well, that's all I can do. I hope it's enough to save your arm."

James laid back and let out a deep breath. Jean sat on the edge of the bed. Neither said anything.

"I guess I made a mess of things."

Jean sighed. "Nobody will argue about that."

James wished Jean had not come, not if she meant to lecture him. "I didn't mean for all of this to happen."

Jean stood and walked across the room, stared out the window. "Two men are dead, James. Feeling bad isn't going to fix much." She quit talking, wanting her words to sink in.

James started to apologize again. But the resentment boiled up in him. "Well, they're not dead by my hand."

Jean whirled around. Her face went from white to crimson red. The tears building in her eyes began to fall. Shuddering, she screamed. "Not by your hand? Who the hell's hand was it? You may not have pulled the trigger, but you killed those men. It was your doing; Gray and Alan said you wouldn't quit." Her body shook. "You could've dropped your guns, but you wouldn't quit. Then that fool boy yanked at his gun. Now, two boys are orphans, and you're going to be a cripple for the rest of your life—if you live." She turned her back on him. Silence filled the room. Minutes passed.

"Why'd you come out here lookin' for me?"

She turned back toward him, the color draining from her face. She couldn't focus and struggled for balance. She leaned against the wall, afraid she would collapse without support. Jean started to remind him she grew up with him, as close as a brother—to tell him after her Fiancé died that she would have wed him if he had asked her. But she didn't say any of that.

Instead, she said, "Because I didn't want you dying. I don't want any more dying." Neither said another word for almost an hour. James fell in and out of sleep. Jean sat, staring out the window. Later, she walked toward the kitchen. "I'll fix you something to eat," she said, unsure if he was awake.

If he was, Jean suspected storms crashed through James' brain: one-minute anger, another guilt. She was right. He wanted to scream at Jean and unleash all of the reasons he took the cattle. The next minute, he wanted to weep.

Jean should have lit a candle before stumbling back to James with bread and some stew. "I left more of this on the stove. It can sit and simmer all night. Rest will be the best thing for you. But I wouldn't stay for more than a few days."

Hungry, James started to eat without responding. Jean wouldn't say anything, but she resented that the man could eat so easily in the current circumstances.

"I found quite a bit of food in the cupboards. You can pack some to take with you. I tore up some more rags and left them by the sink. You ought to change the bandage at least a couple of times a day. If stripes show up, they likely mean blood poisoning, and you better find a doctor. You'll probably lose your arm, but he may save your life." Jean picked up his Navy revolver. "I'll put this on the table. I'll leave your horse saddled; you'd never be able to saddle him. I'll make sure he has hay and water. I can't do anything else for you." Her words sounded so decisive. She stopped for a moment. "Such a disappointing day."

Jean turned and walked out. James heard her lay the gun on the table. He didn't hear the paper money.

Chapter Twelve

The town dubbed it "The Joseph Incident." Almost a month passed before High Meadows population stopped talking about James and the Bowdens being so despicable. Gray got angry with Sanchez when he didn't find James and started calling him "that worthless old Mexican."

Nellie, the only one other than Jean and Annie Laurie, aware of the errand Wehr sent him on, believed the old man did his best and made it clear to Gray she resented her cook's treatment. "If you were so all-fired worried about James, you should have brought him to the doctor instead of sending him off into the rain."

Irritated, Jean pointed out Alan, not Gray, sent James "riding off into the rain."

Marcus and Clint Bowden stayed at the Wehr home only two days past their father and brother's shootings. As a going-away present, they stole food, ammunition, and two horses. Alan Joseph declared them not worth the effort to catch.

Once Zach Joseph got over his zeal to chase down his

brother, he started trying to talk Gray into traipsing to Fort Laramie to find out about the Indians. Gray didn't debate the need for someone going, but he held to his resolution not to leave the valley again. "I'll not deny the importance of going, but somebody else can go. I'm content right here."

Chapter Thirteen

Gray said he had never seen a better animal than the stud he received for his birthday. Annie told him a fine horse heals a broken soul. Gray laughed and named him Luke, after the physician.

Gray rode up to Annie's door on a bright Sunday morning. Carrying a picnic basket, she came down the steps to meet him. "I declare, Annie, you are the prettiest thing. I believe you get more gorgeous every day."

Annie strolled right past him. "Come on, Romeo, saddle my horse."

Gray stepped up his pace to catch her. "Annie, I think a woman as beautiful as you, on a day as beautiful as this, ought to have a man ask her to marry him."

Stunned, she stopped, turned around—slowly—took one step toward him, stopped again. "When do you think we should marry?"

Gray shrugged and smiled at her, mesmerized by her simple response. He hadn't expected such a practical question. He thought she would laugh him off, doubt his sincerity.

"September is a nice month."

Her eyes glistened as she put her hand to the side of his face. "Do you intend to be here in September?"

Gray kissed her forehead. "September, October, November, why I'm thinking about March." Annie Laurie was a happy woman.

Chapter Fourteen

Sweating in the July sun, Millie tied her horse to the hitching post in front of Annie's house, a gabled two-story white house with black shutters. Flowers lined each side of a stone walk leading up to a wide porch surrounding the house's face and sides.

Millie walked up the steps and through the door without knocking. "Annie? Annie, are you here?" She went through the downstairs and called Annie's name up the stairs. A rhubarb pie sitting on the kitchen counter caught her attention. As comfortable at Annie's as her home, she cut herself a piece and poured a glass of milk. She sat down at the table, ate one slice, and helped herself to seconds.

A beautiful seventeen-year-old girl with dark hair, olive skin, and brown eyes, Millie occasionally struggled with loneliness. Only four young men her age lived in High Meadows. She showed no interest in any of them. After finishing the pie, a bit on the tart side, Millie puckered her lips and made a loud, kissing sound. She washed her plate and glass, put them away, went out the back door, and headed toward the barn.

She found Annie negotiating a deal for some horses with a Calvary sergeant from Fort Fetterman. When soldiers came into the restaurant, they were loud-mouthed and rude. A few of them thought they had some right to slap her on the backside. Those who tried ended up with a lap full of hot coffee or whatever happened to be in her hand.

"Did you escape or earn a day off?"

"Begged it off. Mother dear is making me clean the inside of the stoves tomorrow."

Annie chuckled at her young friend. Nellie would indeed give her extra work in return for the day off.

The sergeant and Annie decided on a dozen horses with an agreement on cash when the Army picked them up on Saturday. Millie busied herself, scratching a colt's ears as the sergeant left, avoiding being called a pretty girl, or hearing some comment about being "the little waitress."

Hanging the lariat back up on the wall, Annie took a sigh of relief. She always did when she made a transaction. "I need to check the weanlings out in the pasture. Want to come along?"

"Sure. Poncho is out front. Oh, by the way, Aunt Annie, I've been stealing rhubarb pie."

"It turned out a little sour."

"I don't think so. Are you saddled?"

"No, but Rusty's in the end stall."

Rusty, a rust-colored gelding, a little too lazy for Annie's taste, was getting fat and needed exercise. She saddled him while Millie went off for her horse.

The twenty-three spring colts and fillies didn't need checking on. Annie enjoyed being around them. She didn't put them in stalls or corrals because a pasture baby would grow up more intelligent and independent than one kept in a stall. Still, she liked to go out and handle them.

Millie loved watching the babies. "The little yellow one, he's precious."

"She, she's a little filly. She is a cutie. Her mom is over

by the oak."

"They sure look alike. Will she let me go up to her?"

"Probably. She's a friendly little thing, but don't let her kick you."

Millie walked within ten feet of the little weanling. "Hello, can I give you a scratch? Will you let me touch you?" Millie kneeled on one knee to be at eye level with the young horse. The filly put her head down and nickered, kicked her heels up a little, and moved a little closer. Enthralled with the horse, Millie kept talking to her. "Come here. Come on. I'm not going to hurt you." The young palomino took a couple of steps toward her, jumped away.

Finally, she let Millie stretch her hand out and touch her. She came close, with her nose down toward the ground, ran away, only to come right back. When mom moved toward another area of the pasture, the baby went with her, offering Millie a little cow kick as a goodbye present.

After amusing herself with some of the other babies, Annie sat under a tree watching Millie and the filly play. Millie rubbed her leg below her knee, where the young horse kicked her and started walking towards Annie.

The girl plopped down by Annie. "You know old lady Parish?" It was a silly question; Annie knew everyone.

"Do you mean Mrs. Parish?"

"Yeah, her," Millie said, pretending to miss Annie's point. "The ol' bat asked me last Sunday after church if Nellie ever told me who my real folks were. I told her my mother was either the Queen of Egypt or a whore."

"Millie Jayne Bascomb! You didn't say that to her."

Millie started to laugh. "No, but I wanted to." Millie's personality was what a lot of the town folk referred to as "perky." She took few things seriously and considered life something to be enjoyed. The girl saying such a thing would not have surprised Annie much. "She said Nellie's hiding who my real mother is." The girl turned away, pulled some of the grass between her feet. Her shoulders slumped. "She's lying, isn't she?"

"Yes, she is. None of us, not Nellie, not any of us know who your parents were or what happened to them. What a terrible thing to say to you." Anger boiled up in Annie towards Freda Parish, but she didn't let it show. A show of temper wasn't Annie's way. "Millie, you've been told everything." Annie paused. "I can't imagine any way to find out about your parents. Your mother did everything to find out something, anything about your folks."

Whether Annie understood or not, her peaceful way comforted the girl. "It's not I don't think Nellie loves me. She does. And I love her like she were my real mother. If my other ma is the Queen of Egypt, I'll still stay here and work for Nellie, the little slave driver. Still, I wonder what happened to my folks, where they came from, where they were going."

There was nothing to say. No answers. Annie, Nellie, and Gray made a trip down to Nebraska in 1851 for supplies. While there, they heard talk some Sioux had a white child with them. Though they weren't sure which group of Sioux, Nellie became obsessed with finding the infant. So Nellie Bascomb, Annie Laurie, and Gray Wehr set off into the plains looking for the Sioux and a white baby.

Three days later, they rode into the camp of Spotted Tail. They received a cool but not hostile welcome. Gray, adequate in Lakota, stressed their close friendship with the Teton Lakota and how the young chief, Paints His Horse, lived in peace with them.

Based on their relationship with Paints His Horse's people, they found out the child was not in this camp, but the talk was a white baby was in the lodges of A Man Afraid Of His Horse on the Republican River. Gray talked a young Sioux who spoke some English, a young man named White Buffalo, into taking them to the other village.

Persuading White Bull took little effort because A Man

Afraid Of His Horse was an influential chief among the Ogalala. The young warrior would have a chance to impress an important man and gain considerable status as a brave.

A day and a half later, they rode into the Ogallala camp and found a white girl about six months old. The Indians said they stole her from a Crow village about four moons earlier. They did not know how the Crow came to have a white infant. Despite the woman who adopted the baby putting up some fuss, reasoning with A Man Afraid Of His Horse and leaving the camp with the white child turned out to be easy.

Annie thought back through the memories before speaking again to Millie. "Well, I can tell you this, Millie. Your real folks are dead. There's no doubt." The girl shrugged her shoulders a little but didn't object or rebut Annie's statement. Annie sat back against the tree and continued, "Nellie put stories about you in every paper from here to St. Louis. No one ever responded. They died, somehow; otherwise, they would have come for you."

Millie snapped a twig. "The worst is they laid out on the plains, with nobody alive to bury them. If they had family back east, they likely never found out what happened to them."

Annie put her arm around the girl. She couldn't help feeling a little sorry for her. Nellie Bascomb loved the girl with her whole heart and gave her everything she ever needed. Still, nothing changed the fact she lost her real parents, depriving her of the benefit of a father in her home. The girl started calling Gray "Daddy" as soon as she could talk. Gray took immense pleasure in that and tried to be a father to the girl. He was such an easy touch; Millie never received any disciplining or guidance from him.

Annie rose and pulled up the girl. "When's the last time somebody gave you something?"

Millie brushed some ants from her pants. "Well, Nellie gave me a couple of swats on the butt last week for breaking a plate. She made me bend over a table to get them." God, or someone, blessed the girl with wit. "Old man Cain gave me another cussing yesterday."

"How'd you like me to give you that little yellow filly?"

Millie's mouth dropped open. She couldn't speak, an infrequent occurrence.

Annie smiled at her. "You'll need to leave her with her mother until she's weaned, and she'll be your responsibility to break. But, she's yours." Annie was as fine an example of sternness for the girl as Gray.

"Lord, I'm coming out here and cry on your shoulder more often." Another swat on the butt.

Chapter Fifteen

In town, to pick up a few supplies, Annie stopped in at the restaurant. Nellie sat down next to her. "All Millie can talk about is the little horse you gave her. "

"She's a sweet little filly. You need to give Millie a little time off to come out and enjoy her."

Worried about Millie's welfare, Nellie asked Annie if she thought the girl was happy.

"She's fine, Nellie. She's growing up."

"Do you think she wants to work in the restaurant? I love having this place, seeing people, and working inside. I guess I figured Millie would want to do this, too. I planned to give it to her someday. But I think she likes to be outside. Should I tell her she doesn't have to help here?"

Annie shrugged her shoulders. "Did she say she wants to quit?"

"No, but she did ask if I thought you'd let her come out and help with the horses."

"Sure, I'd love her to come out."

Very organized, Nellie immediately assigned Tuesdays as

the day Millie could come, assuming Annie agreed.

"Tuesdays will be fine, Nellie. Tell her we'll start next week."

The front door opened, Adrian Cain came shuffling in, sat down, and demanded coffee. Annie told Nellie she needed to say something to Adrian before walking over and sitting next to the old man.

Something she got an ugly scowl for. "Who invited you to sit?"

Smiling, she shifted toward him, but not too close—he stank. "Did you hear Gray and I are getting married?"

"Well, don't be expecting any weddin' present from me."

"Oh, that's not why I mentioned it." She paused, leaned a little closer to the old man. "I thought you should know Gray will do about anything I ask him." She put her hand on Adrian's shoulder. "Be clear on this, Adrian, the next time you give Millie a cussing, I'm going to have Gray come in here and," her voice got louder, a lot louder, "kick your hind end so high you'll need it sized for a hat! Do you understand me?" Annie stood with a scowl on her face, indicating it was better for Adrian to keep his mouth shut. "And get a clean shirt."

Finished with the old man, Annie stopped at the door to speak to Nellie. "Tell Millie I'll expect her." She went out and climbed in her wagon to head home. Coming up the street carrying a sugar bag, Millie waved at Annie, who slowed down as she drove by. "Your little filly tried to bite this morning. Plan to start teaching her some manners Tuesday."

"Tuesday?"

"Go ask Nellie."

Chapter Sixteen

Gray Wehr and Zach Joseph were cutting yearlings from the north pasture, with Zach talking as fast as possible. "Why you are being so hardheaded about going. Everybody in the valley says somebody needs to go find out about this treaty."

Gray pulled Lena quickly to the left to prevent a calf from escaping. "Let everybody else go."

"If you're smitten, we can take her with us."

Gray glared at his friend as if Zach lost his mind. "Take Annie along? To Fort Laramie? I doubt she'd be too interested."

Zach slapped his rope on his leg to start a steer moving. "Well, have you asked her?"

Gray's voice became emphatic. "No, I haven't asked her, and I'm not going to."

One of the calves separated from its mother rammed into Zach's horse. The horse spun to its right, losing Zach in the process. Gray laughed at his friend. "I swear, Zach, it takes a good horse to throw you. Just doesn't take him too long."

Chapter Seventeen

Trent Thaxton pulled his horse up at the Sioux encampment outside Fort Laramie. He stepped down and led his bay through the tepees and fire rings.

Now twenty-one, the son of fort traders, he ran his fingers through his dark blonde or light brown hair, depending on one's eye for color, tied his horse to the hitching post, and walked up the three steps into the Sutler's Store. Trent loved the smell inside. A mixture of leather, spices, rope, new clothes, coffee, and candy all rolled into one.

His mother, waiting on a Second Lieutenant fresh from back east, smiled and nodded at him as he ambled in. The Lieutenant, complaining about everything he was purchasing, seemed a whiney fella. "The army doesn't pay for any of these supplies?"

Trent's mother was trying not to sound frustrated, a difficult task. "No, son, they issue you what they deem necessary. Unfortunately, two shirts and two pairs of trousers aren't enough."

"OK, I'm getting three shirts and three pairs of trousers.

You're sure they'll let me wear this straw hat while I'm on duty?"

Mrs. Thaxton answered reassuringly. "Yes. A lot of men do in the summer because they're cooler."

"And, you'll give me credit?"

"You can pay on payday."

"Why do I need different ammo? I don't understand why I should buy bullets; the army supplies them."

Trent interrupted. "The army's issuing you copper-cased cartridges. They're too soft. They tend to jam those Springfields. You'd be better off using cartridges with brass casings."

"This is my son, Trent. He does some scouting for the military. He can tell you most of what you'll need."

The soldier about the same age as Trent appeared happy to meet someone other than officers. "So the copper ones they gave me will jam my gun?"

"Yeah, you'll end up trying to pry them out with your knife or something," Trent said, digging a fingernail into one of the casings. "Not exactly what you want to be doing in a fight." Trent's advice was easygoing and not offensive to the green officer, who realized he had forgotten his manners.

"Thanks, I appreciate your help. By the way, my name's Ned Carpenter."

Trent stuck his hand out. "Where you from, Ned?"

"Fredericksburg, Pennsylvania. This is my first time west of the Susquehanna."

"Well, I've never been east of the Susquehanna. Got as far as St. Louis and Indiana back when I was a kid."

Trent's mother decided this eastern boy was in capable hands with him. "Listen, you assist this young man. Your father's out back loading a supply wagon. I'll go help him." She patted the young officer's arm. "Enjoy the west. Come in any time you need anything."

Carpenter smiled and nodded his head. "Thank you, ma'am. I will."

Trent flipped through the pile of supplies his mother

stacked up for the new soldier. "This ought to do you for now. I'll toss in a box of brass cartridges. A Second Lieutenant's pay doesn't go far." Thaxton picked up the straw skimmer. "The only thing is this hat."

"Your mother said the straw ones are cooler."

"Some wear them." Trent put the skimmer on but didn't say a word. Ned Carpenter passed on the straw hat.

"I need to care for my horse. I'll walk with you," Trent said as they left the store. "When did you arrive?"

"Day before yesterday. So far, no one has noticed me much. All the senior officers are involved in this treaty. I'm not sure they'd notice if I deserted." While the two walked along, Trent decided he might have been wrong about Ned being a whinny sort. "Red Cloud came this morning. He strutted around, a huge headdress hanging almost to the ground in the back. The newspapers back east write a lot about him. When General Terry sat, Red Cloud sat across from him, looking mad enough to stick a lance in him. He'd stare Terry in the eyes until Terry would turn away. Red Cloud smirked every time."

Trent's horse kept nudging him in the back. He gave the bay a light tap on the nose. "Get back, Sundance." He began to tell the young officer a little more about which Indians he'd have the most reason to fear. "People around here are starting to call Red Cloud a peace chief. Rumors are many of the Indians think he's making too many concessions."

"Isn't he the Sioux chief?"

Trent shook his head. "Well, the Sioux don't have a single chief. He's influential. Some of the other leaders and chiefs: Gall, Crazy Horse, and Sitting Bull, in particular, are more hostile. Crazy Horse refused to come in at all, and from what I heard before I left, Sitting Bull and Gall are balking about signing this thing."

"I'm surprised people consider Red Cloud a peace chief. All the papers in the east are calling the fighting Red Cloud's war. Have you met any of these chiefs?"

"Naw. Since the treaty negotiations started, I've seen 'em around the fort, especially Red Cloud and Spotted Tail." They turned toward the stable as Trent continued to talk. "I saw Sitting Bull before I left last week. After I put Sundance up, we'll walk over to the treaty talks. I'll point Gall out to you. He's not too friendly toward whites and is balking about everything in the treaty."

Ned said he wasn't familiar with Gall. "Back East, they mostly write about Red Cloud and Crazy Horse, and," Carpenter continued, "Crazy Horse is considered a devil."

Trent pulled the saddle off his bay and brushed him down. "I know an Ogallala about our age named Two Dogs. I met him out scouting with some patrols. We're kind of friendly." He put his saddle on a rack and hung up his bridle. "Anyway, he says Crazy Horse is sort of a loner or something. I think Two Dogs is a little afraid to talk about him. He says Crazy Horse is a great leader. He also says he's quiet, solitary, even among the Indians."

The Lieutenant was curious. "Does your friend, what was his name? Two Dogs? Like him?"

Trent thought a minute. "I suppose. I think he admires Crazy Horse more than anything. Crazy Horse scares white eyes. It's probably his name. Two Dogs told me one time it's Sitting Bull who hates the whites."

"Some of the papers back east call him 'Slightly Reclining Gentleman Cow'."

Trent laughed. "I don't believe I'd call him that, if you ever meet him."

"Is he a chief?"

Trent shook his head. "No. He's a holy man of some kind, quite the muckety-muck with the Sioux."

"Is he an Ogallala?"

Trent thought Lt. Carpenter was woefully uninformed about his potential adversary for an officer in The United States Cavalry. "No, he's Hunkpapa."

"My God," Ned said, shaking his head. "I'm virtually ignorant about these people. At West Point, we thought they were Sioux, or Cheyenne or Crow. The Point told us to learn our enemy. But they neglected to teach us anything."

The army officers and other representatives of The United States Government gathered outside under a canopy discussing the terms of a treaty with the chiefs and holy men of the Lakota and Cheyenne nations. The whites sat in a semi-circle of straight-backed wooden chairs. A few of the Indians sat in the chairs, but most on blankets.

How well the talks were going depended on who was describing them. Rain In The Face and Spotted Tail were supposedly ready to "pick up the pen," indicating signing the treaty. Gall, Sitting Bull, Red Cloud, and others, determined to live in the old ways, were reluctant. Rumors were Red Cloud favored a treaty but wanted more concessions.

When Trent Thaxton and Lt. Carpenter slid quietly into the circle of men surrounding the participants, the talks were nearly over for the day. A Cheyenne Shaman objecting strenuously to something an Army Major said before they came up, waved his arms, shook some kind of a rattle, and paced back and forth in front of the American officer.

Ned wiped sweat off his hatband. "What's he so upset about?"

"I can't say. I don't understand much, Cheyenne. I do all right in Lakota, but not too well in Cheyenne." Trent listened a little longer. "Near as I can tell, he's saying something about being dead, and I think something about honor or lacking it. I'm not sure." Trent nodded toward the officer. "The Major is from Fort Phil Kearny, so possibly it's something to do with them." He glanced around at the Indians. "Two Dogs would tell me what's going on, but he's not around, at least not now. He probably doesn't have enough standing in the tribe to be here." Trent pointed out Rain In The Face, Gall, Black Moon, and a few others to the new officer. "Sitting Bull isn't with this group, but he's supposed to be here."

American Horse stood after the Cheyenne Holy Man finished venting. He told the men from Washington the Indians would think about the terms. The Sioux headed back to their encampment outside the fort, the government officers and military men to the post headquarters.

Ned turned to Trent and offered his hand again. "I better head over to the troop and find out if I'm on an assignment list tonight." The men shook hands, and Thaxton went back to Fort Traders' store and a hot meal.

Chapter Eighteen

"Such a pleasant evening," Jean said as she walked into Annie's parlor.

"Nellie, Millie, and Zach are out on the back porch," Annie said. "We've got a pitcher of apple cider outside or tea in the kitchen if you'd prefer."

"Cider is fine. It's a rare treat. But I can't stay long. We're moving cattle in the morning. I promised Alan to help Martha cook breakfast for the hands by first light." The two women stepped out on the porch, a wide, long one with a swing on each end. A little white table with six white wicker chairs sat to the left of the door. The chairs had yellow down-filled cushions.

"You look tired," Nellie said as Jean sank into the cushion of the chair next to her.

"We've been working from sun-up 'til after dark every day this week. I'm wearing out." Nellie poured a glass of cider for Jean. "Where did you tell the men you were going?" Jean asked, looking over at Zach.

"I told them I had to run a couple of errands."

"Well, Paxton and Ethan are as mad as hornets about you

being gone," Jean said as she took a sip.

Zach yawned. "Let 'em sting each other. Did you say anything to your brother?"

"No, I told you I am not going to be the one to ask him." Hot and grumpy, Jean pushed her blonde hair away from her face.

"Annie should be the one. She's the one who can persuade him," Millie said as she pulled her bare feet up into the wicker chair.

"I'll talk to him. But, I'm not going to push him about this," Annie said.

"Well, you want to go, don't you?" Zach asked.

"Yes, I want to go. But I'm not going to make Gray mad."

"Listen," Jean said, "if Gray doesn't want to go, Paxton and Ethan will go. They'd probably like to make the trip."

A frown clouded Nellie's face. "I want Gray to go along."

"Why?" Zach stiffened, agitation spread all over his face. "What difference does it make if he goes? Hellfire, he ain't the only man in this valley. Paxton and I, or Paxton and Ethan and I can take you."

"You three can go, go to Fort Laramie or wherever you please. But you're not going to take me," Nellie said in a matter-of-fact voice. "Or my daughter."

Zach turned dark red; veins popped on the side of his head. "Why not?"

"Because I'll be a lot safer going to Fort Laramie with him than with you and Paxton. Or you and Paxton and Ethan, all three," Nellie snapped back in a tone indicating her last word on the matter.

Millie shifted in her chair, got up, and sat in one of the swings, looking disappointed. "Now, what's wrong with you?" Jean asked her.

"Nothing. I wanted," Millie stopped in mid-sentence. "Nothing."

Jean crossed her arms; Nellie noticed her lopsided smile and tight eyes. Nellie raised her eyebrows a little and shook her head slowly but said nothing.

"I said I'll talk to him," Annie said.

"How dangerous do you think this trip will be?" Nellie asked, looking straight at Annie.

"Well, I don't think it should be particularly risky. I mean, something can always happen. But I'm certainly not afraid to go."

"Are you sure?"

"Nellie!" Millie said in a half-whiny voice meant to tell her mother she was foolish and overprotective.

"You be quiet. We're not going off on some fool's mission," Nellie said as her eyes shot daggers over at the girl.

"Going to the fort is not a fool's mission," Millie said, in what Nellie thought a sassy tone, drawing her disapproval. The girl dropped her eyes and turned away. "I'm not trying to be smart. I want to go."

Annie smiled at Millie before looking at Nellie. "Well, do you want to go if Gray goes?" Annie asked Nellie.

"Yes, but not without him."

Zach grunted, twisted in his chair, took a long drink of lemonade, all while giving Nellie a *damn, you woman,* look

"I'll ride over and talk to him sometime tomorrow," Annie said. She turned to Jean. "When will he be around the house?"

"He's planning on going over ranch books right after lunch, so he should be in the house for a couple of hours," Jean said.

Chapter Nineteen

It was past mid-day and hot when Annie Laurie walked into the Wehr home. She found Gray sitting at a walnut table in the parlor, going over the ranch books. "Isn't Jean with you?"

"No, she wanted to do a little more shopping." Annie gave Gray a light kiss on top of his head. Gray thought it a little odd Annie had not stayed and shopped with his sister, but he didn't say anything. "You want a glass of water or anything?" Annie asked.

"I'm fine. As soon as I finish going over these numbers, I'm going out to the south pasture and help Alan and Ethan separate calves. Are you staying for dinner?"

"I thought I might." Annie pulled up a straight-backed wooden chair and sat next to Gray. "Gray," she began in a hesitant voice. "We want you to take us to Fort Laramie."

Gray laid his pencil down and put his face in his hands. He sighed before looking up. "Annie, we've been through this. There's no point in our going. Likely as not, the treaty talks will be over by the time we'd get there. If the negotiations are still ongoing, they're not going to ask for your opinion."

Stiffening, Annie leaned aggressively toward Gray. "There is a reason for us to go. The people in this valley want to understand the situation with the Sioux. No one else will go." Both Annie and Gray knew that was not entirely so, but Gray did not challenge her statement. "And, as far as my opinion is concerned, I may give it to them whether they ask for it or not. Someone needs to bring up High Meadows and find out how this treaty is going to affect us."

Arguing would be pointless. Nevertheless, Gray did not like having the responsibility dropped in his lap. "Why can't somebody else go? I guess they're no busier than I am."

"No busier, but the truth is, you're the most capable."

"Of what? Are you telling me nobody in our valley can find Fort Laramie?"

This was not going to be as easy as she hoped. She thought Gray might give in because she wanted to go. But so far, he was showing no sign of surrendering. As a result, she decided to change her strategy. "Yes, they can find Fort Laramie. Except for the Josephs, though, they're all afraid to go." She paused, hoping Gray would look up at her, which he did. "But more, I want to go. It's something important and a contribution I want to be part of. I think I would be a capable spokesman for the town."

Gray almost laughed at the idea of a woman talking for High Meadows residents, but Annie's eyes kept him quiet. "Also," she said in a more hushed voice, "it would be an adventure, at least of sorts. Life can be a little slow here. Not for you. You go off and see the rest of the world. This valley hasn't trapped you, but it has me." She took Gray's hands in her own, "Gray, I want to make this trip, and I'm asking you to take me. Can't you do this for me?"

Jean and Zach came in the front door almost, Gray thought, on cue. He frowned at his sister. "I guess you're going, too."

"Well, of course, I'm going. I haven't been out of this valley for almost a year," Jean said in a flippant voice.

Zach was smiling when Gray told him, "I ought to kick

your hind end."

Zach had a satisfied air about him. "Nellie and Millie said they'd be ready at first light."

Something unexpected. "What?"

Zach shrugged his shoulders. "I told them dawn, and they said all right."

"Fine," Gray pushed his chair back, stood, almost knocking the chair over. "Now, I'll be responsible for all these women."

"I'll be along," Zach said, a little too impertinently to suit the already irritated Gray.

Gray turned on his friend with his eyes flashing. "You don't grasp what may be out on those plains with all this treaty tension."

"And you do?"

"You're damned right I do." Gray rarely swore and almost never in front of Annie. The sharp words and burning face revealed the extent of his anger. He grabbed his hat and headed for the door. "Kick my butt and call me Charlotte." The screen door slammed behind him.

Zach did a mock jerk when the door slammed. "He took that rather well, don't you think?"

"Oh, shut up," Jean snapped.

Gray walked out toward the barn to the stall keeping his new liver chestnut stallion. He reached up and took a halter and lead rope off the horseshoe they turned into a tack hook. The stud asleep in the back corner didn't notice his visitor until the bolt rattled out of its loop. He perked his ears and gave a slight snort as Wehr slid the door open. The chestnut took two steps forward and tossed his head up and down.

Gray stepped into the stall and slipped the halter on the colt's head. "You're a good boy, aren't you?" he whispered to him as he scratched the horse's neck. "You're a smart boy," he told the stallion as he patted him on the chest. "Come on out here."

After leading the horse out into the barn, Gray tied him to one of the posts and picked up a brush out of an old wood bucket. "The gal who raised you, she's got some blame foolish idea in her head about heading down to Fort Laramie." Gray brushed the horse's mane. "Wants to find out about the Indian treaty. Plans to negotiate it, I guess." Gray spit in his hand to loosen a little mud on the stud's wither. "The others, don't ever listen to what they say."

Gray finished the mane and started to brush the chestnut's neck and back. "What Nellie and Millie, and probably my sister, want to do is go to Cheyenne on the way home and buy a bunch of clothes. I don't know who they think they're fooling...well, they may be fooling Zach, I guess." He said stepping around and rubbing the front of the colt's face. "I believe I'll do a little business of my own in Cheyenne. There are a half-dozen or so horse breeders around there. I can pick up a few head to add to Annie's herd. Might bring a couple of sweet little mares, so you can start earning your keep."

Gray put the brush back in its bucket and led the colt back into his stall. "This will be our little secret." He took the halter off, slid the door shut, and latched the bolt.

By the time Gray finished the day's work and got back to the house, everyone had already gone to bed. "Jeannie, are you awake?"

"What do you want?"

Gray couldn't quite decipher the tone of her voice. Undecided whether she was sleepy or irritated, thinking he was going to try to talk her out of the trip. He cracked the door and stuck his head inside.

"Think about something tonight, for me." He spoke in a calm voice because he did not want to sound angry or irrational. "If those treaty talks happen to go bad, being out on those plains might be a poor idea."

"Graham, you worry too much," Jean rolled over in her bed, pulling her blanket up around her shoulders. Gray closed the door, leaving her to toss and turn for the next two hours as she struggled with what her brother said.

Gray went to his room. He washed his hands and face in the bowl of water, undressed, and lay in his bed. For an hour and a half, Gray thought about all the things unpredictable about this trip. Struggling with whether he should still refuse to go, he finally fell into a light, fitful sleep troubled by gunfights and civil war charges. *Go to the sound of the shooting.* The ghostly cry echoed through the night.

Chapter Twenty

Annie had been able to wake up at about any time she wanted to for as long as she remembered. She checked the time on the gold pocket watch Gray gave her for her sixteenth birthday. Four-fifteen. Before slipping out to knock on Jean's door, Annie pulled on her pants, socks, and shirt, a soft dark blue flannel one with cream-colored embroidery around collar and cuffs.

"Jean? You awake?" Not hearing any answer, she opened the door and stepped into the room. "Jean... Jean. Time to get up."

Rolling over and sighing, Jean still sounded half-asleep. "What time is it?" When Annie told her, she asked if Gray was up yet.

"I'm going to knock on his door now."

Jean managed a sleepy laugh. "Well, good luck. I hope he's in a better mood."

When Annie tapped, Gray answered immediately. "I'm getting up. I heard you come out of your room."

Annie smiled on the other side of the door, finding

something warm in hearing Gray's voice so early in the morning. She hungered for September to come. "I'm going down and start breakfast. Do you think Zach is awake?"

Gray grumbled back. "He better be. This was his idea. If he's not here by the time I come downstairs, I'll go roust him out."

Annie was getting the coffee ready when Jean came down. Gray followed a couple of minutes later. "Has anybody stuck their head out to see the weather?" he groused.

"It's not raining," Jean said, wondering if the weather, too, would be their responsibility.

"The sky is full of stars," Annie said in a pleasant voice. "The sun will come up in a while, and it'll be a glorious day."

"Hmph," Gray grunted as he took his hat off the hook next to the door. "I'm going out and feed the horses." Annie and Jean both held their tongues. "Kick my butt and call me Charlotte. I hope we don't start this fool's mission in a storm."

Zach rode up as Gray was opening the barn doors. They were taking two packhorses with gear and two extras in case they wanted to buy supplies. Gray, still not happy, dissuaded Josh from speaking.

"This is a dangerous trip we're making," Gray growled while Zach tightened the girths on the last packhorse, a stocky cream-colored mare.

Zach slapped his friend on the back. "Oh, don't act like such an old woman. Fort Laramie ain't at the end of the world."

"Four women and ten horses, you're gonna think you've been around the world by the time we're back. We'll be twelve, probably fifteen days each way."

Zach perked up, ready to counter the argument. "Twelve or fifteen days? Why I can sure make Fort Laramie faster than fifteen days, ten at the most."

Unknowingly, Zach put his foot in it. Gray planned on taking a little hair off this dog. "I usually make Fort Laramie in eight, and I agree, I can make it in ten dragging you along." Gray tapped a finger on Zach's chest, not a friendly tap. "That's making about thirty miles a day. We'll be lucky to make twenty with this entourage. Then we have to come back home. Instead of a direct line," Gray paused and made a sweeping motion with his arm, "we're going to swing down through Cheyenne."

For a moment, Zach shut up, unaware the Cheyenne secret he conspired in was out. Still, his silence didn't last. "Well, I guess I didn't know we were taking one of those."

"Those what?"

"One of those entourages. What is an entourage anyway? Couldn't we leave it behind?" Always the borderline fool, Zach got to laughing aloud when his friend muttered something about having his butt kicked and being called Charlotte.

"Let's go up to the house. The girls have probably got breakfast ready, and we're as prepared as we'll ever be."

Biscuits smothered in sausage gravy were waiting for them, and Zach announced he would bless the food. "Father, we thank You for this nourishment. We pray for Your protection on us, and please protect this entourage thing we're taking along. Amen." Passing a glance back and forth, Annie and Jean decided not to ask any questions.

A little over an hour later, they rode into High Meadows. Nellie, Millie, their saddle horses, and two packhorses were ready to go. Gray snarled at Zach. "Four women and twelve horses."

Gray stepped down from Lena, took the lead ropes of all six-pack horses, tethered them together, and handed the rope to Zach. Not a word was spoken as the group headed out of town south, with Annie and Jean laughing to themselves.

Chapter Twenty-One

Marcus and Clint Bowden dragged into Fort Laramie four days before Ned Carpenter received his first official assignment: correct the Bowden boys' behavior. The boys set up a camp behind the enlisted men's barracks, and although Clint didn't know where he was getting the whiskey, Marcus stayed drunk most of the time. A hot wind was blowing as Lt. Carpenter headed off to tell the Bowdens they had become general nuisances and to improve their behavior or be thrown off the fort.

Trent Thaxton was watching his bay gelding canter around a round pen when the Lieutenant passed by.

"I'm supposed to go tell those two vagrants; if they don't straighten up, we're going to toss them out. Come on along. They're back in the south end of the fort someplace," Ned said.

The Bowdens were not at their campsite, but finding them took no effort, considering the trail of mad people they were leaving behind. Trent and Carpenter soon caught up with them in the married men's housing area. They appeared to be sober but were delighting in harassing a couple of fourteen or fifteen-year-old girls.

The Lieutenant motioned for the Bowdens to come over to him. "You, men, I need to speak with you a minute."

"What do you want, soldier boy?"

Being called "soldier boy" by someone at least four years younger struck Ned Carpenter as a little funny. He vaguely heard Trent, who had been around boys and men like the Bowden's all his life, mutter "oh boy," under his breath.

Ned glanced at Trent. "Don't worry; I can handle these two."

"They're gonna be a pain in the hind end. Keep an eye on the older one. He's packing." The armed boy concerned Trent since he was unarmed, and the Lieutenant had his army issue holster snapped shut.

This time careful to put his need in the form of a request, Ned spoke to the Bowdens again, "Can I talk to you boys a minute?"

For his courtesy, he got insolence. "I thought I asked what you wanted." Purposely belligerent, Clint spat on the ground close to the Lieutenant's shiny boots.

Marcus Bowden now turned from the older girl and faced Carpenter. "You ain't smart. We ain't in the army. So we don't take orders from you."

Less than three months out of West Point, the Second Lieutenant maintained its full protocol and politeness as part of his demeanor. He smiled and tried to be as pleasant as possible. "Well, I understand you are not military men. However, you are camping on a military base and taking advantage of our hospitality. So I do need to speak to you."

Marcus curled his lip, "Go to hell."

Now, things could go bad. Trent wondered if his new friend was going to be able to handle the Bowdens. Those questions disappeared when Ned's tone of voice changed. "Get your asses over here before I drag them over."

The Bowden's started toward the young officer. As Marcus moved in front of Trent, he jerked his pistol, a big mistake. Before the gun cleared the holster, Trent grabbed

Marcus's arm, jerking him down while slamming a knee into his chest.

The younger Bowden pulled back a doubled-up fist, another blunder. The Lieutenant brought his army issue quirt down across the side of the kid's face.

The Lieutenant squatted to see their faces, both glum. "We could have done this a lot easier, settled things between us, but now we're going to have a little discussion with my commanding officer." He asked Trent if he'd help him take the two over to company headquarters.

Trent took the older Bowden boy's gun out of his holster, slapped him on the back of the head. "Move before I give you a swift kick." Both Bowdens struggled to their feet. Trent gave Marcus a slight shove in the back to urge him on his way. The boy turned toward Trent but quickly thought better.

Lt. Carpenter's report persuaded his company commander the Bowden boys needed to learn some manners. The stockade would be their schoolroom. On the way over to the army jail, Lt. Ned Carpenter, returning to his military politeness, reminded them three more times none of this should have been necessary.

Chapter Twenty-Two

By dusk, Gray and the group traveled only fourteen miles. Nellie's packhorse threw his gear three times before Gray Wehr gave him three or four swift kicks to the rump and a crisp slap with the lead rope.

"Ow!" Millie said aloud, causing Gray to glance up at her. The expression on Millie's face made Gray embarrassed and a little ashamed of his behavior, although it was nothing to what many men would have done. "I'm as fond of a horse as any man alive, but enough is enough." He mumbled in a weak voice. Annie glanced at Jean, who only raised her eyebrows in response.

The group found a little stream with willows along the bank. Dark settled while Gray and Zach unsaddled the horses and tethered them for the night. Annie and Jean got the camp set up while Nellie and Millie started the evening meal.

By Annie's gold pocket watch, it was eleven-thirty. "I didn't think it was so late," Annie said.

A breeze drifting along the stream eliminated some of the mosquitoes. The four- or five-feet wide stream ran about two and a half feet deep. Running clear, the stone bottom was visible in the moonlight. Millie let cool water caress her tired feet in its ripples and swirls.

Jean laid back and put her head in her brother's lap. "Look at all those stars. Now, this isn't such a bad trip, is it?" She considered his silence, affirmation.

Millie came walking back from the water, with her pant legs rolled up and carrying her shoes and socks in her hand. She bent down and gave Nellie, asleep, a little shake. "Nellie? Nellie? You better crawl under your blankets. You're going to freeze before the night is over." Nellie stirred enough to slip in her bedroll and ask what time they would be going in the morning.

"Well, I want to be traveling by seven or seven-thirty. So, I suppose we need to roll out by five-thirty or six at the latest," Gray said.

The leaving time relieved Nellie, who assumed Gray would want to be on the trail before daylight. Millie wondered if anybody was going to stand guard over the camp. Zach telling her they would make a decision the following morning irritated her.

Within the next thirty minutes, all six slept. Gray did not sleep well, however, and by the time the sun added an orangish glow to the eastern sky, he rebuilt the fire, started the coffee, took out enough food for breakfast, and loaded the packhorses. He worked quietly, not to wake the others. Gray wanted them as well-rested as possible for a long day.

Finally, he gave Zach a light kick on his foot. His sleepy partner sat up and ran his hands through his hair. "What time is it?"

"I'm not sure—six—a little after. Why don't you start cookin' breakfast? We'll let the women rest."

"Why didn't you wake me up? I'd a helped with this."

"I couldn't sleep. No point in everybody missing out."

Millie started to stir under her blanket before pulling her bedroll tighter around her. "It's cold."

Gray offered her his hand. "I imagine before the day's

over, you'll want some of this crisp air back."

The young girl let Gray help her up. She shivered and stretched. "What can I do?"

Gray nodded over at Zach. "Why don't you supervise breakfast? We don't want him burning the rolls. I'll fetch some fresh water."

Millie walked over to the fire. Zach smiled at her. "You're a pretty girl in the morning."

"Yeah, I'll bet. What should I do?"

Zach held out a slab of bacon. "Why don't you start this and wake the others?"

Nellie and Jean were awake. Jean was looking around for one of her boots, lying six or seven feet from her bedroll. "How'd my boot wind up way over there?"

Nellie stood and stretched. "Who knows, but I'd check for snakes before I stuck my foot in, least if it was mine."

Jean, hating snakes, gave her boots a vigorous shaking. Once she worked up enough nerve to stick her feet in them, she gave Annie a slight nudge.

Annie woke easily despite not sleeping well. "What time is it?"

Nellie gave her blanket a hard shake before brushing the remaining dirt and leaves off. "I think you've got the only timepiece with us."

Annie pushed her long fingers down in her pocket and pulled out her watch. "Ten after six. Am I the last one up?"

"You're the late sleeper today," Jean said as she bounced up and down while trying to roll up her blankets.

Nellie stopped rolling up her bedroll, "What's wrong with you?"

"I've gotta pee."

"Well, go before you bust."

"I'm going to! I want to roll this up." She got her blanket rolled and bounded off into the willows.

Gray came back from the stream. "Well, Annie Laurie, you're a beautiful thing in this morning light. Was your bed soft?"

"No, and I sure slept poorly."

Zach announced breakfast was ready. He pointed out the considerable amounts of grounds in the coffee but noted Gray prepared it before he arrived in the kitchen. The bacon, sourdough bread, and white gravy took the chill out of the morning air.

Jean returned from the willows and poured herself some coffee. "Is there anything left?"

"I believe as much as you can eat," Annie said.

"Did you hear us talking while you were down in those bushes?" Zach asked. "'Cause we heard you."

Millie almost choked on her sourdough.

"Don't pay any attention to him," Jean told the girl. "He thinks he's a funny fella."

Loose rock and steep canyons spoiled Annie's sleep, not the hard ground. Today they would ride into Crazy Woman Canyon. They would have to lead the horses across narrow ledges where the canyon walls would drop two hundred feet. A slip and you might fall to the bottom, or bounce off outcrops of rock, perhaps not dying the first time you hit, bouncing further down the wall breaking bones, and tearing flesh until you fell far enough for the impact to end your life.

When they left High Meadows, Annie intended to insist on avoiding this route with its steep and narrow passageways, loose rocks, and rattlesnakes every few feet. But they were behind schedule, so she would say nothing about swinging east and crossing Crazy Woman Creek after it ran out of the canyon, losing another three-quarters of a day. She would simply swallow her anxiety and move down the steep trails without saying anything.

Jean had no fear of heights and would scale a horse up a crevasse or through loose rock fissure without a second thought. Surprisingly, Nellie, with all her cautious ways, had no qualms about walking across mountain ledges. So Annie wouldn't complain.

"It's a gorgeous day, Annie." Gray smiled at her as they shook the grass and leaves off their bedrolls.

"I'll bet it turns into a hot one."

Jean also slept little after throwing her bedroll down on a rough piece of ground and woke in a sour mood. Not wanting to be part of any more conversations, she went over to saddle Jack. The gelding's attitude matched hers. Once she threw the saddle on him, he wouldn't quiet down, kept prancing back and forth under the tether line.

He soon caught the saddle horn in the picket line. Fighting to break loose, he somehow got the lead rope looped around his head and neck, leading to a rearing up and pulling back against the tangled lines fit.

Yelling at him to stand still, Jean started jerking on the rope, trying to free him. None of this helped. Behaving like a blame fool, Jean caught her hand in the picket line, ending up with a nasty burn across her knuckles. Jack proceeded to strike out at the ropes he was tangled in, catching a front hoof sending him over backward. The horse's weight crashing to the ground snapped the ropes.

"What the hell are you doing?" Gray yelled at his sister.

"Nothing. This jack ass of horse is pitching a fit." The horse, back on his feet, continued to fight. "Damn you, Jack!" Turning her wrath toward her horse, she yanked at his lead. "Quit! Quit, I said." Once Jack got the saddle horn pulled free, he settled down. Gray and Zach got the other horses under control before the disturbance spread.

"Are you all right?" Gray asked.

"Mind your own business!" The horse might have calmed down; Jean had not. "What got into him?"

"He wants breakfast. You should have let him graze before throwing your saddle on him." Gray stroked the horse up and down his face. "Whoa, whoa, easy. You're fine, Jack." Gray took another minute, settling the gelding. "The rope cut a gash across the horn and cantle," Gray said, rubbing his fingers over the leather.

"I ought to put a rope burn across his ass!"

"Well, kick my butt and call me Charlotte. Who bit you this morning?"

There should have been an apology to her brother, except she was still mad. "Shut up. Go away." Between her and Gray, that meant "I'm sorry."

"Is she OK?" Nellie asked, looking up from frying bacon.

"Better cut her a wide swath for a while," Gray laughed. Laughed a little too loud—causing him to duck the rock that sailed past his head.

Once on their way, Annie rode with Jean a little away from the others. They said little, but Jean appreciated her friend sticking with her. Annie mentioned she hated scaling down through the canyons up ahead.

"Oh, don't worry," Jean said. "Those ledges are reasonably broad; walk along at your own pace. We can work down in about an hour, three-quarters maybe." *It'll be the longest hour of my life,* Annie thought but did not say.

"Looky," Zach was pointing to the right. The group turned to the west. Buffalo. Four hundred, possibly five hundred head grazed no more than a quarter-mile off.

"Lord, they're a grand sight, aren't they?" Annie said.

Millie stood in her stirrups, hoping to improve her view. "I always want to chase them."

"Well, we're not chasing them," Nellie said in a tone of motherly authority.

"Nope, not today," Gray added. "You can do your buffalo chasing another time."

"How long do you think they'll last?" Jean asked. Gray ignored her—meaning apology accepted.

"Anybody's guess, I suppose, but there sure ain't as many as there used to be," Zach said, looking out at the extensive herd.

Millie and the others sat for a few more minutes taking in the spectacle of the huge animals grazing across the plains. Occasionally, a couple of young bulls would joust or try to mount one of the cows. Otherwise, the animals were almost motionless as the mid-day sun started to bake the dry ground.

An hour later, the canyon rim spilled forth a view everyone, except Annie, found exalting. "I suggest we go on down to the floor, eat some lunch, and head up the other side on full bellies," Zach said. The walls were steep, red, and gray. Indians used the red dirt to make dyes and stains. It was quick to grind into clothes, leaving reddish-brown smudges everywhere.

Annie forced herself to peer down the wall she would traverse. A narrow trail, originally a game path, switched back and forth as far down as she could see. She might be able to see the floor if she wanted to lean out enough, but Annie was content not to see the bottom until she was standing on it.

Millie wrinkled her eyebrows. Her mouth turned down at the corners. "I've never been through this canyon before. How come we're going through here?"

"We're behind schedule," Jean said. "Going through the canyon right will save us two-thirds of a day."

"We'll go the other way on the way home," Zach added. "Now we need to make up some time."

Gray put his arm around Annie. "Listen, we can swing around the east end. A half-day won't make any difference."

Annie almost said, "Let's go around," but she didn't. "No, this is fine. We can go through the canyon."

"Are you sure?" Gray asked again.

Again, Annie wanted to say no—or throw up—but a glance at Jean and Zach confirmed they would be displeased about not taking the canyon route. The expressions on their faces irritated Annie. Decent people would have happily agreed to a detour if one of the others feared walking down a two-foot-wide trail on the side of a cliff. Still, Annie shook her head, "no, let's go this way."

"Let's walk the horses down," Gray said.

"What? Why would we want to walk them down?" Zach had the sensitivity of a box turtle.

Gray gave Jean a distinct, sour frown, thinking she might wise up and say something to Zach. Jean realized how callous she and Zach were about Annie's fear of heights. "We've been sitting these horses all morning; won't hurt us to lead them down," she said. Zach continued to protest until Jean cut him off. "Go on if you want to ride, but the rest of us are walking."

"Well, I'll be damned. Walk if you want, but I'm riding down." Zach turned his horse and headed down the narrow trail.

"Why don't you go ahead," Gray suggested, looking over at his sister. Nellie, you and Millie follow her; Annie and I will come up the rear." With no more talking Jean started down the canyon wall with Nellie and Millie following. "Do you want to go in front of me or behind?" Gray asked Annie, who had turned an ashy gray color.

"Either way, I don't care."

"Let me tie the reins around Lena's saddle horn; you do the same with Fury. Once they tied the reins." Gray turned to Annie. "OK, give me your hand, and we'll walk on down. Lena and Fury will follow along." Annie almost objected but decided to go ahead and let Gray be gracious to her. Should anyone say anything about Gray leading her down, she'd tongue-lash them, put them back into their place.

Annie squeezed Gray Wehr's hand as they started down the ledge. By the time they made it about one-third of the way, the trail wasn't so narrow. Two people could walk side by side in several places, which they did, with Annie hugging the wall. "Quite a view; you have to admit that." Annie admitted nothing. She kept walking at a slow but steady pace with her eyes to the ground, never looking more than four or five feet ahead.

By the time they got to the bottom, Annie was in a cold sweat and taking short, shallow breaths, "Are you all right?" Gray asked.

"I'm fine. I need to sit down." She put her hand on her chest. "Lord, my heart is pounding."

"I'll bring you some water. Do you want to go over with the others?"

"Not a chance. I have absolutely no interest in listening to Zach's opinion about how heights affect me. I'm going to stay right here." Annie gingerly sat on a flat rock. "Give me some water and let me rest."

"Lunch will be ready here in a minute," Nellie said as Gray walked up. "Is she all right?"

"I guess so if being scared half to death is being all right. I think as soon as she catches her breath, she and I'll cross the creek and head on up."

"You're not eating?"

"I don't think she's any too hungry."

Chapter Twenty-Three

Gray started back toward Annie with a full canteen. He handed it to Annie, whose color was beginning to return. "I thought you and I might start up. You can rest on top while I bring the horses and everyone else up."

Annie thought for a minute about whether she wanted to wait alone while the others worked their way up. She glanced over at the canyon wall. "Is the trail any wider than the one we came down?"

"About the same," Gray answered, not wanting to lie to her. "But going up is easier. We'll leave Fury and Lena down here. I'll come back down for them." Annie almost insisted on taking Fury with her. She said nothing, deciding to do this the easiest way possible.

"Let's start. The canyon won't get any lower."

Gray smiled as he reached down to pull her up. "Well, I guess it won't get any higher either."

"We're going to head on up," Gray told the others. "I'll come back down to help with the horses and gear." The trail started spacious enough and ran for well over a hundred yards before making its first switchback. A rock outcrop made for a narrow turn, which Annie slid around by bellying up against the wall. It left a red smear on her face and stains down her shirt and pants. For two more switchbacks, the trail allowed them to walk side by side.

As the trail narrowed, Gray put Annie in front of him. He took hold of her belt, and they continued to move toward the rim. They reached the halfway point in about twenty minutes, some a hundred and fifty feet above the floor.

"This is kind of strange down here," Millie said as she studied the walls.

"I think the canyon is beautiful in a harsh sort of way," Nellie replied. "So many colors in the sides. Red and green, with a gold reflection, when the sun bounces off it."

"Gray and Annie will be at the top in another quarter-hour," Zach said as he watched them move up the last half of the climb. "We'll hike a lot faster than they are."

"We should have gone around," Jean said.

"We'd have lost the best part of a day," Nellie countered.

"We still should have gone around for Annie. If I hadn't been in such a cranky mood, Gray would have taken us around. I feel terrible about this."

"I guess now's a little late," Zach grunted.

Millie pointed toward the top of the canyon. "They're almost up. Annie will be alright once she gets up."

"Stop a minute," Gray said, looking past Annie.

"What's wrong?"

"Let me slip by you a second." An icy chill shot through Annie.

"You're not going to leave me standing here?" Gray put his hands on Annie's shoulders. "Lean back against the wall. You'll be fine. I'm going to walk up the trail a little."

Gray's statement did not comfort Annie. "Why? What's wrong?" She took hold of Gray's sleeves and tried to peek around him. "Don't tell me we are going to climb back down and up the other side."

"Relax. I'll be right back." Gray walked about thirty feet.

Annie pressed hard into the canyon face taking slow, deep breaths. What Gray found was a break about six feet long, where the outside had started to fall away. He stomped on the edge, wondering how loose the ledge was. Nearly a foot broke away. Rocks bounced down the face glancing off boulders through brush, sounding far worse than the damage done.

When the falling rock thundered down, Annie leaned harder into the side of the cliff. She wanted to yell and ask Gray if he was all right, but fear choked the words off. "Kick my butt and call me Charlotte." He pushed and kicked a few more times, but no more rocks fell. Gray turned and headed back down to Annie.

Annie's eyes squeezed tight, shutting out everything. Everything except her fingers desperately digging into the rock wall and the damp granite smelling like a wet dog. Weak and shaking, this was the end. She was going to fall.

Gray stepped out in front of her and took hold of her arms. "You ready to go on up?"

She opened her eyes, a little, squinting. "What was all the noise?"

"I kicked some loose rock off the path. I didn't want you to slip on it." Annie didn't fully believe his explanation, but she didn't want any more detail.

"How much farther?" she asked, taking short quick breaths, twisting toward the trail in front of her.

"We're three-quarters of the way. We'll be there before you know it."

"No, we won't."

Gray didn't know how he would persuade Annie to go across the broken section. In only a couple of minutes, they were standing at the break. "OK, we're going to have to be a little careful right here. Watch where you're stepping, and stay as close to the wall as you can." The break froze Annie.

"I can't cross there. Dear God, Gray, I can't."

"Yes, you can." Gray swore at himself. Not only was the path shattered, but there was also a slight downward slant to it. "Come on, a few steps, and you will be across."

"Oh Lord, I can't. I can't do it," Annie kept repeating.

"Yes, you can," Gray told her. But she would have none of it. He slipped his arm around her waist. "You can do this; relax. Here let me slip your belt off." Gray opened her buckle. He pulled the belt out of its loops.

"What are you doing?"

"I'm going to buckle our belts together; we'll each tie one end around a wrist." He looped the belts and tied one around Annie's right arm and the other to his left. "Now, let's face the wall." Annie turned into the canyon. "Lean in; we'll slip right on across. Slide along the face. You'll be fine." Reluctantly, Annie did as Gray told her, and they started to shuffle across the broken trail. Annie would only move her feet a few inches at a time, drawing out crossing the seven-foot gap. Once on the other side, Gray tried to be light-hearted. "Now, it wasn't so bad."

"Don't stop. Keep going. I want out of here."

"Keep my gun," Gray said as he handed her his colt after they reached the top.

"What am I going to need this for?"

"You might want to shoot a whistle pig or some varmint while I'm gone."

"I'm sure I will."

"I swear it's pleasant to hear you laugh again."

By the time they finished lunch, they could no longer find Annie or Gray. "Well, they made it to the top," Zach said. "We may as well start. We'll meet Gray on his way back down."

Gray was halfway to the bottom by the time the girls and Zach got the lunches packed and started up. Zach stepped up on his gelding and reached for the lead ropes to three packhorses Jean tethered together. Gray waved his arms frantically at Zach.

"Wait! Stay Put!" Gray could not yell loud enough to catch the attention of the others. He picked up his pace, coming down the narrow trail in a half run. "Get off the horses! Hold on!"

Zach was on his way to the first switchback, with Nellie,

Millie, and Jean following along. "Stop! Stop!" Once Gray waving his hands back and forth, had their attention, they pulled their horses to a halt and waited as Gray moved down to them.

"The trail's got a break about three-quarters of the way up. We'll have to walk the horses."

"Is it bad?"

Gray's frown told the story. "Bad enough. Let me slide by you and go back with Lena." Gray's mare was in the back of the line. Jean held her reins, with the last two packhorses tied behind. Zach started up as Gray went back past everyone, describing the washed-out section. He untied the tethers from each horse, looped their lead ropes around their necks as he shifted to the back.

The procession moved at a brisk pace until Zach got to the brake. "We'll have a little fun here," he called back to the others. Zach slipped back to the side of his gelding and tied the reins around his neck. He jumped out to about the middle and onto the other side. "Come on, Tom, jump over here." The sorrel threw his head but did not start forward. "Come on, Tom, come on."

The horse, while anxious about being left, still would not step out on the broken ledge. Zach called again. This time he turned and started on up the trail. Tom whinnied but still would do no more than move to the edge of the area. "Nellie," Zach yelled. "Throw a rock at his butt the next time I call him." Nellie picked up a small stone and stepped out enough to see Tom. "Come on, Tom." Nellie flung the rock, skipping the stone off the horse's hind end and sending it bouncing off the canyon wall. Tom jumped forward but stopped again short of the ledge.

"Do you want me to go slap him on the butt?"

Zach thought for a moment. "I'm afraid if you do, and he jerks back, he might knock you off."

"He's not going to knock me off." Nellie slid around the two packhorses between her and Zach's sorrel.

"Once he crosses, I expect the others will follow along,"

Zach said. "You be careful those horses don't cut loose behind him and run you over."

Nellie was now behind Zach's gelding. "All right, holler to him."

"Come on, Tom. Come here."

Nellie brought her open hand down on the horse's rump. The slap echoed through the canyon. The gelding lurched forward, with Nellie taking another swing at him as his hind end left her range.

The packhorse behind Nellie did what Zach feared. He bolted past Nellie, and, making matters worse, he chose the inside of the trail. Nellie tried to duck away from him. The pack brushed over her back, ripping her shirt as the horse shot up the trail. That was not the worst; the chestnut gave his tail a whip as he passed Nellie. The dark red tail raised a welt across Nellie's cheek.

"Oww! Oww! Spit!"

"Are you all right?" Zach shouted.

Nellie saw the next packhorse dancing behind her in a fit of nerves. She threw her hands up. "Whoa! Whoa!" She moved toward the horse and grabbed the lead rope, jerking down, trying to gain some control of the nervous animal.

The frightened mare would not settle down, so Nellie stepped to the inside and let the cream-colored horse go by, giving her a solid, loud swat on the butt as she went. None of the three horses had any difficulty negotiating the broken ledge.

Zach ran up the trail fleeing from the charging horses. Once they passed, he called back to Nellie. "Are you all right?"

"I'm fine. The blame gelding whipped me in the face with his tail. My cheek stings like fire." Rubbing her face, Nellie turned to her saddle horse and took his reins. "Come on, and don't you give me any trouble." She led her horse as she gingerly tiptoed across the break. Millie, Jean, Gray, and Lena, and Fury all followed without incident. The last packhorse, however, balked when he reached the break.

"I'm going after him," Gray said. "Take them on up. Tell

Zach to come back. One of us may have to be in front and one behind this stubborn sap." Gray took the lariat off his saddle before Jean led the rest of the horses to the top.

When Jean and the others came over the rim without Gray, Annie got upset.

"I'll go rescue him and the horse," Zach said as he started back down.

"You tell him to be careful!"

"What about me? Aren't you concerned about me?" Zach laughed, looking back over his shoulder at Annie.

"Both of you, be careful."

"Let me have the loop of your lariat," Zach said when he got back to Gray. He slipped the loop under his arms and around his chest to keep his hands free. "I'll put it over his head, you can pull, and I'll push from behind." Zach jumped about halfway across the gap, intending to land on one foot and leap over to the other side. When he hit, another piece of the broken trail gave way, causing him to slip and careen off the side of the canyon.

Zach came down on the side of his hip, bounced, and tumbled for about fifteen feet before the rope snapped tight, jerking him back against the wall, knocking the wind out of him. "Hmmph."

When Zach fell, Gray dropped to the ground and dug his heels in to gain balance for when the rope would catch Zach's weight. The force of breaking his friend's fall pulled Gray right to the edge.

"Zach? Zach?"

Zach dangled, only about half-conscious. Wehr strained to regain a more secure position in his precarious perch. "Are you all right?" he yelled again.

Zach mustered a weak reply. "I think I busted some ribs. I can hardly breathe. Damn." Zach fought to clear his head. He needed to make some assessment of the situation. "I'm hanging here," he moaned.

"Can you find any kind of foothold or anything to grab?"

Zach pawed out at the canyon with his feet, sending a

shower of rock two-hundred feet to the floor. "I can't. Can you pull me up about five feet? There's a little ledge above me. I need another couple of feet."

Wehr pushed himself up to his feet to lean back into the wall. "How much more do you need now?"

"A foot or so." Gray struggled to take up that much. Zach grabbed at the narrow edge. Catching the edge with both hands, he managed to pull himself chest high on the outcrop. "Keep the rope tight. I'm almost up." He pushed away from the wall a little and threw one foot to the top of the ledge. His heel caught, and for a second or two, held, but his boot slipped, shooting him down the rock like a pendulum taking off on its backswing. Zach moaned as he swung across the jagged canyon wall. "Uhhhh! Ahhhh!" He grasped at every possible handhold, but none held. "Pull back. Pull back!"

Gray made every effort to stop the lifeline as it burned through his gloved hands. It kept slipping. Zach cried out over the rattle of rock and debris flying down the side. Then, an odd silence. The rope stopped ripping through Wehr's hands. Gray stepped over the rope, raised it behind his rump to gain leverage. "Are you all right?"

"I think so. Can you hold me?"

"I can hold you, but I don't know if I can pull you up." Wehr fought for a foothold, slipping at first, before finding a stable place to stand. "Do you have a grip?"

The lariat snapped closed around Zach's wrist on the first fall, cutting in so tight he could not let go if he wanted to. "The rope's got me. I'm caught in the loop. I'm hanging here."

Wehr tried for a firmer hold and managed to take a couple of shuffling steps back up the trail. "I'm in a better place. I think I can pull again."

Zach spun at the end of the rope like a top coming off a string when he fell the second time. He was having trouble connecting with his surroundings. When Gray yelled again, Zach regained some of his wits. He peered to each side before looking up. With nothing to grab on to, he looked down. Relief flooded over him. "How much rope have you got?"

"What?"

"How much rope do you have? I'm only eight or ten feet above the trail down here."

"Six, seven feet. How's the trail?"

"Fine. Lower me as much as you can. The drop won't be more than a couple of feet."

Wehr started to question his friend, but alternatives were minimal, so he let the rope slip through his hands. "No more rope," he said as he felt the knot at the end. "How far down?"

"Two, three feet at the most. Count three and let me go, but count out loud." Wehr did. Zach dropped to the trail and fell forward to his knees. He kneeled for a second. "I'm down."

"Are you all right?"

"I ain't dead."

"Are you hurt?" Wehr yelled, angered by Zach's flippant response.

"Hell, I don't know yet. Give me time to stop shaking."

Gray leaned out over the edge to see Zach kneeling on the ledge, shaken. The packhorse on the other side of the gap posed a perilous threat. By their nature, horses, being herd animals, do not like being deserted by their companions. Gray glanced down the trail in time to see the horse rear-up. His front feet hit the ground only long enough to start a run at the broken path.

Gray kneeled right where the beast was going to land. He lunged out of the way, but he was not quick enough. The horse came crashing down, almost on top of him. A hoof burrowed into his thigh as the gelding's chest hit him across the head and shoulders knocking him to a prone position.

For a brief moment, he could see the horse's underbelly, the cinch, and flashes of horseshoes as the packhorse fought to get a foothold before his right rear foot slid from the trail. The bay's shoes dug at the soft red rock. Momentarily, Gray thought the animal would live, but he was too afraid, too frantic. He spun, sunfished, striking out as he lost balance. The horse fell, stretching out his neck and screaming. Then he was gone.

Gray closed his eyes, but he could not shut out the picture

of the horse lurching and tumbling backward. The twelve-year-old gelding had made one last tremendous effort at life but failed, crashing to its death. He left the ledge with all four feet in the air, with the pack on its back spilling supplies, all careening to the canyon floor and splashing into Crazy Woman Creek.

The world went silent. Zach peered down at the dead packhorse. "What the hell happened?"

"He jumped across. He hit me and lost his footing, went nuts and over the edge." Zach took one more look down at the horse before starting back. When he got back to the break, he put the lariat's loop around his waist before throwing the other end to Gray. Zach stepped out on his left foot, placing it as near to the wall as possible. He took one step with his right and leaped for the other side, with Gray giving the rope a yank toward himself.

"Well, that didn't turn out so well," Zach said.

The men took only a few minutes to hike the remainder of the canyon. When they got to the top, the others had moved several hundred yards back from the rim and were unaware of the accident. "Wonder whose idea that was?" Gray muttered.

The loss of the horse shook up all three women. Jean wondered if they should try to salvage some of the supplies now on the canyon floor, but Annie sternly ended any discussion of salvaging supplies. Silently, they checked cinches and gear.

Finally, Zach spoke. "Well, I guess we should have gone around."

Annie whirled toward him. The fire in her eyes belied the calmness of her voice. "Yes, Zach, we should have gone around, but going around would have cost us precious time. Time, instead of a faithful animal."

"I'm sorry, Annie. It's my fault," Jean said, feeling the responsibility more deservingly lay on her than Zach.

Annie, regaining much of her composure, shook her head at Jean. "It's nobody's fault. I didn't mean to be so nasty. No one is to blame." Annie stepped over to Gray and wrapped her arms around him. "I'm glad we didn't lose one of us," she said as she put her face into Gray's shirt.

"Are you all right?" Gray asked Zach as he held Annie.

"Oh, I banged my ribs up, and I got a rope burn around this wrist, but hell, it's a long way from my heart."

"I'll find some salve," Nellie said after looking Zach's wrist over.

Fifteen minutes later, everyone was mounted and riding south. This time, the two men each led three packhorses.

Chapter Twenty-Four

Zach hated the sadness settling on the group. For a half-hour, he tried to lift their spirits by teasing Millie about her horse, a sixteen-hand Appaloosa, being too tall for her.

"Leave Poncho alone. He can outrun your sack of bones any day of the week."

"Well, maybe so. But at least if I fall off mine, I'll hit the ground the same day."

Jean's gray had been grumpy about getting back on the trail but settled down after a mile or so. The shadows shifted in the trees. Light, dark, there, gone. Jean first noticed him off to the southeast. She moved her horse over next to her brother's. "Do you see him?" The rider was no more than a silhouette against the hazy sky.

"Relax. We're all right. If they meant us any harm, they'd be attacking. Take these horses. I'm gonna find out if he's in a mood to talk." Wehr handed the packhorse rope to his sister. He turned to Zach. "Keep moving along at the same pace. I'm going over and say hello." Wehr nudged Lena into a light lope. As he did, the Indian started his horse toward him in a walk.

Running Wolf, the brother-in-law of Paints His Horse, held his hand out when Wehr got close. He spoke English, so Wehr did not worry about his Lakota.

"Hau Running Wolf."

The Teton Lakota brave, about Gray's age, had long hair streaked with gray. He wore only a breechcloth. His skin shined from bear grease.

"Hau Wehr. I am surprised you are riding this far from home with women. Why are you doing this?"

Gray still wondered the same thing. "We're going to Fort Laramie to learn about the treaty."

Running Wolf slipped off his horse. Wehr did the same. "No good will be made in the talks."

Gray didn't want to offend Running Wolf by disagreeing with him. Neither did he want to confirm the negotiations would be fruitless. He'd be verifying white men weren't trustworthy. "Has Paint His Horse sent anyone to the fort?"

"He sends no one. We will not go to an agency. So no need to talk."

Gray did not respond to the Lakota warrior. Running Wolf was wrong. White men would never be content, letting Indians keep land the whites might want. Running Wolf would someday be forced to a reservation. One of the white man's choosing.

Gray, anxious to move on, put Lena's reins back over her neck and swung back up on the mare. "We need to make up for some lost time," he told the brave. "Give our greetings to Paints His Horse. Tell him if meat becomes scarce in the winter, we'll cut him some cows."

Running Wolf said his goodbyes and sprung back on his spotted pony. He headed off in a slow walk to the north. Wehr loped Lena back to the others.

Annie smiled at him. "The conversation was kind of brief."

"I'm not much of a talker."

"Was that Running Wolf?" Zach asked.

"Yeah, and I suspect he has some friends up in those

pines."

Jean stared back in the trees. "I don't like him."

Gray did not want a lecture on the Sioux or Crazy Horse, so he discouraged her. "Oh, Jeannie, you don't like any of the Sioux." That was far from accurate.

Jean didn't care for the tone of her brother's "Jeannie." He used the name to show affection for her, when she frustrated him, and he wanted her to do something—like shut up.

Whatever they argued about, Jean made sure to have the last word. "I like the Sioux, and you know it. I like Paints His Horse, better than I like you. Spotted Woman is a sweet friend. I just don't like Running Wolf."

The afternoon stayed hot and grew more humid. By early evening, they put over twenty miles behind them despite the canyon problems. Threatening clouds were building off to the west. Gray told them they should make a small stream in an hour or so. With any luck, they would be there and in their canvas tarps before the rain started.

As they got closer to the river, a hot wind blew itself into a frenzy, whipping off Nellie's hat, a funny-looking one, like a top hat but only half as tall. She called it a Victorian Riding Hat. Gray called it silly-looking. Zach chased the thing for over two hundred yards.

The stream, never big, was running a little low for the time of year and was a bit alkaline. Gray and Zach let the horses drink before they unsaddled and tethered them. The women started a fire with the abundant dry brush while the men unpacked the canvas tarps and built a lean-to with the back facing west. The storm held off until dark, allowing them to eat and move all their gear into the make-shift shelter. By ten-thirty, a slow, steady rain fell.

"Are you ladies all warm and comfortable here, enjoying all the pleasures of home?" Gray asked.

Annie, always the optimist, said if the wind didn't start whipping around, they should stay dry in their shelter.

Rain put the fire out in less than thirty minutes, leaving the camp pitch dark. Despite the length of the day, everyone was too wet and too gloomy to sleep. In the middle of their small talk, Zach asked Millie, "Has Gray ever told you about the time he and Danny Tucker killed the little Tucker girl's cat?"

"I didn't kill any cat."

Jean backed Gray's claim, at least to some degree. "No, not a cat, a kitten."

"I didn't shoot any cat or kitten. I didn't shoot anything," Gray said, angry at Zach for bringing the damn story up.

"You may as well tell her," Nellie said. "Zach won't quit until you do."

Gray brushed his hair back, frowned at Zach. Most men, because they had been boys, laughed heartily. Seldom were ladies amused. He decided to finish as quickly as possible.

"Danny Tucker's dad gave him a new rifle. We shot tin cans, hand-drawn targets, and tree limbs until about three or four in the afternoon. Bored, we sat on the front porch with a jug of apple cider, hoping it had turned hard. Danny's mother and his little sister turned up their lane in the wagon, with Susan yelling, 'Danny, Danny, see what I got.' They stop and out hops this little yellow kitten, Susan's yapping 'isn't he cute? Danny's sitting with his rifle pointing up in the air, he points the barrel down, and crack...goodbye kitty."

Millie—well—Millie disapproved. "He shot her kitten?"

"He didn't mean to," Gray said, wishing Zach Joseph had been born mute. "I guess the cat zigged instead of zagging."

"What did his mother say?"

Gray shook his head a little. "I can't say. I thought I heard my mother calling."

"My brother, the loyal friend. He deserts in your time of trouble."

"The summer got hot early that year. Every kid in High Meadows almost lived at the swimming hole in the river. Our frog white skin turned tan and then a deep brown. Over a month slipped by before anyone saw Danny," Gray said. "We were all surprised; we figured he'd been hung."

Millie pinched Gray's shoulder before hitting him with

her fist. "How old were you?"

"Oh, I don't remember. Eight or nine. I suppose Susan was four or five. The kitten shooting might have been a bit traumatic for her."

"I guess so."

Annie laid her head in Millie's lap. "Ask him about the time he and Danny were roping cows. The story is funny."

"Oh, you went from kittens to killing cattle," Millie exclaimed.

Gray slapped at Annie's knees for bringing this up. "No, we didn't kill anything."

Annie jumped in to clarify things. "No, this time they killed a lariat."

Gray started to tell the tale. "I guess we were about eleven when this happened."

"You and this Danny Tucker kid?"

"Yeah, me and Danny Tucker."

"I don't like him."

"His dad had about a dozen steers and cows up in a lot, and Danny and I, for who knows why—decide we're gonna rope one. So, we fetch his pop's best lariat out of the barn. We whirl this thing and throw the loop for about thirty minutes. We didn't come close to roping one. His dad's got a shed built, six and a half or seven feet tall with a door on each end. Well, one of the cows goes in."

Millie gave Gray a light kick. "What'd you do grab a rifle and shoot the poor beast?"

Gray slapped at her foot. "Danny has an epiphany and climbs up on the roof. I'm to go in and chase the cow out the other door, where Danny will drop the noose over her head. I gotta tell ya, worked slicker than a whistle...right up to where the cow gets to the end of the rope, in a hard trot. I'll say this though, ol' Danny held on. I mean, he comes sailing off, like a big bird. 'Course he doesn't fly long. The cow, mad as a hornet, drags him around the lot two or three times before Danny gets the rope wrapped around this scratching post. Now she's caught, but she's pulling for all she's worth. Next thing, she's choking. In a little while, her tongue is hanging out, and down she goes. Well, when she falls, she's got the rope so tight we can't pull any slack. Big ol' heifers too heavy for us to scoot or move. By now, her tongue's out about a foot, and she's making this awful sucking sound. We're getting desperate; time to grab a knife. We saved the cow, but we lost the lariat."

To Gray's relief, Millie found this story a little funny. "What did his dad say about you ruining his rope?"

"He never knew. It sorta disappeared at the bottom of their pond."

"And his dad never figured Danny had something to do with the rope missing?"

Zach jumped in. "Naw...like when Nellie's fancy butcher knife vanished."

Nellie's jaw fell. "What did happen to my butcher knife?"

Millie made a run at ignorance, but Nellie wasn't having any of it. "Millie Bascomb, what about my butcher knife?"

Millie covered her eyes with her hand, spread her second and third fingers a little, and peeked through. "Do you remember when that coyote kept tearing through the garbage behind the restaurant every night?"

"What about the coyote?"

"Well, he got into the garbage one night while Sanchez and I were cleaning up the kitchen. I opened the door to throw something at him." She paused for a moment. "Happened to be your butcher knife in my hand. Oh, Lord, you are not going to believe this, but I hit him."

"She's a regular mountain man."

"And, uh ...the knife stuck in him but didn't kill him. He kind of ran away, with your knife sticking in his butt."

Jean and Annie, even Nellie, laughed. More stories would have followed, except for a gust of wind blowing a corner of the tarps loose. Zach and Nellie grabbed the flap and tied it back down before anything or anybody got too wet. Gray suggested everyone try to sleep.

Chapter Twenty-Five

The bugle cut through the misty gray sunrise, filling the air with a piercing whistle. To Annie's surprise, the shrill sound didn't wake anyone else. Groggy from sleep and disoriented by the fog, Annie wondered what was out there, if anything. Half-afraid, she hoped she might be dreaming. The noise shredded the early morning again, a bull elk.

The weather hadn't improved through the night. Before morning, the temperature dropped, and the rain turned to hail. Annie wanted to pull her blankets up over her head and go back to sleep. Instead, she reached over and shook Gray. "Gray, **it**'s morning."

"What time is it?"

Annie pulled out her watch. "Six-thirty, and the weather is terrible." A rain and hail mix was trying to turn back to rain. "Shall we wake the others?"

Gray wanted to stay in his warm bedroll, but laying in bedrolls wasn't his way. Sleeping in wouldn't get them to Fort Laramie. "Let me put my boots on. I'll go out and see what the sky's like before we decide."

Dark gray, rainy clouds rolled in every direction. Annie watched Gray pull his coat collar up around his ears and walk to the stream. Because of the hard all-night downpour, the water was rushing.

Gray looked miserable slushing around in the drab morning. The lean-to wasn't much, but it did keep the rain off. Annie hoped Gray would decide the wiser thing would be to hunker down for a while and hope the weather cleared. Gray plodded back under the shelter, drenched from his short time outside. He shook his head at Annie, took off his coat and boots, and crawled back into his bedroll.

Two hours later, Annie woke again. The skies had improved enough for the rain to stop, and a few patches of blue peeked through. Annie rousted the others, and in a few minutes, they finished breaking camp and packing the horses. They again headed south.

The blue didn't last long. A long soggy day lay in store, and the group would spend hours in misery.

Chapter Twenty-Six

Down at Fort Laramie, American military leaders were growing frustrated as days passed. Many tribal chiefs, including Spotted Tail, A Man Afraid Of His Horse, and Standing Elk, signed the treaty on April 29th. Red Cloud, Gall, Lame White Man, and others continued to hold out, making new demands. Red Cloud said he would not sign until the forts closed.

Generals Sherman and Terry wanted the Northern Cheyenne included as well as the Sioux. Roman Nose and Dull Knife were leading their tribes further north into the Black Hills and Powder River areas, joining with the Sioux in raids against whites.

The Thaxtons sat down to breakfast before a corporal knocked on their door. "Beggin' your pardon, ma'am, but General Terry is dispatching a reconnaissance and wonders if your son would be willing to go as a scout?"

"Well, why don't you ask me? I'm sitting right here."

The soldier was young and afraid of breaking the decorum. "Yes, sir. General Terry is sending out Major

Crenshaw, and he requests you go along."

"I got that part. Where are they going?"

"I believe up toward the Powder River." The corporal stayed at attention.

Trent's dad told him to relax. "We're not officers."

Mrs. Thaxton asked the boy if he'd like some coffee or a biscuit. "No, thank you, ma'am. I'm only here to inquire about your son."

"Sit down. You don't need to stand to inquire," Trent said. "What's Terry want to go up toward the Powder for?" The corporal didn't consider it his place to answer questions. "You'll have to ask General Terry."

Trent poured another cup of coffee. "Take a guess. I won't tell the General."

The corporal swallowed hard. "I believe—I'm not sure— but I figure he wants to find out if Northern Cheyenne moved into the area."

"You go around doing too much 'figuring,' they're liable to make you an officer."

Trent's mother, always a mother, felt sorry for the young soldier. "Trent, mind your manners."

"Well, Corporal, when does the general want us to leave?"

"I believe tomorrow morning. General Terry said to tell you that you'd be gone only a couple of weeks."

Trent tossed the rest of his coffee down the sink. "Tell him I'll go. I'll be ready at first light."

"Yes, sir. The general also would like you to eat lunch with him. He's meeting with the officers and scouts."

"Pleased to. Elizabeth is a fine cook."

The corporal thanked Mrs. Thaxton and apologized again for his interruption.

By mid-morning, rumors spread through the fort about Sitting Bull leaving without signing the treaty and taking several

Hunkpapas with him. Agitated by Sitting Bull's behavior, General Sherman was surly with everyone around him, white man and Indian alike.

Red Cloud grew more stiff-necked about fort closures. Sweat ran down General Sherman's face and into his beard. Puffing hard on his cigar, white smoke hung around his head. He considered every word he said. "Now, listen, Red Cloud, I do not have the authority to promise the closure of Fort Fetterman." He unbuttoned his blue dress coat and tugged at his tie. He took out a red handkerchief, mopped his forehead, and leaned forward with his feet crossed at the ankles. "All I can do at this point is make recommendations back to Washington, and I am not going to recommend closing every single fort in the west."

A glass of tea sat on a small table next to the general's chair. He picked it up and rolled it across his forehead before holding it against his neck. "You may as well understand the white man is not going to leave. Those forts protect settlers heading toward Oregon, as well as serving as supply depots. What you're asking is out of the question." He sat the tea down and snapped at an enlisted man to fetch more.

General Sherman ground his teeth and frowned at Red Cloud. "I've asked you every day since these talks started if you can control your people, if you can promise a lasting peace. You can't bring leaders like Crazy Horse in to talk. Sitting Bull leaves every time the wind shifts direction. How can I think white men would be safe if all the forts are closed?"

Despite Red Cloud speaking some English, a translator repeated everything Sherman said. Red Cloud started to answer, glancing first at the translator, an Ogallala Sioux, and then at Sherman. Further irritating Sherman, he kept speaking in a combination of English and Lakota. "We want no white man in the Black Hills or from the Platte to the Bighorns, the Wolf Mountains. If no white man comes to these lands, there is no need for the forts."

Sherman bit the end off a new cigar and spit it out. "You would cut the white men off from everything west of the plains? Deny us the right to cross on our way west?" The general stood and threw his cigar on the ground. "These are not negotiations, and I have no intention of giving away everything from the Mississippi to the Snake. The terms of this treaty are set and signed by most of your chiefs." Sherman stomped off, leaving his officers to work out the details of more meetings.

Chapter Twenty-Seven

Trent Thaxton tapped on the door of Terry's quarters at noon. An old black woman answered the door and told him the men were in the dining room.

General Terry, Major Crenshaw, two other officers, and a regular army scout were around an oak table. Terry stood and extended his hand, "Morning, Trent. I appreciate you joining us."

"Thank you, Sir. My pleasure."

Alfred Terry was a casual man—for an Army Officer. Sitting at the end of the table with a glass of sherry in front of him, he was gracious and approachable—for an Army General. Not fussy about his appearance, he wore black slacks and a white shirt with the sleeves rolled up and collar open at the neck. Major Crenshaw was very formal in his dress uniform.

Terry motioned for Trent to sit next to Major Crenshaw. Two more Lieutenants, one of whom was Ned Carpenter, came in, completing the group. Terry walked to a bookcase pulling out a map and rolling it out on the table. "I appreciate your coming, gentlemen. Lunch will be ready shortly, but I thought we might take this time to study where I would like you to go and what your purpose will be."

Major Crenshaw and Thatcher put some glasses on the map's corners to prevent them from rolling up.

"My concern is," Terry began, "over rumors the Northern Cheyenne under Dull Knife, and Roman Nose, are moving up along the Powder River." The general circled the area on the map with his finger. "We've had some reports of raids on wagon trains, killing some, harassing others, and driving most out of the territory." Terry sat down. "What I would like you to do is take a troop and a few extra men, scout the whole vicinity for Cheyenne. The country is full of Sioux, but I'm concerned about the Cheyenne moving north to join them."

Terry took a drink of his sherry and motioned for one of the Lieutenants to roll up the map as his cook started to bring lunch in. "I don't want you to engage. This is a scout and locate mission. Still, we'll supply you well enough to defend yourselves should you be attacked. I think you can be back within three weeks, perhaps as little as two." Terry waved his hand at the food. "Help yourselves, help yourselves."

The old black woman served lunch, a tureen of beef stew, two loaves of bread, and a small bowl of butter.

"You'll be a sizeable enough force the Indians; if they are there, they may spot you first. I want you to be of enough strength to deter them from attacking if you are spotted. You'll want to send the scouts out ahead every day." He looked at Trent and Thatcher. "Don't get too far to gallop back in a hurry if need be, and I want you to stay in sight of each other. Out on those plains, you can view a lot of ground while still keeping each other in sight. Any questions?"

Trent and Tad Thatcher understood well enough, and Lieutenants avoided asking Generals' questions. So only Major Crenshaw had a question. "Should we come across an Indian village, what do you want us to do?"

Terry dipped his bread into his stew, stirred it around ceremoniously before stuffing it in his mouth and talking around it. "Pull back and skirt around. I don't want them threatened. If they act in any hostile or threatening way, use your judgment about engaging." There were no more questions, so after lunch and various small talk regarding Sitting Bull's departure and Sherman's disposition, the guests departed with orders to meet again at first light.

Chapter Twenty-Eight

By their fifth day out of High Meadows, travel turned routine for the Wehr group. Except for the rainy day, the weather stayed pleasant, although a bit on the warm side. Gray figured they were only a day behind schedule because of the slow start, the rain, and a half-day lost drying out gear. He believed they would make the Powder River and camp by late afternoon or early evening.

They crossed a series of ridges, hills, coulees, and drainages for the rest of the day. The grass waved knee-high and green for a few miles before turning stubby and brown. It was the hottest day of the trip, making everyone's clothes damp with sweat.

Perspiration ran down Nellie's back, and her face was as red as the middle of a watermelon. Gray handed her his canteen. "Drink a little of this, but not too much. We'll camp in a stand of cedars along the Powder. We should be there in less than two hours."

Nellie took three swallows. "My lips are so chapped I don't think they'll ever be soft again."

Gray's sympathy cheered her—a little. "We'll stop early, likely before five. You'll have a good rest, and you'll be better in the morning."

"I don't think my swollen hind end will ever improve." The affliction hit Nellie with a vengeance because she rode less than any of the others.

An hour or so later, Gray recognized they were within a couple of miles of the Powder River. He told Zach he wanted to ride up to the far bluff, where he believed—he hoped—he'd see the river and be able to gather his bearings to find the cedar grove where he wanted to camp. Zach started to go along, but Gray didn't want the women left all alone.

Annie volunteered to take the three packhorses Gray was leading. Gray handed her the horsehair lead rope, and Millie asked to go with him. Nellie did not object, so the two loped off toward the bluff a mile or so away.

Jean let out a deep sigh. "Let's wait here until he decides which direction he wants to go; no point in riding straight ahead if he's going to want us to head off to the right or the left."

Nellie dismounted before anyone else. "Amen. I may walk to the river."

Zach, never one to shirk his responsibility to rest, climbed off his sorrel gelding. He wanted to tie up the horses, but the sage in the area wouldn't hold them. He hung his hat on his saddle horn and wiped the sweat off his face. His curly brown hair, thin on top, revealed some of his white scalp. "I swear, Zachary," Jean said, "put your hat back on before Indians see the reflection bouncing off your white head. We'll all be scalped."

"Oh, button your lip. I still got hair."

Nellie sat on her reins and took her boots off. She pulled off her damp socks and shook them out. She rubbed her feet, wishing for some rubbing alcohol to pour over them.

Annie and Jean remained mounted. "For heaven's sake, Nellie, are you going to camp here?" Annie asked.

"I might. At least my butt wouldn't hurt. And Zach's snoring wouldn't keep me awake half the night."

Zach took a cake of tobacco out of his saddlebag and bit off a chaw. "Well, you can all go to blazes for all I care. I'll ride off and leave you sittin' here."

Nellie, standing now, wrapped her arms around him and gave him a wet kiss right in the ear, a loud one. Insulted and with his ears ringing, he put his hat back on and climbed into his saddle.

"And another thing," Jean added, "spit that nasty tobacco out."

Zach pulled his horse over toward Annie. "Don't be sidling over here. I'm not going to protect you." Annie motioned with her head for Jean to come over next to her. Jean stepped down off her horse, and they walked a little ways away from the others. Annie wanted to ask Jean about the incident. This was the first time she had been able to slip off. "What got into Gray when he kicked the packhorse?"

Jean sighed. "Frustration," Jean said. "Gray has a bit of a temper sometimes. He hides his outbursts from you."

"Well, he tries."

Jean smiled at her friend, an awkward, crooked smile. "It's a flash temper. He gets over the outbursts almost immediately." She turned away. "I think he lets things build without saying anything until they burst out. After he blows up, he falls into terrible guilt," she said, looking at Annie. "Gray can be a funny person," she said in a lighter voice. "He's giving, sweet, kind...still sometimes he is so sad." Jean smiled. "My brother is a good man, Annie. I love him with all my heart. He'll be a fine husband."

Annie put her arm around Jean. They started back toward Zach and Nellie, who were still laughing and bickering about Zach's chaw of tobacco. "I understand all those things about him, and I love him," she said. "I was surprised he got so mad at a horse. Lord, he's so crazy about them. I wondered if something else was wrong."

"No, I don't think so. I think he's a little worried about something happening to one of us. He can let the smallest things bother him."

Millie and Gray sat looking down at the Powder River. Gray squinted, fighting the sun's glaring reflection up and down the banks. Off to the left, about a half-mile up, the river bent through a grove of cedars where he wanted to camp.

Being unable to tell if anyone else was camping in the trees concerned Gray. He wished he hadn't let Millie come. He needed to move closer. While he doubted he would find anyone, he would still be putting her at some risk. He pulled a Navy Colt in a Walker holster from his saddlebag and strapped rig crossfire on his left side, sitting along his hip rather than down his thigh. Buckling the gun belt, he turned to Millie.

"We're going to ride down to that grove of trees. I doubt anybody's around, but I want you to drop back and let me go on in alone if we do spot someone. If everything is all right, I'll wave you in. If not, I won't. Shooting means turn Poncho around and kick him back for the others as fast as he can run."

Millie's Appaloosa, anxious for a drink, crow-hopped once or twice. She pulled his head around and snapped at him to stop. Gray told her to pull him up on the other side of Lena.

"I don't see anybody, do you?" Millie said.

"No. Let's go on down. We'll water the horses and go back for the others."

The bluff was steep. They picked their way down with some care, snaking back and forth to hold their footing. Once down, Gray let Lena wade out into the river. Because Poncho loved to roll in water, Millie dismounted and made him drink from the edge of the bank.

As his bay drank, Wehr studied the bluffs for a shallower place to bring the others down. Past the trees, a game trail came down a drainage. He turned Lena, and they splashed out in the river.

"Well, are you ready to go back?"

Millie mounted her horse, and the two started back up the bluff. When they reached the top of the ridge, Annie, Jean, and the others were barely in sight, way back where they left them.

"They didn't move an inch. They're still in the same place."

Gray pulled the dragoon out of his holster. He cocked the weapon and pointed it in the air, and fired once. "You got their attention," Millie said. Gray stood in his stirrups and waved his hat. The little group remounted and headed for the river bluffs.

Nellie rode up barefooted. "I hope there's no Indians around here with you shootin' off your gun."

"You're sassy again," Gray said. He patted her bare foot. "You're about halfway to what you should be."

"This is as close as you'll ever find me."

They traveled along the bluff and down through the drainage Gray and Millie found to the river. The shade from the trees made the air at least ten degrees cooler. A breeze drifted up, and the lush green grass made this the most pleasant spot they camped so far. Clear skies meant they wouldn't need to put up shelters, which pleased Zach, who opposed all work.

Once they set up camp, Gray and Zach decided to walk along the bluffs to scare up some quail or chuckers for dinner. Jean suggested heading down to the river to catch a few fish while the men hunted. The fish would be a pleasant change from the dried beef if the men failed at their hunt.

Gray and Zach grabbed their shotguns and headed upriver. Annie's head ached, so she decided to lie down for a nap while the others fished.

Meandering slow and lazy in the late afternoon heat, this was the largest river they'd encounter. A couple of frogs jumped in the water as they approached. The bank flattened out into a grassy area where the women sat down.

Millie rigged up a pole from a willow branch with a safety pin for a hook and caught a grasshopper for bait. Jean and Nellie decided to let Millie handle the afternoon's fishing. They would sit and watch unless the fish proved to be biting like mosquitoes.

Jean took off her shoes and socks and started to run her feet back and forth through the thick grass. She laid back and put her hat over her face to block the sun.

"Is Gray still mad about this trip?" Nellie asked.

"No, he's fine," Jean said. "Soon as Annie told him how much she wanted to go, he caved in." Jean chuckled under her hat, "and don't let all his complaining bluff you. He's got wanderlust so bad, down deep he probably wanted to go."

Millie caught her first fish, a bluegill too small for eating. She unhooked him and tossed him back in the river. "Go find your big brother."

Jean drifted off into a light sleep, listening to Nellie hum some song she wasn't familiar with. Nellie flipped off an occasional ant or bug crawling on her. Millie caught a few more fish in the next hour or so, none worthy of the frying pan.

The temperature was in the nineties when Jean awoke from her nap. Nellie was lying next to her. "How long have I been asleep?"

"Not long. Thirty minutes."

Jean sat up and tugged at the front of her shirt. Sweat rolled down her neck and along her chest. "I'm about melted. Let's go swimming."

Nellie looked back around at the trees. "I wonder where the men are?"

Jean stood and stretched, pushed her hair out of her face. "They're off looking for something to shoot. Come on, let's jump in the water."

Nellie snickered and started taking off her shoes and socks. Millie turned around to find Jean unbuttoning her shirt and Nellie undoing her trousers.

"What are you two doing?"

"We're going skinny dipping."

Millie tossed her willow branch fishing pole up on the bank. Giggling like schoolgirls, they were in their birthday suits in no time.

Splashing around about knee-deep, Zach's calling out mortified them—sort of. "I've seen two full moons in the same month but never three before."

The air filled with screaming women and belly laughing from Zach and Gray.

Once in the modesty of deeper water, Nellie took charge. "Get out of here, you two."

"Go?" Why me and Gray came down here to do a little swimming of our own."

"Well, go find your own river to swim in. This one is ours," Nellie yelled over all the commotion.

Not too embarrassed, or self-conscious, Jean laughed at the silly situation. "Graham, If you don't get out of here, I'm going to yell for Annie. She'll pin your ears back."

"She's asleep."

"Fine, I'll come out and get our clothes. I'll tell everybody back home you made your sister go parading around naked in front of the whole world."

"The whole world's not here," Gray said. "But don't go parading around naked." Gray paused and laughed some more. "Let Nellie parade around."

"I'll drown first," Nellie shot back.

The two men started toward camp. Zach turned back around. "You be sure to remember what gentlemen we were about this."

Chapter Twenty-Nine

Before first light, Major Crenshaw of the United States Calvary and B Troop men rode out of Fort Laramie's gates, heading north to the Powder River. Most of the Sioux slept when the soldiers passed by their encampment. Except for a few barking dogs, the only sound breaking the morning stillness was the clanking of sabers as the horses moved into a trot.

Crenshaw planned to lead the men along the North Platte to where the river turned due west. He would leave the Platte and head straight north to the Powder River.

Of the officers, only Miles Crane, a lanky Hoosier, had been more than twenty miles north of Fort Laramie. Crane was stationed at Fort Phil Kearny at the time of the Fetterman disaster. After the Fetterman fight, he commanded several patrols between the two forts and as far north as the Wolf Mountains. Crane engaged the Sioux on two different occasions, both times outnumbering the enemy and taking easy victories.

Tad Thatcher, the regular army scout, was in his early fifties. His thinning hair was gray and curly. He wore a full beard and a rawhide necklace around his neck, from which hung the bones of the ring and little fingers of his left hand, he lost to a bear trap at fourteen. He was rough of character and manners. In truth, Trent Thaxton didn't like having him along. Thatcher was a man of crude humor Thaxton didn't appreciate.

"Well, boy, did you leave your ma and pa with a hug and kiss this morning? Or did you do a little business with some of the doves last night?" Trent didn't answer the burly scout.

"'Cause I figure this green Major from back east is as likely to git us all kilt as to git us back to the fort in one piece. I doubt he'd know his stump from whiskey if he gits us into a fight." Thatcher bellowed loud enough for most of the troop to hear.

Trent stared out into the morning's first light. "I kind of thought we're to keep him at arm's length from the Indians."

Thatcher growled back. "Let's hope he's got the sense to stay at arm's length." The scout loped his horse up toward the front. Trent pulled over closer to the column.

Trent was shooting the bull with one of the privates, one Slocumb Dillon, late of London, England, when Ned Carpenter came lopping up.

"Hello, Lieutenant. All quiet this morning?" Trent asked, holding out a slice of beef jerky to the Lieutenant.

"The Sioux haven't attacked us, and nobody's fallen off his horse yet," Carpenter said after declining the beef.

"That's good, Lieutenant." Trent laughed.

Carpenter motioned up toward the Major. "Major Crenshaw wants you and Thatcher. He's wondering if you ought to be moving out."

Trent turned back to the English private. "Well, Dillon, I guess it's time for me to go to work. Don't let the sun bake your brain."

Trent and Lieutenant Carpenter loped their horses back to the front of the troop, where Major Crenshaw acknowledged Trent's arrival with a nod of his head. The older scout was with the officers. "We're over three hours from the fort," Crenshaw began. "I suppose you two men should move on out ahead."

"I guess that's what we're along for," Thatcher said, meaning to be insulting. Thatcher's mood was worse than usual. Because of the early start. Thatcher liked to drink deep into the night and meet the day sometime around noon.

The Major ignored Thatcher's surliness. "Will you come in for the noon meal?"

Trent patted his bay on the side of the neck. "Probably not, Major. Unless we find something to report, we'll stay out 'till the night camp. I'd move over a ways from the water, half-mile or so. As the day heats up and the horses get thirsty, some of them may be a bit grumpy, wanting water if they're walking right along the river."

Thatcher nodded in agreement. "Pull back over to the river when you break for the mid-day meal. Give 'em a drink and have one yourself. Slide away from the water again 'till night."

The Major turned to Captain Crane. "Start moving the men away from the water. Let's keep them at a rapid pace but short of a forced march."

Thatcher bit off a chunk of tobacco, a habit evident in his stained beard. "You ready, boy?"

Trent swallowed the urge to mouth off to the older scout. Instead, he told Thatcher to go ahead, and he'd follow. He turned toward Ned Carpenter and waved his hat. "Save me a little something from tonight's meal."

The two scouts urged their horses into a lope as Ned Carpenter and the rest of the troop veered off to the right to put a little distance between them and the river. The morning sun was turning the plains hot and uncomfortable.

Chapter Thirty

Annie and Gray rode a few yards from the rest of the group, talking about everything from what time of day to hold the wedding to which pasture to put the mares in when fall came. Annie wanted an evening ceremony in the flower gardens behind the Baptist Church.

"What'll we do if it rains?"

"We'll move inside the church. But it's not going to rain. I want to go by Douglas or Cheyenne on the way home. I bet they have a nicer frock coat than they do at the Keller's." Now the truth was out. Gray chuckled to himself at the easy way Annie slipped the little Cheyenne surprise into the conversation.

"You don't want me ro buy my outfit from Keller's? That may not go over so well." Gray couldn't care less where he purchased his wedding coat; he liked a little fun with Annie.

"I bought the material for my dress there. Jean and Nellie got the material for their dresses from them. They should sell something more fit for a groom as handsome as you. Back when my folks owned the store, they kept a better selection for special occasions."

Gray smiled at her. "Well, whatever you say. I want the wedding the way you want."

They rode along together without saying much of anything else, enjoying the quiet of each other's company for another half-hour before Jean joined them. "Lord, I always forget how these plains stretch on forever with no shade," Gray's sister complained. She hung her hat on the saddle horn. For someone blonde and fair-skinned, Jean's face never burned. She got a deeper tan. She took a string out of her pocket and tied her hair back. Her face's features were sharp, and with her hair back, her high cheekbones became more distinct, almost chiseled looking.

At nineteen, Jean fell in love. Her twenty-one-year-old beau was an easygoing only child of an older couple who came to High Meadows in the summer of 1841. Though the winter snows of 1852 piled deeper than anyone had ever seen, hot weather arrived early in the spring.

Flash floods thundered down through streams and creeks a man could typically step across. Seven Brothers Creek roared out of its banks. Andy, her fiancé, and Ethan Joseph were trying to move cattle across when Andy's horse went down, and the creek sucked him down. Ethan dove under the cold water over and over until he was exhausted, but he did not find Jean's brown-eyed lover.

Three days later, they found his body almost four miles downstream. For all appearances, Jean gave up on life for the next several years. Not until Gray took her with him on a trip down into Kansas did she regain some of her old glow. Still, she never showed much interest in being courted again, although many, including the dashing J.B. Hickok, tried. Zach Joseph still made no secret of wanting to walk the aisle with her.

"Listen," Jean said. "I didn't come over here to interrupt. Let me lead those packhorses for a while. Millie already has Zach's. It gets stale and tiring dragging those all day."

"Jeanie, you're a saint."

She took the lead rope from her brother. "I'm not sure I'm a saint, but you might be right. I'll leave you two alone." She turned with the three packhorses and headed back toward Zach and the other two women. Gray looked up at the sun. "Close to noon. We should start looking for a place to take a short rest."

"Any chance of finding some water out here?" Annie asked.

Gray shook his head. "Not much. We'll cross a few streams and creeks if they haven't run dry. The Lightning is the next river. We won't be there 'til tomorrow night or the day after."

Annie unbuttoned her collar. "That'll be hard on the horses."

"It'll be hard on Nellie, too," Gray said. "I hope we'll come across some running streams. Keep your eyes open for trees or spots of green."

A hundred yards or so, off to the left, a gully ran east and west. Gray climbed off Lena and waved for Annie to bring the others. The gully, no more than a ditch, was dry and dusty. Its bank washed out on the west side was deep enough to provide some shade.

Nothing resembling a tree grew anywhere in sight. A little water might flow through early in the spring, but any trickle would be long since dried up. Millie and Jean picked out some of the biggest sagebrush to tie the horses. Once done, they jumped down into the shade with the others.

A hot breeze was blowing, stirring up some dust. A few clumps of brush jutted from the side of the bank, full of spider webs and their spiders, making the place a miserable spot for a picnic. The women wanted to move on without stopping at all. Still, Zach insisted the horses needed some rest, and it wouldn't hurt the females to be out of the sun for a little while.

Nellie's reins wore a blister inside her thumb. Annie had some salve in her saddlebags. They climbed up the side of the ditch. From the top, Nellie called back, telling Jean she had not done much of a job tying horses because two were wandering around loose.

Annie volunteered to catch them, but Jean told her to take care of Nellie's thumb "before gangrene sets in, and we have to cut her arm off at the elbow." Jean scampered up herself. The packhorse, nibbling at a patch of dry cheatgrass, made no effort to escape. She re-tied him and started for her gray a little further down the top of the gully, looking for more grass to nibble on.

"Come here, Jack." The horse took a few steps away from her. "Whoa, Jack. Stand still." He took another step or two, but she soon caught him and tied him to a stronger-looking piece of sage.

Jean started to walk back to the others. *Buzz.* Silence. *Buzzzz!*

The bunny shuddered again, went into convulsions. An eight-year-old couldn't help the little rabbit. But she would never forget. Never.

Where was the devil? He sounded a little to the right— right next to her. He rattled louder. Satan always comes in the form of a snake to sink his fangs deep and shoot his victim full of poison. *Don't move.* She shut her eyes. *Think Jean, think. What am I supposed to do? They strike at heat and movement. Their vision is poor.*

The snake stopped rattling. *The demon wanted to trick Jean into moving*, stepping in the wrong direction, stepping closer. Give him a reason to strike. He started again, louder and madder. Jean was not scared or afraid. Her terror was far beyond those emotions. Her body shook in a pulsating rhythm. More color fled from her face with every rattle. *He's to the right. Should I jump to the left? Oh, God, what if he bites. They're almost deaf. Call Gray. Do it now.* In the feeblest, quivering voice, she managed to say her brother's name.

He didn't answer. *Damn you, Gray, come up here. Call him again. Holler louder.*

Her throat was too dry, too tight. She was choking. *Dear God, coughing means shaking, don't let me cough.*

Finally, Gray came to the top of the bank. The others followed. They'd all see her die.

"What's wrong?"

Jean wanted to be small, a child again, to rush into her brother's arms. She would settle for speaking. She stood staring straight ahead, tears running down her face.

Her brother pulled his pistol. "What's wrong?"

Snake. Aren't you listening? He's rattling so damn loud.

"I hear him. Calm down! Don't make any move provoking him to bite. Turn your head as little as possible, but try to find him."

Jean moved her head—slowly—only because her brother said to. A half a turn. There he was, a yellowish viper, coiled and ready to strike. "It's huge."

"All right, do you think he can strike you?"

"He's right by me. Do something!"

"Stand still! I can't find him. I need to move around behind you. He's not likely to strike if you don't provoke him." Gray had no idea if the old rumor was true or not.

"Hurry up, damn it!"

"Don't swear at me."

Gray crept behind his sister, feeling for his knife at the same time. If the snake struck, he wanted to cut the bite open as quickly as possible.

Jean felt him bite, violent, horrible burning, right below her knee. It would be worse if he did strike.

Gray found the snake—Jean's Lucifer—big, ugly yellowish-brown, cat-like pupils, coiled with his head up high to strike.

Jean closed her eyes, swallowed her tears, prayed to stand quiet, prayed the snake would not bite—but mostly, she prayed her brother would not miss.

The Colt's report shattered the air. Jean started screaming, jumping up and down, and brushing her pants like she was on fire. Annie rushed to her, grabbed her, but holding on to her near-hysterical friend proved quite a task. "You're safe. You're fine, Jean. The snake is dead."

Jean went limp in Annie's arms. She took a deep breath, exhaled, then another deep breath. "I've never been so damn scared."

"He's about five feet long, but he won't be rattling at anybody else," Gray said in a more cheerful voice.

Zach picked up the rattler, holding him at arm's length. "He'd make a hearty lunch if you want to cook him up."

"I'm not cooking that filthy thing," Nellie put an end to any argument about eating snake.

Chapter Thirty-One

The snake incident ended the mid-day rest; Jean rode close to her brother for the remainder of the afternoon. Everyone welcomed the evening's arrival. The men shot some scrawny sage hens Nellie cooked, along with cornbread. Zach and Jean both fell asleep before dark settled over the campsite.

Coyotes, in full chorus, mystified Millie. "What do you suppose they're howling about?"

"How on earth would we know?" Nellie said. "Ain't none of us ever been a coyote."

"For heaven's sake, aren't you the old grump?" Gray chided, defensive about Millie.

"What do you think they're howling about, mister coyote expert?"

"They're singing to the moon and each other. Tellin' each other about their day, what they ate for lunch, how far they had to chase it. Mostly, I believe they're singing to the moon like a man does to his horse when he's out all alone."

Nellie stood and brushed the dust off her pants. "You sing to your horse? Well, I'm going to bed before you start." She reached down and patted the side of Millie's face. "You better head to bed, too, little girl." She turned back toward Gray. "'Cause we have to be on the trail by first light."

Gray raised one eyebrow. "Well, you can sleep 'till noon. Course we won't get to Laramie before the first snow."

Nellie started toward her bedroll, turning around once to stick her tongue out at Gray, giving him a little smirk before shaking her backside at him and moseying off.

Millie stood. "I better go with her. Otherwise, I'll be in trouble if I'm not the first one up."

Annie told the girl goodnight and called out to Nellie, "sleep tight." Annie laid her head on Gray's stomach. "Do you sing to your horse?"

"You bet. Lena likes opera."

Annie laughed at her man. "I can imagine you singing opera."

"I sing opera quite well, thank you."

"Oh, I bet you do. And I'll bet the coyotes sing that night."

"They do. They join in and accompany me."

"You mean they all want to jump in and drown you out."

"Well, now you've gone and hurt my feelings," Gray said in his most pitiful voice.

"Oh, I'm sorry. Let me give you a kiss." Annie rose and kissed Gray's lips. She ran her fingers through his hair. "Are you tired?"

"A little, how about you?"

Annie sat up and pulled her knees up between her arms. "Not like last night. Everybody else is worn out. Are you glad we came?"

"I'm glad I came with you," he said, putting his arms around her.

Before leaving High Meadows, Annie decided to find out about two parts of Gray's life, areas of mystery to her. He would be reluctant to talk about the second.

"Gray? Why did you go off and fight in the war? I guess I never understood. We were so far removed. No one else in the valley went."

Gray fumbled with Annie's ring. "I thought the nation to be something worth preserving."

"Sometimes, I wonder if we're a part of the country."

"I think we are. I think we're where the growth will be. I think we'll be the heart of this country someday."

"They say brothers fought against each other, families lost all their children."

"Sherman was right. War is Hell," Gray answered, looking down at the ground. "I remember reading newspapers about battles I fought in. The papers declared 'glorious victories,' but nothing was glorious." His face grew somber, almost sorrowful. "Men paid a bloody and terrible price, saving this nation. If a man was shot in the arm or a leg, they didn't try to save the limb; they amputated. Wounded men begged friends to kill them. Men who wanted to surrender were gunned down or run through with a bayonet. Men sat alive in pools of their own blood with their insides spilled out in their laps. War is a cruel thing. It takes brave men to fight for what they believe in. The rebs were wrong. Their cause was despicable. Still, many confederates fought bravely. I talked with some who were captured. Some claimed Christ. But none could justify enslaving another human."

"You're a brave man," she whispered, laying her head on Gray's shoulder.

"I didn't mean me, Annie. I had no idea what courage or honor was...until I saw it in others. This may surprise you, Annie. In my heart, I think I'm a pacifist. But," he gazed at Annie's face shining in the moonlight. "Some things are worth preserving, taking a stand for, and," he said quietly, "dying for." He wiped his eyes before looking back at Annie. "I hate a fight, Annie," he said, pausing to touch her knee. "I'll also say this; if I'm in one, I'm going to fight to win."

Annie sat quiet for a while, thinking about the character of the man she loved. After a time, she took his hand from around her shoulder and kissed each finger. "I want you to tell me something else."

Gray kissed her behind the ear. "Must be my night for

confession."

"Are you going to be content in our valley raising horses, not riding off whenever the mood strikes you?"

"Ah, the wanderlust. I wondered when that was going to come up."

"Be serious with me."

Gray sighed, leaned closer to her. "Annie, I want to stay in the valley as your husband. I have for as long as I can remember."

She lay her head on his shoulder. "Why haven't you?"

Gray turned his eyes away. She repeated her question, taking his chin in her hand to make him look at her. Her brown eyes, soft and warm, made answering difficult. "You know why."

Annie rattled off Gray's oft-used explanation: "Because you shot a gunman named Jack Winslow and got a reputation with a gun, which every gunman and young fool in the territory wants to take away. And you don't want them coming into High Meadows looking for you." When she slipped out from under his arm and turned to face him, he thought back to the morning when Jack Winslow walked into the Comanche Bar in a crummy little Kansas town.

Winslow wanted to settle down with a woman after drinking all night. He grabbed a blonde-haired saloon gal named Blue Tooth Sally, who objected to his manner. She jerked away and slapped him across the face. Winslow struck her hard enough with the back of his hand to split her lip and send her sprawling out on the saloon floor. She tried to sit up, covered with sawdust and whiskey. Almost without thinking, Gray, not yet nineteen, reached down to help her up.

"Git away from my whore!" The drunken Winslow grabbed for his gun. Gray pulled his pistol and shot. He didn't remember squeezing off the second and third rounds; he only remembered hearing the Navy Colt's explosions.

The sheriff called it "justifiable." Blue Tooth Sally made a considerable effort to comfort him with her charms, but Gray, although tempted, shunned her overtures. "Justifiable," or not, the killing troubled Gray for a long time.

Rumors flew all over Kansas Winslow's family, of no higher morals or social standing than Jack himself were hunting for Wehr, intent on gunning him down. None of Winslow's kin ever showed up.

Others did. With blood in their eyes, they came looking for a name. None matched Wehr with a gun, and they all paid a high price for their recklessness. Still, the more men tried, the more others came.

"Gray," Annie said, looking into his eyes. "I don't believe you're telling me the real reason." To her, the whole thing was preposterous. Gray left searching for freedom from something, although she had no idea what. "Why do you think a gunman will ever come?" Annie paused for a moment. "Are you sure, or does the idea make for a convenient excuse?"

It was not a convenient excuse. But Gray didn't respond; he stared into the night.

"What are you thinking about?"

"Nothing." He lied. "I was listening to you breathe."

"Gray, if you don't think you can live in our valley, I mean if for some reason you have to go away sometimes, I'll live with that. I love you. If I have to, I'll settle for as much time as you'll give me. I'll take it." Annie drew a deep breath, "unless you keep another woman somewhere."

"What?" Gray Wehr had never loved any woman other than Annie Laurie. How could she imagine the possibility? "Annie, I've loved you all my life, you and only you."

She smiled at him, put her arms around him with her head on his shoulder. "I believe you. I don't think you've ever loved anyone else. Likely been with a few, though."

That was startling. Gray wondered what she knew—or thought she did. Nellie? Ally Hart?

"Why Annie Laurie," Gray laughed. "How can you say such a thing? And you, the joy of my life. When I think of you, it's like a lady with a lamp. I see you pass through the glimmering gloom and flit from room to room. And slow, as in a dream of bliss, I, the speechless sufferer, turn to kiss your shadow as it falls upon the darkened walls. As if a door in heaven should be opened and closed suddenly, your vision came and went, the light shone was spent."

"What a beautiful little speech. Gray Wehr, 1868?"

"Longfellow, about 1857."

"I still want an answer to my question. Will you stay home?"

He held her and thought about how to answer. He wanted to tell her the truth, whatever the truth was. Something deep within him made him wander, something he feared. He sat back. "Annie, I'm not sure I can answer." Her searching eyes cut into him, troubled him. "When I come home, I want to stay forever. This will sound like I'm insane, I guess. At home, everything can be fine. I'm happy until dark feelings inside of me take over." His voice was pallid, toneless like the face of a dying man. "I can't describe them; they're like drowning in muddy water. I can't sleep at night. I'm terrified. The war and gunfights haunt me. I'm lonely, even when I'm with people. I suppose those feelings are the reason I leave."

He crossed the line he held his emotions behind. He was too honest. He fell back on his old excuse. "Annie, what if somebody did come gunning after me?"

"Graham," Annie's voice trailed off. "No such thing is going to happen."

She was wrong. His excuse was valid because many had, just not to High Meadows. "Annie, strangers fear me because of rumors I'm a vicious killer. Some of them have hate in their eyes. They're wondering if they're fast enough with a gun to cut me down."

Gray turned back toward the woman he loved. "Annie, these are men I never as much as insulted. What if some terrible thing happened to someone in the valley, to you, Jean, or the little girl asleep by the fire? I try to convince myself there's no reason to be afraid, but I can't. The whispering haunts my sleep. I wake up seeing the flash of a gun--so I leave." He sat for a minute, listening to the quiet night. He wanted to tell Annie more about the nightmares and about the darkness he suffered through. He had become settled in his mind there would be retribution or consequences of the prodigal life he had often led. He didn't say any more about his private demons. "I guess I want to run away from myself," he said. Gray stopped talking. He put his arms back around Annie. "I start missing you, and I come home."

"I think you're a poor judge of your friends. I don't know a soul who wouldn't be proud to stand behind you. I'm going to ask you something I've never asked you before." Gray feared this was not going to be good. "How many men have you killed?"

He hoped she would never ask him. The answer might stop her from loving him. "None who didn't deserve killing."

Annie let his answer pass.

They held each other and talked through most of the night as Gray tried to open up to her. Millie woke up twice and asked, "Are you two still talking?"

Finally, they crawled into their bedrolls to steal a couple of hours of sleep.

Zach awake at first light, rebuilt the fire to start breakfast.

As they were saddling up, Nellie asked Gray if he thought they would make the Lightening River by nightfall.

"I'm not sure." Gray checked whether Annie was close. "Nellie, can I ask you a question?"

"Well, sure, why couldn't you?"

Gray buckled the cinch and lay his arms across the saddle's seat. "Annie and I talked almost all night. I told her things about me that I didn't ever plan on telling anyone." He fumbled a little with the reins. "You talk to Annie...a lot. Do you tell her everything?"

Nellie laughed at Gray. Not much of a laugh, a little one. "Well, I tell her almost everything," she said. "Course, I'm not going to marry her." She took a step closer and gave Gray's hand a little rub. "Gray, she doesn't expect perfection out of you. And she doesn't want to judge you. She wants to understand you and love you. And for you to love her back." She smiled at her old friend, mischief in her eyes. "And if she knows about that little scar way down low on your back, it's not because I told her."

Chapter Thirty-Two

By mid-morning, the sun blazed down, raising the temperatures to over a hundred degrees. The plains flattened out. No hills or bluffs, nothing but dry grass laying limp against the breezeless horizon. The horses were sweaty and thirsty. One of the packhorses Gray led kept walking up against Lena's backside and rubbing his halter against her rump. Finally, the mare, tired of his behavior, gave him a kick with her left foot. Before Gray reacted, the sorrel packhorse jerked the rope out of his hand and commenced into a fit.

The horse broke the tether to the two horses tied behind him. One bolted to the south. The other whirled twice before running head-long into Jean's gray, setting him off bucking, twisting, losing Jean on his third lunge. Zach got the horses he was leading out of the commotion before they joined the ruckus.

The animal that started the whole thing continued sunfishing wildly, all four feet off the ground. His nose nearly touched his hoofs at the peak of every jump. He whirled, kicked, and turned, throwing supplies in every direction.

The flour sack burst open, sending flour over a twenty-square-foot area. Bacon flew one way, jerky another. Finally, he landed on his lead rope. He threw his head back, snapping the rope off at the halter. This sent him into a wilder fit, the highlight occurring when he tripped on his own bucking feet, fell, and rolled over the pack saddle, breaking it in two places.

Gray jumped off Lena and, while the packhorse was in the process of getting back to his feet, managed to grab its halter. The horse jerked back two or three times, trying to free itself from his grasp, but because Gray held on out of sheer anger and the horse had about worn himself out, he gave up on freeing himself from Wehr's hold. Once the rogue calmed down, the other horses settled down. Jean's horse and the other packhorse stopped about a quarter-mile away and stood snorting at the air.

Annie helped Jean to her feet. "Are you hurt?"

Jean moved her head in a circular motion around her shoulders. "I don't think so. When he threw me, I bounced against the stupid gelding. I guess he broke my fall."

"You're sure you're all right?"

Nellie, having her own problems settling her horse down, noticed the blood on Jean's shirt. "You're arm's bleeding."

Jean did not feel any pain, and once they pulled her sleeve up, they found a nasty scrape, nothing more.

Zach handed Annie the rope to the other three packhorses and headed over to catch Jean's gray and the black packhorse. Millie and Nellie tried to salvage as much flour from the burst sack as possible. Jean and Annie started picking up the supplies, scattered from "hell to breakfast," according to Zach.

Gray assessed the damage to the packsaddle and found it unfixable. Fortunately, they had brought the two extra horses, both with packsaddles. Gray pulled the straps off the busted saddle. "The rest isn't worth haulin' back. We'll pick up another one at Fort Laramie."

The better part of an hour went into packing the scattered supplies and gear. As they remounted, Zach motioned for Gray to come over a little ways away from the group. "We probably don't want to tell the women, but there are a lot of pony tracks over by where I caught those horses, unshod ones."

Gray took off his hat to wipe the sweat from his brow. "Which way?"

"South, same as us." Zach turned his back. "They're—I'd guess two days or more. Ten or twelve of them, it's not a village moving."

Gray tapped Lena's reins against his leg. "Well, I agree. Let's not say anything right now. Keep our eyes open." Both men mounted and eased their horses back to the others.

The rest of the day went without incident until about two-thirty when they spotted a small grove of trees. Zach gave the rope to the packhorses to Jean and loped over for a better view. He found a stream about three feet across.

Chapter Thirty-Three

Trent Thaxton and Tad Thatcher scouted little more than two miles out in front of the troop. With Thatcher to the east and Trent to the west, they kept as much ground between themselves as possible while maintaining visual contact.

So far, they found no signs of Indians, not Sioux or Cheyenne. Trent scared a few prairie dogs and one rattlesnake, but nothing else moved. Thatcher started up a small hill when something at the top caught his attention. He pushed his paint horse into a light gallop. He found what they were looking for.

Thaxton was too far away to hear Thatcher yelling, and looking off in another direction, he didn't see the rough old scout waving his hat. The shot came from his right. When he looked, he saw Thatcher standing on the hill's crown. He and Sundance covered the distance to the army scout in a gallop. As Thaxton rode up, Thatcher yelled down to him, "The Cheyenne are up here! One of 'em is right over there." Thatcher found a burial scaffold, on which lay a Cheyenne woman. "She's likely a couple of weeks dead."

Trent stepped off Sundance and walked over to the

scaffold. The poles were dyed red and yellow and adorned with feathers and ribbons. A broken clay pot lay at the foot, probably knocked off by a buzzard or some other scavenger. The corpse, gaunt and leathery, was clothed in a buckskin dress and moccasins and lashed to the platform. Someone, a husband, perhaps a son, had folded a gray and red blanket under the head. Alongside the body, the family placed jerked beef, tobacco, a sewing awl, several strips of rawhide, and a well-worn leather pouch, making her, as Thatcher said, "Ready for her trip to the happy hunting grounds."

Trent didn't answer Thatcher's question about how long the woman had been dead. "I guess we better head back to the Major and tell him. If all the army's interested in is knowing if the Cheyenne are this far north, I guess we can tell them." The scouts headed back to the troop.

Major Crenshaw ordered a halt an hour later when the two scouts returned. "Did you find anything?"

Since Thatcher was the regular army scout, Trent believed he should be the one to report. "Found a dead squaw about two miles up. She's Cheyenne."

"You're sure she's Cheyenne?"

Thatcher spat a brown stream of tobacco, wiped his hand across his mouth. "Well, Major, I'll tell you. I've been out here all of my life. I believe I can tell the difference between Cheyenne, Sioux, and Crow. And the dead squaw is Cheyenne."

The Major turned to Captain Crane. "Our mission is to discover if the Northern Cheyenne moved up this far. Based on what Thatcher and Thaxton found, they have." He tugged at his collar while looking over the landscape. "The question now is, do we continue on toward the Powder or turn back to the fort." The Major rubbed the back of his neck. "I realize I'm the commanding officer, but you've been out here longer. I'd appreciate your opinion."

Captain Crane, unfamiliar with superior officers asking advice, hesitated.

"Go ahead, Captain. I won't be offended."

"Major, as you say, the decision is yours." Crane glanced at the scouts, perhaps seeking confirmation for what he was about to say. "My opinion is we should move on up toward the Powder. I believe we would be well served to make an effort at knowing a little more about how many Cheyenne came north and, if possible, exactly where they are."

The Major stepped around and remounted his horse. "Your input is noted. Do you still believe we can make the Lightening River tomorrow?" Thatcher pressed his thumb against one side of his nose and blew snot out the other before affirming Crenshaw's assumption.

"Well, Thatcher, you and Thaxton move back out to the front. Scout on up to the river and wait for us."

Chapter Thirty-Four

It thrilled the women when Gray told them they would camp at the stream for the night. He said the horses were extra tired, going all day without water. And since he couldn't guarantee to make the Lightening River by dark, Gray decided to stay and move early in the morning.

Annie took every horse out into the water, filled her hat, and poured water over them. She rubbed each one down. Along the neck, and withers, down their back and legs. She stroked and kneaded their muscles with her gentle hands.

Zach walked up the stream finding a hole four or five feet deep full of pan-sized trout. In a little more than half an hour, he had enough fish on his stringer for supper. Jean found some wild onions not far from Zach, in which Nellie sautéed the catch.

After the meal, Millie started down the creek to stretch her legs. "Hold on a minute. We need to talk before you stray off," Gray said. For some reason, the tone of his voice scared the girl. She sat next to Gray. "We're going to stand guard tonight," he said with no explanation.

Millie and Nellie's mouths both dropped open. "Why?" Nellie stepped closer to Gray and Millie. "Did you see something?"

Gray aggravated at himself for not doing a better job explaining put his hand on Nellie's shoulder. "When Zach went over to catch the horses this morning, he found pony tracks."

Nellie felt sick. She placed her hand on Millie for support as she sat down. She didn't fear the Lakota who lived by High Meadows, but this was different. These Indians, Indians they didn't know, might be hostile. "How many?" she asked.

"Ten or twelve ponies heading south, and the tracks were two or three days old."

Despite herself, Jean was a little angry at the way Nellie was reacting. "Nellie, you knew we were going through Indian Territory before we ever left. There is always a chance of seeing Indians."

"I thought Gray would avoid them."

Gray shook his head, laughed a little. "How am I supposed to know where they are going to be? I'm not some fortune-teller."

"You cross back and forth across these plains, and you never talk about meeting any," Nellie countered.

"And we haven't seen any either. Now relax," Annie said.

Nellie took a deep breath, trying to calm herself. "I thought if we saw Indians, we'd spot them from a long way off, and we'd ride around them or something." She turned to Jean for moral support. "I guess I didn't expect to come across signs of them and not know where they were."

Jean tried, speaking in a softer voice, to reason with her friend. "Running Wolf didn't scare you. I was more concerned than you."

"That close to home, I figured it would be somebody from Paints His Horse's people. I'm not scared of them."

"Paints His Horses' braves might have attacked us," Jean said.

"That's ridiculous," Nellie answered. "Don't patronize me."

Gray hated listening to the women talk this way. "There is no reason to worry. If Zach or I thought the Sioux were anywhere around, we wouldn't have built a fire to cook over." He smiled at Nellie, his voice calm. "Nevertheless, we'll take a few precautions. We'll keep someone awake through the night, and tomorrow Zach and I will scout out as we move along. Don't worry." He patted Nellie on the knee, which she also considered patronizing.

Despite her irritation, Nellie gave into the men's judgment, and Millie asked to go ahead and take her walk. "Don't fall in the water and drown," Gray said.

With dark settling down, they took Annie's gold pocket watch and, by drawing lots, decided the order in which they would stand watches of an hour and a half. Annie drew the first guard, luck that pleased Gray because it would give her the best chance at a decent night's sleep. Nellie would be second, followed by Gray, Millie, Zach, and Jean.

Annie nudged Nellie for her turn.

"Do I sit someplace, or do I walk around camp? I've never been a sentry before."

Annie smiled as she changed into a warmer shirt for sleeping. "Sit by the fire, stay warm. Keep an eye out and listen for strange noises. You'll be all right. If you hear something, nudge Gray. He'll wake right up."

"Should I carry a gun?"

The thought of Nellie packing a firearm—Annie had scary visions of a crazy woman blasting away wildly through the camp. Thank the Lord a shotgun held only two shells. The survivors could disarm her before she reloaded. Annie pointed out a shotgun to her friend. "Be careful with this. We don't want you shooting one of the horses or, worse, somebody who gets up to go to the toilet." Annie rubbed Nellie's hand and assured her everything would be fine.

Nellie meant to sit calmly by the fire, listening to the sounds of the night, but the first screech in the dark caused her to yelp out loud.

"It's only an owl, Nellie," Gray chuckled. "He won't hurt

you. You're too big for him to carry off." A few minutes later, Gray was snoring, meaning she was all alone in the night.

The wind picked up, and a dingy mist snuck through the air. Lightning occasionally lit up the sky. Each time the night brightened, Nellie strained her eyes to capture as much of the landscape as possible. Annie might like watching storms roll in. Nellie didn't. At least not all alone amidst strange sounds and unidentifiable shadows.

She memorized part of the horizon during every lightning flash: a few rolling hills, half-hidden in thin clouds and gray fog. Hostiles hiding behind every bush, predators, real or imagined, it didn't matter. They were waiting to strike.

Halfway through her turn, Nellie wondered why she wanted to make this trip. The days had been as hot as hades or wet and miserable. Now, she was sitting by the campfire, shaking. Still, there was a reason, and she figured if she lived through the next forty-five minutes, she might survive long enough to accomplish her purpose.

Finally, boredom overcame her fear and grew so intense she decided to take a little walk and check on the horses. Stumbling around in the dark seemed no worse than sitting frightened in the middle of the shadowy camp, alone and afraid of being scalped. In the end, Nellie regained her senses. At last, her time as a guard ended. She bent down and shook Gray. "Hey, your turn."

"You made it, huh? Is everything peaceful?"

"Everything makes too much noise in the dark."

Already hot and humid, when the sun turned the horizon red, Zach urged everyone to keep their dusters on top of their saddle rolls. "That sky is worrisome."

"Better to ride in bad weather during the day than sleep in it," Annie said.

Nellie woke in a much better mood, living through the

night without being scalped. She said she could make breakfast herself and told Millie to help with the horses and breaking the camp.

The sky turned from red to dark gray while they mounted. Gusts blew from the south right into their faces. The wind and the smell of rain spooked the horses. Zach's sorrel wanted to stop or turn around, and Zach repeatedly kicked him in the flanks.

It came in sheets once the rain started, blowing across the plains instead of falling from the sky. Annie held her hand in front of her face, trying to block the wet. Jean and Nellie cursed. Millie urged Poncho in behind Jean's gray. She ducked her head, with her chin tucked into the collar of her coat, letting her appaloosa follow the gray's tail.

Gray rode to Annie's right to shield her. Vicious gusts blasted them with sand and dirt-loaded rain. The drops stung when they hit and left splotches of mud on the horses and riders. Gray ducked his head down to see Annie.

"Ain't this a fine time?"

"I always love storms like this when I'm at home," Annie repeated it; Nellie groaned. It was true. Annie loved to sit on her west-facing back porch, watching the gray clouds and rain roll up the valley. A gust of wind blew hard, forcing Annie to hold her hand over her face, between her hat and her slicker. "I admit, though, it's a little more peaceful sitting in the house next to a fire."

Lena kept twitching water out of her ears. Gray squinted, looking for something on the landscape to offer a little shelter. Only rolling hills and sheets of blowing rain lie ahead.

Despite the showers, the day stayed miserably warm. The oilcloth dusters blocked out the downpour, but at the cost of being hot. "I swear," Jean said, "I'm sweating so hard inside this coat, I think I'm almost as wet as if I didn't have it on." Rain pounded down, the coats became heavier and more uncomfortable, chaffing at any bare skin they touched.

Three hours later, the downpour stopped. The clouds disappeared, and, indignant at having been blocked out all morning by the storm, the sun came beating down. Progress through the weather had been slow, and they still hadn't reached the Lightning River.

"Damn, Gray, did they move the river since I was here last? I didn't think we were more than an hour or so away when we camped last night," Zach griped.

"An hour? I wouldn't have stopped an hour away. We may still be two out."

"Once we find the Lightning, how far is Fort Laramie?" Millie asked.

"Two, two and a half days," Gray told her. "Most of its right down the Platte River, the easy part of the trip."

"The Platte's is what I remember from the last time you took me to Fort Laramie,"

"How old were you?"

"I think about twelve or thirteen."

"When we get to the Lightning River, let's stop for the day," Annie suggested. "I mean, everything is wet, it's hot as Hades, and I want a bath."

"Me too," Nellie added.

Gray didn't argue, just asked Nellie if she'd like him to wash her back.

Annie whacked Gray in the arm. "Your days of washing Nellie's back are over."

Gray turned beet red. So did Millie.

They would make the fort in ten or eleven days, not the twelve to fifteen he predicted. The women beat his expectations with the effort they put in. They had done no real complaining, not even when the plains hit them with two nasty storms.

A sorrel horse wandering a couple of hundred yards to the left snorted and took a few steps toward the Wehr group before grazing again on the brown grass. "You ladies stay here. Zach and I are going to take a little ride to that horse."

Annie reached for Gray's arm. "You don't think he's bait for an ambush, do you?"

"If he was standing in taller grass, I would. Over there,

they'd have no place to hide."

Gray and Zach moved off toward the horse. The light sorrel with a star on his face did not attempt to run or escape. "Whoa, whoa," Gray gently said as he stepped off Lena and walked over to the slightly underweight horse. A horsehair rope hung from around his neck. "Easy now, easy." Gray reached out to take hold of the halter. He stroked the Indian pony along the chest and back. A blue handprint on each hip and yellow lightning bolts painted down his front legs alarmed Gray. "Sioux war markings," he said.

"Where do you suppose he came from?"

"I can't say, but this is a bad sign." Gray gazed out over the landscape. "I wish we knew where those Indians he was with are." Gray and Zach studied the horizon seeing no signs of dust or anything to indicate Indian movement or presence. Gray slipped the loop off the horse's neck and yelled at him, waving his arms and causing the horse to bolt off. "Let's head back to the others before they start worrying."

Gray minced no words in his explanation about the Sioux pony. The women took the news of the war markings without comment. Nellie did ask why Gray ran off the horse.

"I didn't want him following us. If they're out looking for him, I want him as far away as possible."

About mid-afternoon, they made the Lightening River. Right after tying the horses, they started to scatter out the gear and supplies. The tarp covering most of the food leaked; they could only salvage one loaf of their bread, water poured out of the cornmeal sack. Zach shook and brushed water off the bacon and jerky.

"I'll try to save the cornmeal," Millie said, "but I may be wasting my time."

Nellie picked through the rest of the supplies. "Our coffee's damp but not ruined."

"I'll start a fire, and you can brew some," Zach said.

Once everything was spread out to dry and the camp well set up, Gray mentioned taking Lena across the river and up to the top of the highest hill to look around.

"Why? What do you think is over there?" The anxiety in Nellie's question irritated Wehr, who thought it evident enough. "I wish we'd stayed in High Meadows," she mumbled half under her breath.

"Well. It's a little late for wishing. Save some coffee for Lena and me."

As he was about halfway across, Annie hollered, "If you find any Indians, ask them if you can borrow some dry food."

"I will, Annie. I'll ask for a leg of lamb with some mint sauce."

"You ask, but I don't want it without the mint."

Zach, who didn't sleep well the night before, laid under one of the cottonwoods. "Be sure and wake me up if we git attacked by the Sioux."

"Why?" Jean wondered aloud. "You couldn't hit one standing right next to you."

"I could too. One right next to me."

Nellie and Millie found shade of their own and, despite worries about the Indians who lost the sorrel pony, fell asleep before Gray made it halfway up the hill. Jean regretted what she said to Zach. She regularly made him the butt of her jokes, although he never complained and always remained good-natured. She asked Annie if she thought she hurt his feelings.

"Course not. He knows you like to tease him."

Jean still decided she would be sure to say something warm to him before the day ended. No one liked teased continually.

Once they started up, Lena wanted to lope, getting them to the crown in only a few minutes. Gray breathed easier, not seeing any teepees dotting the plains. He stepped off Lena to let her graze a minute or two. Someone called out.

"Hello, on the hill!"

Hearing a voice gave him a bit of start, and he reached for

the handle of his gun.

"Hello."

The voice echoed from across the ravine. At first, Gray couldn't spot anyone in all the sagebrush. Then he caught sight of him, alone on a bay horse, carefully moving along the steep bank. Gray waved his hat at him.

Gray pulled his canteen off his saddle and took a long drink to wash the dust out of his mouth and throat while he watched the bay and his rider work toward him. By the time they hit the ravine's bottom, Wehr recognized him. He walked Lena over toward where the slope started down. "Well, kick my butt and call me Charlotte. What are you doing here, Trent?"

"Scouting for the army. What brings you out here?"

The two men knew each other from Wehr's passing through Fort Laramie. Thaxton and his father also delivered supplies to High Meadows over the past several years.

"I'm going down to Fort Laramie to find out about the treaty talks," Gray told him.

"I can tell you," Trent said. "The treaty with the Sioux is mostly negotiated, but the army's concerned about Cheyenne movement."

"How many soldiers are out here?"

"A troop, they're five or six miles back up the river. Tad Thatcher is with us; he's scouting up the other direction. They're supposed to meet me down here sometime before dark. You by yourself?"

Gray laughed. "Not hardly. Zach Joseph and four women are with me, including the official town spokesman."

"Women? Why didn't you bring men?"

"Lord, it was their idea. They think they're on some kind of blame holiday."

"Where are they?"

"Over on the other side of the river. We put up a camp in that grove of trees before I rode up here." Gray stepped back up on Lena. "Cheyenne, you say?"

"Roman Nose and Dull Knife."

"What about the Sioux? Any concerns about them?"

Trent took his hat off and wiped his sleeve across his brow. "Well, a passel of chiefs signed, but not Red Cloud. Sitting Bull left, threatening war."

"We found a Sioux pony wandering lose this morning," Gray fiddled with his reins. "He was painted with war markings."

"There's been a few reports Crazy Horse moved south from the Tongue River. Rumors are he has fifty or sixty warriors with him. The army doesn't put too much stock in the stories."

Gray thought for a moment about Trent's revelation. "Let's head on back to camp. Coffee's on, and I think you know everybody with me. Annie Laurie, she's the spokesman, my sister, Nellie and Millie Bascomb, and Zach."

The two men rode slowly down the hill and across the flat area back to the river. Annie and Jean both recognized the Thaxton boy, and Jean gave Millie a shake. "Wake up; we have company."

Annie chuckled at Jean waking Millie while she let the other two sleep. Over the years, Millie had developed quite a crush on Trent.

Millie was having a hard time shaking off her nap. "What did you say?"

Jean leaned over her and tapped her fingers on the girl's nose. "I said company's coming."

"Who? When?"

"Right now, and you better sit up and see who."

The girl sat up, rubbed her eyes, and pulled on her face when she realized two people were crossing the river. The one on the left was Gray, but she couldn't identify the younger man with him, at least not for a moment.

Trent Thaxton. Panic. She had been lying on the ground asleep. She was a mess. She got to her feet as fast as possible while trying not to call attention to herself. She ran her fingers through her hair to brush away any leaves, grass, or twigs. She tried to hide behind Jean, but Jean kept stepping out from in front of her. Finally, with one last quick sweep of her hand across her pants, Millie had done as much as she could. Someone should have warned her.

The men stepped down off their horses, two nearly identical bays.

"Well, where did you come from?" Annie put her hand out to Trent.

"Hello, Annie. I came up from Fort Laramie. I'm scouting for the army." He smiled at Jean. "How are you, Jean?" Millie moved a little bit forward. Trent glanced at her but immediately looked away without saying anything.

"Aren't you going to speak to me?"

Trent shifted from one foot to the other, shrugged his shoulders. "I wasn't sure you knew me."

"Do you think I'm stupid? I've met you as many times as Annie and Jean."

Trent had no idea being shy would get you in trouble with a girl so quickly. "I didn't mean to offend you," he muttered, shifting back and forth.

A little ashamed, Millie wished she had kept her mouth shut. Sadly, she still couldn't. "Well, I guess my memory's better than you think, isn't it?" Millie had no anxiety talking to the boys around High Meadows, at least not the ones she wasn't interested in, which was all of them. But she liked this young man, and she kept making a fool of herself.

The boy made another attempt at an apology before escaping to tie his horse. Annie went over to give him a little advice about handling females. As she walked up, Trent flashed a nervous smile.

"I didn't try to make her mad."

"Oh, you didn't. She's a just little smitten." Annie idly started scratching Trent's horse. "Go tell her how pretty she is."

Trent said, "All right," and walked toward Millie and Jean to Annie's amazement.

Annie rushed to follow along.

Trent stopped a few feet away from Millie. He leaned over

a little and smiled. Rather a charming smile. "You're not going to bite me, are you?"

"What?" Millie backed away, a little stunned.

"I wanted to come over and tell you I didn't recognize you at first. I mean, you've become such a beautiful woman since the last time I saw you. But you snarled at me once today. So caution was called for. I didn't want bit."

Another step back. Dumbfounded, mouth agape. Until, she blurted out, "Annie Laurie!"

Annie burst into laughter. She backed away and threw up her hands. "I didn't tell him to say anything."

"You did too."

"I didn't. I swear."

Trent stepped up to Millie. "She didn't." He took the girl by the hand. "Why, when Gray and I crossed the river, I wanted to say to him, 'my, what a beautiful young gal you have with you.' I was thinking that exact thought when Jean woke you up, and you started pulling grass out of your hair and wiping drool off your mouth. I said to myself, 'well, ain't she an elegant little thing?'"

Millie yanked her hand away and headed off in her walking across a plowed field gate. "I need to check my horse."

Trent waited a couple of minutes and slowly slipped toward Millie, trying not to catch the others' attention. As he walked toward her, he thought she indeed was a beautiful girl, the prettiest he had ever seen.

She was brushing the horse's mane and pretending not to see Trent coming. The hair around her face was damp with sweat and hanging limp. Again, she thought she must be a mess. Trent thought she looked wonderful standing in the bright sunlight.

"I didn't embarrass you, did I?" he asked.

She smiled at him. "You couldn't do anything to embarrass me in front of those people. They spend half of their lives trying to embarrass me."

"Probably because they like you." Without realizing it, Trent was looking deeply into Millie's eyes.

"What are you looking at?"

Her question snapped him out of his daydream state. "Nothing, nothing."

"Yes, you are. You are looking right at me. Why?"

"Nothing, I was...looking at your eyes. They're real pretty." He sounded like a fool. The boy had read a couple of dime romance novels soldiers loaned him on various scouts. The heroes always talked with silver tongues, sweeping beautiful women off their feet with flowery prose. Awestruck, the best Trent could do was mutter about her eyes, which men and boys probably told her daily.

She was likely used to men delivering soliloquies to her, spouting phrases worthy of the poetry books. *If I did come up with something beautiful to say*, he thought, *I wouldn't have the nerve to say it.* He was again looking into the girl's eyes.

"Now, you are embarrassing me," she said.

Chapter Thirty-Five

Major Crenshaw and his troop arrived about five-thirty and set up camp on the Lightening River's other side. Trent, Gray, and Zach crossed over to meet them. The Major told them about the new treaty. He said most of the Sioux chiefs signed or made their mark in April. "Red Cloud is refusing to sign. He's still making demands the peace commission has not given in to."

Annie and Jean fell asleep early. Nellie and Millie sat around the campfire wishing the men would come back across the river.

"Nellie," Millie said, "do you remember when I was eleven or so, and you let Gray take me to Fort Laramie?"

"I do."

"Well, do you remember when I came back all excited about some boy, and I told you he's the boy I want to marry?"

"Yes," Nellie laughed. "You pestered me for two months for a hope chest."

"You told me he was my first puppy love. I'd get over it and forget all about him."

"I guess I did."

Millie took her eyes off Nellie and gazed into the fire. "I didn't."

With only a sliver of moon and few stars, the night was very dark. Nellie and Millie heard the horses splashing in the river before the silhouettes of the three men danced along the bank. They pulled their saddles and tethered the horses before coming over to the campfire. Trent Thaxton, with his bedroll, flopped over his shoulder.

"You were gone long enough," Nellie said as they walked up.

"We were," Gray replied. "I'm worn out. You four can sit up talking if you want to. I'm gonna crawl into bed."

"The Major told us everything the army's been doing for the past six months," Zach said as he poured himself a cup of coffee. He took one swallow and threw the rest out on the ground. "I swear, Nellie, this stuff would stand a fork on end."

"That's because it's been sitting next to the fire for four or five hours." Nellie pitched the remains of the pot out behind the flames. "Are you going to let us in on what the army's been doing? Or are you going to let us sit here and wonder?"

"We can tell you," Zach said. "I don't know what it'll benefit you."

"Knowledge keeps us from being ignorant," Millie said. The girl wasn't going to be belittled in front of Trent and would not take deriding from Zach Joseph.

"Well. Annie ain't gonna be happy when she finds out. I guess the agreement is signed, but we don't know the details important to us," Zach said as he shook his head. "The government people have been sitting down with a bunch of Indians arguing about a treaty since early spring. From what the major says, the whole affair is a done deal."

"Already signed?" Millie asked.

"By most of the chiefs," Trent told her. "Not Red Cloud, Sitting Bull, or Crazy Horse."

"If the treaties complete, what's the army tramping around out here for?"

Trent told her about the rumors the Cheyenne, particularly

Dull Knife and Roman Nose, had been moving north, and we're trying to confirm that. He also told the women about the burial scaffold, something Nellie did not want to view on their way into Fort Laramie. At Gray's request, Trent did not mention the rumors of Crazy Horse's movement south.

"Are you and the soldier boys still going the rest of the way up to the Powder?" Millie asked. "What's the point? We came from there and didn't run into any Indians."

"Well, hellfire, girl. We didn't exactly cover everything between here and the whole Powder River area." Zach growled. Millie's face flushed, but she held her tongue.

Trent considered Zach's comment mean-spirited and uncalled for. He turned his eyes toward Millie to catch her reaction. The remark hung in the air like the stench of burnt cooking. Trent decided not to let the insult pass.

"Well, nobody can cover everything between here and the Powder. The army can't do any more than you did."

Millie appreciated the quickness with which Trent interceded for her. She wanted to say something back to Zach, but there was no reason to spark an argument or fight with everyone already tired.

"Anyway, to answer your question," Trent said, smiling at Millie, "the troop is going on up to the river, but the Major's sending me back to the fort with you. I'm going to report on what we've seen so far," he said with a little bit of a laugh. "And the Major also thought," Trent continued with a glance at Zach, "it would be a good idea to have another man along with you ladies."

Zach headed to bed and suggested the other three do the same thing.

As they prepared their bedrolls, Trent caught Millie looking over at him. He smiled at her. She smiled back and gave him; he was almost sure, a little wink before she turned around and crawled into her blankets. The thought of the wink kept Trent company and awake for nearly two hours.

Chapter Thirty-Six

Fort Laramie's stockade was a dark, dreary, stinking, damp place inhabited chiefly by spiders, ants, flies, and drunkards. On Thursday morning, the Post Commander decided Marcus and Clint Bowden served enough time and released them with the provision they leave Fort Laramie.

The oldest Bowden boy had been sick and still reeked of vomit when they made the fort stable. A Corporal was cleaning stalls when the Bowdens came in and went straight into the stall for their horses. "Can I help you, boys?"

"We're getting our horses, and we don't need any help from you. Stay out of our damn way," Marcus said, glaring at the Corporal.

Dewey Smith was an army veteran who made Sargent on four different occasions, only to be busted back, generally because of fighting or his love for Irish Whiskey. He had no interest in complicating his day by bashing a couple of snot-nosed smart alecks heads.

The Bowden's saddled up and galloped the horses out of the barn and toward the front gate. "You boys leavin' us?" A young private standing by one of the corrals asked.

"Git the hell out of our way," ordered the younger boy.

The Bowden's kicked their horses in the flanks and stormed through. Either intentionally or because he wasn't much of a horseman, Clint knocked down a Sioux woman as they ran the horses through the Indian camp. The Private shouted a couple of obscenities at the Bowden's and went over to help the woman back to her feet.

"You alright?" He asked.

The Lakota woman did not speak English and stared blankly at him as he tried to lift her. To the Private's astonishment, a Sioux warrior shoved him away from the woman and screamed at him in Lakota. Fortunately, the woman interceded on his behalf, pointing and yelling at the Bowden's. The brave, a compelling figure in a breechcloth and deerskin leggings, listened to the woman who the Private thought might be his mother. The soldier tried to explain he only intended to be helpful, but neither Sioux understood him.

The warrior, probably in his late twenties, accepted the woman's explanation and didn't threaten the corporal anymore. The private, scared witless by the screaming Indian, smiled and, for some reason, started nodding his head, yes, as he eased away from the encampment. The Indian muttered something at him as he left, but the trooper had no idea whether it was "thank you" or "if I catch you outside the fort, I'll lift your scalp."

The Bowdens decided to ride down to the Yellow Dog where "Wild Bill" Hickok shot "Buffalo Face" Jack Terry, although neither one had any more than a vague idea of where the place was. They rode south along the river for more than two hours before deciding to give their horses and hinds ends a rest. Both were more concerned about their asses than the horses. Clint, not one of God's brighter creations, sat on the riverbank. He suggested they ought to sneak back to Fort Laramie after dark and set the whole place on fire.

Marcus took a long slug from a bottle of whiskey he pulled from his saddlebag. Why'd ya let us ride so damn fer?

You shoulda said something. I ain't ridin' two hours back now.

"By damn, I may," the younger boy answered. "I'll kill a bunch of soldiers and damn Indians all at the same time."

"Well, you go ahead. I'm going down to Yellow Dog," Marcus said, drawing out another long drink.

"You don't know where Yellow Dog is," his brother countered.

"It's right on this river. All I gotta do is follow the blame river. Hell, even you can follow a river."

The two boys sat in the sun for another half-hour, arguing and swigging down the whiskey. When they finally finished off the bottle, they broke it against rocks, dragged themselves back on their horses, and kicked them up to the top of the riverbank.

The screams were blood-curdling, except Clint didn't hear them because the arrow slammed into his throat, knocking him off the horse and back over the riverbank into the broken whiskey bottle. The shaft broke off as he bounced and rolled back down the steep rocky bank.

Marcus half-jumped and half-fell off his horse; he leaped down to the riverbed, breaking an ankle when he landed. He managed to yank his pistol, an old Navy Dragoon, out and start shooting wildly at the top of the bluff. He grabbed his brother and rolled him over. The younger boy's eyes were wide open, bug-eyed, but frozen in an astonished stare. The only sign he had ever been alive was blood bubbling out around the broken arrow and the sickening gurgling sound emanating from the wound.

Horrified, the older boy emptied his gun at no more of a target than a dirt bank. As he decided to run, three painted Indian ponies with screaming riders flew over the edge. One of the horses hit Marcus Bowden, kicking and stomping on him as he landed. All three leaped off their horses and onto the boy before he screamed again.

Marcus couldn't breathe; he couldn't make sense of what was happening. He didn't want to. He tried to scream for help, but no sound came out. It didn't matter. No help was coming.

Black paint covered the Sioux's face from his eyes down, making his otherwise mundane features brutal. He was wearing a beaded necklace and had rawhide thongs around both arms. The feathers in the back of his hair were the last thing Marcus was conscious of before the burning pain on the top of his head. The Sioux tore off Marcus's scalp with a ripping motion, stood up, waving the trophy above his head, and screamed.

The second warrior rammed a knife into Marcus's side, ending his life. A third cut off his fingers. The Sioux believed the boys would enter the next life as they left this one. They slashed their arms and legs and plucked out their eyes to cripple and blind them.

A few minutes later, the three Sioux warriors rode back toward Fort Laramie, leading two new horses. They left the disemboweled and mutilated bodies of Marcus and Clint Bowden at the edge of the river.

Chapter Thirty-Seven

Zach shot a good-sized prairie chicken before mid-day, which Nellie roasted and served along with a few biscuits left-over from breakfast.

"I swear, I'm going to be glad to make Fort Laramie and eat something besides jerky or one of these stringy old birds," Zach complained.

Nellie took his plate and scraped the crumbs into the fire. "Shoot younger, tenderer birds instead of the oldest, toughest ones on the prairie."

Tired of the bickering about food, Annie asked Gray to walk up the bluff and sit with her. The ridge rose several feet above the river and sloped gently to the bank where the grass was a little more tender, and a soft breeze drifted out of the northwest.

They sat at the top and watched a coyote hunt, unsuccessfully. "What are you going to do about the ranch after we've married?" Annie asked.

"Well, I thought I would turn my part over to Jean and Paxton. We can lay claim on another couple hundred acres across the river."

Gray's statement surprised Annie. "You're going to give them your share?"

Gray tossed a few rocks and pebbles at the river. "Jean would never let me. Paxton might, but not Jean. She'll make sure we get a fair payout. We'll spend a little time with her at Fort Laramie. We can talk easier without Paxton around." Gray leaned over on one elbow facing Annie. "I want to raise more horses than you are now. This territory is going to flourish in the next few years. There'll be a greater need for horses. We'll deliver the best ones a man can own."

Annie laughed a little. "From a girl with a dry goods store to a woman who raises the finest horses a man can buy. Quite an accomplishment." The next few minutes passed quietly. Annie put her arms around Gray's elbow and laid her head on his shoulder. "What a glorious day."

"I'm glad we've made this trip. I'm enjoying being out here with you."

Annie squeezed his arm and sighed. "I'm thrilled we ran into the army. I feel safer now. Their coming up here without any trouble is reassuring."

"Running into Trent surprised me," Gray said.

"I like him."

Gray agreed. "I think he's dependable. He comes from solid people."

Annie picked up a little yellow caterpillar and sat it on gray's knee. "Millie thinks she's in love with him. Nellie told me this morning."

"You didn't need Nellie to tell you, did you? A half-blind man could see it."

"I hope they marry," Annie said. "They'll make a sweet couple, and they'll sure have beautiful kids."

"How do you know?"

"Are you blind? Millie's endowed with beauty, and he's a handsome young man. Why wouldn't their children be attractive."

"No reason, but nothing guarantees they'll be gorgeous. I

mean, what about Pott's youngest girl. Her parents aren't necessarily any uglier than most, and her brothers and sisters are all right, but I swear if she's not the ugliest girl ever born. She's at least in the competition."

Annie slapped Gray's shoulder. "What a horrible thing to say."

"Why? I'm not making it up. I'm not passing judgment. It's a fact."

Millie and Trent walked up behind them. "How soon do you want to start on the trail?" Trent asked.

"Let's rest another thirty minutes or so," Gray said. "We're sitting here discussing what an ugly kid the youngest Potts girl is."

"We are not! You said that, not me. There was no discussion."

"They are ugly, though. You can't argue that." Millie laughed.

Annie sat straight up. "Milicent Bascomb. You must be hanging around with this one too much," Annie grinned, giving Gray another smack on the arm.

Zach kicked some dirt on the fire as Jean and Nellie finished picking up the little bit of gear they unpacked for lunch.

"I guess everybody except us has someone to be in love with," Jean said, looking over at the two couples sitting on the bluff.

"That ain't true. I'm in love with you." Zach said to her.

"You wouldn't recognize love carrying a sign," she countered, flashing her blue eyes and the tiniest hint of a smile.

"I would too. Why can't you see that?"

"I guess I must be blind." Jean threw the leftover coffee on the dying campfire and turned away.

"You are to me," he said as he headed off to put the gear back into the packsaddle.

Nellie propped herself up on her elbows with her feet straight out. "He is a decent man."

"I didn't say he wasn't, but that doesn't mean I want to

take him into my bed every night for the rest of my life."

Nellie smiled. "Do you ever wish you had married?"

Jean sat back down next to her. "I honestly don't think about marriage much anymore."

Nellie shook her head a little bit. "I sort of do wish I had a husband. I would enjoy a man loving me. Of course, it would have to be a man I loved."

Jean hesitated. She shouldn't say it, but she did. "Like my brother?"

"No," Nellie said. "He's taken. Always has been."

Nellie was one of her two best friends, yet it surprised Jean, Nellie wanting to be married. In all their conversations, Nellie never indicated wishing to wed.

"Well, you're a beautiful woman, Nellie. You could take your pick of men."

"We both ought to select one down at the fort, a couple of high-classed officers with gentleman's manners."

"Lord, if we're going for husbands, we better be on our way. You grab the horses, and I'll go tell those four to get a move on."

Nellie headed over to the picket line. "Come on, Zach. Let's go. Jeannie and I are going to find ourselves a couple of fine young officers to wed. You can catch one of their sisters."

The afternoon turned to twilight amidst small talk about when they would reach the fort, how the treaty talks might be going, and enjoying riding along the river after so much time out across those plains.

The evening meal consisted of fish rolled in some cornmeal they managed to dry out after being soaked in the rainstorm. The skies clouded up again before dusk, making the night a dark one. With almost no breeze, the hot, close air prevented Annie and Nellie from sleeping, and they had been sitting over on the riverbank for over an hour when Millie joined them.

Nellie yelped and almost jumped out of her skin when the girl walked up behind them.

"What did you think I was? A bear?"

"You scared me half-to-death," Nellie wrapped an arm around Millie as she sat down.

"How long have you two been sitting here?"

"Quite a while," Annie answered. "Are the others asleep?"

"Yes, but how Trent and Jean can sleep through those other two snoring is beyond me. They sound like a couple of old bears."

"Did they wake you up?" Annie asked.

"I'm not sure. Something did."

"I can tell you why Millie can't sleep," Nellie said. "Because her heart's pounding so hard over the boy lying over there."

Before Millie figured out what to say, Annie jumped in. "There's nothing wrong with having your heart pounding over a boy. A lot of things are worse than being in love."

Millie leaned over against Nellie. She wanted to ask so many questions, but with her emotions running so high, she was afraid she'd start babbling. Instead, Millie let her thoughts drift along with the river, at least for a while. "All right, but don't be giving' me a bunch of guff," she grumbled in her no-nonsense voice.

Her voice trailed off. She stumbled over her words. "How do I?" Her eyes bounced back and forth over the two women, "how do I know if I'm in love?"

"Oh, dear God," Nellie gasped. "I was afraid of this."

"Stop it, Nellie!" The corners of her mouth turned down. The glint in her eyes disappeared. "You're my mother, and you're supposed to help me with this."

Nellie's stomach tossed. She had never been in love—a short flirtation with Gray—before she was twenty, but never in love. "Annie's the one you should ask."

"No, she ought to ask you, Mom. Now you behave yourself and answer her. I'll go back to the camp and leave you two alone." Annie stood up and walked away. She turned back, smiled, "Millie, I will say this. When you love someone, your heart will tell you. And don't let anybody talk you out of it."

The tall willowy woman turned and headed for the campfire.

"Why did she go?"

Nellie thought for a minute and squeezed the girl against her. "I guess because she's my best friend."

"Well, she didn't need to leave."

"She thinks something this personal should be a private privilege for me." Nellie paused for a long time, "Do you love him?"

Millie thought that over. The answer was easy. Saying it was hard. What if Nellie objected? The girl knew she loved the young man, but convincing her mother it was real might be tricky. "How do I know?"

Nellie didn't answer. She played with the girl's fingers, rubbing them and stroking them. They sat quietly for a few minutes.

"I love him, Nellie."

"I know. Everybody knows. They can see it in your eyes, in the way you act when he comes around."

"You're not going to tell me it's too fast?"

"Well, how long have you loved him?"

Millie chuckled. "Since I was eight years old."

"Then it's not too fast."

The river flowed along; Millie waved her hand to chase gnats away, they came right back. "So I guess the only question, my only problem, is does he love me?"

"What?" Nellie exclaimed. "He is crazy in love with you."

"I like being in love."

"Well, I'm glad." Nellie patted the girl's knee. "If you want to be sure about his feelings, I can run over and wake him up and ask him for you."

The girl hugged her mother. "Don't you dare."

Chapter Thirty-Eight

The cloudy night produced no rain, and the sun broke bright. Zach, always a talker, was incredibly full of himself this morning. "We ought to be at the fort by mid-afternoon, on the eleventh day, not the fifteenth day like some people said. Annie will straighten the treaty up by evening, and we can start back home tomorrow morning.

"Zach, if we do run into any hostile Indians, I hope they cut your tongue out," Jean said as she tossed the scraps from breakfast into the fire. "Trent, you came from Laramie. How long do you think it'll take us to make Laramie?"

"Mid-afternoon easy. If you want to push real hard, we can make it about noon."

"Afternoon will be fine," Gray said.

Annie's heart sank. Gray was strapping on his gun, the .45 caliber colt, not the dragoon he usually wore on his left hip. This one hung from his right hip, and he tied it down to his leg. Blood rushed to Annie's head, making her a little dizzy. She sat down, hoping no one would notice.

Only Jean did. She walked over to Annie, held out her

hand to help her up.

"Come on, let's check the canteens."

They found three of them almost empty and went over to the river to fill them.

Jean bent down to the water and took a canteen from Annie. "Don't worry, Annie. He's a cautious man. It doesn't mean anything."

"I hate seeing him wearing that gun," Annie sighed. "The Colt revolver is the part of him I don't understand. The part that makes him leave home."

Jean handed the full canteen to Annie and took another one. "If you ask him not to, he won't wear it."

"No, that would make him feel obligated not to or guilty if he did. You're right. He wears the Colt when he's going to be in a town or fort with a lot of strangers."

"Well, keep in mind," Jean said. "If something does happen, we want his protection."

As they walked back to the others, Annie took little solace in her friend's thinking.

"Are you ladies all ready to go find Laramie?" Gray asked.

Jean, always direct, was again. "Isn't that why we came?"

Gray had no idea what misstep he made, but he sensed from the tone of his sister's response he committed some kind of a social blunder. He thought about asking her but decided he would be better off continuing in what his mother used to refer to as "ignorant bliss." Besides, it was probably too late to fix his mistake anyway. So he swung up on Lena's back and nudged the bay mare south.

At noon, Trent said they were "an hour and a half, two hours from Fort Laramie." Gray asked the women if they wanted to stop for a meal or head straight to the fort. First, they picked riding on in, but a mile or so down the river, they climbed a hill above a good-sized stand of cottonwood trees. A little creek ran through a half-circle-shaped meadow and into the Platt. The grass waved lush and deep, and the field overflowed with blue, yellow, and red wildflowers too pristine for a female to pass by.

They arrived at Fort Laramie a little before two. The size of the Sioux and Cheyenne encampment surprised everyone except Gray, worried Millie. "I've never seen so many Indians at one time!"

The makeshift village was a collection of tepees of all sizes. The largest was the Medicine Lodge, made of tanned and brightly painted buffalo hides, sewn together with rawhide thongs and stretched around thirty lodge poles, stood more than fifteen feet tall.

On their migrations into the Black Hills or Big Horns, they would cut trees each fall and winter, strip the limbs, and drag them from camp to camp until they were so worn and broken as to be of no further use. Poles for each tepee were lashed together at the top radiating out into a circle. Smoke curled out the opening of many, and those with open flaps revealed shadows darting about inside.

Five to seven-foot poles, reminiscent of maypoles, stood throughout the village. From them, rags and cloths dyed red, green, blue, and yellow blew gently in the light breeze. Tied into the fabric strips were medicine bags filled with roots and barks meant to keep away evil spirits. Dogs scavenged the camp for scraps of meat or garbage. A few babies sat outside the tepee entrances crying. The dust, noise, and general confusion bothered Millie.

Once they put their horses up, Trent and Gray headed over to deliver Trent's report to General Terry, who Gray briefly served under in the war. Because he respected Gray, General Terry insisted Annie and Jean stay in his home, the most comfortable at the Fort. Nellie and Millie took up residence in the Thaxton home. Gray and Zach would bunk in the B Troop barracks. Thus settled, they drifted over to listen to the treaty talks.

Nellie tugged on Trent's sleeve. "Is A Man Afraid Of His Horse here?"

"Has been. I think he's out in the encampment. At least I don't see him around." Nellie's interest in a Sioux Chief puzzled Trent. "Do you know him?"

"We've met," Nellie replied. "Will you come out with me and help me find him?"

"Sure. I'll be glad to," Trent answered, bewildered.

"Wait here a minute. I want Millie and Gray with us." A few minutes later, she came back with Millie, Gray, and Annie. "All right, let's go."

They walked through the Indian village, asking anyone who understood their English/Lakota mix where they would find A Man Afraid Of His Horse. An older brave pointed to a lodge about two-thirds of the way to the end of the encampment.

An old woman puffing on a pipe sat out front. After Gray asked her in Lakota for A Man Afraid Of His Horse, the old woman got up and went inside the tepee. An old man came out, his hair almost white, his skin rough and weathered. He wore a calico shirt with a red sash around his waist. He spoke in broken English, a tremendous relief to Nellie. "I am A Man Afraid Of His Horse."

Nellie stepped forward. She smiled, caught his eyes with her own. "My name is Nellie Bascomb." Nellie patted her chest. Tears filled her eyes. "My heart is full of thankfulness for you."

The old man understood her words, but not why she would say such a thing.

"Seventeen summers ago, I came to you, along with these two friends." She motioned at Gray and Annie. "You were camped on the Republican River, caring for a white child. You and your people were treating the infant with much kindness. I asked you for her."

"I remember this," the old chief nodded his head but showed no emotion.

Nellie took Millie by the shoulders and pulled her forward. "This is the child," Nellie said, smiling broadly. "I came from my home in the Bighorn Mountains, the rough animal horns. I came to show her to you and to thank you again for giving her to me."

The old chief's expression softened; he reached out and touched Millie's face. "The child has grown to be handsome."

"She is a wonderful daughter." Nellie's voice broke, tears ran down her cheeks.

Millie put her arms around the Lakota Chief. She kissed his cheek.

Millie's behavior stunned A Man Afraid Of His Horse, making for an awkward moment. He again touched her face before looking back at Nellie. "You have done well," he said. "She is not too filled with hate to touch a Lakota."

The old woman who had gone in the tepee for A Man Afraid Of His Horse said something in Lakota. When he answered her back, she motioned for them to come in.

When they sat down, Nellie asked A Man Afraid Of His Horse if the woman who initially adopted Millie was with them in the encampment.

"She is dead seven summers now."

"She died of the running face sickness," the woman, Comes In The Sun, told them. "She was my cousin, Iron Dog Woman. She died on the Tongue River after we moved from the Black Hills and The Greasy Grass."

After Annie expressed their sorrow, they talked for over an hour about Millie. Both A Man Afraid of His Horse and Comes In The Sun smiled, showed some affection to Millie. Gray asked about the treaty. A Man Afraid Of His Horse remained polite but not what anyone would call friendly. His resentment apparent, the old chief did not understand what gave the white man the right to restrict the Lakota to reservations. Why didn't the Sioux have the right to be free and live where they pleased. "Why do the white men have the right to do this? Who gave them the right?"

Gray told the old man how white men wanted the best for the Lakota. He tried to convince the chief the army would protect the Sioux. They would give the Lakota food when the winter came. No one, including Gray, believed anything he said.

Nellie told him they would like to eat a meal with him

before they went home. The old chief became standoffish, and Annie wished Nellie would let it go. Out of a grateful heart, Nellie pressed the issue, assuring the Sioux she would bring the food. Finally, plans were made for supper the next night.

Annie didn't think A Man Afraid Of His Horse wanted a meal with them, but he no longer had the boldness to tell white people no. She thought about somehow providing the old man with an escape, but Nellie meant the gesture as kindness, so she let it pass.

Once they got back in the gate, Nellie kissed Gray on the side of the face. "Thank you for bringing me."

"I wish the woman who gave me to you still lived. What is running face sickness?" Millie asked, putting an arm around Gray's waist.

"Cholera," Gray said. "Something they can thank the white man for."

Zach and Jean came walking up. "There's a dance tonight," Jean said. "It starts at eight, and I thought we should sleep a little, so we can kick up our heels."

Chapter Thirty-Nine

Annie, Gray, Trent, and Millie came early so they wouldn't miss a dance. Zach arrived and got caught up in a conversation about Montana beef prices with some of the officers. Nellie and Jean came about twenty minutes later. Officers and enlisted men alike lined up to dance with them.

After her fourth dance, Jean walked over to Zach, sitting in a chair against the wall, looking about as comfortable as a long-tailed cat in a roomful of rocking chairs.

"Come on."

"What do you mean, come on?" Zach asked in a pitiful voice.

"You want to dance with me. You'd like to shoot every man who has so far, so come on."

"Well, you're awful full of yourself."

Jean reached down and pulled him up. "Come on. I like this music. Now stand up."

Without saying anything, Zach got up and took her in his arms, closing his eyes as he held her close to him. He danced gracefully, and Jean felt warm in his embrace, nothing like with those officers. Zach made her comfortable, happy. When the song finished, she gave him a squeeze and a little pat on the back.

"Thanks, I enjoyed dancing with you." He let her go and turned to leave.

Jean grabbed his hand. "Come back here. Don't you leave me standing here like a woman scorned."

Gray touched the orchestra leader lightly on the arm as he whispered in his ear. He walked back to Annie as the sound of the music started again. A Corporal with an Irish tenor voice stepped forward to sing. Annie smiled at Gray and slipped back into his arms.

"Annie's father named her after this," Millie told Trent. "Whenever we had a dance back home, he'd have this sung and waltz Annie all around the room." The Corporal's voice pealed clear and crisp with a beautiful Irish lilt.

> *Maxwelton's braes are bonnie*
> *Where early fa's the dew*
> *and 'twas there that Annie Laurie*
> *Gave her promise true.*
> *Gave her promise true.*
> *Which ne'er be forgot will be*
> *And for bonnie Annie Laurie*
> *I'd lay me doon and dee.*

Annie laid her head on Gray's shoulder and let the words and melody take her back to those long-ago wonderful times when she danced with her father.

> *Her brow is like the snowdrift*
> *Her throat is like the swan.*
> *Her face it is the fairest*
> *That e'er the sun shone on*
> *And dark blue is her e'e*
> *And for bonnie Annie Laurie*
> *I'd lay my doon and dee.*

Jean smiled at her friend, nodded her head, and clapped lightly. She put her arms back around Zach, and they started to dance as the orchestra struck up "Little Footsteps." Zach let his hand stroke her back as they danced. The light fragrance of her perfume, the softness of her hair, this might be as close to heaven as he would ever be in this world.

"Jean." He half-whispered as he held her, "How long are you going to burn a candle for a man sixteen years dead?"

She immediately stiffened, pushed him away, and took a step back. "I should slap you." She whirled around and headed for the door.

Zach's knees buckled like someone hit him in the stomach. The color rushed out of his face. For a moment, he thought he was going to fall over. Then he followed her. By the time he got out the door, she was down the steps and almost running across the parade grounds. He began to run after her. He called her name twice, loud enough she'd hear, but he hoped not to catch anyone else's attention.

She stopped, spun toward him, her face ablaze. "What? What do you want now?"

He wished he had let her go. "I'm sorry. I didn't mean to make you mad." For all of his gift of gab, a trait he was proud of, he turned into a stammering fool. "Hell, why was it such a terrible thing to ask."

"Go back into the dance." She spoke with no sentiment, no emotion at all.

"Will you go with me?" Zach put his hand on her elbow.

She jerked her arm away. "No." Her voice filled with anger, bitterness wrecked Zach. She turned and walked away from him.

Zach stood numb, mad at himself, enraged at Jean, and disgusted with the world in general. He never said a harsh, let alone mean word to Jean Wehr in his entire life. Every day Zach tried to do something to make her decide to love him. Right now, standing in the dark like a damn fool, he hated her.

Jean walked around quietly, crying for more than a half-hour. Sixteen years was a long time to carry something.

"Are you all right, ma'am?"

Jean jumped. "You scared me!" she gasped.

"I'm sorry, ma'am. I didn't mean to scare you." The

young soldier, not used to being in the presence of a beautiful woman, may have been more shaken than Jean. "I saw you out here, and I thought I should check on you."

"I'm fine," Jean smiled, dabbing at her eyes before putting her hands across her chest. "Don't worry about anything."

"Well, I'm sorry for scaring you. Can I do anything for you?"

Jean started to turn away but changed her mind. "Yes, would you go to the dance and tell somebody I need to talk to her out here?"

"Happy to. Who do you want me to find?"

"A woman. She's thin, not too tall. She has dark wavy hair. She's wearing a light blue dress with white cuffs. Her name is Nellie."

"I'll find her right away. I'll tell her you want her."

The young soldier hurried away. Minutes later, Nellie came out. Jean motioned for her.

Nellie ran down the stairs toward her friend. "What's wrong? The Private said he thought you were upset."

Jean took Nellie by the arm. "Come on. Let's take a walk." They crossed the parade field where they would be alone. "I hurt Zach's feelings."

"Well, for heaven's sakes, it's not like this is the first time. He never has any trouble getting over it."

"This time maybe a little worse." Jean gave a quick sigh. "Who am I kidding?" she groaned. "This is a lot worse. Usually, I'm joking with him. Not this time." Jean was crying again, but not hard enough, Nellie noticed. Her eyes filled up with tears. "Damn him, Nellie. He wants me to love him so bad."

Nellie fought the urge to chuckle. "Well, that's not exactly a terrible thing."

Jean stopped walking and turned away from Nellie. "Yeah, well, I've been wondering if I could love him. Tonight dancing with him, I was so comfortable in his arms. Then, he asks me how long I'm going to carry on over a guy dead sixteen years." Anger built up in her again. "What the hell kind of a question is that?"

"An inconsiderate one," Nellie said. "Zach isn't exactly genteel. Maybe he didn't mean it."

"He meant it, but it doesn't matter. I can't let him love me anyway. I can't let anybody." Jean turned around and faced Nellie.

"You're crying."

Jean wiped her eyes. "Don't look at me."

Nellie put an arm around her. "I can't remember seeing you cry before."

"I try not to make a public spectacle out of bawling."

"I always thought you talked to Annie about this tender kind of stuff," Nellie said, rubbing her friend's back.

"Well, I guess I can't talk to her about this."

"Why not?"

"Really? Have you ever strolled up to her and said, 'Oh, Annie, I need to tell you something about your future sister-in-law. I'm a slut."

Nellie Bascomb didn't say anything. She didn't move. She couldn't. She wasn't sure she could keep breathing.

"Well, have you?"

Nellie stood with her arms around Jean and looking straight ahead. Jean pulled away from her.

"No, I didn't think so."

"What are you talking about?" Nellie finally mumbled.

"I made love to Andy before he died, and not once, every night for about two weeks. I don't think righteous girls are supposed to before they are married." Jean started to walk across the parade field. The dry dirt broke into powder under her feet.

Nellie took a second or two to realize Jean was walking off. She scurried to catch up. "You're not a, uh ... a"

"Slut," Jean helped her.

"Right. A...what you said."

"You're a lot of comfort. You can't even say the word," Jean said, half-crying and half-laughing at herself.

"I can too," Nellie shot back. "Slut, there, I said it. Slut.

See, I said it again. Said it straight out. Slut. And you are not one."

"Lord, you are ridiculous,"

"At least you stopped crying," Nellie pointed out as she gave Jean, now sitting on one of the fort wells, a kiss on the forehead. "But Jean, what I don't understand is why you're bringing this up. It was a long, long time ago."

"Don't you think this might be a little bit of a problem on a wedding night?"

"I didn't think you were marrying him."

"I'm not, but I might want to marry someday."

Laughing erupted from Nellie. She couldn't stop. "Oh my, have you got the wrong opinion of men. You need to talk with your brother. He'll clear your head."

"You're not telling me he and Annie?"

"No! I didn't say that! I didn't mean that!" Now Nellie was laughing harder. "I'm sure they haven't. I meant he can tell you how men view women."

Both women started to laugh together. Jean almost told her Gray already knew, but she didn't. "You're a wonderful friend, Nellie. You made me feel a lot better."

"Is that why you never give Zach any hope? Tell me no."

Jean stopped to think about Nellie's question. "I'm not sure. I don't think so, not with Zach, but it is why I try not to fall in love. Any man, marrying me would be getting..."

Nellie helped her out. "Seconds, we call it in the restaurant business." The women laughed and talked about men and life in general for another hour. A few people started coming out of the dance. "It must be about over," Jean said.

"I wonder if I should go check on Millie," Nellie mused.

"Don't worry about her. Trent will see her home."

Humor returned, "We should check on Millie." They didn't. They sat and chatted, gossiped a little.

"Did Annie ever tell you I was forced once?"

"Nellie, who?"

"A Lakota." Jean's mouth dropped, and unbelief flashed in her eyes. "I was fifteen. He caught me one day by John

Creek." Nellie told this as if a third person was talking. "He ruined me, made me so ashamed; I didn't tell anyone for three years. I wanted to die. Finally, I told Annie. We cried all night one night. About three months later, Paints His Horse became chief. I rode out to his village, and I told him what happened."

"What did he say?"

"Not much." Nellie stopped, thought back all those years. "But I'll never forget his eyes, the compassion, and kind-heartedness. He hurt for me. He was my friend; he cared about me. He asked me who—I pointed him out." Nellie hesitated. "Paints His Horse picked up his lance, walked over to the man, and shoved the lance right through him. He didn't give him a chance to stand up." Nellie took an intense breath. "He pulled the lance out and handed it to me. I lifted it above my head and thrust the thing in him as hard and as deep as I could. I don't know if he was alive. I hope so. I hope my face was the last thing he ever saw. I wonder if he thought I was worth it?"

Jean ignored Nellie's humor. "Did you tell Annie that part?"

"We cried about that too. Annie held onto me when I asked God for forgiveness."

"Graham held me one night in Kansas when I asked." Jean breathed.

They sat beside each other for a long time, with neither speaking. Eventually, Nellie broke the silence. "So now we both know why we're not married."

Annie was asleep when Jean got back. She slipped out of her clothes and into bed as quietly as possible. Over at the Thaxton place, Millie had started to worry about her mom. When she came in, Millie asked, "Where have you been? I was about to come looking for you."

"Out walking around and talking to Jean. Go on to sleep. It's late."

Chapter Forty

The anger burned toward everyone. Gray shook—violently. Rage overcame him. Most of the hatred he directed at himself over his meanness toward Annie and Jean. Yet, he couldn't stop his wrath. He swung at Jean, shoved Annie, screamed at Millie. He lashed out to hurt the people he loved the dearest. He meant to inflict pain on them, wound them emotionally. He wanted them to hate him back because he hated himself. The madness continued; his yelling and swearing raged on. He managed to stop short of physical violence.

Gray's body jerked. He woke, his bed soaked with his sweat. The nightmare ceased, hell stopped raging, thank God.

Gray's sleep was like this for nights in a row. Disturbed sometimes by the war, other times gunfights, and still, other times fear and hurt. Sometimes, the nightmares would go away, leave him in peace. They always returned. Always the same, they either brought back harrowing memories of bloody battles or thundered with anger, bitterness, and sadness. The turmoil targeted the people he loved, those he would never want to harm or hurt.

Still dark outside, sleep impossible, he lay in the black, empty barracks, praying to God for release from the torturous dreams. Across the room, Zach breathed deeply in a peaceful rest. Gray ached to find rest far away from sorrow. He closed his eyes and tried to go back to sleep.

Another thirty minutes passed—slowly. Gray struggled to bring or allow sleep to come back. He failed, as he always did. He might as well go outside. Perhaps he'd find a sentry who'd like someone to talk to as he walked his rounds.

Private McIlhargey, an eighteen-year-old recruit who only shaved once a week, had been on the plains for about eight months. He pulled out his pocket watch: Three fifty-five, still an hour and a half or two hours before morning's light. Gray walked with McIlhargey through the fort.

They climbed up in the observation tower, studied the Sioux encampment, and discussed the assimilation of the Indian, something Gray did not believe either right or possible. No one moved anywhere in the village. Other than some dying campfires and a few dogs wandering around, nothing stirred in the camp.

Gray kept the private company on his rounds until five-thirty when the eastern sky began to show a little bit of a dull orange haze. With the breaking of the dawn, weariness washed over Gray. He decided to go back to the barracks and lie down before breakfast and before he would escort Annie to church.

Chapter Forty-One

Sunday morning broke blue and sunny. A gentle breeze, enough to make the warm morning bearable blew. Annie, Jean, Nellie, and Millie went to the Protestant Church services with the Thaxton's. Zach went to the enlisted men's mess for breakfast. By late morning he still sat, drinking coffee, sharing tales and lies with several off-duty soldiers.

Mostly they talked about the new treaty. The older, more grizzled troopers claimed the whole thing a waste of time. An old Sargent said there was no point to the effort at all. "Why, hell, we signed one with 'em back in '51. How long did it last? I'll tell you how long. 'Til some damn politicians back in Washington City decided they didn't like the Indians having as much as they got. Soon as they decided that, white men and the army started, breaking everything in that document. Turned it into a pack of lies."

He spat a wad of tobacco at a brass spittoon. "It ain't gonna change none out here. I read this thing. They'll give the Sioux and, I guess, the Northern Cheyenne all this country up here. The damn politicians, or the railroad, or somebody else white will start wanting the land. Them Indians will be crap outta luck. And we'll be the ones to fight the stinkin' war, a bunch of kill'n and dyin' on both sides. Those Sioux ain't leavin their land, and we, by damn, will never let 'em keep it. We might as well go kill 'em right now and be done with it."

Zach tired of coffee and cigars and took his leave to go out and find the others in his party. He found Annie out looking for Gray. He told her he left Gray sound asleep in a bunk almost three hours ago. At Annie's request, he went to roust his friend.

About thirty minutes later, Gray and Zach knocked on the door of the Thaxtons' living quarters. Everyone except Millie and Trent sat around the family dining table.

"Annie Laurie, you're a beautiful sight this morning," Gray kissed the top of her head.

"You're sure a late sleeper," Jean mused.

"You missed church," Annie added.

Gray told them he didn't go to sleep until about five-thirty. When Annie wondered why—he gave her some story about the barracks being hot and the bed uncomfortable. She poured him some coffee and rubbed his shoulders. She knew he often struggled with sleep, but he never described the nightmares in detail.

Jean and Annie, now guests in General Terry's home, told them the general wanted everyone, including the Thaxtons, for lunch at one-thirty.

Gray asked about the whereabouts of the other two. MyraThaxton laughed and asked Nellie to tell Gray. "Well, after church, Millie became struck by an overwhelming need to tour the rest of the fort. Why she hasn't been here in years, everything's changed so much. Mira, so kind, told Trent he should act like a gentleman and show this poor girl around. So, they are on a tour of Fort Laramie. After they left, I realized Millie might not be carrying any money for keepsakes. She's going to want some to remember her trip. I was about to go looking for her and give her some money, but Myrasaid she thought Trent had cash on him, and he might be willing to loan her some."

"They're going to meet us over at General Terry's," MyraThaxton said.

Gray and Robert Thaxton were talking about old times when Robert asked Gray if he had seen that scoundrel Jimmy Hickok anytime recently.

"I did. I ran into him back in the spring. He just left Yellow Dog to go down to Kansas where he's a marshal."

"I guess he's going to make himself right famous. 'Wild Bill' Hickok. It's got a ring to it."

"Didn't you say he shot some buffalo hunter at Yellow Dog?" Jean asked.

"Yeah, he did. Over an issue of personal cleanliness. He said the bullet went clean through the man's shoulder."

Trent's dad slapped his hand on the table. "Why, I'll bet it was old Jack Terry. Somebody plugged him down there this year."

"I don't think he knew the guy's name," Gray said. "He did say he was ugly. Ugly enough to scare little children."

Robert glanced at his wife and laughed. "That's him. Old 'Buffalo Face.' I swear. I can't wait to see him again and tell him none other than 'Wild Bill' Hickok shot him. Heavens, he'll feel a lot better now. That'll give him something to brag about."

Jean hopped up, catching everyone's attention. "Here's the difference between men and women. Can you imagine a woman saying," Jean stuck her thumbs in her belt and did a little swaggering motion, "Yeah, I got plugged. Right here in the shoulder, but," she made a sound imitating a man spitting tobacco, "hell, it were 'Wild Bill' Hickok done it."

Jean started a round of laughter, including Zach, quiet all morning, still stinging from Jean's words the night before.

Trent and Millie were already at General Terry's home when the others arrived. Gray questioned Millie thoroughly about all the changes at Fort Laramie. She was greatly relieved when General Sherman came and diverted Gray's attention.

Once everyone sat at the dinner table, Terry's cook brought in hot rolls, butter, creamed peas, and a vessel of chicken and dumplings. General Terry patted her hand. "You're all in for a treat this afternoon. Lizabeth here makes the finest chicken and dumplings I've ever tasted, and I have sampled a many."

Annie kept tapping Gray's foot with her toe. Jean, Nellie, and Millie glanced at each other, at Gray. Gray hated chicken and dumplings. When they finished eating, everyone grandly praised Lizabeth's chicken and dumplings, especially Gray, who apologized profusely for not being able to hold more than his one helping.

General Terry gushed over the little colored woman. "Lizabeth, you have outdone yourself. Such praise from Miss Bascomb? Why that is high praise indeed. After all, she owns a restaurant. I believe I might detect a bit of jealousy in her."

Lizabeth thanked them all for being so kind to her. She brought in coffee and peach cobbler. She told the General he should ring for her if he needed anything else.

She went back to the kitchen, where her nephew sat, finishing off the chicken and dumplings. She started cleaning up. "Isaac, did you hear that? 'Lizabeth, you have outdone yourself. And such praise from Miss Bascomb? Why that is high praise indeed.'" She dropped a bowl into the dishwater. "They can all kiss my colored rump."

Annie hoped all through the dinner and dessert, one of the Generals would start a conversation about the treaty talks. They talked about everything else from the number of sage hens on the plains to what influential men they'd become if Ulysses Grant "gets himself elected President."

Once it became apparent neither Terry nor Sherman would accommodate her, and both Gray and Zach intended to sit complicit in silence, she took on the task herself. She leaned forward with her elbows on the table, "As you know, Generals, our home is in a little valley in the Bighorn Mountains. That makes us quite interested in the exact terms of this treaty."

Annie liked Alfred Terry. General Sherman, a man she hadn't yet formed her opinion about, seemed capable of killing the mood in any room. Neither responded to her.

"You do know our home is in the Bighorns? West of Fort Phil Kearny?"

Terry spoke first. "Yes, of course, I'm familiar with your valley." He turned toward Sherman. "I guess General Sherman may not have been aware."

"Exactly where in the Bighorns do you live, ma'am? I didn't realize anyone lived in those mountains." The General's eyes darted between Annie and General Terry. Sherman did appear to be truly surprised. "You have a town or only a few scattered homesites?"

"High Meadows, General. It's been there since before 1830. Frankly, I'm a little angry. This treaty sounds as if you gave away our homes and, further, banned whites from the land." Annie, having said her piece, locked her jaw, her eyes burned into the military men.

Sherman, unaccustomed to having a woman talk to him in such bold language, paled and turned to Terry for help. "Alfred, are you aware of this problem?"

Terry, now put on the spot, wanted to disengage himself as soon as possible. "General, I'm not sure High Meadows would fall under the terms of the treaty."

"Well, my god, man, this may be a bit of an issue. Retrieve a copy."

"Yes, sir." Terry went to the roll-top desk in his study and came back with the treaty. He handed the paper to Sherman, who thumbed through it quickly.

"Miss Laurie, here is the definition of the land to be given to the Indians. I'll let you read this yourself." Annie took the document from Sherman.

Article XVI

The United States hereby agreed and stipulates that the country north of the North Platte River and east of the summits of the Bighorn Mountains shall be held and considered unceded Indian territory, and also stipulates and agrees that no white person or persons shall be permitted to settle upon or occupy any portion of the same; or without the consent of the Indians, first had and obtained, to pass through the same; and it's further agreed by the United States, that within ninety days after the conclusion of peace with all the bands of the Sioux Nation, the military posts now established in the territory in this article named shall be abandoned, and that the road leading to them and by them to the settlements in the territory shall be closed.

"Does High Meadows fall within the boundaries of the treaty?" General Terry asked with what sounded like a genuine concern in his voice.

Annie stared at the paper. She read the paragraph a second and a third time. "This says 'east of the summits.' Our valley is in the heart of the mountains. You go up into the Bighorns. You drop into a high valley. We're sort of in the summits. You enter from the south. Peaks surround us on three sides." Annie handed Gray the document.

It struck Gray he had been making his own choices his entire life. No one told him what to do. No one would force him to leave his meadow home. Still, he didn't like the inconvenience this treaty might cause. "The thing concerning to me, as I read this, is Fort Phil Kearny. It's on this land. You plan to desert it?"

Sherman was more direct with Wehr than Annie. "The forts along the Bozeman Trail will be closed within ninety days, including Fort Phil Kearny."

"What exactly does 'within ninety days' mean? Have the ninety days already begun?"

Sherman's eyes darkened, and a frown bent his lips. "Phil Kearny will close by the middle of August. The process is underway."

"Fort Kearny is the closest place we can go for supplies," Jean said as she took the treaty document from Gray. "What about Fort Fetterman?" Anger started to show in her voice.

Terry told her Fort Fetterman remained an issue of negotiation. He told them of Red Cloud's insistence on its closing. Sherman, however, said the closure would not happen. He guaranteed them, Grant, should he be elected, would never stand for Fort Fetterman to be abandoned.

"Which Indians signed this?" Annie asked.

General Terry produced the list from the roll-top desk. The document continued for several pages, breaking the names down by tribe;

The Brule Band of Sioux,

The Ogallala band of the Sioux,

The Miniconjou band of the Sioux

Sherman pointed out numerous chiefs and

leaders listed on the treaty:

Poor Elk

High Wolf

American Horse

Four Bears

Sitting Bull

A Man Afraid Of His Horse

Yellow Robe

Gray glanced over the list. One name jumped out at him. "Sitting Bull? I thought he was refusing to sign."

Sherman let Terry explain whether or not Sitting Bull signed the document was a matter of some debate. "He picked up the pen, an indication of agreement," Terry said, before admitting the Hunkpapa leader claims not to have signed and now had left the fort.

"Red Cloud is holding out for more forts to be closed?" Zach asked.

Sherman put his cigar in an ashtray. "Red Cloud is a stubborn man. He's going to have to come to an understanding that negotiations, by their definition, mean no one gets everything he wants."

Gray's eyes darkened. "I hate to rain on your parade, Generals, but unless you get Red Cloud's signature, and Crazy Horse's, and Sitting Bull's and Gall's on your treaty, I'm afraid you've got nothing, no peace, and no solution to your problem."

The discussion carried on for another forty-five minutes or so. The afternoon visit heated up with Annie accusing the army of being derelict of their duty regarding High Meadows and the people who lived there. "The fault rests entirely on you, General Sherman. What happens if we don't want to leave our homes?" Her eyes bore into Sherman. "Do you plan to march your army through and burn our homes?"

"Madam," Sherman shot back. "I have been sitting here wondering why a woman as attractive as you is not married, but now I can see why."

Gray started out of his chair, but Annie put her arm in front of him. Sherman, certainly no fool, laughed. "I believe I am lucky you are not armed. I might now be dead."

"I wouldn't push it, General," Gray growled.

Sherman retreated deeper into his chair. "I apologize, Miss Laurie. I rarely have anyone, especially a woman, speak to me in such a blunt manner." Annie leaned back and glanced at both Generals and the window across the sitting room.

Alfred Terry made a move at peace. "Is it clear your town is in the land given to the Sioux?"

Zach stopped sipping his coffee. "Do you have a map drawn up?"

Terry squirmed. "I'm afraid the cartographers are a bit behind."

Sherman spoke again, surprising everyone, including General Terry. "Surely you would not consider moving your homes too great a price for peace with the Indians. Think of the lives that you would save. Did either of you men fight in the war?" he asked, looking at Gray and Zach.

"Captain Wehr fought under me," Terry said. "He earned a battlefield commission under me. Served with me until Sheridan stole...I mean had Gray and about forty more of my men transferred to his command."

"Where did you fight with Sheridan?"

"I joined him at Perryville. Fought with him at Chickamauga, Chattanooga, Yellow Tavern, and Meadow Ridge."

"Did you go down the Shenandoah with him?"

"Down the Shenandoah and fought at Saylor Creek."

"You appreciate the terrible cost in lives war brings,"

Sherman said. "You and your friends can rebuild somewhere."

"General, we worked, bled, and died to settle the valley. We'll not leave our homes."

"Then, sir, you may be considered hostile to the United States," Sherman snapped.

Annie leaned forward, intercepting Gray, fortunate for Sherman. "What kind of a military do you run? You come out here and make a treaty without knowing whose lives are being affected. What Gray told you is right. If Red Cloud, Sitting Bull, and Crazy Horse don't sign the—thing," she said, intentionally demeaning the document, "you may as well throw it in that Cherrywood fireplace. I, for one in this room, have no respect for the military or its leaders." Annie stood and threw her napkin on the oak table. "We'll realize more success in living in our valley at peace with the Lakota than the Sioux ever will in getting your army to honor any treaty with them." Annie, on her way out of the room, stopped and apologized to General Terry. "I'm sorry, sir, but he made me mad." She walked out of the dining area and upstairs to the room where she and Jean were staying.

Everyone else sat around the table for quite a while without saying anything. "Your fiancée is a fiery woman," Terry finally said, smiling at Gray.

Gray laughed a little, although not finding any humor in the observation. "Annie rarely gets so angry. I don't remember her ever being so mad."

"Jean's usually the feisty one," Millie cracked, drawing a nasty frown from Nellie. William Tecumseh Sherman sat his eyes on Millie and allowed the corners of his mouth to show the slightest smile.

"Well, Alfred," Sherman said as he stood, "perhaps those delayed maps should make sure the border of this treaty stops short of the edge of their valley." The General folded his napkin and laid it carefully alongside his plate. "If you folks will excuse me, I am rather given to a Sunday afternoon nap." Everyone stood as Sherman left. After his departure, Terry motioned them back into their seats.

After a short silence, Zach glanced toward the stairs. "Well, she said she was going to come down here and help negotiate the treaty."

Millie laughed. "Yeah, but I didn't realize she was so high-spirited."

Chapter Forty-Two

Nellie made a deal with one of the army cooks for ten steaks for the meal with A Man Afraid Of His Horse. Gray enjoyed the beef more than the chicken and dumplings. The old Lakota and his two wives ate, but except when A Man Afraid Of His Horse said he liked elk better, they ate in silence. Little more than tolerated, the Wasichus received no invitation back.

Montana daylight stays late in July. When they slipped out of A Man Afraid Of His Horse's teepee, dusk was only beginning to shroud the camp in strange hues of blues and deep orange, giving an almost mystical presence as Indians danced and skipped around small fires to the sound of drums and chanting. Feathers and paint gave them an otherworldly appearance in the fading light. Curious women with children clinging to them watched and stared as the white eyes left the village.

Annie and Jean dreaded returning to General Terry's home to go to bed, so Gray said he would walk them home and perhaps speak with his former commander. Jean playfully pointed out Annie was the "old witch." She, after all, said hardly anything. Much to Annie's relief, Alfred Terry was courteous, to the point of expressing regret for some of Sherman's gruffness.

He offered them a cup of coffee. Annie, anxious for an opportunity to apologize, accepted on behalf of all three. "General, I am genuinely sorry about my outburst this afternoon. It was ill-mannered."

Terry chuckled warmly. "You were negotiating terms for your town. They should be grateful to you. Your efforts were magnificent."

"I was rude."

"You were persistent." Terry leaned over and patted Annie's hand. "Rarely are difficult negotiations conducted with the high decorum and diplomacy politicians and military leaders would like the public to believe. My next letter home will detail you putting old Bill into his place."

Terry's joking relieved Annie. "Well, I'll assure you, General, my career as a diplomat is over."

"Amen," Gray said, lifting his coffee cup as if in a toast. After a little more casual conversation, Gray headed to the enlisted men's mess, figuring to share a few tales and cheap cigars before going to bed.

At the same time, Nellie sat and visited with Trent's parents, taking advantage of the rare privilege to talk with someone from outside her valley.

Millie and Trent meandered down toward the river. A warm breeze drifted gently through the cottonwoods while crickets breached the quiet evening. Trent bent down and caught one. "They're noisy little devils."

"I like hearing them. Let it go." Trent took Millie's hand and set the cricket in her hand. "He's cute." The bug showed Millie no affection. It immediately jumped to freedom.

They sat under one of the trees along the river's edge. Trent leaned over and kissed Millie softly on the lips. "Did that scare you?" Millie whispered as she put her arms around him.

"What would I be afraid of?"

"Well, that I wouldn't let you." She slipped her face into

the crook of his neck and gave him a gentle kiss. "Or my breath would...be unpleasant." She sat up and played with her hair. "Or I'd bite."

They strolled along the river enjoying the summer evening, talking about things important and unimportant for nearly an hour. They laughed, hugged, kissed, and fell more in love.

Annie, Jean, Nellie, Gray, and Zach spent the first three days sitting in on the treaty talks where Red Cloud demanded Fort Fetterman's closure. General Sherman was always quick to give Annie a wink or nod. Anytime the opportunity arose, he delighted in introducing her to the other officers as the "female who bested him in negotiations." As the week moved along, Annie started to like the General.

Millie spent her time, all she had, in the company of Trent Thaxton. The others mostly hung around the treaty talks. In mid-afternoon on Wednesday, Annie announced she would like to head for Cheyenne the following morning. It surprised no one when they found out Trent would make the trip back to High Meadows with them.

Later in the afternoon, Gray went over to General Terry's home to discuss the terms of his leaving the ranch with his sister. General Terry's cook and housekeeper answered the door and sent her nephew upstairs to fetch Jean. Jean and Annie both came down. "I thought we might talk a little while the others aren't around."

"I should go back up," Annie said, feeling a little awkward.

"For heaven's sake," Jean said to her, taking her by the arm. "You're going to be his wife. There are no secrets from you. Let's go out on the porch. It's hot in here," she said as she opened the door and stepped outside. A cool breeze wafted across the open porch, just enough to disturb the heat without ruining the stillness of the afternoon.

Jean sat on the porch swing. "Well, what's on your mind?"

Gray shifted his feet, not quite sure how to begin. Jean

pushed her blonde hair back away from her face while pushing the swing into motion. "Would this be about wanting your sister to buy out a ranch partner?"

"Yeah, I suppose so."

Annie sat in a wicker chair. "Listen, I can wait upstairs if you want to talk in private."

"Stop being silly," Jean told her before looking up at Gray. "You may as well know; Paxton already gave me a lecture about this. He came over to the house as soon as he found out you two planned to marry." Jean grabbed at but missed, some insect flying annoyingly around her face. "He figures you should give us your share."

Gray eased into the swing next to her. "What did you tell him?"

"I told him he's a bigger horse's ass than I thought." Annie blurted out a laugh. Jean shook her head at her and smiled. "Are you sure you want in this family?"

Annie nodded. "I'm sure."

"Anyway," Jean continued, "I went over and talked with Alan. We went through all the ranch books to figure out what your part is worth." She handed Gray a folded paper. "Agreeable?"

"That's a lot of money, Jeannie," Gray said before handing the note over to Annie.

"It's a fair price. If our little brother doesn't want to pay half, I can do it myself. It would be kind of fun to have two votes at the family meetings."

Gray sat back in the swing. "I appreciate this, Jeannie. You're a first-rate sister."

"Yes, I am. But I'm a tired one, too. I'm going to take a nap. I'll see you after a while." Gray stood with Jean. Annie hugged Jean as she went into the house. She turned to Gray, raised on her toes, and kissed him before heading into the house and up the stairs.

Chapter Forty-Three

The Thaxton's asked everyone to dinner. Trent's mother sat quietly throughout most of the meal. She had taken to Millie, but Trent making the trip to High Meadows saddened her. After they ate, Trent and Millie went off on their nightly walk. The others took chairs out to the back porch.

"We're glad you folks came down," Myra said as she poured coffee for her guests. "I'm sorry the treaty is still vague about your valley. But from what Trent says, Annie took care of it. Bested Bill Sherman. The old scoundrel needed humbling."

"In my opinion, little will change at home," Zach said.

"It will send us farther for supplies," Nellie countered.

"I suppose a little extra travel is not too high a price to pay for peace," Gray responded.

"Fort Laramie is three times as far away as Phil Kearny," Nellie said. "And we've been at peace."

"I guess I don't understand the ways of government." Annie shook her head, her jaw tightened. "We have no right to restrict the Lakota's freedom?"

"Manifest Destiny, I suppose," Gray answered.

"I think it's manifestly unfair." Annie brushed a red ant off her knee. "After all, they were here first."

Gray stood and walked to the edge of the porch before looking back at the others. "We're a stronger nation. The strong to rule over the weak." He sat down and leaned back against the rails. "The Crow held this land before the Sioux. But the Sioux pushed the Crow off."

"And the Crow hate the Sioux to this day," Zach added.

"True enough," Gray said. "And I suppose the Sioux will forever loathe the white man. Way of the world, I suppose."

"We would do better to make the Indians Christians than to conquer them," Myra said.

Jean spoke for the first time. "Annie's our resident theologian. You'd need to ask her."

"Well, what do you think, Annie?" Myra Thaxton asked.

"I believe Christ died for the Lakota, the Crow, and the Cheyenne as he did for everyone. But I don't think we can force Christianity on them. They must accept Christ out of a free heart, as I did, as Gray did, and as you did." Annie laughed a little, smiled at Jean, "I'm not the resident theologian."

Gray stood and put his hand out to Annie. "Let's you and me take a walk along the river."

"As long as I don't have to be swatting off mosquitoes."

Annie and Gray walked out the back gate and down toward a grove of tall trees. "I'm eager to start home," Annie said. "I think Nellie is getting a little concerned about the business."

"Well, I don't suppose she has too much to worry about, being the only restaurant in town."

Annie snickered as they walked. "I guess that's an advantage for her."

Later, sitting almost a mile downriver, a warm breeze came up off the water. The moon cast a white reflection across the river, like a silk ribbon you could reach out and touch. Annie turned toward Gray. He had his eyes closed and wore a peaceful expression. She almost said something but sat quietly.

Black, quick-moving shadows caught her eye. Squinting, she made out seven or eight deer down for an evening drink. Two came out belly deep. They splashed around for a few minutes before heading back into a gully and out of sight.

All of this convinced Annie living in the west, with its wildness and untamed beauty, made her the most fortunate woman in the world. "Are you asleep?"

The slightest hint of a smile crossed Gray's mouth. "No, but I'm thinking about it." Annie reached out with her hand and ran her fingers through Gray's blonde hair, pushing it back away from his face. Gray took her hand and kissed her palm. She leaned over and kissed his lips. Annie loved his hand brushing through her hair and stroking her face. She closed her eyes as he rubbed a finger over each brow and down the side of her nose.

Chapter Forty-Four

The group packed everything before sunrise. As they left the fort for Cheyenne, many of the Sioux were striking their camp. "I'm not the only one who decided it's time to go home," Annie turned toward Gray. "Are you concerned over Indians leaving, going the same direction?"

"I'll admit, I wish they would stay here, at least 'til we're a day or so away."

A little anxious herself, Millie wanted to learn to shoot Trent's pistol and begged him to let her. Trent kept telling her she'd blow her foot off.

The second morning out of Fort Laramie, four Sioux warriors approached the Wehr camp. They stopped about fifty yards out and rode in a slow circle, two in each direction. Millie took Trent by the arm and mumbled something about how he should have taught her to shoot. Zach reached for a rifle. "Don't,"

Gray said. "I don't think we need to fight here. Relax."

One of the Sioux was Two Dogs, Trent's friend. At least, Trent hoped. Trent raised his hand to him. Two Dogs said something to the one next to him, and they moved back toward the other two. As Gray walked out toward them, Annie slipped up beside him.

"Should you leave your gun here, so they know you're friendly?"

Gray glanced at her. "I prefer they know I'm dangerous. You stay here. Trent and I will go on out. Tell Zach not to touch that rifle."

Jean whispered to the other women the Lakota, particularly the second from the left, were magnificent-looking men. Two Dogs wore only a breechcloth, as did the two other men. Their bodies shined from the grease rubbed on them, their raven black hair hung in braids to the middle of their chests. The oldest brave bore scars on his chest from sacrifices at a Sundance.

The second from the left, the one Jean thought exceptionally handsome, was lighter-skinned. His brown, and not dark brown hair, flowed halfway down his back. He wore a buckskin shirt and breechcloth. One eagle feather adorned his wavy hair, pointed down. A flat pebble hanging from a leather thong draped over his left ear.

Two Dogs introduced the bare-chested warriors as Touch The Clouds and Yellow Elk, the shirt wearer as Tasunke witko, a name he said emphasizing each syllable. Trent turned toward the man. Gray spoke in Lakota to the light-skinned warrior.

The Sioux answered back. He didn't smile or show any hint of emotion. The tone of his voice wasn't threatening, but not matter-of-fact either. He slipped off his horse, a paint with yellow lightning bolts painted down his front legs. The other three Indians stayed on horseback. "We are from the Bighorn Mountains," Gray told him. He corrected himself, using the term rough animal horns, the Sioux name for the Bighorns. "Paints His Horse is my friend." Gray doubted that would make any difference, but he figured there was no harm in mentioning the friendship. "We are coming from Fort Laramie. We listened to the treaty talks. Now we are going home to tell our families about them."

Yellow Elk mumbled something to Two Dogs, but Gray couldn't make out what. The shirt wearer said nothing. Gray shifted around, glanced at the other Lakota and Trent, trying hard to think of something else to say. "We're about to eat; do you want to share with us?"

The light-complexioned Sioux, Tasunke witko, took one step toward Gray, stood still, as if distracted, or sizing Gray up. "What promises did the soldier chiefs make?" he asked, ignoring Gray's invitation to breakfast.

"Some," Gray said, nodding his head and shrugging his shoulders. He thought about telling them the treaty had been signed but thought better. Deciding vagueness might be the best policy.

"Your government will offer food and blankets and clothing," the light-skinned shirt wearer said. "They will say they will put borders around some of the land and say it is ours, promise white men will stay off. Lies." The warrior shot two fingers in the shape of a V, the sign of a forked tongue across his chest. Gray shifted his weight but didn't speak. "How can the white eyes own the earth? Who can own the earth? The Indian came here first. Why must we leave?"

The answer was simple. Sioux will move for the same reason the Crow moved. The Crow could not defeat the Sioux, and the Sioux cannot triumph over the whites. Gray did not respond.

Tasunke witko grunted, swung gracefully back onto his spotted pony. "Leave this land. Go back to your mountains. Live in peace with Paints His Horse. I will honor your friendship with him instead of killing you." He moved his lance to his right hand. "If I find out you are not his friend, and I see you again, I might yet kill you."

Gray's eyes narrowed, his voice calm but decisive. "I do not lie about Paints His Horse. To show myself kola, I offered you food. If you ever decide to kill me, you might be the one to die."

The warrior smiled—a little—"kola."

Two Dogs again said something to Trent. Gray didn't hear what. The four Lakota turned their ponies and loped away at a comfortable pace. The encounter was brief, only ten minutes from its beginning to end. "What did he say to you?" Gray asked, waving a hand toward Two Dogs.

Trent stood, staring out at the departing Sioux. "He said, 'It is wise to be brave, but not a fool.'"

"I wonder which he thought we were."

After they moved back over with the others, Gray spoke first. "I guess since we kept our hair, things went all right." Nellie gave him a sour eye, sensing the meeting had not been a light-hearted conversation.

"What did you say to him? And what did he say to you?" Jean demanded.

Gray fidgeted with the Colt on his leg. "I asked them to breakfast."

Annie slipped her arm in Gray's. "I guess he declined?"

"He called me kola."

"Friend. A good start," Annie said.

Jean resented the lighthearted crack about breakfast, considered it insulting. "Who were they, anybody important? What went on?"

Gray smiled at his sister and put his arm around her shoulder. Another pompous gesture she didn't appreciate. "The one in the shirt, Jeannie," Gray paused, "That was Tasunke witko… Crazy Horse."

Chapter Forty-Five

After two more days of begging, Millie wore Trent down about letting her shoot his pistol. He handed her the gun and told her to aim at a dry stick about twenty feet away. She held the weapon in both hands and pulled the hammer back. The pistol went off with an ear-shattering crack. And, the blamed gun kicked so hard Millie almost dropped the heavy thing. The bullet tore into the ground about four feet from Trent's bay horse. Sundance, unaccustomed to being shot at from close range, whirled and headed north up the river.

Nellie came running and hollering to find out what happened. "She tried to shoot Sundance! I've got to catch him before he goes all the way home."

Trent went to swing up on Poncho. Not used to such a tall horse, he didn't make the saddle. Poncho disapproved of this much excitement. The explosion, Trent bouncing off his side, sent the appy into a state of nerves. He started backing away from Trent, pulling on the reins and trying to free himself. Trent yelled for him to hold still, sprinkling his speech with a few bits of colorful language directed at the horse.

After three failed attempts, he got his foot into the stirrup and on the horse. He spun the horse around and kicked him north. Sundance had a long head start. Despite the tall Appy's speed, they galloped almost a mile-and-a-half to catch the bay gelding.

When Trent came back, leading Sundance, the other six stood waiting with their horses. He stepped off Poncho and handed the reins to Millie. Taking them, she told Trent he needed to keep a tighter rein on his horse; otherwise, the trip home would take a long time.

Chapter Forty-Six

The Magic City of the Plains, at first, an end of the track camp, snowballed. Only a year after the first settlers arrived, Cheyenne boasted two hundred businesses and a population of five thousand. In many ways, the new metropolitan area was sophisticated, with dry goods emporiums, restaurants, one fancy, schools, and churches. In other matters, Cheyenne remained a rough railroad town. Saloons, gambling parlors, and brothels still lined several streets.

Gray didn't like this detour, but Annie and the other women wanted to shop in Cheyenne's larger stores and enjoy a fine meal at its most prominent and fanciest restaurant.

They first checked into the hotel and ordered seven hot baths. A quick shopping trip followed to buy the men, who had shown so little foresight to come without suitable clothes for fancy dining, including a brand-new beaver hat for Gray. Annie thought its tan color complimented his blonde hair.

At eight, Annie, Jean, Nellie, and Millie walked into the vestibule of the Maggy McGuinn, the finest eating establishment in Cheyenne. The woman he would soon marry took his breath away. Her hair was up and pulled back from her face. She wore an ivory dress with long sleeves, on which pearl buttons ran up the sides to the elbows. There, the sleeves, fitting tight from her wrists to her elbows, puffed out up to her shoulders. The collar made of a long piece of lace cloth wrapped around her neck and buttoned to the left of center, under her chin. A silk bow behind her head caught the light enough Gray would have sworn he was looking at an angel. "Annie Laurie, you are a beautiful sight."

As the restaurant's host seated them, Gray had never been happier or prouder. One at a time, the gentleman pulled out a burgundy leather chair for the ladies. A white linen tablecloth covered the long table, silver napkin rings held matching napkins, rose petals lie around the long-stemmed water glasses. With the dining room's west wall glass, the sunset's soft glow bathed the entire room in a warm orangish blush.

The host left with the promise their waiter would arrive soon. "I'll bet nobody spits tobacco on this front porch." Millie immediately regretted her silliness. "I'm sorry, I'll behave."

Nellie had never seen so many choices on one menu. It featured steaks, fresh trout, duck, lamb, pheasant, and pork chops. The waiter, a young and personable lad, recommended the duck and the lamb. "Our steaks are also excellent. We cover them with black pepper grounds and prepare them over an open fire." The choice of white and red wines came with the counsel to match your wine's color to your meat. The exception, he said, in his opinion, would be the pork chop. He suggested a gentleman might prefer fine sipping whiskey before the meal.

Zach asked the waiter to bring the wine before dinner and proposed a toast upon its arrival. "To my friends, may our caring for one another remain a cherished part of each of our lives."

Jean made a point of sitting next to Zach, put her hand on his. She mouthed the words "I'm sorry" and squeezed his hand. The meals and the evening turned out excellent. The six old friends talked, laughed, and made Trent comfortable among them for a little over two hours.

Chapter Forty-Seven

Annie roused Gray out of the hotel early to go shopping. Her soon-to-be husband's younger, boyish good looks over the years turned to a rugged handsomeness. The black frock coat hung perfectly from his shoulders, curving in along the waist and following the slightest bend over his hips.

"Well, what do you think?"

Annie raised her eyebrows and took in the full measure of him. His blonde hair pulled back off his tanned face, bumped down over his collar in the back with enough curl to give him a slightly rakish appeal.

"I think we need to buy you new shoes. You can't be coming to my wedding in those beat-up old boots."

"Hats and boots, Annie, hats, and boots." The clerk shot off to fetch wedding-appropriate footwear. Annie leaned against Gray and slipped an arm around his waist. She laid her head on his chest and slid her other hand inside his coat. Annie loved his smell and the softness of his breath down along her face and throat. If a preacher walked in, she would marry him standing right in the middle of the Emporium for Men.

After a moment, she lifted her head and gave him a soft

kiss under his chin, in the curve of his neck. She removed her arm when the sales clerk returned, proudly displaying a pair of shiny black shoes, "perfectly suited for a wedding groom. This elegant dress boot laces up with a combination of both eyelets and hooks while a padded tongue and collar offer extra comfort."

Gray resented the interruption, thinking the sharp-nosed, bespectacled man must be the dumbest fella God ever created.

They walked back to the hotel café with Gray carrying his new frock coat, trousers, and shoes. They sat at a table in a corner out of most people's way.

"I can run up to my room and climb into this wedding outfit, and we can find ourselves a local justice of the peace." His seductive expression, the best he could marshal, delighted Annie. "We can be Mr. and Mrs. before the next thirty minutes pass," he whispered, his lips touching her ear.

"Well, you're a romantic sort."

"I am. That's why I want to find a justice of the peace." Annie didn't want him to know, but what an awful strain not to agree.

They drank coffee and tea before Annie told him she had to meet the girls for a shopping spree. She laughed about him having the afternoon off to spend with the boys. Annie gathered up the new clothes and took them to her room for safer keeping. Jean, Nellie, and Millie met her when she got upstairs.

Inside Cheyenne's long row of saloons, a man with a paltry sum could find a few card games needing an extra player—and more money. Zach, who seldom left High Meadows, figured he'd find a chair waiting for him at one of those tables. Gray didn't mind going along; he just would have preferred lounging around the hotel all afternoon. Saloons are all the same: drinkers talking in loud voices, inept or half-drunk piano players pounding pianos badly in need of tuning, the stench of beer, whiskey, and smoke hanging over it all.

Zach decided The Blue Moon Saloon offered the best opportunity. As they walked over to the bar, he searched for an empty chair at one of the poker tables. The bartender, a friendly gent in his mid-forties, wore a white shirt, frayed at the cuffs, a black tie, and a vest. Despite the forty or fifty extra pounds he carried, he slid back and forth with a certain amount of grace. "What'll it be, boys?"

"Whiskey for me," Zach said. "I can't say what my friends favor." Although neither drank much, Gray and Trent both ordered a beer.

The bartender, who introduced himself as Pete, asked Zach about his preference for whiskey. Gray figured Pete overdid the service thing because he pegged Zach out of his usual surroundings and decided on a bit of fun. Zach grinned back. "Well, what kind have you got?"

Pete took an immediate liking to his new customer. "Well, I've got Rye, Scotch, and Irish. I recommend the Irish myself."

"Irish it is."

"Irish it is!" Pete went to the trouble of wiping the shot glass before pouring three fingers of the amber-colored liquid. Zach slugged the whole thing down in one swallow. Pete turned his head and gave Gray a bit of a wink. Gray slapped Zach on the back and suggested he try some of the Scotch. Zach Joseph, a good-natured man, happily joined in on the laugh. Pete raised the bottle of Scotch. "Shall we have a go at the Scotch, Laddy?"

Zach held up his hand. "I think I better have a beer, Pete. It's a little cooler on the way down."

"A beer it is, my boy. You're probably right. I serve a higher quality beer than whiskey."

Zach laughed again. "Well, to tell you the truth, I surely wouldn't know. Being right honest with you, I can't say if you gave me Irish or Scotch the first time." Zach took a sip, hoping to cool the trail of fire the whiskey left. "You think I might get into one of these games?"

Pete motioned at one of the card tables. "Well, I believe those boys over by the wall would welcome a fifth. Go on and tell 'em I sent ya."

Zach headed off to the poker table, announcing his arrival with a smile, a slap on the dealer's back, and his recommendation from Pete.

"I hope yer friend plays cards better'n he drinks whiskey."

Gray shook his head as he watched Zach wander off. "I sorta doubt he does."

"Well, if you'll be needing nothing else, I guess I ought to head for the other end of the bar. Yell, when you want your beer topped off."

"Is he always like that?" Trent asked.

"He's one of a kind."

"For the life of me, I can't find the attraction to hanging around a saloon," Trent said.

Gray surveyed the room. Three whores kept making the rounds, trying to drum up a little business. One man sprawled passed out on a table back in the far corner. Besides the one Zach joined, four or five poker games progressed, complete with the drinking, smoking, and swearing accompanying the winning and losing.

"No, I don't see too much attraction here either," Gray answered, thinking back over all the times he had been in a saloon and how little positive ever came out of the experience.

One of the back corner games broke up when two of the poker players lost their finances. A rough-looking man picked up his shot glass and headed toward the bar. After Pete slid down and refilled him, the card player drank it in one gulp and whacked the glass back down on the bar, got the glass filled again. The man, unwashed, unshaven, uncouth, was nothing but a saloon mongrel, a cur, and an obnoxious drunk. He growled at Pete to leave the bottle, poured, and knocked back two more shots before turning toward Gray and Trent. "You two, come on over here. We need a couple more players."

Gray rubbed his hand over the rough bar, smiled. "Sorry, poker's never been too kind to me."

The man, half-drunk, got surlier. "Well, this might be your lucky day."

"Thanks anyway, but I'm not much of a card player." This fellow didn't plan to take no for an answer. The troublemaker swigged another shot of whiskey, this time straight out of the bottle while glaring at Gray. He staggard down the bar toward Wehr and Trent. He carried a single-action Colt, similar to the one Wehr wore on the trail, strapped on a belt his belly hung over. The cuffs on his shirt were dirty and frayed. Hard liquor stains spotted the front. He walked up to within three feet of Wehr, stinking of rye.

"You figure you're too gentlemanly to play cards with us?"

"I'm not a poker player." Gray briefly closed his eyes, shook his head at Pete in a reassuring manner. "Don't worry about it. It's only the whiskey talking."

Bill flushed, swore, and grabbed at his pistol. Only fools are so imprudent. Wehr snatched his Colt out of his holster and jammed the end of the barrel into the man's face. Hard into his face, "Go ahead! Pull that pistol, you damned fool."

The saloon went deathly quiet, with everyone's eyes fixed on the stranger thumping one of the town bullies. Wehr pulled the gun back and gave Bill a couple of stiff pokes in the face with the end of the barrel. "You think this is worth dying over? You want to die now?" He gave him three more sharp jabs to the cheeks and forehead. Each one cut a little circle in his sweaty face. "Answer me, you jackass. You're the curly wolf. Is this something to die over?"

Wehr waited for an answer. None came. Gray pulled his gun back and, in one flowing motion, bashed the side of Bill's head. Bill wobbled. His fall was most ungraceful. One of his arms swung over the bar, knocking off glasses and the half-full whiskey bottle. He went down on his hind end and flat on his back with his head bouncing off the brass foot rail. He came to a rest with his mouth gaping open. Blood gushed from a gash, extending from his ear to his eyebrow.

Zach got up from his card game. "I'll bet he wakes up with a headache."

Pete leaned over the bar. "He's needed whacked for a long time." He motioned for some men at the other end of the saloon. "Drag him out of here for me." Two of them each picked up an arm and pulled him across the rough wooden floor and out into the light of day. "Let me give you boys a fresh beer on the house."

Gray waved him off. "I'm not much of a drinker," he said as the cowboys who dragged out the unconscious drunk came back through the swinging saloon doors.

"We drug him around the corner and left him lying in the street. In a pile of horseshit," the shorter one laughed.

"I hope he doesn't cause you a lot of problems over this," Gray said to the Irish bartender. "I hate to bring a man grief when I won't be around to help clean up the mess."

"Naw, he'll be no more trouble than he always is. Hopefully, a little less."

"Well, anyway, I'm sorry about the problem."

Gray and Trent finished the two beers. Trent asked Zach if he planned to rejoin his poker game, but Zach decided he preferred the excitement of standing at the bar with Gray. Wehr had all the saloon he needed. He thanked Pete for the beer and apologized for the third time for the trouble.

Gray wanted to look at some horses and was going over to the livery to inquire about local horse ranches. The three men bid their farewell and left the Blue Moon.

The bright light of the day contrasted with the Blue Moon's smoky darkness. All three squinted as they went through the batwing doors. They walked down the steps and out into the street a few yards, not knowing the three other men from Bill's card game had followed them until a coarse voice cut through the air.

"Hey, you sons-a-bitches, you ain't getting away with what you did to Bill." A revolver cracked but missed its target. Gray spun toward the saloon, yanking his Colt and returning fire. Trent also shot back.

They hit one man in the collarbone and another through the groin. The third man, not a complete fool, desired to go on living. He threw his gun down in the street, raised his arms, and begged not to be murdered.

Zach was standing between Gray and Trent with his weapon still holstered. Fear paralyzed him. His face turned a sickly white, and he wondered for a moment if his knees were going to buckle, leaving him in an embarrassing heap on the ground.

Pete rushed through the swinging doors. "Well, I'll be damned. You fellas sure ain't to be messed with."

"How bad are they hit?" Trent yelled.

Pete and a couple of other men bent down over them. "Well, they got holes in 'em. But neither's dead." Pete stood up and came down the steps laughing. "Ol' Harry's probably gonna be obliged to find a new way to have fun, though." Harry, his trousers already blood-soaked from the buckle to the knees, was trying to sit up, screaming for a doctor.

Gray walked back up on the porch. "I suppose somebody better go for the sheriff."

A cowboy with an oversized red bandana tied around his neck spoke up. "He won't care if nobody's kilt. He still don't care none if it were a fair fight unless one of the killed ones is a particular friend of his, and these two ain't. And they ain't dead neither."

Zach swallowed his whiskey and beer back down for a second time. "Are you at least going to bring them a doctor?"

Pete told some cowboys to throw them in a wagon hitched across the street and haul them over to Doc Goodrich's office. So much screaming and swearing. "For two hellcats," Zach said. "They sure holler a lot."

As the commotion died down, Gray turned toward Trent and Zach. "Are you both all right?" The two men nodded as Gray's eyes worked Zach over. "Ain't you the dependable one?"

"I guess I was a little slow figuring things out."

"What's to figure out about a bullet zipping past your head?"

The episode dampened Gray's interest in horses, so he headed back to his hotel room alone. He closed the door behind him. He lay on the lumpy bed. Embarrassed and angry about what happened, he wanted to keep it hidden from Annie. Familiar emotions erupted inside him—crushing sorrow and anger. Exploding in sudden fury, he flew off the bed, grabbing and tearing at its linens. He tore them off and violently hurled them around and across the room.

He grabbed a pillow, beating it against the head of the bed before slinging it at a pitcher and washbasin. They went sailing off the chest of drawers, crashing into a wall, sending pieces of the clay basin and pitcher all over the room.

He tore at his shirt, ripping the front open, popping off all the buttons. Gray sank to the floor and leaned against the bed. He yanked a boot off and flung it through the air. He hit himself in the face repeatedly with the other boot before slamming it against the door to the room. Breathing hard, he grasped two handfuls of hair and pulled as he sat with his head between his knees.

Almost an hour passed while he lay, unmoving, under the window. Finally, he raised his head. His bloodshot eyes assessed the damage to the room. He took two deep breaths, letting each one out slowly. Minutes later, undergoing guilt, he straightened the room. None of the linens were torn or ripped, merely thrown about the room. The pillow lost a few of its feathers but otherwise survived. He remade the bed and picked up the pieces from the broken pitcher and bowl, a matching set made of clay and painted blue with white flowers.

Once he put things back together, he took a faded red shirt out of his pack and lay back down on the bed, right before Annie tapped on the door.

"Gray, are you all right?"

He got up and grabbed his hat, wondering why Annie would ask if he was all right. He opened the door and stepped through, trying to block her view of the room. "I'm fine. Let's find a horse ranch close in and ride out for something to do."

Annie put her arm around him. She started to question him but changed her mind. With Gray opening up to her on this trip, she decided not to pressure him but continue letting him set his own pace. "Looking at horses sounds like fun," she said as she walked with him down the hall toward the stairway. Annie didn't yet fully understand the darkness that sometimes took hold of her man. She resolved he'd be safe from those demons when with her.

Albert Clement owned the closest ranch. They asked Jean if she wanted to ride along, but she sensed Annie's desire to be alone with Gray and declined their offer. Gray assumed from his sister's demeanor neither she nor Annie knew anything about the Blue Moon shooting.

As they left the main road at Cheyenne's outskirts and headed to the Clement ranch, the route soon disappeared down to a couple of wagon ruts. Only a few cottonwood trees and some scrub oaks dotted the landscape. Before the house came into view, they spotted some Clement horses grazing off to their right. Though some distance off, they appeared to be quality animals.

Annie was a little concerned about what they would say to the rancher once they met him. "You're not planning on buying horses, are you?"

"I thought you wanted to come out here," Gray said in a cheerful tone.

"I did until we got his house in sight. Now I feel a little silly. I mean, we're not interested in buying any horses."

"If I found a real calm-natured stud or a solid-looking mare or two, I might surprise you."

Annie's eyes widened. She had no idea they might indeed be in the horse market. "We raise horses. Why would we buy from other ranches?"

"How many head have you got?" Gray asked her matter-of-factly.

"We've got about sixty-five head of horses, counting the mares, yearlings, and the geldings."

Gray stopped Lena. "You keep saying we. Annie, you own sixty-five head. I have three, and one of those you gave me." He shifted a little in the saddle, absorbing her curiosity. "I'm going to bring something to this marriage besides extra laundry and aching knees."

In his late fifties, Albert Clement, a lanky fellow, started ranching horses on this spot before Cheyenne existed. For the last three years, since having his kneecap broken by a rank dun, he and two of his ranch hands tried to geld; he walked with a severe limp. When Gray and Annie rode up, he stood at the corral with his wife, a short and extremely skinny woman with red and gray hair, watching one of their hands work a sorrel mare.

Figuring they should wait until asked to step down, Gray and Annie stayed on their horses while Gray inquired about Mr. Clement. The lanky string bean wiped his hands on his shirt. "You found him."

"Mr. Clement, this is Annie Laurie. My name is Graham Wehr." He started to tell them they raised horses in the Bighorn Mountains, but Mrs. Clement interrupted.

"I know who you are. I watched you kill Rudy Gates in Denver, in what, '64 or '65?" Her proclamation jolted Gray, embarrassed him in front of Annie.

Annie jumped in immediately to change the subject. "I raise horses in a little valley north of here. Gray and I are going to be married on the first of September." She added the marriage information, hoping Mrs. Clement would catch on to the idea she didn't want to discuss Gray's past. "We thought we might want to expand our herd. Do you have anything for sale?"

"Everything on the place," Mrs. Clement shot back. "You can't make any money-raising horses unless you sell them. You ought to understand that if you raise horses."

I do, Annie thought. But she held her tongue instead of telling the woman she also understood a little something about politeness.

Gray intervened for Annie. "Yes, ma'am. We'd like to see anything you'd like to show us."

You might, Annie thought. *I'd like to tell the old bat there are other places in this territory to buy horses.* Finally, much to Gray's relief, Mr. Clement spoke up. "How many you think you'll be interested in?"

"I'm not sure. A half-dozen, a few more."

Annie gasped before deciding seven people should be able

to move six horses down the trail, though Nellie would be little help.

"Well, step on down," Mr. Clement said. "We've got some penned behind the house you might like. By the way, my name's Albert. This is my Mrs., Mary."

Annie smiled brightly. "Pleased to meet you both."

As they started toward the corral, Mary Clement moved in beside Gray. "I'll tell you, I never seen anybody else ever jerk a pistol as fast as you did when you popped Rudy."

Gray wanted to crawl in a hole or push this big-mouthed woman down one. But again, Annie intervened for him. "How long ago did you say he shot this Rudy fella?"

Mrs. Clement recalled the killing as in sixty-four or sixty-five. She knew it was spring because she remembered Denver's streets bogged with mud on the day of the shooting.

"Why, Mary, in '64 or '65, you saw nothing. You should have seen him before he got old. He's so old and slow now he's putting up his gun and getting married so he can watch a few horses graze from the rocking chair on the porch." Albert Clement laughed over Annie's rebuke of his wife, effectively ending the talk of Gray's ability with his pistol and lifting Annie's opinion of the man.

All mares and their foals, thirty or forty horses, grazed in the pasture behind the Clement house. Gray slipped through the split-rail fence. Annie and the Clements stayed outside.

Two of the mares, both with babies and a two-year-old filly, caught Wehr's eye. They all stood about fifteen to fifteen and a half hands with solid hips. All three had bright eyes, good confirmation, and straight legs set solidly under their chests. "How old are these two?" Gray asked.

"Six and Eight," Albert responded, pointing out each. "We bred the six-year-old to the same stud again this year. I planned to breed the filly, but one of my daughters broke her in the spring and has been using her for a pleasure horse. She's got an awful sweet gait."

"How much for the five of them?"

After some haggling and negotiating, Gray bought the two

mares, foals, and filly. Clement agreed to bring them into town the day after next and save Gray a trip back to his ranch. The Clements invited Gray and Annie to supper, an unexpected bit of courtesy from Mrs. Clement, but they declined, wanting to be back in Cheyenne before dark. They thanked them for the horses and headed back to meet the others for dinner.

Jean, Nellie, and Millie sat in the hotel lobby, waiting anxiously for Gray and Annie to return. Trent and Zach had not come down from their rooms. When they went in, she whispered to Gray, "Uh, oh. I think we're in trouble."

Jean grinned at her brother. "Well, we almost sent out a posse. Of Course, we had no idea where to head them."

"I thought you went to the justice of the peace's office," Millie said.

"We went out to a ranch and bought five head of horses," Gray told them matter-of-factly.

"I'm sure you did," Jean answered, assuming her brother wanted a rise out of Nellie and Millie. "I'm starving," she complained before telling Gray to go upstairs and fetch Zach and Trent so they could all go to supper. Annie and Gray both headed up the stairs to change clothes and retrieve the others. Ten minutes later, all four came back down.

Nellie started into the hotel restaurant. "No, no. Not there." Millie grabbed Nellie by the arm. "Trent and I found a little place down the street we want to eat at tonight. It's homier."

Jean nudged Nellie, smiled at Trent. "Must mean dark and romantic." She was wrong.

The café, Fat Annabelle's, was not dark—or romantic. Annabelle was fat. When Anabelle recognized Gray, she caterwauled across the cafe. "Lord, save me. I figured you were dead by now."

"I almost died once after eating your cooking," Gray replied.

"Would have served you right," Annabelle laughed. "You cost me a regular customer back in Denver when you shot Rudy Gates." She waddled over and grabbed Gray around the shoulders. "You ol' reprobate. I'll go fetch you all some coffee."

Annie turned toward Gray. He couldn't interpret what was in her eyes. "Was the whole town of Denver there when you shot that poor fella?"

"No, the whole town wasn't," Gray answered. "He wasn't a 'poor fella,' either. He was a mean old barn rat."

They pulled tables together to accommodate the entire group. Gray, Annie, and Jean sat on one side with Trent, Millie, Nellie, and Zach on the other. Zach slumped in his chair about Jean sitting on the other side.

Gray tapped on the table in front of Zach. "We told Jean, Nellie, and little bit here," he said, pointing to Millie, "we bought five head of horses this afternoon. I got them from a guy named Clement. He's going to bring them into town for us the day after tomorrow."

Jean's mouth dropped. "You bought horses?"

"Yeah, I told you I did."

"I guess I didn't believe you. I thought you were feeding Nellie and Millie a tale."

"We're driving horses home?" Nellie's eyes bulged.

"Won't be any problem," Zach said, definitely excited about this new event. "Mares, geldings, or what'd you buy?"

"Two mares, their foals, and a little filly," Annie said. "One foal is a filly; the other's a little colt."

"How are we going to move the babies across the rivers?" Nellie asked.

"They'll be easy to cross," Trent told her. "Lots of shallow spots in the Powder this time of year."

Encouraged by his friends' enthusiasm for the horses, Gray told them he and Annie planned to ride out to another ranch about six miles east in the morning if anyone wanted to come along. Much to his surprise, the entire group decided to go.

"What'll you have, folks?" With a keen eye, you could pick out most of the menu on Annabelle's apron. "Tonight's specials are beef stew and chicken and dumplings."

Gray sat back in his chair and smirked. "Annabelle, I'm sorry to tell you this, but I hate chicken and dumplings. I despise chicken and dumplings so bad; I abhor being in the same room with them."

Annie dropped her eyes and shook her head, but said nothing. Fat Annabelle towered over Gray. She leaned over, putting both hands on the table in such a manner Millie shifted away from Gray in case Annabelle picked up something and hit him. "Unless my memory is trickin' me, I threw you and a no-account army Sargent out of my place the last time you drug in. When was that? Two, three years back? If you can't mind yer manners, I'll pitch you again."

"Pitch away, but you'll lose all this business."

"Not mine. I'm having chicken and dumplings," Jean said.

"I hope you've got the money to pay for them," Gray cracked.

"If she don't, I'll let her owe me," Annabelle retorted, giving Jean an unexpected solid slap on the back, amusing Millie.

Gray winked at Millie, glanced up at Annabelle. "Where's Ed tonight?"

Wehr's question cast a pall on Annabelle. Her eyes drooped, her voice softened. "Dead, nearly a year now. He suffered awful more'n two months. His passing was a relief, to be honest with you." She sighed, shrugged at Gray with a lost, sad smile. "Mary Lou went back to Denver. She never did like Cheyenne. Sometimes I figure I ought to do the same." Once everybody gave her their orders, Annabelle shuffled back into the kitchen. Annie asked Gray if Ed was her husband.

"Her son, I never met her husband. He ran off from them back when the kids were little."

"Mary Lou's her daughter?" Nellie asked.

"Pretty girl, too," Gray said. "Thin, nothing like Annabelle. At least not the last time I saw her. She's a strawberry blonde, real quiet. Never said much." Wehr tilted his head toward the kitchen, where Anabelle disappeared. "Old Annabelle, she may not be stunning, but the woman's got a good heart." Gray slid his chair back and stood. "I'm going out back. I'll be right back."

When Gray left, an older gentleman at the next table leaned over toward Annie. "Is that your husband, ma'am?"

"Not yet," Annie smiled, "but soon."

"Well, he doesn't know me, but I know him. Two of my sons fought in the war with him. We lost one of them." The woman sitting with him bowed her head as his words slipped out so quietly. "My other son said your man made a valiant effort to save my boy. Amos's blood poured over your man's hands while he pressed on the boy's chest, trying to stop the bleeding."

The old man paused and turned in his seat to face Annie more squarely. "You hear a lot of fancy language about courage and sacrifice when people talk about war. Mostly from fools. My son says your man understands what sacrifice for a cause, and another human being is, says he stood and faced down the horror of war without a hint of self-concern in him. From what my boy says, you got yourself a fine man. From what he says, he's worth the trouble to hang on to." The old man sat back down. "I wanted you to know."

Annie struggled with what to say to the old gentleman. When tears started welling up in Jean's eyes, she knew her future sister-in-law would be no help. Relief flickered across Annie's face when Gray walked back in the door. As he sat, she touched his arm. "Gray, this gentleman says you and his sons fought together in the war."

Both men stood as the white-haired man introduced himself. They whispered for a few minutes before he told Gray, he and his Mrs. "best pay Annabelle and head on home before it gets too dark."

Gray took the man's hand and laid his other hand on his wife's shoulder. "When you write Charles, tell him hello from me. I'd like to see him again. Serving with him, sir, was my honor."

Annie smiled at Gray when he sat down and took a drink of his coffee.

Being a slow night in the restaurant, after Annabelle served the meals, she pulled up a chair and joined the conversation. Annie thought primarily out of loneliness. Walking back to the hotel, she said something about feeling a little bit sorry for the woman.

"Do you feel sorry for me? I'm a single woman running a restaurant."

"But you have people who love you," Annie replied.

"Name one," Jean said.

"Not me," Zach said.

"Me either," Gray added.

"Well, I do." Millie put her arm around Nellie. "You short little slave driver."

When they got to the hotel, Trent and Millie said they wanted to walk a little longer. Nellie told them not to go far or for too long. Jean and Annie invited her to come up to their room with them, but being tired, she decided to go to bed.

Alone, Nellie gathered a quilt around herself and slumped into a chair next to the window in the hushed room. There was no chatter in the downstairs lobby, and with no one on the street below, everything fell quiet. After a few minutes of looking out, she started to rock, mainly for the comfort the creaking provided as the rocker teetered back and forth.

"Well, old girl," she said out loud as she thought about Millie and Trent, "I guess you need to learn to enjoy silence." Her chin dropped to her chest when she fell asleep in the chair. She still slept when Millie came in from her walk with Trent.

Millie touched her shoulder to wake her up. "You better climb into bed. You'll have an awful stiff neck if you sleep in that chair all night."

"Did you enjoy your walk?" Nellie stood and stretched.

"We did. We only walked a block. We sat in front of the hotel a while."

Nellie opened her arms, taking the girl into the quilt. They looked out the window for a few minutes, wrapped up together. Nellie kissed the side of the girl's face. The time raising her, seventeen years, had been much too short.

Chapter Forty-Eight

In the morning, Annie and Jean woke to the sound of angry voices below their window. Before she realized neither voice was his, Annie feared Gray had gone down in the street and been challenged by some gun hand looking for a reputation.

One man was swearing at another over an argument unsettled the night before. Poker seemed to be at the center of the quarreling. Annie told Jean it was more likely liquor.

Jean pulled Annie away from the curtain. "Stay away from the window. We don't want to catch a stray bullet." Outside, the men were still pulling on whiskey bottles. Their swearing became so slurred the argument turned into indiscernible nonsense. Both men were falling down drunk. One was on his knees, puking.

Gray's tap on the door startled them. "Are you two awake?"

"There's a couple of drunks below our window hollering back and forth at each other."

"They woke me up an hour ago. I doubt they're dangerous. Why don't you dress and come down for breakfast?

I'll knock on the other doors."

"Give us about twenty or thirty minutes, and we'll be down."

Zach joined Gray, sitting alone in the hotel restaurant. The morning waitress poured him coffee, which he filled with sugar and milk. "I swear, Zach, why do you bother putting coffee in your cup if all you want is sugared milk?"

"You drink your coffee the way you want, and I'll drink mine. I guess I don't need your advice on how to take my coffee."

The two men sat for a minute before Zach brought up the purchase of horses. "Did you buy decent horses from the Clement fella?"

"I did. But I'll tell you this, the woman he's married to is a fright. I thought she and Annie were gonna get into a catfight." Gray took a drink of his coffee and laughed as he thought back about the visit. "From what I found out yesterday down at the livery, this fella we're going to meet today raises prime stock."

As Zach started to reply, the argument outside the hotel diverted his attention. Curious, he got up and headed toward the door.

The clerk at the front desk said, "Don't pay no mind. They rooster up about two or three times a week." He came out from behind his counter and scurried over to where Zach stood watching the two drunks. "They liquored up at one of the saloons, and then this happens. They're a blamed nuisance."

"Do they ever start shooting at each other?"

"Naw, they only yell about shooting each other. They'll either wear out and go home in a little while, or the marshal will come down and run 'em off." The deskman walked out on the porch. "Hey! You two. Shut up out there! You're disturbing our guests. Scram out of here."

The older one, a ragged cowboy in his late thirties, yelled for the clerk to come out and kiss him on his ass. He dropped his pants and waved his bare backside.

The clerk's face boiled red. His eyebrows bounced so high

his forehead disappeared. He shook his pencil at them. "You git. I'm sending the boy down for the marshal. You two, scram!"

The clerk, wearing a white shirt, blue vest, and what Zach thought to be a woman's garter around each arm, right above the elbow, shot in from the porch and dashed back to the desk, yelling toward a room in the back, the hotel office. "Jason, Jason, where are you?"

A freckle-faced, red-haired boy about thirteen came out into the lobby. "Jason, go fetch the marshal. Tell him those two drunks are causing trouble in the street again." He started pushing him toward the front door. "You tell the marshal to hurry over here." He shoved the boy out the door, stepped back out on the porch, and began waving his pencil again. "I sent my boy after the marshal. You two better skedaddle before they come back."

The drunks yelled a few obscenities at the pencil-waving clerk before heading down the saloon row. Zach turned and went back to the restaurant.

"What happened?"

Zach sat down and put his napkin over his lap. "Couple of cowboys drunk from last night." He took a drink of his coffee. "The desk clerk ran 'em off. You best not provoke him. He's a dangerous man with a pencil."

The four women came into the room. Dressed in pants and shirts, ready to ride. "Where's Trent?" Zach asked.

Millie said he overslept. "I woke him up when I knocked on his door. He'll be down in a few minutes." She also knew what he wanted for breakfast, enabling them to go ahead and order.

Trent walked in right as the breakfasts came. Annie said grace, and Zach started talking about being anxious to see the horses.

"It's almost seven-thirty; we better hustle up." As they left the hotel, Zach edged over to Gray, "for a guy so concerned about making this trip; funny, it ain't bothering you to complicate things by driving horses." Gray made some off-handed remark in response.

George Jensen's place was only about four and a half miles out of town, but the house sat almost a mile back. The partly cloudy sky made the day hot and humid. Zach and Nellie had been overly talkative all morning, making Gray happy when he finally saw the ranch house. Gray knocked on the front door of a two-story farmhouse in need of whitewashing. The footsteps inside sounded like those of a woman.

"What can I do for you?" The woman answering the door appeared to be in her mid-twenties and about ten months pregnant.

"Might Mr. Jensen be around?"

The woman sized Gray up. "What'd you want with him?"

"I thought I might be interested in a few horses if he has any for sale."

"You with the military?" Her tone was nasty.

Gray chuckled. He didn't think he looked too army. "No, ma'am. I own land up in the Bighorns. Raise horses and thought I might like a little fresh blood in them."

"Well, George is out behind the barn," she said, making no effort to make introductions. "He and his son Joe are with my husband cuttin' some studs."

"Much obliged," Gray said, hurrying to spit the words out as she closed the door in his face.

Gray got back up on Lena and told the others Jensen was out behind the barn. They found Jensen, his boy, and three ranch hands cutting the young horses. Millie gasped at the sight of the bloody men.

The oldest man, who Gray assumed to be George Jensen, started over toward them. "Morning. What can I do for you?"

"Thought I might be interested in a few horses if you have any for sale." Gray stepped down and shook hands with the rancher.

Jensen was a small man with white hair and rock-hard hands calloused from years of ranch work. Gray figured him to be in his late fifties or early sixties. "Where you from?"

"A little town called High Meadows. Sits in a valley up in

the Bighorns."

"I heard of the place," Jensen said. "Ain't never been there but heard of it. They say it's a little piece of heaven and jist about as hard to git to. You folks have been in the place a long time, I guess."

"All our lives. We're on our way back from Fort Laramie."

Jensen gave Wehr a funny sort of a double-take. "And you say yer on the way back to the Bighorns?"

"We rode down to find out about the treaty talks with the Sioux."

"All of you? The women, too?"

"Yep, rash behavior," Gray smiled. "We picked up the boy at the Powder on our way down. He was scouting for the army. Now, he's going back home with us."

Jensen chuckled. "I can see he is." He scratched Millie's horse and turned back to Gray. "I hope I ain't out of line by asking, but you do know the Bighorns are in the opposite direction from where you're headed."

"The opposite direction?" Gray played at being stunned.

Annie piped in, saying they, the females, were at fault. They wanted to shop in Cheyenne.

"I figured something like that. You had a safe trip?"

"Not bad," Zach said.

"Well, what kind of animals are you looking for? Weanlings, yearlings, or broke ones?"

Gray untied the faded red bandana from around his neck and wiped the sweat off his face. "Breeding stock, mares, a weanling stud or two. I might be interested in an even-tempered yearling colt, but I don't want to fight a real bossy one, trying to mount everything in sight all the way home. I'm after smart horses, pleasers."

Jensen reached into his shirt pocket and opened an old pocket watch. "Well, looky here, it's plum noon. Why don't you folks come on up to the house? We'll eat a few beans or whatever the women are cooking up, then look at the horses on full stomachs."

Gray glanced at the others and shook his head. "I don't believe we ought to drop seven strangers in on them for lunch."

"Not a problem. The females cook up stew or something to feed twenty hands. The problem today is I sent all but five out on the range. You'll save me a hind end chewing from the daughter-in-law. She's full-blossomed, and the heat's got her cranky about everything. She'll pitch a holy fit about cookin' extra food and nobody here to eat. So tie yer horses to the rail and come on up to the house. In good weather, they usually set the meal on some tables I built out back."

Everyone was as surprised as Gray about being invited to dinner and were a little stand-offish about accepting. When they got up to the house, Mrs. Jensen made them right at home. She assured them the food would have gone to waste had they not come along since her husband never did remember to tell her he was sending most of the hands out, and she wouldn't need to cook for them.

Mrs. Jensen was a wiry woman who appeared to be eight or ten years younger than her spouse. The scent of the hot rolls and stew flooded through them as they went behind the house. It was a yeasty aroma, warm like being wrapped in a quilt on a cold winter evening.

"I don't know if you are praying folks," Mrs. Jensen said, "but we are, so we'll ask you to bow your heads with us before we eat."

"Effie don't want anybody eating any unblessed food," Mr. Jensen said after she finished the blessing. "What she don't realize is I ate a lot of unblessed meals out on the trail, and they ain't never killed me."

"Only because God in His grace blessed you even when you haven't thanked him."

"Well, I can't argue with you. When are you folks heading back to your little valley?" he asked, turning his attention towards Annie.

"We hope to be on our way by mid-morning tomorrow. I suspect it'll take us more'n two weeks with the horses."

"You're brave women to drive horses into those

mountains," Mrs. Jensen offered. "I would have thought you'd have made men do that alone."

"Well, when we started, someone forgot to tell us about the horse purchase," Nellie said, curling both her lip and nose.

Mrs. Jensen and the daughter-in-law were anxious for information about the treaty talks up at Fort Laramie. Annie was careful to tell them everything. Everything except her spirited exchange with William Tecumseh Sherman, which Jean delighted in describing.

When everyone finished eating, George Jensen stood and patted his belly. "Well, let's go select a few horses to fit your fancy."

Nellie offered herself and Millie to help clean up the dishes. Millie wanted to go pick out horses, but her upbringing kept her from protesting. Jean also stayed to share in the cleanup. Annie volunteered, but no one would stand for her helping since the animals were for her ranch. Mrs. Jensen said Annie needed to go down and supervise the selections to ensure the men didn't make poor choices. She said she wouldn't let anyone help, except she enjoyed the company of new folks so much.

Jensen pointed out everything in two pastures as for sale. He named one fixed price for all the mares, another for the yearlings, and another for the weanlings. Jensen said most of the broodmares ranged between eight and ten years old. He told them to select anything they liked.

Annie and Gray slipped through the rails of the fence and walked out among the horses. An hour later, they selected a chestnut mare and her foal, a coal-black filly, and two brown yearling fillies out of the first pasture. They chose a dark brown mare, her stud colt, and three yearling fillies out of the second.

"You've got quite an eye for horses," Jensen said. "Picked yourselves out ten winners. Let's go over to the house and settle up."

Zach and Trent pushed the stock into a corral next to the barn while Gray and Annie went to the house with Mr. Jensen.

Jean, Nellie, and Millie sat in the house with the Jensen

women laughing about Jean's snake incident when Mr. Jensen, Gray, and Annie came in. "Your sister is lucky you're a fine shot with a pistol," Mrs. Jensen told Gray.

Gray took off his hat and chuckled a bit. "Well, he was a sitting target. It would have been more challenging if he had been moving." Gray laughed a little harder. "I'll tell you this, Jeannie wasn't laughing like she is now."

"Except for your packhorse...the rain...the heat...the snakes...and a sore backside or two," she grinned, looking at Nellie, "sounds like an enjoyable trip, but I guess I'm getting too old for so much enjoyment."

Around mid-afternoon, they started back. The day wasn't as humid. They pushed the horses to Cheyenne with no difficulty or incidents. Before dark, Gray dealt with the livery keeper to keep the horses for the night. The friends ate a quick meal and headed to bed early.

Chapter Forty-Nine

Gray was up before dawn and at the livery long before Albert Clement brought the other five horses into town. His skinny wife came with him. And without Annie for protection, she started in on Wehr's notoriousness with a gun. She speculated about being a "famous and fearsome fella."

Able to slide a word in, Wehr told her he would give about anything to rid himself of the reputation, and he would not talk about it anymore. His bluntness took the starch out of her, and she let the matter drop. After a brief thank you and goodbye, Wehr headed over to the hotel.

Annie and Jean were sitting in the lobby. "Where are the rest?" Gray asked in an agitated voice.

"Well, morning to you, too." Jean shot back. "What did you do, get up on the wrong side of the bed?"

His sister's sauciness annoyed Gray. "It doesn't matter which side of the bed I got up on; I want to hit the trail. Have you seen the others yet?"

Gray wouldn't like it, but Annie told him, "Nellie and Millie are upstairs packing, and Zach and Trent are finishing breakfast."

All the gear was outside the building, except for what Nellie and Millie still had in their room. Gray and the two women went into the hotel's restaurant and found Zach and Trent with only their meal's remains in front of them.

Zach held up the coffeepot. "Want some coffee?"

"I had my mine over two hours ago."

"You'll have to excuse him," Jean said. "Brother's in a surly mood this morning."

"I'm not surly. I want to be on our way."

"Well, we're ready to go," Zach said, standing up and getting some money out of his pocket to pay for his breakfast. "Shall we go up for the other two, or do you want to leave them here? I sure wouldn't want to delay you none."

"Annie and Jean can," Gray answered in a dictatorial tone. "You two come with me. We'll load the packhorses, and we can start for home."

Zach snapped a salute to Gray, and the three men headed over to the livery while the women started up the hotel stairs. "Millie's sick," Nellie told them.

The girl was sitting by the window, ghostly pale, pulling her hair back to tie it off her face with a string. "I'm fine. My breakfast didn't sit well."

"Are you going to be able to travel?" Jean asked.

"Yes. Leave me alone!"

"Don't you talk to me like that. I'm not your mother," Jean bristled back.

Millie said nothing more. Instead, she gathered up the gear. As she worked, she set her jaw and clenched her teeth to hold her stomach down. Jean and Nellie picked up two armfuls of supplies and left the room. Annie and Millie busied themselves gathering up the rest.

"Did you wake up sick?"

"No, I was fine until I ate breakfast. We came back upstairs to pack, and I started puking all over the floor. I couldn't reach the basin."

Annie put a hand on the girl's forehead. "Well, you're not

feverish. You're kind of cold and clammy."

"I'm better. Let's haul this stuff down. Gray'll be mad if we don't show up right away."

Annie laughed. "Don't you worry about Gray. I can handle him."

Once Annie and Nellie got their gear out front, Gray and the others had the packhorses ready. All that remained was to put in the packs Annie and Millie brought down, pick up the new horses, and be on the way home.

When they got to the livery stable, Gray's mood improved. "Trent, why don't you and Millie take the left flank like you did yesterday. Jean, you and Nellie take the right. Zach, Annie, and I will take the back and push. Let's hope these two groups of horses tolerate each other."

Annie and Zach held the packhorses while Gray and Jean pushed the little herd out of the corral.

Leaving Cheyenne, they rode up the street, where several children pointed at them and commented to their mothers or playmates.

"If I expected such an audience, I'd have put on a big red nose." Zach waved and tipped his hat to a couple of women with parasols over their shoulders. "I swear, I bet we don't see any more ladies walking down the street with yeller parasols. I don't ever remember seeing a yeller parasol in High Meadows, do you, Annie?" He didn't give Annie a chance to answer. "And I'll tell you something else we ain't gonna have for a while, a soft bed or a stove-cooked meal."

"Well, kick my butt and call me Charlotte. With all this bitchin' and moaning' you're doing, you must have forgotten whose idea this little trip was," Gray told him.

"For heaven's sake," Annie said. "Am I going to listen to this all the way back to High Meadows? That's going to make for a long two weeks."

Gray's face lit up. "Annie Laurie, it's good to hear your voice. I wasn't sure you were going to say anything all day."

Annie, wearing a dark blue shirt, light tan pants, and tan-colored hat, reached over and patted Gray's arm. "I guess I'm the quiet type."

They headed northwest out of Cheyenne, hoping to hit Horse Creek by putting in a long day. The little herd of horses moved along with no complaints for more than two hours. Zach was pointing out they would grow grumpier as the day wore on with no water when Annie noticed Millie off her horse and bent over at the waist.

"Gray, we may need to stop. Millie's sick."

"Ride over and find out how bad she is," Gray said.

"She got sick on her breakfast."

Nellie left Jean and rode to the back of the herd. "Is Millie throwing up again?"

"Apparently so. Why didn't you tell me she was sick? We would have stayed in Cheyenne."

"She said she wanted to travel," Nellie said as she and Annie headed over to Millie. The horses, especially the weanlings, were ready for a rest and did not scatter or stray off. Annie came back over to Gray and Zach. "She's not going to be able to ride. She's thrown up everything in her, and now she has the dry heaves."

Gray stepped off Lena, glanced over toward the girl. "I wish there was a little shade around here."

"We can put up one of the lean-to's," Zach suggested.

"Trent wants us to move on. He says he'll stay back with Millie and catch up when she's better," Annie told them, "but I don't think Nellie is too hep on the idea,"

Gray got a little indignant. "Well, we're not doing that. I like Trent, and I suspect he can handle himself, but I'm not leaving Millie back here with him."

Gray and Annie walked over to talk to Nellie. Zach stayed in the back. "You're going to have to drive these horses to water," Trent said. "Otherwise, we'll never keep them together."

"Well, that may be true," Gray said. "But she can't ride sick."

"Why don't I stay back here with her and catch up with you at Horse Creek tomorrow?"

"Nope. We're not leaving her with anybody but me," Gray said.

"I told you 'Daddy' wouldn't go along. It wouldn't be proper."

Trent wanted to protest, but arguing would be pointless regarding the propriety issue. Gray told Trent to push until they made Horse Creek, even if after dark. "If Millie and I don't catch up tonight, sit tight. We'll come in the morning."

"I'm going to stay with you two," Nellie said.

"No, you're not." Gray's voice was insolent. "They're going to need your help with these horses, and you wouldn't be any value to me."

Gray's impertinence agitated Nellie. "This is my daughter," she vehemently protested with her eyes spitting fire.

"And mine, and I'm going to keep her safe." His declaration stunned Nellie. Millie's jaw dropped; what Millie always wanted, what had always been in her heart, her dad, her daddy, confirmed. Gray's voice softened. He put his arm around Nellie. "Now, the God's truth is you'd be an added burden. If something happened, you'd be someone else for me to worry about."

Nellie turned to Annie. "Do you think I should?"

Annie nodded her head, "Yes, they'll be fine."

"Give her some oil of turpentine," Zach said. The man never understood when to keep his mouth shut.

The girl put up a spirited disagreement about the cure, one likely to busy her at both ends. But she lost the argument when Nellie and Annie considered the treatment prudent. After administering the oil, Nellie hugged Millie and whispered something in the girl's ear, making her laugh. Gray gave Nellie a boost on her horse, patted her knee. "I promise you; I'll bring her back to you."

After the others left, Gray pulled the saddles off Lena and Poncho. Millie was at it again. Down on her hands and knees, retching, throwing up again. Dark green, orange, dull yellow in wretched stomach tearing heaves.

In a chivalrous act, Gray let her finish before walking over to her. He knelt beside her and rubbed her back the way a real father would. "What did you eat for breakfast?"

"Those bastards poisoned me." Millie sat down and put her head between her knees. Gray, the disciplinarian, shook his head, failing to stifle his laugh. "Sausage and fried eggs," she said.

"Well, maybe we ought to ride back into Cheyenne and chat with the cook."

"I'm sorry to slow us up." She wiped her mouth and rubbed her sleeve across her forehead.

"No rush," Gray told her. "We'll arrive when we arrive. There's nothing important about driving those young horses in a hurry. I wouldn't have sent the others on ahead except for how dry this area is." Not giving any thought to the question, Gray asked, "What did Nellie whisper to you when she left?"

"She said my pee's going to smell like violets," Millie laughed, knowing she would embarrass her 'daddy.'

Wishing he minded his own business, Gray pulled Millie's blanket off her saddle and spread it out on the ground. With no shade anywhere around, he didn't want the girl lying on the dry dirt. Millie laid down and fell asleep in a few minutes.

Trent handled the right flank while Jean and Nellie rode to the left, and Annie and Zach pushed from the back. "I should have stayed with Millie," Nellie said to Jean as they tried to move the horses back into a tighter group.

"Why? She's safe with Gray. He's the most capable if anything happens."

"But she's sick, and I need to be back with her, comforting her."

"You should be more concerned about her protection than comfort. And I'm sure they'll catch up by the time we make camp or soon afterward," Jean said. "We need to keep these horses moving. They'll start getting grumpy if we don't find water by dark." Jean slapped her reins against her leg, attracting the attention of one baby starting to lag. "Has Millie said anything about marrying?"

Nellie took a deep sigh. "She hasn't come out and said anything. But she loves him, so a wedding is coming. I hope they make High Meadows their home. If he wants to take her to Fort Laramie, I'll die." Nellie had been worrying since the second night at Fort Laramie. She decided she would allow them to live at Laramie only after putting up a hard fight. She started crafting her argument to persuade the Thaxton's to come to High Meadows. Nellie slapped at a mosquito biting the side of her neck, waved her hat back and forth to disperse the horde remaining. "What do you suppose they'll do to make a living?"

Jean thought for a minute. "I'm not sure what you do is as important as who you do it with. I always figured I'd be happy doing about anything with the right one."

"Well, it doesn't put food on the table because you're with the right one. A person in love can starve to death, as easy as anybody else."

"Are you trying to start an argument?"

"No," Nellie shot back. "I'm concerned about my daughter."

"Well, stop worrying about her. Lord, Nellie, if she and the boy can't find a meal, I'll give them one." Jean pointed over at Trent for a moment. "Besides, he strikes me as being intelligent, even if he is a little exciting."

"What?"

Jean smiled and pulled on her collarless white shirt to let a little air down the front. "I think a little excitement adds to the fun of life." She nodded over at Zach and lowered her voice. "I mean, take Zach. He's as solid a man as you'll ever find. He's steady, patient, reliable, has a sense of humor, and is smart in certain ways. But he's not exciting." She put her hand on Nellie's arm and laughed a little. "You always know what Zach is going to do tomorrow."

Jean pulled her horse back a little. "I think we should push these animals a little harder. We want to hit water tonight."

Zach agreed. "I don't relish the thought of trying to drive thirsty horses after dark."

Annie slapped the rope coiled in her hand against her leg. She made some kissing noises at the horses, pushing them into a faster walk.

After staring at the eastern horizon for about thirty minutes, Gray saddled their horses. Millie had been sleeping for over three hours when he bent down and shook her shoulder, causing her to roll over on her back.

"Wake up, sweetheart."

She blinked and squinted her eyes. "How long have I been asleep?" she asked without sitting up.

"A while. How are you feeling?"

The girl sat up and stretched. Her stomach was sore from all the throwing up, but she wasn't sick anymore. "I'm better," she said. "Do we have any water? Some dog must have slept with his butt in my mouth."

Gray handed her a canteen. "Why don't you walk around a little? I think we ought to try to catch up with the others."

Millie sensed the strain in Gray's voice and jumped to her feet. "Is anything wrong?" she quizzed him, glancing around her surroundings.

Gray motioned to the east. "See the smoke over in the far horizon? I've been watching thirty minutes or so."

Millie stopped rolling up her blanket. "What does smoke mean?"

"I'm not certain, but I think we should move on."

Gray's demeanor frightened the girl. She tied her bedroll on the back of her saddle. "What are you worried about?" she asked. "Daddy," she said when he didn't answer.

Hearing her call him 'daddy' brought a smile and chuckle

to Gray's lips. "I told you. I think it's smoke. I'm concerned about why it's there. A homestead sits over about there." Wehr climbed up on Lena's back, took a long gaze at the sky. "I suspect that's what's on fire." Gray's tone was more somber.

Millie mounted up. "Shouldn't we go see?"

"It's farther than it looks, and there'd be nothing we can do. If their barn or house caught fire, by some accident, they'll have to build them a new one."

"You think Indians are burning the place, don't you?"

Gray took a deep breath; no point in lying. "Well, my guess is a Sioux raid."

"What about the treaty they signed?" Gray shrugged his shoulders without responding. "Shouldn't we try to do something? They might still be alive."

Gray's expression was both stern and yet soft. "If the Sioux set the fire, Millie, those sodbusters are dead. That is the bitter truth. What we need to do is clear out of here." Wehr hated the despair on the girl's face. "It sounds cruel, but it doesn't change the facts. We can't help those folks, and we best think of ourselves."

Gray turned Lena to the north, and both kicked their horses into a gallop. They rode at a stiff pace for three hours, stopping at the top of a bluff. Wehr peered at the horizon when they stopped, looking for dust or any sign showing Indian movement.

Trent and Zach insisted on pushing the little horse herd reasonably hard all day, making Horse Creek an hour before dark. Nellie didn't hear Annie and Jean walk up behind her as she sat staring at the sagebrush-covered hills and ridges. Thick clouds gathered in the west. Although there was still some daylight, it was impossible to see far.

"They'll be here soon," Annie said, sitting down beside her friend.

"He said they would catch us before dark."

"No, he didn't," Jean said while standing. "He said if they didn't catch us tonight, to wait here, and they would meet us in the morning."

Nellie didn't respond. She stared into the falling dusk, thinking she made an unforgivable decision by leaving Millie behind. She should have insisted, sick or not, Millie stay with the rest of the group or refused to let the others go off without her. No matter how expert Gray was with a gun, he could not protect Millie from an entire Sioux or Cheyenne raiding party. Or what if they ran into some plains trash? Whites can murder you as fast as any hostile Indian.

"Let's light a fire and start supper."

Nellie numbly reached up and took Jean's hand. Jean pulled, helping her to her feet. To stop Nellie from worrying, Annie asked her about what she wanted to fix.

"Some of the beef and a few of those potatoes," she said as they walked back toward the men.

The three women had loaded up one pack with new potatoes and onions. They had also put in two roasts, figuring they would cook them the first two nights on the trail. Otherwise, they packed the same things they left High Meadows with: bacon, jerky, cornmeal, flour, and several loaves of bread.

Zach was walking back from the remuda as the women came back into camp. "They've taken care of their thirst and are quieting down. I put hobbles on the mares to keep them from wandering off," he said as he pulled off his boots.

"Wait," Annie said, trying to catch him before he got both off. "Would you take the coffeepot and bring Nellie some water?"

"I swear, how would you make it without me around?" None of the women responded.

Jean threw dry brush and sticks on the fire while Nellie cut the meat up into strips. Trent finished putting up the canvas shelters. "I faced those to the east. I believe we're in for rain from the west."

Chapter Fifty

Gray and Millie rode three hours into the dark before giving up on making Horse Creek. Millie up early was saddling the horses when Gray woke. "Well, I swear, if I knew you saddled horses that good, I'd a slept late every morning." Gray stretched and tried to loosen up his stiff, aching bones.

"I don't see the horse tracks anywhere." Millie turned toward Gray.

"I was afraid we lost them in the dark last night." Gray's lack of concern eased her mind—some.

"How will we find them again?"

"Won't need to. We may have to ride up and down Horse Creek instead of right into their camp, but it won't be much trouble." Gray was not happy about riding up and down the creek for a couple of hours, trying to find the others, but he didn't want to worry the girl. "So, how are we feeling this morning?" he asked in a cheerful tone.

"A lot better than we were yesterday," she laughed. "I guess I'll live, which I doubted for a while." Gray kept limping around like an old cripple as he gathered up the gear. "You're moving worse than old man Crane. Are you all right?"

"Oh, yeah, this knee's a little grumpy. I'll be loosened up here in a little while."

"Do you want to start a fire and cook some breakfast and warm your old bones or climb right on those horses?"

Gray, stiff and hungry, believed any delay in climbing on a horse would be one of life's pleasures. Still, he thought better. "I think we should get going. Nellie's going to be worried sick since we didn't make it in last night."

"I don't suppose there's any doubt about that. The sky's blue and sunny, so are you ready to go find us the others?"

Gray moaned as he put his foot in the stirrup. "I hope we don't have to search too long."

They had been on the trail for over an hour, talking about all sorts of issues important to Millie when Gray became less talkative. At first, Millie thought he might be tired of listening to her ramble about silly topics. "Do you want me to be quiet?"

"No, I'm enjoying you."

"Well, what's wrong?"

"You're sure an inquisitive little thing," Gray said before pointing to the sky over to their right. "Those are buzzards. I thought so, but we're getting close enough, I'm sure."

"That means something's dead, doesn't it?"

"Probably." The innocent tone of Millie's question amused him. They would find a decaying antelope or elk and ride off to join the others. "I better go up the hill."

"I'm not staying here by myself, so don't tell me to."

Gray started to tell her to stay put, but she wouldn't mind him. When they hit the crown, the bile in Millie's stomach erupted into her mouth. "Dear Sweet God," Gray muttered before realizing Millie was about to slip off her horse. He jumped off Lena and caught her in his arms. "Don't look down there, don't," he told her. But she couldn't help herself; some strange force overtook her, forcing her to look. Her eyes darted back and forth across the slope.

"Gray, they're all dead." Hot tears started streaming down her face.

"I know, honey, I know." Gray tried to bury her face into his chest. He studied the area for some movement, some sign of life. Nothing—nothing except pale, lifeless bodies lying among dead horses in the dry brown grass. The naked corpses lay ashen in the bright sunlight.

Deep, grueling sobs shook Millie. Her tears soaked the front of Gray's faded red shirt. He rocked her and whispered, "I've got you, sweetheart." The girl felt so small in his arms. She was a little girl again, a child. If he didn't hold her, keep her safe, she might disappear.

After a few minutes, he pushed her back to see her face and wiped some tears away. "I'm going down. Somebody might still be alive. I'm going to leave you here a little while. Nothing will hurt you."

The girl's face was red and wet. Too numb and too afraid to speak, it took all her strength to nod her head. Gray took a deep breath and let it out. After one glance at Millie, he started down.

Major Crenshaw had seven Sioux arrows in his back and two in his left leg. Gray continued to walk through the bodies of Troop B. Tad Thatcher lay toward the bottom of the hill, stripped, and disemboweled, his gray dead eyes open, staring at the blue sky. The horses near him were rigid, bloated, and stank. The blistering sun had swelled some to almost twice their size. Ned Carpenter was among a small group of enlisted men. His army issue Colt in his right hand. He had powder burns on his temple, indicating in desperation he took his own life.

Gray trudged back up to Millie. "They're all dead. They even killed the horses," he said as if killing the horses was more curious than the slaughter of the soldiers.

Millie put her arms around Gray's neck. "Can we bury them? We can't let them lay here rotting." She squeezed him with all her strength. "I want to bury them. We're not leaving them here to rot on these horrible plains."

Gray untied two shovels from a dead mule's packsaddle. He found a sandy spot, and for the next few hours, they dug a common grave for the soldiers.

Once the pit was deep enough, they went to the nearest body, and with Gray at the head and Millie at the feet, they lifted the soldier off the ground. Once they carried the dead man, a dark-haired private, not over twenty, to the edge of the newly dug hole, Gray sensed Millie unprepared for what they would do next. Of course, she was unprepared. What could prepare a young woman for what they would do next?

"Hang his feet over," he told Millie in a voice filled with humanity. Sympathy for the soldier and for whatever family they left. But mostly, compassion for the girl. Millie followed his instructions, and Gray let the body slip down into the bottom of the pit. The private hit on his feet before lurching forward, landing face-first with a sickening sound.

"Oh, God," Millie cried out. "Oh, sweet God."

Gray grabbed his daughter into his arms and held her. He put his hand on the back of her head and pushed her face to him; she clutched at his shirt with both hands—squeezed fists full of cloth and muscle with all her strength.

"I'm sorry," she wept. "I'm sorry."

"Don't be sorry," Gray whispered to her as he stroked her hair. "You're tender-hearted. Nothing to be sorry about." He paused. "A lot of people would benefit from being more tender. Don't be sorry, sweetheart, don't be sorry."

Millie shook, sobbing again, much like when they first discovered the bodies. Gray rocked her as her tears again dampened his shirt.

"I'm scared, so afraid."

"Because you are a human being. A gentle soul." Gray closed his eyes as he held Millie. *Go to the sound of the shooting. Go to the sound of the shooting.* He hated those words. Fools—fools who thought themselves heroes must have authored the command. *Go to the sound of the shooting…*a high-minded and noble idea, filled with honor and glory. But it held nothing dear for humanity—*Go to the sound of the shooting.* Go to the place of death.

Gray squeezed the girl.

Chapter Fifty-One

By noon, Nellie was in a complete frenzy. Twice she saddled her horse to go searching for Gray and Millie. Twice Annie and Jean stopped her. Now she determined Trent or Zach should go back, but Annie and Jean refused to allow it. They argued for over an hour before Nellie gave up and went to pout alone by the creek.

Jean hated Nellie being so upset. She hated it more because she didn't know what to do. She, herself, worried about her brother and the girl, but sending someone back for them would be a foolish thing to do. They might miss each other by a bluff or two, and two parties would be unaccounted for. Still, that would be the ultimate decision to be made: whether someone would go back searching or push the horses on toward home.

Jean sat down next to Annie at the camp's edge. "What are we going to do? They should be back by now."

Annie thought a moment. "I don't think we should do anything until tomorrow morning. Then we can send Trent back. I'm sure he can pick up their tracks and find them. I doubt

Zach can."

Jean fretted over Annie's response. "That's a long time to wait."

Annie turned toward Jean. "I hope you're going to be my sister-in-law."

Jean thought this an odd thing for Annie to say. A moment passed before she grasped the meaning of what her friend said, and a cold, deep fear cut through her. Jean realized she had never given any thought to the possibility of Gray dying somewhere out on those plains. He came and went for twenty years, but she never worried hostile Sioux or some gun-hand in a dirty saloon might kill him. Now, with him, only four or five hours overdue, she was thinking the worst possible thoughts. "Maybe Trent should go now."

"No," Annie responded, shaking her head. "They're going to show up here." She got to her feet. "That's where I'm putting my faith." She touched Jean's sleeve. "I'm going over to talk to Nellie."

Jean watched Annie walk away. She turned and headed over toward Zach and Trent.

"How's Annie doing?" Zach asked, as Jean walked up.

"She has faith."

"Nellie?" Annie said, walking up behind her.

Nellie turned to Annie. The sunlight brought out the bit of auburn in Annie's hair, and Nellie thought how attractive Annie was standing next to her. "Do you think they're all right?" she asked as Annie sat down.

The sweetest hint of a smile crossed Annie's lips. "Well, I'm trying not to think about them. Because if I do, fear takes over." She wrapped an arm around Nellie. "Look up at the sun and clouds in the sky. The same God who put those in the sky and hung those stars last night is the one I'm counting on to bring Gray and Millie home safe. I figure, by comparison, it shouldn't be hard getting those two into camp," she said with the slightest laugh. "So, I keep concentrating on His abilities instead of Gray's or Millie's."

Annie made Nellie feel better. Still, Nellie couldn't stop

asking, "But what if He doesn't bring them back?"

"He'll be the God who will comfort and carry us through."

Zach and Trent carved a circle on a tree and were throwing a knife to see who could come closest to the center. Trent bounced the blade off the tree as often as he stuck it in. Zach, however, was extraordinary. He never missed the circle and was seldom more than inches from dead center.

Zach's skill impressed Jean. "You're a strange duck, Zach," she laughed. "You can't hit anything with a pistol, but you're a crack shot with a knife."

"The noise throws me off," he laughed. "Here, why don't you take a turn? You might be an expert at this. You sure knifed me plenty."

"Ohhhhh." Jean raised her knee and bent over in mock pain. But she had knifed Zach more than a few times. More than she ever realized.

"Come on over here," Zach chided.

"All right, all right." She reached out, taking the knife from him. "Do I have to hold this thing by the blade?"

"Yeah, like this." Zach held the blade and went through a throwing motion.

"I hope I don't cut a finger off."

"You won't. Throw at the middle of the circle."

Jean reared back and flung the bone-handled Bowie knife, missing the entire tree by at least ten feet. "Goodnight," Trent yelled. "You're worse with a knife than Millie is with a pistol. Don't fling that again 'till I get Sundance away from here."

Jean and Zach both started laughing. "I'll go get it. I want to try again," Jean declared.

"No. You stay here. I'll go. I don't want to be downwind of you with a pig sticker in your hand." Zach told her.

Zach jogged out past the tree, pointing out she almost threw it in the creek. "Yer a distance thrower. I'll give you that," he yelled. He picked up his knife and turned around to walk back. "Well, looky here who's dragging in," he hollered, waving his arms in the air.

Annie and Nellie turned, and seeing Gray and Millie,

Nellie broke into a full run toward them, almost tripping over an exposed tree root, which would lead to a nasty fall. Annie stood and let a satisfied smile break across her lips. "Thank you, Lord." Smiling, she started walking to the man she loved.

"Where on earth have you been?" Nellie asked as she hugged her daughter.

"Well, we got a little lost," Gray said. "We hit Horse Creek way too far to the north. I thought we must be south of you, so like a couple of borderline fools, we rode north up the creek for over two hours. 'Course we had to turn around and double back, and well, we're just now getting here."

For being safe in camp, Millie was downcast, troubled. "We're starved! Have you got anything to eat?"

"We'll warm you up some of last night's meal to tide you over to supper," Nellie said, leading the girl toward the campfire, with Trent and Zach following along.

Annie and Jean were both giving him a "you're lying" glare. "What happened?" Annie asked, skipping any small talk.

Gray took his hat off and checked to ensure the others were out of earshot. He wiped the back of his hand across his mouth. "We rode about three hours after dark trying to make it. With all the clouds, it was black last night. We lost the tracks and ended up about a mile and a half or two miles to the east." Gray put his hat back on. "We got an early start, and I would guess around eight, ran up on all those soldiers. Massacred." Neither woman said anything. Gray always struggled to read Annie's emotions, but Jean was shaken. "They wiped out the men, the horses, the mules, everything," Gray continued.

"Did Millie see all this?" Annie asked.

Oh, yeah, everything," Gray said. "We spent the majority of the day digging a common grave. She got right in and dug with me. Shovel for shovel full."

"How long had they been dead?" Jean asked.

"My guess is three, four, or five days."

"Were they Sioux or Cheyenne? Or, do you know?" Annie asked.

"Sioux. There were plenty of arrows to tell by."

"Could you tell which way they went?" Jean asked, almost whispering.

"Off to the east." Gray kicked at a clump of grass. "But I suspect they'll swing north. I wanted to follow their trail a little while to find out. But, I knew Nellie'd be wetting herself."

"North is the way you think they'll head? That doesn't sound good." Concern crept into Annie's voice, into her entire demeanor. She slumped down on an old tree stump.

"Well, they're east of us, Annie. I'll wager money they hit the Powder far northeast of where we will, and they'll likely follow it straight north to the Crazy Woman. We'll cross clear at the south end. We'll be miles from them, twenty or thirty."

"You don't think they'll stay around here?" Jean asked.

"No, the army will send somebody out looking for those troopers. They won't stay in this area. They'll more likely head back to Fort Laramie and the treaty talks than hang around here."

"Do you think so?" Annie asked.

"Well, you can never tell about the Sioux," Gray answered. "I do think they'll head north and either over into the Black Hills or up into the Tongue River area." Gray paused for a moment. "Listen, I don't want Nellie to know about this. I'm going to tell Trent. I want to find out if he has any idea why those soldiers made such an about-face in their movements. They were at least six days south of where we ran into them." Gray glanced around. "I don't think I want to tell Zach about finding them either."

Jean understood not telling Nellie but was a little skeptical of not telling Zach and asked why not. "I'm not sure, Jeannie; I don't trust how he'd react."

"He did all right when he found those tracks on the way down," Jean countered. "I don't think it's right to hide this from him."

Weariness pressed down on Gray. His knees were stiffening again, and a sharp ache shot between his shoulder blades. "You may be right," he sighed. "Let me rest and think a bit."

Trent was telling Millie a joke as they walked over to the fire. Millie's laughing refreshed Gray because it seemed like a long time since anyone laughed. "What a welcome sound," he told her. "I was afraid you threw up all your laughs with everything else in your belly."

"Don't make me laugh too much. My stomach is still sore."

"When you eat a little dinner, it'll settle down," Nellie said.

During the evening, the setting sun put on a spectacular show along the western horizon. It started with a burst of orange and softened into pinks and lavenders and a dozen blue shades. By the time the quarter moon came up, Nellie and Millie lie on their bedrolls, sleeping.

After thinking about what Jean said and getting Annie's opinion, Gray told Trent and Zach about the troopers. Zach said little, other than to agree with the decision not to tell Nellie. Trent took the news about Ned Carpenter hard and related how Tad Thatcher predicted the green Major would get them killed. A prediction Trent put little stock in. He did not know why Troop B changed directions.

"You would think the army would stop sending out boys and greenhorns to do a job sized for a man who knows his surroundings," Gray said.

"You sure would think the Fetterman massacre would have taught them," Zach added. "But they never learn much."

"Well, I've learned when folks suffer bad days like this one, a good night's rest helps," Annie said as she stretched her arms out behind her back. "I suggest we all turn in."

Gray threw his bedroll down next to Annie's and fell asleep listening to her soft breathing. The night was sultry, and none of the group used any sort of blanket. Zach snored like a bear with his arm over his eyes, and Millie kept moaning in her sleep as she rolled from her right to her left side, trying to escape Sioux arrows and the anguished cries of dying soldiers.

Chapter Fifty-Two

They put in long days, all dry. At night, Nellie dreamed she was lost, traveling in circles. Day after long day, drug on. She baked during the day and froze at night.

An hour after daylight, Jean sat on her gray gelding belly deep in the Powder River, trying to urge one weanling the rest of the way across. She spent the night slapping off mosquitoes and listening to men snore. The lack of sleep increased her aggravation over the colt, remaining stubborn about getting into deeper water. He refused until his mother reached the other side and whinnied.

With all the horses across, the worst of the trip home was behind them. Gray knew one creek about eighteen miles away that would still be running. They would camp at the stream this evening and make it a simple day tomorrow, spending tomorrow night along Crazy Woman Creek. Then a simple two-day or two-and-a-half-days to home.

Everyone took up their usual position: Trent and Millie on the right flank, Gray, Annie, and Zach in the back, and Jean and Nellie to the left. Riding at a leisurely pace, Zach kept updating Gray on some of the horses' personalities. "The Clement mare over there," he said, pointing out one sorrel, "she's cantankerous."

"She's bossy," Gray answered. "But I suspect she'll settle in."

"That little black filly is sure sweet," Annie said. "She's as curious as can be and sure wants to be gentle. If you walk among them, she'll come right up to you."

Gray handed the packhorse's lead rope to Annie and turned a little to the left to roust one yearling, wandering back a little. Gray's bay took to pushing the extra horses along the trail. He figured they cut the boredom for her. "Lena is enjoying this," Gray said as he moved next to Annie and Zach and took the packhorses back.

"If we can raise a bunch of animals half as desirable as Lena, we'll do well," Annie said. "Even prosper."

"You should have ridden your chestnut stud this trip. I could have ridden your black stud," Zach said.

"Oh, fine," Annie laughed. "Luke and Billy fighting and mounting these mares all the way home."

"Well, they would enjoy themselves," Zach claimed. "I'm surprised you ain't tired of all this company and gone off on your own," Zach said to Gray.

"Annie's company keeps me around, not yours."

"Oh, you like my company well enough. I ain't ever taken a shot at you, which is more than can be said for most folks around you as much as I am."

A coyote jumped out of sage a few yards in front of Trent and Millie, startling one of the yearlings. "Whoa, whoa, you're fine," Trent called to the colt.

"That coyote must have been asleep, letting us get so close," Millie said.

As Trent answered her, Zach yelled out, "He didn't have a butcher knife stuck in his hind end, did he?"

Millie started to laugh when Nellie hollered across the horse herd, "Go chase him down and see if he's got my knife."

Of course, Trent didn't know the coyote story, so Millie

took considerable delight in describing the incident to him. "You must be a better knife thrower than Zach is."

"Well, it happened," Millie replied. "Or I broke the blade off trying to open a can of lard. I don't remember. But I figure the coyote's butt tale makes a more exciting story, so don't tell the others about the lard can."

About mid-morning, all four women complained about needing to go to the toilet. There were no trees or thick bushes until they found a little coolie off to the right, and the entire procession halted while, one at a time, they slipped over below the small hill and out of sight.

"Relieving yourself is another advantage of being a man," Zach pointed out. "A woman's gotta find herself a tree or bush to hide behind. The whole plains are one open outhouse for a man. He just needs to face the other way."

Once all four women came back, Gray gave the horses a brief break. They loosened the cinches on both the saddle and packhorses. Jean stretched out on the ground and, using her arm for a pillow, fell asleep.

"How late do you think we'll arrive at this little creek tonight?" Annie asked.

"Oh, early evening, well before dark," Gray answered. "I thought we might ride on awhile past noon and stop when the heat of the day starts to hit."

Nellie started moaning and rubbing her backside. "I think my horse has the hardest gait of any horse God ever created. My butt is so sore. I may walk the rest of the way home."

Annie had also been lying down. She sat up. "If your gelding's too stiff, we can cut you out one of those mares we bought. Clement's daughter rode that dark bay filly all year. She might not be so rough."

Nellie thought about Annie's offer. "Do you think she might be easier on my hind end?" When Nellie asked, she believed the only thing likely to help would be a long soak in her bathtub dreaming little dreams surrounded by warm bath oil-filled water.

"If she has a softer gait, she would," Annie said. "The

Clement girl called her real smooth."

Nellie was interested but a little afraid of getting on a strange horse. There was no point in trading a stiff trot for the chance of being thrown. "Are you sure she's well broke?"

"Kick my butt and call me Charlotte. You are an incurable worrier." Gray took a chunk of jerky out of his pocket, tore off a medium-sized piece, and stuck it between his cheek and gum like a chawing man would a wad of tobacco. "Let me throw your saddle on her. I'll ride her around a little and make sure." Gray got up on his feet, turned to Zach. "Do you know which filly we're talking about?"

"The dark bay standing over there?"

"Would you catch her while I pull Nellie's saddle off?" Zach grabbed a rope, walked over to the filly, and slipped the loop over her head before leading her over to Gray.

Gray threw the stirrup up over the saddle's seat and undid the cinch on Nellie's gelding. "Gray," Annie said. "I think the girl rode her in a hackamore. I stuck one in the packsaddle on the roan."

Trent found the hackamore and put it on the horse while Gray tossed the blanket and saddle on her back. He pulled the latigo tight, stuck his foot in the stirrup, and stepped up. She walked around as sweet as a puppy. Gray trotted and loped her in a couple of circles before pulling her up next to Nellie. "Smooth as she can be. Should give you an easy trip home."

"I appreciate this," Nellie smiled.

"You want to try her out before we start again?"

"No, I trust you. I sure don't need any extra riding."

Annie shook Jean's shoulder and told her to wake up. Jean woke in a stupor. "What day is it?"

Gray stepped behind her, bent down, and pulled her up by her shoulders before giving her hair a light tug. "The same day as when you went to sleep."

Trent tightened all the cinches and volunteered to take four of the packhorses.

Annie held out her hand. "And I'll take the others for a while."

The day passed with the sun beating down and not a wisp of a breeze. The dust and sage gave Annie a headache across her eyes and the bridge of her nose. "I'm ready to be back home," Annie said, licking her chapped lips. "Our valley is never this hot, dry, and unpleasant. Lord, I'm tired of this brown landscape."

"Gold, Annie," Gray said.

"Gold what?"

"The golden plains, Annie. The American Frontier."

"Well, I don't see anything golden."

"I thought the 'golden plains' were in Kansas and Nebraska," Zach laughed.

"This whole area is nothin' but prairie," Gray said. "Flat and windy, But Nebraska, that's a cold place. Winters there make a man ache, hurt you clear down into your soul. Howling winds rip across there colder than a whore's heart."

Gray's fretting about cold weather while sweat was rolling off everyone amused Annie. "Well, I wouldn't mind much if a chilly wind whipped across here."

"You wouldn't want one of those Nebraska northers. They chill you right to the marrow of yer bones. It takes a month of hot weather to recover," Gray told her, not exaggerating a bit. He recalled once getting lost in a winter blizzard in that God-forsaken place. Only by blind luck, he stumbled into Ogallala and saved himself from freezing to death.

Annie wiped the perspiration off her face. "A person can always put on a coat to keep warm, but it's hard to cool off when the weather's like this."

On the other side of the remuda, Jean realized Nellie was riding a different horse. "What happened to your horse?"

"Gray switched him for this filly. You're sure observant."

"When?"

"When you were napping."

Jean stifled a yawn, shook her head, and gave a dismissive wave of her hand. "Napping, my foot. I was stomping on rattlesnakes."

By mid-afternoon, everyone fell half-asleep in their

saddles. Zach did fall asleep for a little while.

Two hours later, the sun scorching the plains, and the air smelling of dust, Gray waved over to Trent and Millie, Jean and Nellie. "Let's give these horses a rest. We've got fifteen miles in." Despite deep tans, everyone in the group suffered from sunburn.

"Suits me fine," Nellie called back.

"How long do you want to rest?" Zach asked Gray.

"Oh, an hour, I suppose."

"I believe I'll take me a little nap." Zach untied his bedroll from behind his saddle. He spread one of his blankets out on the ground and folded the other one up to use as a pillow. In less than five minutes, he fell asleep with his hat over his face. Nellie and Jean also decided a nap would be the best way to spend their break from the horses. Gray and Trent hobbled the mares in case the two of them and Annie fell asleep as well.

"I sure wish there was a creek or something around here to take a swim in," Millie said.

Gray took the top off his canteen and slung some of the water at Millie. "Best I can do."

"You're kind of quiet today, Trent," Annie said.

"Thinking about Ned Carpenter," he answered, after checking to see Nellie wouldn't overhear. "He told me this was his first time west of the Susquehanna."

Hearing Trent bring up Carpenter made Millie sad. She never met him, but Trent mentioned him being only twenty-three. Perhaps thinking about him made her feel so downhearted because twenty-three didn't make for much of a life or because she buried him. Also, Millie figured her parents died at about that age. She thought about how she never liked soldiers, sometimes being rude when they came into the restaurant. She decided she would try to be nicer to them in the future.

"I suppose once we get to High Meadows, I better ride over to Fort Phil Kearny and tell them what happened," Trent said.

"We'll grab fresh horses at our place, and I'll go with

you," Gray said. "We can make the round trip in less than a week, assuming the fort's open."

Neither Millie nor Annie enjoyed hearing this, but it was necessary, so they didn't bother to protest. "Why do you think the attack happened?" Millie asked.

"I'm curious myself," Gray said. "Judging from them being all grouped up on the hillside, I'm certain they fought a defensive battle. As far as who provoked the fight, hard to say."

Annie thought a moment. "Why would the Calvary provoke a confrontation with a sizable band of Indians? From the way you described it, it sounds like a slaughter."

Trent speculated. "I told Gray, Major Crenshaw was a decent man, easy-going, but he hadn't been out here long enough to know how to deal with Indians. He likely provoked 'em without realizing it." Trent took off his hat and hung it on sagebrush next to him. "Remember, some of the Sioux, Crazy Horse, and many others are hostile over the treaty. They want the army out of here now."

"We met Crazy Horse, and he didn't bother us," Millie recalled, thinking back about their brief encounter. She still pictured the four Sioux.

"We didn't threaten him, and we're not military," Annie pointed out.

"I suspect Crazy Horse is a pragmatic fella," Gray said.

"What's pragmatic?" Millie asked.

"He wouldn't start a fight he might not win. The four of them against us would have been nip and tuck." Gray arched his back, trying to push out some of the kinks. "Well, we better head these animals up to water. We can discuss all these deep mysteries of life some other time."

"Millie and I'll wake the others while you two check the saddles and gear," Annie said.

The day continued uneventful, hot, dry, and dull.

Chapter Fifty-Three

The creek was running almost full, odd for this far into the summer. Nellie and Millie slipped upstream a little way for a chilly sponge bath while the others unpacked the gear. As soon as they returned, Annie and Jean went upstream and the three men downstream to take their baths. By the time they got back, Nellie and Millie had supper almost prepared.

"Well, other than Millie's disagreement with her stomach and your awful discovery of soldiers, I'd call it a fair trip," Zach said as they sat down to eat. "I'm almost sorry it'll be ending in a few days."

"Oh, the only thing you're sorry about is the work waiting for you when we get home," Jean said. "Now, let Gray bless this food. I'm hungry."

Chapter Fifty-Four

"Ten or twelve miles, and we'll be sitting in a little grove of Aspen trees on Crazy Woman Creek," Gray said. "Two hoots more, and we'll be home."

Nellie and Millie insisted when they pulled out of camp that since they had not led the packhorses for more than a few minutes, it only fitted for them to take their turn. The morning, fresher and cooler than the day before, got one yearling frisky, prancing and dancing with his head and tail in the air. "About noon when the sun is beating down, that fella is going to wish for some of his energy back," Jean noted.

The day slipped by as easy as sipping lemonade on the front porch. About three in the afternoon, Millie caught sight of some aspens. She turned around and called back to Gray. "Is that the Crazy Woman?"

"I believe so."

The grove of trees and a stretch of green grass along the river made a picturesque scene and lifted everyone's spirits. "This would be a peaceful spot to live," Millie told Trent.

"Except we'd need to cut down the trees to build the

house," Trent laughed. "And besides, I doubt you could endure the loneliness out here."

Within a few minutes of arriving at the aspen grove, the men unsaddled the horses and made a rope corral. The women unpacked some food and supplies before spreading blankets out in the shade.

Everyone was catching a nap when someone yelled out, "Hello in the camp." Gray sat up. It took a moment or two for his eyes to adjust before he saw two men approaching. "We're friendly," the bigger one called out. "Mind if we come on in?"

"Come ahead, but I'd prefer you keep your hands where I can see them," Gray said as he got to his feet. He leaned over and tapped Annie on the shoulder, gave his sister a slight tap on the rump with his foot. "We've got company." Annie and Jean got up, and Jean woke the others.

Judging from their dress, the two men were buffalo hunters. Both tied their horses to one of the trees and walked toward Gray. The bigger man, the one who called out, recognized Gray. "Well, I swear, I ain't seen you in what, five or six years?"

"It's been at least that, Perry."

Perry Dawson, broad, loud, and with quite a taste for whiskey, hunted buffalo on the Kansas, Nebraska, and Montana plains for as long as Wehr remembered. Unlike many in his profession, Perry was an affable fellow who would go well out of his way to avoid an argument, let alone a fight. Gray did not recognize the hunter with him, so he stuck out his hand to him. "Name's Gray Wehr. You boys like some coffee?"

"Gray Wehr? Damn, I heard of you," the stranger said.

Dawson slapped his partner on the back. "And it's all true, so you better be blame cautious what you say to this fella."

Gray poured them each a cup of coffee and introduced the rest of the group, introducing Annie as his fiancée. "Fiancée?" Dawson blurted. "Why would such a bonny gal want to marry up with the likes of you?" Dawson reached over and slapped Gray on the knee as he let fly a boisterous laugh at his joke.

Annie, amused and a bit surprised, delighted in the buffalo

hunter's friendship for Gray. She found him different from what she always assumed these types of men to be. "Oh, I guess I can't resist those green eyes," she smiled.

"Green eyes?" Dawson roared. "Why, by damn, they are green. I never noticed before." He slapped Gray's knee again. "Why ain't you ever told me you roped yourself such a beautiful little filly?"

He turned back toward Annie. "I'll tell you this, ma'am, yer getting a reliable man. I fought next to him in a few skirmishes with Indians and white men both. Treat him gentle."

Annie, touched by the sincerity of his comments, smiled at Perry Dawson. Still, she couldn't help wondering how much this man understood about gentleness.

"I don't suppose you got anything to stiffen up this coffee?" Dawson asked, looking back at Gray.

"Sorry, not even for medicinal purposes."

"I didn't figure you did. You never were much of a drinkin' sort. Dawson laughed loud enough Millie thought they might hear him up in High Meadows. "The chance of runnin' into teetotalers like you is why I always carry my supply with me." Perry reached into his pouch and pulled out a flask. He poured some into his coffee cup and took a couple of slugs straight out of the flask before putting it back in his possibles pouch. Dawson introduced his partner as Piss Roberts. "Piss is from Arkansas, but I don't hold it against him."

Millie burst into laughter, so hard tears sprung into her eyes. She bent over, burrowed her head in Trent's shoulder. Trent lost control, followed by everyone else except Gray.

When he caught a breath, Zach stammered, "This trip has been an educational experience for Millie."

Piss only appeared a little disheartened. "Well, Piss ain't my Christian name. My given name is Harold."

Jean glared at Zach and mouthed the words "shut up" before he asked Harold about the origin of his nickname.

After two more cups of Irish coffee, Dawson took on a solemn attitude. "You might be interested in knowing," he said, looking at Gray, "we ran across Harvey Kehn camped about four or five miles up the Crazy Woman Creek." Gray's eyes flashed at Dawson. Annie and Jean's at each other. An icy chill hit everyone except Trent. "Two others with him," Dawson continued. "One is that half-breed crow; we didn't know the other one. We moved on. Me and Piss don't share fires with men of such cut."

Harvey Kehn murdered, raped, and robbed all over the territory for twenty-five years. His range spread from Montana and Wyoming to Kansas and Nebraska. Not being hung or killed testified to both his meanness and his cunning. He showed no preference regarding killing either. White, Indian, woman, child, it made no difference.

Gray stood and, without a word, headed for the makeshift corral, grabbing Lena's bridle on his way. Annie, quick to her feet, followed him. He slid under the rope holding the horses, and Lena started walking toward him. Gray slipped the snaffle bit into her mouth and the headstall over her ears before leading her back to the rope hanging about four feet above the ground. He raised it for him and Lena to walk under. "Hold this for me," he said to Annie.

"Don't do this, Gray."

"Hold it while she walks under."

Annie reluctantly obeyed. Gray wrapped Lena's reins around a limb and picked up her blanket and saddle. He threw the blanket on her back and smoothed it out before he tossed the saddle on.

"Gray, you don't need to do this," Annie said as he reached under the horse to grab the cinch.

Gray got stiff and curt. "Yes, I do."

Annie took a step back, trying to think of some way to stop him. She glanced at Jean, who, when she saw the expression on Annie's face, walked over to her side. "What are you doing?" Jean demanded in a sharp-edged voice.

"You know what," Gray snapped back, reaching in his saddlebag for his Colt and its gunbelt. He buckled it around his waist and was tying the holster to his leg when Annie touched his back.

"Please, Gray."

Trent and Zach started pulling their horses out of the remuda.

"I'm sorry, Annie. Don't interfere."

Annie's shoulders slumped. She stepped away from him. Her disappointment hiding in the dark, she was defeated. "Fine. Do what you want."

"I will."

Zach and Trent were cinching their saddles. Gray did not ask others for help—ever. "What are you two doing?"

"You going to fight three of them?" Zach asked.

Gray stopped for a moment, pointed at the Remington on Trent's hip. "Make sure that's loaded." Without looking at him, Gray told Zach, "You're staying here."

"What the hell do you mean, I'm staying here?"

Gray's eyes shot over at him. "I mean, you're not going with me. Somebody has to stay here with the women."

"Let Trent stay. I'll go with you."

"No."

Gray sought Annie's eyes. She turned her face away. He turned it back, kissed her without receiving a kiss back. "Don't worry."

Annie refused to acknowledge Gray as he stepped upon the bay mare and turned her upriver. Trent swung up on Sundance without stepping into the stirrup. Zach parted his lips to speak, thought better of it, and watched with his jaw set in silence as the two men rode away.

Chapter Fifty-Five

"You seen the knife I use to cut bacon?" Harley Blaine asked.

"I ain't had your damn knife," Kehn shot back. "Crow, you seen his knife?"

Crow, a half-breed Crow Indian, had been killing and raping with Harvey Kehn for six or seven years. "I ain't seen yer blade either," he said to Blaine, a short ugly man who hooked up with them about six months back. "Are you plannin' on frying side meat again? By God, I'm getting awful tired of salt pork."

"Get off yer ass and go git us something else to eat," Blaine snorted back, tossing the hunk of meat into a frying pan over the campfire.

"I can't shoot what I can't find," Crow said. "We ain't seen as much as a jackrabbit in blame near a week." Crow spat a good-sized wad of tobacco into the fire. "Harv, is there any whiskey left in the jug you got?"

"Some, but I'm workin' on this one. You can grab the one off Harley's horse."

Crow fetched the other jug and sat by Kehn. Harvey Kehn

was fifty-three years old, showed every day of it, but age had not tempered his meanness. A medium-sized man, Kehn had huge hands. Greasy salt and pepper hair hung limp past his whiskered jawline. His skin was a sickening fish belly yellowish-white. His right eye, clouded over by a cataract, matched his wretched disposition. Losing its sight had been a significant irritation because it was his 'gun eye.' Learning to shoot "left-eyed" had been a tedious and aggravating task. "How long you figure 'til we make Cheyenne?"

"Ain't going to Cheyenne," Kehn growled back. "Decided to head north to Bozeman. The weather will be cooler. Nothing in Cheyenne. Hasn't been a decent saloon or a big-bosomed whore since Al Nelson's saloon burned down."

"The whores are all right in Cheyenne," Crow responded. "You want their bosoms to fill up them huge paws of yours. Hell, they wouldn't be able to sit up."

Harley sat down with the other two men. He took a long swallow out of the jug Crow took off the horse, picked something up off the ground, and started to scrape on it with his skinning knife. "You ain't got that scalp scraped off yet?" Crow asked.

"I'm doing an extra careful job. The riverboat captains on the Yellowstone are paying fifty dollars each for Sioux and Cheyenne scalps if they are in top shape."

"Hell," Kehn said, "A few more squaws in camp, we could of become rich men."

"There's other Injun camps, I suppose."

"Leave the horses here," Gray whispered. He and Trent tied the horses to scrub oak and crept toward the campfire. Gray stopped in a clump of willows along the river. He motioned for Trent to kneel. "The one in the middle is Kehn. The half-breed is Crow. The other one is a stranger to me." Gray and Trent crouched down. "You handle the third one. I'll take care of

Kehn and Crow."

"Are we going to walk right in?"

"Unless you want to shoot them from here." Trent never heard of Crow, but he knew about Kehn, a ruthless killer. Shooting from here made perfect sense to him. Gray spoiled the idea. Pulling his revolver, he walked straight in.

Harley Blaine growled at the two men walking into the camp. "Who the hell are you?" he bellowed.

Kehn raised his head, squinting his cataract-free eye to identify the intruders. "I'll be damned," Kehn stood in mid-sentence, grabbing at his gun. Before Kehn cleared the leather of his holster, a forty-five-caliber bullet from Wehr's Colt blew a gaping hole in the center of his chest, spinning him around. The next one hit Crow in the belly, exiting through his kidney as he tried to pull his hunting knife. He shot Kehn two more times, as the killer crumbled to his knees, swearing, and still trying to return fire.

While Gray did in Kehn and Crow, Trent put two slugs into Harley Blaine, one in the jaw and the other in the chest, leaving three men lying dead within a few seconds. As Trent's eyes bounced from Blaine to Kehn to Crow, he thought he wouldn't want Gray Wehr mad at him. A funny thing for him to be thinking.

Of the three murderers and rapists, only Blaine got off a shot as he fell, dying. Although mortally wounded, Kehn was trying to shoot back when he took the last two bullets. Gray gave all three bodies a swift kick. Trent assumed he wanted to make sure all three were dead, which made sense if you didn't want to be shot by a man you thought you already killed. That was the reason Trent decided on, although he didn't rule out the possibility Wehr kicked them all because he didn't like them.

"Let's unsaddle their horses," Gray said.

"What do you want to do with the saddles?"

Cutting a halter with a knife sheathed on the back of his belt, Wehr grumbled something about leaving the saddles and turning the horses loose.

"Aren't you going to take the horses with us?"

Wehr kicked dirt on the fire. "I don't need stolen horses."

Trent almost asked Gray how he knew they were stolen. A foolish question. While looking around the campsite, Trent found a pile of hair next to Crow's body. "Gray, there must be a dozen scalps lying here."

Wehr walked over to Trent. He picked up some of the scalps and sorted through them. "All women and children," Gray muttered in disgust. He tossed the hair back down on the ground. "Mighty brave men," he grunted.

"These might be what got Ned Carpenter and the rest killed," Trent said as he stood looking down at the pile of black hair.

"Well, something got those boys killed. Might as well blame this trash." Gray took the guns off the three dead men, unloaded them, and flung them into the river. He threw all three upriver, grunting as he let each gun loose. Trent watched the pistols sail off into the night, turning over and over until they disappeared before splashing into the river. *So much for "to the victor go the spoils,"* Trent thought.

"Damn," Gray shouted as he let the last pistol go. "Somebody should have caught up with this trash years ago." Wehr was breathing heavily, staring into the darkness. "Hickok had a chance once. But he drug him into some little town on the Kansas and Colorado border instead and locked him up. Two days later, he killed a deputy with three kids and escaped."

Trent stood for a while, not knowing what to do. He went through the shirts, pants, and boots of the three corpses. "What are you doing? We're not going to keep anything," Wehr snarled.

"I wondered what they had on them." Crow's pockets were empty except for some tobacco. Trent found a piece of paper folded up in Harvey Kehn's pocket. "Gray, this fool is carrying around a copy of his wanted poster."

Wehr walked over to the body, and Trent handed him the poster. The flyer had an artist's drawing, although a poor likeness, of Kehn's face and information about a $1,500 reward, dead or alive. It described Kehn's activities as murder, rape, robbery, and debauchery. Wehr wadded up the poster, grabbed Kehn's nose, and shoved the paper in the man's mouth. "If somebody finds him, they can identify his worthless ass."

"Are we going to bury them?"

Wehr was detached. He barely answered. "They've done nothing to deserve burying."

Wehr and Trent didn't talk much on the ride back to camp. When they arrived, they put their horses back into the rope pen and headed toward the campfire, where Annie sat cutting up a couple of sage hens. She was slamming a butcher knife into the birds so hard Nellie finally said, "Annie, the bird is dead. It's not attacking you." Annie threw the knife down, didn't say a word, just walked off up the riverbank.

Jean went over to her brother. "You best talk to her. You mucked yourself up."

"What am I supposed to say?"

"I can't tell you," Jean snapped, "but you better say something." Her piercing blue eyes cut deep. "I'll tell you this, Graham; you need to learn your self-righteous sense of right and wrong needs to take other people's feelings into account. You brought back a nightmare she's been trying to escape for years." She turned away from her brother and marched over to help Nellie with the evening meal, leaving Gray standing alone in the cooling night air.

Millie signaled to Trent, wanting him to step away with her from the rest of the group. "What happened?"

"Killing." Trent caught the girl's eyes with his own. "We walked right into their camp, bold as you please. Gray doesn't say one word, no drop your guns, no raise your hands; he started blasting away at Kehn and a half-breed Indian with him." Trent shook his head. "As soon as Kehn saw us, he went for his gun. He meant to kill us but didn't clear his holster. I don't know what Gray would have done if they'd thrown their hands up to surrender." The young man did know. Wehr would have shot them.

Some of the color left the boy's face. "It was like being lost in the middle of something dark and dirty. I realized the third guy pulled his gun. I'm not sure who he intended to shoot. I sure didn't wait to find out. I shot him."

The boy stopped talking. Millie put her arms around him and lay her head on his chest. "I wonder what Kehn did to make Gray hate him so much?" Trent did not expect an answer.

Millie's breathing was shallow, sad; if breathing can be sad. She whispered. "He killed Annie's brother, and he raped and killed her sister."

Annie was staring upriver, her spirit broken, ready to surrender her will, when Gray walked up behind her. He stopped a few feet away. "Annie?"

She turned toward him. "I cut my finger."

Gray took her hand. Her left index finger was bleeding. "Let me see." He took his neckerchief off. She held her hand out to him, and Gray wiped away the blood. "I don't think this is too bad; squeeze on your finger with this," he said as he wrapped the pale blue bandana around her finger. Annie still had not as much as peeked at Gray. "Are you all right?" he asked in an unsure voice.

She spoke without looking up. "So, you kept your promise." It wasn't a question to be answered. She didn't sound critical, but her tone left Wehr wounded, empty, and not knowing what to say. At last, after what seemed forever, his eyes locked on hers. But she broke it off. She shook her head, staring into the darkness. "I love you with everything I am, but Graham...don't you ever kill for me or mine again." Annie started back to the campfire, but realizing Gray was not following, she turned around to him. "Come on; the meal's ready. We waited for you, and everyone is tired."

Jean had already told everybody, except Gray, she wanted a chance to talk to Annie alone after supper. When Zach and Gray checked on the horses, Nellie, Millie, and Trent went walking along The Crazy Woman. Jean sat down next to Annie. "Are you going to be all right with him?"

"I suppose. I'm not sure."

Jean was taken back by the indifference in Annie's response. "I hope so, Annie." The nervousness in her voice surprised Jean. "My brother loves you with all his heart. But he has some powerful ideas about honor and loyalty." Jean didn't think his ideas so odd. She wanted Annie to understand Gray placed a higher value on honor, loyalty, and promises given.

Annie's eyes flashed with momentary anger. "My mother did not ask for that promise he gave her to avenge her children," she said, her words sharp and cutting.

"No, Annie, she didn't." Jean hesitated, wondering if she should let the issue drop, but she wanted Annie to understand something. Moreover, an urge to defend her brother caused her to speak. "Your mother didn't, Annie. Your father did." The fire in Annie's face disappeared, replaced with disbelief. "Maybe I shouldn't have told you," Jean continued, but it is the truth, Annie. Your father made Gray promise him what he did tonight if he ever found Harvey Kehn."

"I don't believe my mother or my father told Gray to kill somebody."

"Annie, we don't have children. We don't understand that kind of loss."

"They were my brother and sister."

"But not your son and your daughter." Tears glistened in Jean's eyes. "I don't want Gray to lose you."

The emotion of Jean's statement shocked Annie. She reached out and pulled her friend into her arms. Gray and Zach came back from checking on the horses while the women embraced.

"Come on, Zachary, take me for a walk along the river," Jean said as she and Annie let go of each other.

"My feet hurt," he answered without looking at Jean. "So let's go soak our feet," he suggested when he did.

"Good idea."

Gray sat across the campfire from Annie. He had been thinking about what to say to her ever since they walked back for supper. "Life's a hard thing." Gray paused and stirred the fire with a stick. "Half the time, I'm not sure I ever do the right thing." For some reason, fear, embarrassment, he couldn't make eye contact with Annie.

"I think you do fine," Annie said quietly, not because she believed it but because she didn't want to push him down into a still darker mood.

"Fine can sure cause a lot of sleepless nights," Gray answered half-heartedly. "Do you remember the night I came home from going after the man who killed Ben Green's boy? Jean said I got Ben some justice."

Annie had been in the kitchen when Jean told him, but she overheard and remembered Gray's answer.

"You said you weren't sure it was yours to give."

"Annie, I want you to understand something, and I can't say if this makes me a better man or a worse one. I never set out to get justice for Ben or your folks either." His eyes locked on Annie's, seeking understanding. "I'm not sure what justice is, but it sure ain't for me to define." He sighed; his eyes jumped from one place to another, at Annie, into the fire, out into the dark. "I made a reckoning. I guess punishment is a prettier word." He stirred the embers. "I made Kehn pay for what he did...cold hard revenge. If you want a full confession, I didn't care whether it was just or not."

Annie studied his face and features; the man she loved came across tired and aging. She wanted to reassure him. At least she wanted—to want—to reassure him. She couldn't. He wouldn't believe her, anyway. He would think she was saying it because she loved him, which would be the truth.

"How mad are you? Do you still want to marry me?"

Home, she thought. *Home is the answer, home where I can keep him safe, where we can bury this part of him.* "I asked you this before, and now I'm going to ask you again. Will you stay home?"

It wasn't a yes, so the question bothered him. Gray touched her face so softly in the fire's glow. "I'll try, Annie."

Her eyes and her heart dropped. "That's not enough. Anyone can try." She turned away from him. "I want," her voice broke, "no, I deserve more. I want a commitment. I want a real husband."

Gray closed his eyes and turned his head away. For the first time, he realized how much character mattered to this woman. *My God*, he thought, a*re you fool enough to sit here and lose this woman?*

"Annie Laurie, if you'll marry me, I'll never leave our valley again." Either the sound of his voice or his eyes made her believe him. She didn't care. She believed him. "The wanderlust part of me will be dead and buried forever. There'll be no more promises to keep, except never to leave you again."

Annie got up and walked around the fire. As Gray stood, she put a hand on each side of his face. "I love you, and I always, always will. But you have to talk to me. If I'm to be your wife and part of your life, I want to help you through those black periods. You cannot push me away every time you're disheartened. Nor can you ignore my opinions every time they differ from yours. I'm going to give you all of me, Gray. Now, despite what I said on our way to Fort Laramie, I expect everything from you in return."

"How long are we gonna sit here by the river?" Zach asked. "I feel like when my ma sent me out of the room cause she didn't think I was old enough to hear about breeding the cows."

Jean spoke without looking over at Zach. "We'll give them a little longer."

"What are they talking about?"

"I'm not sure." She lied, not wanting to pursue Annie and her brother's issues with Zach. She pulled her feet up out of the water and turned toward Zach. "I, uh," she began, finding difficulty in choosing her words, as she always did when circumstances required an apology. "I need to apologize for the night down at the fort."

"You apologized in Cheyenne."

"I am sorry, Zach. You're important to me." Zach sat still,

staring out across the river. "But," she said, sending a chill through him.

"I knew there was a 'but' coming."

"I need to be truthful with you." Truth was going to be more challenging than she thought. "I can't marry you. I'm flattered," she said, her voice breaking a little with emotion. "I'm very touched you think so much of me, and I care about you, Zach. But not in that way."

She did not want them to, but her words hurt. Nevertheless, she felt it best to make herself understood. "Now I'm going to cry," she said, wiping at her eyes. "Gray says I'm the most emotional woman he's ever met."

"Emotional hell, I think you like being a bitch." Jean was caught off guard. Zach's reply cut deep into her.

Jean sat for a while without responding. He had hurt her. "If I am one, our life and the land make one. We're building something here, homes, dreams. I like to think we have a hand in building a country. It's hard. If I'm unfeeling, that's what made me so. But, if you think I'm trying to be harsh with you or to hurt you, well, you're wrong. Annie, Nellie, my brother, and you are the most important people in my life. Everyone knows how I adore Graham, and I couldn't live without Annie and Nellie. Zach, I put you up with them."

The tears overcame her a little. "You mean more to me than Paxton." The corners of her mouth turned up into a warm little smile. "You treat me better, you're kinder, and I feel more affection for you than I do for him. But I love you like a brother and a friend."

Having decided back in Cheyenne, Zach said nothing; Jean would not hurt him again. They sat in silence until Jean went back to the campfire. A minute later, he got up. He didn't care anymore.

As everyone came strolling back, Annie laughed. "I'll swear you all look worn out."

"It's been a long day," Jean replied. "Nellie and I will clean up these dishes. Trent, why don't you and Millie set up the tarps?"

Zach sat by the fire next to Gray. After Trent and Millie walked off, Zach's frustration with Gray came out. "Why wouldn't you take me along, but you took the Thaxton kid?"

"Zach, you're a fine hand with a horse," Gray laughed, relieved at a shift in the evening's tone. "And regarding cattle, I can't name a better cattleman. You're a loyal friend," Gray paused for a moment and chuckled, "and if I was going to a talking contest, you're the man. But when it comes to shooting, you couldn't hit a barn, standing in it with all the doors closed."

Zach took off his faded yellow bandana. He wiped the sweat off his hatband and his face before tying the ragged cloth back around his neck. "Ain't true, and it gets a little tiresome. My old man told me once I couldn't hit the river if I was standing in the middle. So I got up and threw a stick out in the river, a small stick. I waded out, and bang, bang, bang, bang, four times out of four. So, I could blame sure hit the barn."

Gray poured two more cups of coffee and handed one to his friend and one to Annie.

"I swear, Gray, I think you'd take Jean to a fight before me."

Wehr stretched out his legs. He took a sip of his coffee, cold; he spat it out. Gray threw the rest on the ground and pushed down on his left knee, trying to relieve the ache. "Hell, Zach, I'd take Millie before you."

The two men and Annie sat for a few minutes. "You hit a stick four times out of four?" Annie asked.

"No, I hit the river all four times."

As Annie listened to the two men laugh, so shortly removed from death, she wondered how life had so little value.

Chapter Fifty-Six

The smell and popping of bacon cooking woke Annie. "Well, Annie Laurie, You're a lovely thing in the morning," Gray said.

"You must have terrible eyesight." She pushed some of her tangled hair out of her face, touched his four-day beard as he gave her a morning hug. "You've got gray in your beard. Go shave. I'm too young for an old man. Is everyone else awake?"

"Except Zach," Jean answered.

Nellie had quite a bounce in her morning. "Guess what Trent and Millie told me last night?"

"Oh, I can't imagine," Annie said, smiling at Millie.

Nellie beamed at the two young people. "Are you going to tell them, or can I?"

"Go ahead," Millie laughed.

Annie didn't think she had ever seen her friend happier. "They're getting married."

Maybe it wasn't the time, but Gray loved teasing the girl. "So, is breakfast about ready?"

Millie flung a wet dishrag at him. "You're not getting any."

"When are you two doing this?" Annie asked.

"Well, we hope the second Saturday in October. Trent's folks will have plenty of time to plan, and there shouldn't be any snow yet to spoil their trip."

"This is going to take place in High Meadows?" Jean asked.

"I think the wedding should always take place in the bride's hometown," Trent said. Annie and Jean both wondered whose thinking that was, Trent's or Nellie's.

Millie went over and sat on Gray's lap. "So, can you give me away?"

Gray wanted to make a joke, but too much emotion flooded through him. His voice quivered. "It will be my honor."

"Don't break down." Millie hugged him tighter, with tears welling up in her own eyes. "You're supposed to be happy."

Gray kissed the side of her face. "I am." Gray turned to Trent. "You're getting a sweet girl. Treat her kind."

"I've been given quite the lecture. I believe her mother's exact words were, if you mistreat her, I'll swim rivers of blood to get to you."

"Oh, that's our Nellie, so tenderhearted," Jean grinned.

As everyone laughed, Annie thought about how peaceful and at ease Gray was with Millie sitting on his lap. This gentle and caring side of him, how I love it, she thought.

The work of breaking camp and saddling the horses shared time with talk of the two coming weddings. An hour passed after finishing breakfast before they climbed on their horses to head into the last two days of the trip home.

"We'll ride right along the water about two or three miles and swing off for home," Gray told them as they started to push the horses across Crazy Woman Creek. The Crazy Woman being much smaller than the Powder, none of the young horses experienced any problem crossing.

Chapter Fifty-Seven

An hour into the morning, Annie and Nellie drifted a little to the horses' left into wildflowers growing along a knoll. Excitement over Millie's upcoming wedding kept Nellie talking almost non-stop since leaving camp.

It was beautiful, sunny, with a blue sky. The kind that makes a person happy. The awful thud in her back knocked the breath out of Nellie. For a moment, she expected to fall off her horse. Again, a thud, this time sharp and burning in her left rib cage. Nellie's stomach jerked. Something warm ran over her lips and down her chin.

Delicate bluebells, drooping in clusters, flourished between clumps of sage. They caught her eyes. She wanted to touch them, inhale their sweet aroma. Realizing Annie was trying to pull her down, Nellie leaned into her friend's arms. Screaming for help, Annie laid Nellie down on her right side.

More blood trickled over Nellie's lower lip, spewed as she coughed. "I see Jesus. I see the Savior," Nellie whispered. Annie held her and called her name, but her dear friend was gone.

Millie jumping off her horse made no sense, but she did. She ran toward where Nellie lay. Gray and Lena were at Annie's side when the screams ripped through the air. The Indians tore down the knoll, riding half-naked, faces painted war whoops echoing. Gray leveled his rifle at the one out front and squeezed the trigger. The Cheyenne took the bullet in his chest, flipping violently backward off his horse.

Trent cut through the horse herd toward Millie. As he bore down on her, he leaped off his galloping horse. He stumbled but came up running, jumping over sagebrush and knocking the wind out of her. Still, she kept screaming. Trent let the girl go and spun around to fight.

Jean slid off her gelding, ran to the back of the herd with her rifle. She pulled up, shot at a warrior trying to chase off the horses. Although Jean hit him, she did not kill him or knock him off his paint horse. She fired again, this time hitting the warrior's horse. The wounded animal wrenched back and to the right, crashing down on his Cheyenne rider, crushing the Indian's pelvis. "Start shooting, Zach!" she screamed as she dove next to him. Zach had not yet fired a shot, but now he pulled his pistol and started.

Gray swung his Winchester at a Cheyenne who stormed down on him. The dog soldier took the blow in his rib cage and howled in pain as he toppled off his terrified horse. Gray ripped the knife from the back of his belt and tackled the warrior, stabbing him two, three times as Gray slammed him hard to the ground. He sunk the blade twice more into the Cheyenne's bare chest, taking his life.

Gray again grabbed his rifle, sure five or six enemies still attacked. A brave burst through dust so thick it made vision difficult, with his lance ready to hurl when Gray shot him. Another warrior, this one carrying a Winchester, made a rush at Jean and Zach. Gray leveled his sites and killed him.

The bullet tore into the brave's temple, bouncing him across the high desert. Gray scrambled to his feet and raced towards Lena as the last two Cheyenne whirled and charged their horses toward the crown of the knoll to flee. Gray kicked

Lena into a full-out run through the sage in pursuit of the two fleeing warriors. As soon as he came within pistol range, he jerked the little bay to a stop, aimed his Colt, and shot. The Cheyenne slumped forward before falling.

Trent screamed at Millie to stay put as he tore back up the riverbank. He drew a bead on the last target and squeezed the trigger before the Indian reached the top. Time stopped—the bullet slammed into the Indian's back below the left shoulder blade, catapulting him through the brush and rocks. At first, Gray didn't realize what happened. He yanked back on Lena's reins, spun her around, back toward Annie and Nellie.

Gray jumped off the bay mare. "Are you hurt?" Annie lay with her arms covering Nellie. "Are you hurt?"

"No, no, I'm not. But Nellie's gone. She's gone, Gray." Gray realized Zach was yelling about Jean.

"Jean's hit!" Gray yelled as he grabbed Annie, pulling her with him toward his sister. As they ran by, Gray shot the Cheyenne crippled when his horse fell on him.

Blood soaked the upper left thigh of Jean's pants. "I'm all right," she told Gray when he got to her. Gray stuck his finger in the tear in her trousers and ripped the pant leg open. He tore the sleeve off his shirt to wipe away the blood. After seeing the wound, he put his arm around his sister's head and pulled her to his shoulder.

"It's not bad, Jeannie," he whispered to her, not being entirely truthful. "The bullet didn't go in. It cut a nasty gash but didn't go in."

"An arrow," Jean said as if necessary. Gray reached out for Annie. He sat a moment with them both in his embrace.

"Hold each other; I need to find out about Millie." Gray got up and walked to the creek bank. "Is she hurt?" Millie lay curled up in Trent's arms with her knees under her chin.

"She's not hit," Trent said.

Gray leaned into the steep bank and took his hat off. For a minute or two, he stared at the edge of the water where Trent held the girl. He told Trent to keep Millie down by the creek for a while.

He walked to where Nellie's body lay, dropped to his knees, and put his face in his hands. Gray regained enough composure to pull the arrows out of the woman so dear to him all his life. Gray picked her up and carried her back to Annie and Jean. Every step sent a jarring pain across his nose, eyes, and forehead.

As he lay her down, Jean started to sob. "No, please, Jesus. No." Annie put both of her arms around Jean's neck and pressed her wet cheeks into her friend's blonde hair. Gray chased down one of the packhorses for a blanket to cover Nellie.

"I'm not sure Millie knows she's gone," he said as he headed back toward the stream. Trent was holding Millie. "Millie," Gray said. She trembled as Gray slid down the bank. She fell into his arms. Gray held her with neither saying anything. Without looking up, Millie asked in a whisper if Nellie was gone. "I'm sorry," Gray said as he stroked the side of her face.

"I want to see her," Millie said.

"Are you sure, sweetheart?"

"Yes."

Trent boosted himself up the bank, reached down, and helped Millie to the top. Gray picked up Trent's rifle and climbed back up. Annie, Jean, and Zach sat crouched next to Nellie's blanket-covered body.

Millie started for the others, with Gray and Trent walking behind her, far enough to be out of earshot. "Do you think she'll be all right?" the younger man asked in a hushed voice.

"Eventually, but she's a tenderhearted little girl, probably take a little time."

As Millie approached, Annie and Jean went over to her. They took her in their arms. "I want to see my mother."

Annie took her hand, and the three walked toward the red and black blanket. With Annie and Jean still standing, the girl dropped to her knees and pulled the blanket from Nellie's face. "She looks peaceful." Millie leaned down and kissed her mother's eyebrows. "I love you." Millie sat with her for a minute or two before laying the blanket back over her mother.

Annie knelt beside her, slipping an arm around her shoulder. "She told me she saw Jesus."

When Trent and Gray walked up, Trent kneeled next to the girl. She glanced first at him and then at Gray. "Will you make a travois? I don't want her draped over a horse, and we're not burying her out here."

"No, we're not," Gray whispered. He picked Nellie's body up and carried her over to the edge of The Crazy Woman. "Grab the ax in the packsaddle on the sorrel," he said to Trent. "Why don't you start on the travois while Zach and I gather up horses?" As he and Zach left, Gray turned to Annie and Jean. "Stay right here. This would be the easiest place to defend if anything happens."

"You don't expect another attack, do you?" Jean asked in an anxious voice.

"No. Those were Dog Soldiers. Nobody will be searching for them. Go sit down. Get your weight off your leg. We're going to move as soon as we catch the horses, and Trent gets the sled ready." Gray and Zach got mounted and headed toward the knoll, where the animals stopped running and started to eat.

"Why don't you think anyone will come looking for those warriors?" Zach asked.

"They're Cheyenne Dog Soldiers, Zach," Gray answered, amazed at how naïve Zach was about his country. "Dog Soldiers," he repeated, seeing Zach had no idea about Dog Soldiers. "They're a warrior society. They act as a front or rear guard or a plain old war party. When these braves don't return, the others will assume they've been killed in a battle and move in another direction."

"So, where do you think the rest of the village is?"

"My best guess would be back south of Crazy Woman Creek, a day or so from here. Since the Cheyenne are moving north, this was probably an advance party."

"Dog Soldiers?" Zach said. "You suspect they helped kill those troopers?"

Gray tried not to show his frustration at Zach's questions.

"No. Sioux killed them. We didn't find any Cheyenne arrows."

Rounding up the horses was an easy task, and Gray and Zach returned with the others in only minutes. Seeing the packsaddles on, Jean asked if Gray and Zach re-saddled and packed them. "They were still saddled," Zach answered.

An hour later, Nellie's body tied to a completed travois, they were ready to head west along The Crazy Woman. "We'll follow the Crazy Woman to the edge of the Bighorns, camp on the creek tonight, and head north in the morning. We should be home late tomorrow night."

"Gray, I think you should recheck Jean's leg before we start," Annie said. "Her bandage is blood-soaked."

"I'm fine," Jean protested. "Let's go."

"It will just take a minute."

"I'm all right," Jean snapped, turning her back to limp away.

"Good, I'll only need a minute to be sure." Gray had to force her down on the ground. He untied the bandages and spread the wound with his fingers.

Jean pushed his hands away, took on a haughty air. "Well, Dr. Wehr, can we go now?"

"No, we can't. We're going to sew this up."

"Like hell we are!" Jean tried to stand.

"Stay down; you're bleeding like a steer with its throat cut. Now sit down." After a minor struggle, Gray subdued her. Annie went to the packhorse for a needle and thread. "Zach, go find a stick or a piece of rope for her to bite on."

Jean turned red, shoved Gray away. Her eyebrows dropped and came close together. "I said no!"

"I heard you. But we're sewing you anyway."

Annie came back with the needle and a spool of white thread. She sat down beside Jean and started threading.

Outnumbered five to one, Jean had no choice but to surrender. "Oh God, this is going to be worse than the arrow."

"Do you want me or Annie to do this?"

"What difference does it make?"

Gray chuckled a little as he motioned for Annie to hand

him the needle and thread. "Bite down on this," he said as he took the rope Zach fetched. "Zach, you and Trent hold her down, but don't hurt her," he said as he glanced up at her. Jean lay back flat on the ground, and Zach pressed down on her shoulders. Trent took her feet. "You ready?" Jean took a deep breath as she nodded her head.

She couldn't help squealing and lurching when Gray pushed the needle into her leg for the first time. Jean clenched her fists, driving her fingernails into her palms. The sewing burned; she could feel and hear the thread pull through behind. Eighteen times Gray pierced her and drug the stitch through her raw flesh. Every time, a dull tug followed as he pulled the suture tight and made a knot to hold it in place.

Gray tied the last knot, leaned over, and kissed his sister on the forehead. "You're a brave gal, Jeannie."

Jean let the piece of rope fall out of her mouth. "You better hope you sewed me a pretty scar." She took and let out a few deep breaths. "For a while, I thought I was going to throw up."

As her head cleared and her stomach settled some, Jean protested the thirty-minute rest Gray insisted for her, but she did not protest enough to change his mind. The stitching drained much of her energy, and the break would be welcome.

The day drug on hot and miserable, three times they rode through swarms of mosquitoes, voracious biters. Off and on through the day, one of the women wept. Sometimes they broke down because of the reality of Nellie's death sinking in, other times because of the violent way she died, and occasionally memories of their childhood flooded back.

Annie longed for the end of this horrible day. Dark fell an hour before Gray called a halt to the travel. "If we start early and be home sometime late tomorrow night."

"Let's pull the saddles without unpacking anything," Zach responded. "I'll get some jerky and coffee; we'll eat and head to bed."

As the men unsaddled and put up a rope corral, Jean limped over to Millie, sitting by the river. "Are you all right?" she asked, looking down at her.

"I'll be fine. I wanted to be alone for a while."

Millie's response embarrassed Jean. She almost reached down and patted the girl's shoulder but thought better. Annie scolded her when she came back over to the fire. "Gray will chew us both out if he catches you walking around."

"After riding a horse all day, I guess I can walk to the river and back."

"Are you in much pain?"

"I don't want to go dancing." Jean eased on the remains of an old tree stump hit by lightning in the distant past.

"How's Millie doing?" Annie asked, glancing over at the girl.

Jean shrugged. "She wants to be alone," Jean said indifferently as she rubbed her hand in a circular motion on her wound.

Annie was cutting up some jerky, but the sound of Jean's voice caused her to stop. She stood and walked over to Jean. Annie sat next to her and slipped her arm around her. "Well, I'm sure she meant nothing. She has had no time alone all day." Annie pulled Jean's blonde hair back away from her face and blew on her neck. "You're hot."

"I'm tired. My leg is throbbing." Jean laid her head on Annie's shoulder as a few tears welled up in her eyes. "I think I'm going to go to bed. I'm not hungry."

"We need to change the dressing on your wound first. Let me bring you a fresh pair of pants."

"My brown ones are in the top of my pack. They're clean, and I planned to wear them tomorrow."

"I'll be right back. "Annie headed over to the packs, meeting Gray and the others halfway. "Would you men stay over on the other side of the horses for a little while? I'm going to take Jean another pair of pants and change the bandage."

"How is she doing?"

Annie paused from digging in her pack for the brown trousers, her face tired and drawn. "She's worn out, says she's not hungry, and wants to go to bed. She's hurting, admits her leg is throbbing."

The three men headed back in the other direction while Annie got the pants and returned to the fire. Jean, her trousers off, sat with a blanket draped across her lap. Millie came walking back from the riverbank as Annie unwrapped the bandages. "Are you all right?" Millie asked, sitting down next to Jean and putting an arm around her.

Forcing a smile, she patted the girl's knee. "I'm fine. Annie's going to change the bandage for me. Soon as she's done, I'm going to bed."

"I'm sorry you're hurt, Jean," Millie said, hugging her. Jean would have given anything for the right words to say to the girl. She wanted to tell her how she loved Nellie, how sad she was, but she couldn't speak without breaking down. After a moment or two, Millie stood. "I'm going over to Daddy and Trent."

"We'll call to you when I finish," Annie responded before turning her attention back to the wound across Jean's leg. "I'm going to walk over for some water. I want to wash this out with some soap."

Jean muttered to herself about having a nasty scar as she dabbed at the wound with the bandages Annie removed. The four-inch gash was about mid-way down her thigh and deeper than she thought. So what, being unmarried, no one would see her bare leg.

"I ought to pour some more collodion on this," Annie said as she came back from the river with a coffeepot full of water and a bar of lye soap.

"You don't need to be pouring any more on me! The stuff burned me for two hours this morning." Annie started to argue with her but was too tired.

The men were murmuring on the other side of the rope corral. Zach tapped on Trent's shoulder. "Millie's coming."

The girl stopped and scratched Poncho's ears a little while before walking over to them. "Annie said they'd call us when Jean's bandages are changed." She slipped her arm around Trent's waist. Sweat rolled down her flushed face. "I don't think I'll be able to sleep if a little breeze doesn't pick up."

"I think tonight is going to be still all night, no breeze," Gray said, his voice detached. "I'm going to sit down while we are waiting on them." Millie and the other two men also sat on the ground. When Trent stretched out, Millie laid down, using his legs as a pillow.

Trent started playing with her brown hair. She closed her eyes, enjoying him stroking her hair and cheek. "Your hair is damp."

"I told you I'm hot."

"What time do you think we'll make High Meadows tomorrow?" Trent asked, looking up at Gray.

"By midnight," he said. "I'm not going to wake people up in the morning. We'll let everyone sleep 'till they get up on their own."

"I swear, I think I could sleep forever," Zach said.

Gray scowled at him over his choice of words. But despite her reluctance, Millie had drifted off, no harm done. "You can stay at Zach's," he told Trent. "Jean and I will keep Millie and Annie both at our place tomorrow night."

"I hadn't thought about a place. This day's been like a bad dream."

Annie called over. They had Jean's bandages changed. Trent woke Millie, and they all headed back over to the fire. They crawled into their bedrolls. Within minutes, four fell asleep, everyone except Annie and Gray. He listened to her toss and turn for half an hour. "Are you still awake?"

"I can't get comfortable."

"Do you want to take a walk?" A little later, Annie and Gray walked off along the riverbank as a full moon reflected off the water brightening the night. A quarter-mile or so from the camp, Gray stopped. "Nine," he said.

"What?"

Gray picked up a dirt clod and threw it out over the rippling creek. It broke apart in the air making a hundred little splashes. "Nine," he repeated. "On the way to Fort Laramie, you asked me how many men I killed." He paused and kicked another clod. "But, by damn, not one of them was innocent."

Nine men. Dear Lord, nine men dead. The thoughts raced through Annie's mind. She knew of four: the oldest Bowden boy, the killer of Ben Green's son, the gunman Gray shot at nineteen, and Rudy Gates, whom she learned about in Cheyenne.

That left five men more, so many dead men. "Why are you telling me this now?" Didn't he think she experienced enough dying in the last few days?

Gray tried to think through turbulent emotions. He sat in the grass along the river. He held his hand up and eased her down next to him. "I don't know why. You asked me once. Maybe because of all the recent deaths." He hesitated, not sure how to explain himself. "I guess I figured a little more might not matter much."

Annie sat silent, hoping tears building up would stay in her eyes. Were the tears coming because the man she loved was at last opening up to her or because his life out of High Meadows had been so different? Of course, much of the harshness he brought on himself by putting himself in such rough places. She doubted any of the nine killings took place in a church. His fame, she found out on this trip, reached farther than she realized, and he was not famous as a traveling evangelist.

She thought of two more: Harvey Kehn and the killer with him. *That only leaves three.* Regrettably, she wondered if Gray counted them in the nine. Annie would not ask him. She did not want to know. She knew in her heart.

Gray, pale and downcast, turned toward her. "Precious God, Annie, all those men are dead by my hand. Not counting the eight more I helped kill today."

She stiffened. "Don't count them. They were enemies in battle, and they attacked us."

"Well, they were still men, and they're still dead."

Annie's emotions stormed, vexing her to the breaking point. Anger took over. "Yes, and I hope they're burning in hell."

Gray's eyes locked on Annie before he caught himself.

The harshness was unlike Annie. The look on Gray's face, the disbelief in his eyes, started tears down her cheeks. Her words trembled with emotion. "I'm sorry. That was a terrible thing to say. But, they killed someone I loved, and I hate them."

Gray took the woman into his arms.

Annie closed her eyes and, for a moment, allowed herself comfort before easing him away. "No, Gray, it isn't. I have no right to hate them."

He again pulled her close. "It is Annie. Your feelings are normal."

She let her head lay on his chest. "We committed no wrong in defending ourselves." The words sounded odd to her as she said them. "It's not the killing; it's the hate in my heart for them." She put her arms around Gray's neck and squeezed tight. "Nellie is with the Lord, but I loved her, and this hurts." She took an unsteady breath before she sobbed. "I want her back. I want my friend back."

Gray did not remember the last time tears ran down his face. He wanted to splash some of the creek on his face to wash them away. Yes, clean the hurt and the death away with the cold water of Crazy Woman Creek.

Almost an hour passed before Annie's breathing grew slower and quiet. Gray slid back and slipped her head down into his lap. He lay back and prayed for this tall, thin woman with such a beautiful face. A few minutes later, Gray slept, a sleep filled with anger, violence, and fear.

Chapter Fifty-Eight

At first, Jean was confused. Sleep had taken a firm hold on her and pulled her deep within itself. "Jeannie, Jeannie, get up." Consciousness skirted near enough to recognize her brother's voice.

"I'm awake," she said. Trying to force her eyes open. "What time is it?"

"Almost eleven," Gray said. "I hated to wake you, but we need to go."

Jean sat up and ran her fingers through tangled hair, started to stretch. Her left thigh stopped her. "Lord, my leg is stiff. Did you starch this while I slept?"

"I'm not surprised," Gray replied as she rubbed her hands over the wound. "Let Annie dress this and try to move around a little. Some of the stiffness will loosen up."

Gray went over to help Trent and Zach saddle horses while Annie cared for his sister's leg. "The stitches all held," Annie said as she removed the wrappings. "Didn't bleed much either; that's a positive sign."

Annie started to rip a petticoat into strips. "Where did that come from?" Jean asked.

Annie stopped ripping for a moment. "Out of Nellie's pack. And don't be bleeding too much today, or we'll run out of bandages." Annie finished dressing and bandaging. "You're white as a sheet. Are you all right?"

Jean twisted around, stretched her leg. "I think I need to eat. Is anything left from breakfast?"

"I don't think anybody ate anything. I guess we didn't think about eating." Annie stood and reached down to Jean. "I'll go pull something out; we all better eat something before we start. Are you able to walk?"

"I may be a little slow, but I'll hop around," Jean moaned.

Annie walked over to Gray and asked him to build a fire to cook something up. She nodded toward Millie over scratching her horse's neck. "Is she OK? She's stayed away from everybody almost all morning."

"She's quiet," Gray said. "Trent didn't think she slept much."

"I think I'll ask her to help with lunch. She needs something to occupy her mind a little." Annie headed over to the girl.

Throughout the morning, Millie tried to avoid the others. Silently careening through a range of emotions since Nellie's death, she lay awake most of the night. Overcome by enormous loneliness, when she did sleep, dreams or nightmares disturbed her rest. They took her back to her childhood, to happy times. In the nightmares, again and again, she lived through the Indian fight and seeing Nellie's lifeless body.

Before dawn, the lonely cries of a red-tailed hawk woke her. Since the sun came up, fury twisted inside her, only to be replaced by waves of deep sadness. She went through a burning thirst for revenge, followed by despair. Still, she forced a smile when Annie came toward her.

"How's Jean this morning? She slept a long time," the girl said as she pushed her hair back from her face, revealing her tired and bloodshot eyes.

"She's hurting a little, and I think she needs to eat. You

want to help me fix something?"

"Let's warm up some of the stew leftover in the Dutch oven."

"Zach," Annie called out. "Would you pull the Dutch oven with the stew out of the pack on the sorrel?"

Gray had the fire going and a pot of coffee brewing by the time the women came over. Zach brought the Dutch oven, and they quietly ate until Millie looked over at Gray. "What does Cheyenne mean?"

What an odd question, Gray thought. "It's the French word dog, *Chien.* Early French fur trappers saw them eating dogs. So they called them Chien. Sometime the spelling changed to 'Cheyenne.'"

"They're nothing but savages," Millie replied under her breath. Gray put his arm around her and kissed the top of her head.

Gray did not consider the Cheyenne or any Indians savages. They were doing no more than fighting to keep something, which they would inevitably lose. In their circumstances, Gray would do the same.

As the women busied themselves cleaning up the dishes, a scorpion crunched under Trent's boot right behind Millie. "Better be careful where you step. Everything in this high desert will either bite you or sting you."

The girl turned toward him and slipped into his arms. "I want to go home."

"Tonight, sweetie." he pressed her head against his chest.

Chapter Fifty-Nine

Jean's thigh throbbed beyond any pain she remembered, but she remained determined to ride until Gray decided to break for an evening meal. Besides, they would be heading into the pass in the Bighorns in another hour, which would lead them to their valley and home. Being in the mountains again would ease some of the pain.

Millie rode on the left flank with Annie while Jean and Gray pushed the herd with Zach and Trent on the right side. "There's our pass," Zach muttered to Trent. "I guess we can stop worrying about gettin' attacked by Indians."

Annie Laurie's soft brown eyes darted from ridge to ridge. Every shadow and every movement made her look twice. She came halfway out of her saddle when Millie spoke. "When will they bury Nellie?"

"I'm sorry. Your voice startled me." Annie smiled and paused for a moment, thinking to herself how she hated to answer the question. "I suspect the funeral will be tomorrow or the day after."

Millie's head dropped, she became despondent. "That's

soon." Annie hesitated about responding. The burial would be almost immediate because Nellie's body hadn't been lying in a cool, dimly lit parlor; it had been under a blanket in the hot sun.

"It is soon," Annie said in a hushed voice. So quiet, Millie strained to hear. "But everyone will put aside whatever they are doing to come. We all loved her."

"I wish we had never taken this trip, don't you?" Millie's voice was emotional and muffled. Before answering, Annie whispered a prayer for God's guidance.

"Things turned out horrible." Annie was conscious of rubbing her reins between her fingers and thinking about the smooth leather. "I'm so sorry about Nellie." Tears ran down Annie's cheeks, and her throat hurt, making talking difficult. "Jean, Gray, and I all love you. You'll never be without a family. I wish we could, but we can't have the past back."

Annie drew a deep breath before trying to continue. "Millie, sweetheart, think about what scripture says." She pulled back on her reins. "God's word says He will give us a peace passing understanding."

Annie hesitated again before continuing. "My heart and the scripture. I wish they were telling me the same thing. I wish they were water from the same spring, but our flesh is weak. Our view is only from this side of eternity. Millie, God, says Nellie is with him. He says she is apart from sorrow, pain, and removed from death. No matter how we are hurt, we must put our faith in God. What we face, Millie, does not change the truth of God's word or His promises. He promises to comfort us. We need to open our heart to Him and let Him do it."

Annie forced herself to smile. Her chin trembled when she spoke again. Perspiration beaded on her forehead and throat. "Nellie got to raise you," Annie said. "She got to know you are getting married. She loved you, and now she's with the Lord." Annie's smile grew brighter as she reached out for the girl.

Millie said nothing as tears started down her cheeks. She wiped them away and gave a slight nod of agreement. An hour passed before Millie spoke. "We all die because of what Adam and Eve did. Isn't that what the Bible says?"

"By one man, death came into this world."

"I'm going to speak to those two."

Chapter Sixty

Jean's thigh throbbed as she turned to her brother. "Let's rest and eat something." He glanced over at his sister, struggling off her horse.

"Why didn't you say something sooner?"

"Why didn't you think to ask?"

Gray wanted to apologize, but her face caused him to lead Lena away instead.

"Do you want to find water first?" Zach called back.

"I know where water is," Gray answered. "It'll take us two more hours."

Absent conversation, the meal didn't take long. First, one person, then another, stared over at Nellie's body only a few yards away. As soon as everyone finished eating, Annie changed the bandages on Jean's leg, and the group headed deeper into the Bighorn Mountains.

Trent and Millie were riding together again. Gray and Zach pushed the herd, and Annie and Jean rode the other flank. Annie unbuttoned her breast pocket to check her watch. "Nine-thirty. We've got another thirty minutes or so of daylight. At the pace we're going, we'll be home about one in the morning."

"You take the room you always use. We'll put Millie in the other guest room," Jean said.

"I'll take her home with me tomorrow. She can stay until she's ready to go back home."

Jean couldn't see much—movement in the trees off to the right, no more than an odd reflection in the light or a shadow out of place. Maybe it was real, perhaps imagined. A chill shuddered the length of her body. She was afraid for the first time since the snake threatened her. There hadn't been time to think during the Cheyenne fight, no time to be scared. Now, time crept, with nothing to fill emptiness except foreboding fear made worse because what she feared was vague, faceless.

"What's wrong?" Annie spoke only in a whisper, but her voice still caused Jean to shudder.

"I think I saw something in the trees."

"Like what?"

"I'm not sure."

"An animal?"

"I don't know...something moved...I think."

"Let's go back to Gray. We'll tell him."

As the two women turned their horses, movement came out of the trees, not a light reflection or a shadow. Riders. "Indians!" Jean whirled the gray around, buried her heels into Jack's flanks as she and Annie fled.

Annie, yelling Gray's name, dug her boots into her horse's side and tore toward the back of the little horse herd, panicked at the sudden disturbance. They took off in the general direction Annie and Jean were heading. One mare slammed into Zach's sorrel as several others ran by screaming and whinnying.

"Come on!" Trent screamed, grabbing the reins of Millie's horse. He spun both horses around and kicked his bay into a run as his eyes darted back and forth across the landscape, scouting for something; a downed tree, a ridge, anything offering cover.

Gray stood in his stirrups, waving his arm frantically over

his head. "Whoa, whoa. It's Paints His Horse!" Gray was trying to bring something, people or horses or anything back under control. "It's Paints His Horse!"

Gray's yelling brought the others out of their blind panic and back to their senses. Jean was embarrassed and a little disgraced by the hysteria she started. She thought Indians were tearing out of the pines, whooping and shooting arrows at her.

The Sioux, nine, stopped when Annie and Jean started all the chaos. Gray figured it quite a sight from their view. "I swear," Gray groused at his sister as Trent and Millie rejoined the group. "What set you off?"

"I thought we were under attack."

"Well, no harm done, I suppose," Gray said, showing some empathy and managing a bit of a smile. "Zach, you, Trent, and Millie bunch up the horses. I'm going to take Annie with me over to the Sioux." Gray waved his arm at the Indians, still sitting on their horses outside the trees, motioning them to come over.

"You probably scared them half to death," Gray chuckled as he and Annie started toward the Lakota.

"I think they took ten years off my life."

"We're a little jumpy," Gray said as they rode up to Paints His Horse, the Lakota chief and friend.

"You're lucky your horses did not run further." Paints His Horse smiled. "Are you coming home from Fort Laramie and the talk of a treaty?"

They sat together in a tight little group as Gray told his Sioux friend about their trip. Paints His Horse took the news of Nellie's death hard. He spoke harshly of the Northern Cheyenne and said he was happy for how the fight came out.

Dusk's shadows began providing some welcome relief from the heat when Annie, Gray, and the Sioux rode over to Jean and the others. "Paints His Horse offered us lodging for the night. I told him we wanted to go home, but if anyone disagrees, we can stay in the village." Gray told the Sioux chief he worried about the time already spent taking Nellie's body home, but he didn't want to repeat that in front of Millie.

Millie almost protested about going to the Sioux camp but caught herself and sat, hoping no one would want to stop. "I think we should move on home tonight," Jean said, settling the issue.

Paints His Horse and his warriors rode with them a few miles before breaking off for their village. Minutes after they left, Gray told Annie, he was a little surprised at how hard Paints His Horse took Nellie's death. "I'm not," Annie responded.

"No?"

"I'll talk to you about it someday." Gray wanted to press Annie but decided to let his curiosity simmer. Enough secrets had been shared on the trip.

For the next couple of hours, they rode higher into the Bighorns. "We should be thankful for this bright moon," Annie said as they approached the top of the rocky trail leading down into their valley. "I'd hate to lead these young horses down on a coal-black night."

Gray called to the others to hold up a minute and gather around Annie and him. "Let's make a little plan before we go crashing down this mountain."

Millie was taking over Nellie's role as the group's worrier and set her eyes on Gray. "Zach, you throw your saddle on the sorrel mare we got from Clement and take the lead. I believe the others will follow her right on down. Trent and I will ride right behind. The rest of you stay back some. If any of these horses start down off the trail, let 'em go. I don't want anybody hurt in the dark."

Annie pulled out her gold timepiece and tilted its face toward the moon. "Ten minutes till one. We'll be home by two."

"We're only about an hour behind our expectations," Zach said as he loosened the cinch on his gelding.

Trent looped a rope over the Clement mare's head and led her over to Zach. "I hope Clement told the truth about this mare being broke," he chided Zach.

"If she's not, I'll reach the bottom ahead of you," Zach

laughed. A couple of minutes later, they had the horse saddled and bridled. "Well, we got no whiskey, so we may as well find out if they'll follow mamma home." Zach gave a little wink to Millie and reined the sorrel to the front of the herd. "Come on now." Two colts followed, and as soon as Gray and Trent made kissing sounds, the others started right out.

Zach led at a slow and careful pace, though being so near home made him comfortable in his surroundings. For the first time since they left Cheyenne, Zach was at ease. The relief of being close to home renewed Zach's gift for gab. "I swear, Gray, these are smart horses. They're coming right along."

Gray, too tired to get into a conversation with Zach, didn't respond.

"You remember the little black gelding I used to own?" Zach yelled back.

"I hope nobody's camped out here wanting to sleep," Gray called back. "Cause you'd sure keep 'em awake."

"What kind of blame fool would camp out here on the side of a mountain?" Zach glanced down ahead of himself and reined the mare a little further to the inside. "Now, do you remember my little black gelding or not?"

"Yeah, he had two white socks." Gray gave up any hope Zach would let the ridiculous story drop.

"That's the one. Well, one time, me and the little black started down through here, and damn if we didn't jump up a grizzly."

"You best watch where you're going,"

"Why? This mare can see as well as I can."

Trent couldn't help laughing at Zach. Gray shook his head and told the boy they'd be listening to this the rest of the way home. "So, this bear gets to chasing after us, and that horse decided he'll escape faster without me. He throws me. Leaves me all alone, face-to-face with this Griz."

"So, what did you do?" Trent asked.

"What did I do? What could I do? I got et! A bear's got no moral qualms about eating a man."

"Don't you ever tire of hearing yourself talk?"

Zach hesitated before answering. "Millie. I didn't mean to offend you. I thought I might bring a little laugh to the end of an awful day. I won't say anything else."

Millie wished for her words back. After riding a little farther on, she did apologize. "I'm sorry, Zach. Forgive me."

About thirty minutes later, after telling Millie she didn't need to apologize, Zach led the horses off the mountain trail and out into the long valley of home.

Chapter Sixty-One

Sleep for Millie again came with difficulty, and she didn't wake until almost noon. Annie asked her if she would like some lunch, but she declined. "Where's Daddy?"

"He went into town. Jean's up in her room resting. Her leg is bothering her quite a bit."

"When will he be back?" Millie sat at the end of the kitchen table.

"I wouldn't think much longer. He left about seven-thirty." Annie sat across the table. The red and white oilcloth tablecloth stuck to her bare arms. "We're in for a warm one today." Annie swiped two fingers across her forehead. "But I suppose in the second week of August. We should expect hot weather."

"Has Trent been over yet?"

Annie regretted not mentioning Trent when Millie first came down. "He and Zach came in about an hour-and-a-half ago. They went to take the horses over to my house. They'll be back in another hour or so." Millie got up, walked over to the sink, picked up a cup, and started working the water pump handle. "Do you want to ride over and meet them?" Annie asked, hoping because she was so tired, the girl would say no.

"I guess not," Millie said between drinks. "By the time we saddle, they'll almost be back."

"Let's go sit in the front porch swing," Annie suggested after a few minutes of silence. "Hopefully, there will be a little breeze."

Millie didn't want to go anywhere. It would take an extreme amount of energy and effort to walk back to the table. She couldn't think of any reason for continuing to stand in the kitchen, so she asked Annie if she wanted a glass of water to take along.

The swing hung from the top of the porch by two chains. Millie wondered why they used such heavy chains to hang a swing. It accommodated three people and made the expected funny creaking sound, swinging back and forth.

Nuisance, the Wehr's black dog, came out from sleeping under the porch. He climbed up the stairs and sat down in front of them. "Hello, Nuisance," Annie said in a voice sounding like baby talk. "How are you, Nuisance? Huh? How are you?"

Nuisance whined when Annie said his name. "Come on, come on up here." Annie helped the old dog up. He snuggled between them with his head on Annie's lap. The dog carried a small scar above his left eye, where Gray, teaching him to avoid rattlesnakes, bounced a rock off his head. Gray coiled up a dead one in the front yard, and every time the pup approached, Gray threw a rock at him. Jean called "it a mean thing to do," but Gray countered it was better than what would happen if he ever "tore into a rattler."

Millie rubbed the dog's belly. "I don't think you missed any meals." The two women sat talking for the next half-hour, wishing Gray would come back from town.

Chapter Sixty-Two

Gray cut off the trail and headed for Seven Brothers Creek. A few minutes later, he climbed off Luke at the top of a steep bluff. He tied the chestnut stud to a tree and started down the side. About halfway down, exposed roots zig-zagged through the path. Below, the trail forked around an old tree. Gray wished he could still run down this hill blindfolded and at full speed. Those carefree days had long passed, become lost in time. He kept his eyes open and was cautious about where he put his feet.

Once at the bottom, he stood next to the creek, thinking about the bluff, which gave the two boys so much pirate treasure and many animal bones masquerading as early settlers' bones. They drug a net through the creek countless times, catching everything from fish to crawdads, snakes, and angry snapping turtles.

Once, they cornered a possum along some rocks, but the possum didn't play possum. Instead, he fought. To this day, Gray remembered how savage his pointy teeth were when he bared them and hissed. He made several short charges, forcing the boys back into the safety of the water.

"Kick my butt and call me Charlotte. This was quite a place to grow up, wasn't it, Danny?" There was no answer. Only one boy was alive. Danny Tucker was long gone, dead at nineteen. Not from any terrible illness, no grand accident, no one took his life. He died in his sleep.

His dad died within months, and his mother, about a year and a half later. Without explanation, one day, his sister left the valley. No one had any idea where she went. She disappeared. Gray's memories of her weren't of the young woman who left. He remembered her as an eight or nine-year-old girl. He couldn't remember anymore why he and Danny thought the little blonde-haired girl to be such an aggravation.

Gray sat down on an old stump to think a little about his childhood friends. "Well, Danny, I lost Nellie Bascomb. You remember what a flirt she was. Hell, it may have been my fault. I should never let them talk me into going." Gray sat for the better part of an hour throwing an occasional rock into the creek and remembering one childhood adventure after another and considering death coming too early, so much too soon. The climb to the top was steeper than for a young boy.

Chapter Sixty-Three

"But I would not have you to be ignorant, brethren, concerning them which are asleep, that you sorrow not, even as others which have no hope. For if we believe the Jesus died and rose again, even so, them also which also sleep in Jesus will God bring with him. For this, we say unto you by the Word of the Lord, that we which are alive and remain until the coming of the Lord shall not prevent them which are asleep. For the Lord Himself shall descend from Heaven with a shout, with the voice of the archangel, and with the trump of God; the dead in Christ shall rise first; then we which are alive and remain shall be caught up together with them in the clouds to meet the Lord in the air; and so shall we ever be with the Lord."

"Think for a moment." The pastor said as he finished reading the scripture. "Think about things you enjoy. Think of the people you love. I love my wife. There is no one I would rather be with than her. I love to fish. Alan Joseph and I share that passion." The Reverend turned his eyes toward Annie and smiled. "Annie loves walking through the meadow along the riverbank behind her home, watching the horses graze in the pasture. And, Millie, how Nellie loved and enjoyed you." The pastor scanned the congregation. "While you think about all the things you love and enjoy, think about this: a loving God provides you with all these things. He takes pleasure and enjoyment of your enjoyment in them. But now, let me ask you, is there anything God would give us to enjoy more than Himself? Above all things, God wants you to enjoy Him, to enjoy Him as your God and your Father."

The preacher stopped and stepped out to the side of his pulpit. Another smile flickered across his face. "Some people like to think their loved ones who preceded them to heaven spend all their time looking back down to earth watching us. I can't imagine such a thing. Millie, I believe this with all my heart your mother is having the most wonderful time possible. She is in heaven, a place of golden streets, of jeweled buildings...and, praise God...she is with her Savior and her God. I'm sure her parents are giving her the grand tour," he laughed. "I believe she's being held and hugged by Jesus Himself. She is in glory. Her joy is complete. If she has time to think of us, the thoughts she must be having about us are that she can't wait for us to join her in that glorious place. So the question is this, have you accepted Jesus Christ as Savior? Have you confessed to Him you are a sinner, repented, and asked Him to forgive you and come into your heart as Savior and Lord? Because once having done so, you can rest in total assurance you will one day be in the glorious place Nellie Bascomb is today."

Pastor Haggerty closed his Bible. He stepped down out of the pulpit, took hold of Millie's hands, and whispered to her of his admiration for Nellie. In the next few minutes, Millie Bascomb withstood being hugged, kissed, consoled, and comforted by everyone in High Meadows.

After the funeral, Trent and Annie took Millie back to Annie's house. Everyone else in the valley went to Nellie's restaurant for Gray to tell them about the new Sioux treaty. Eighty-seven of High Meadows residents gathered to learn the truth about all the rumors.

By pre-arrangement with Gray, Zach Joseph acted as the moderator for the meeting. Zach explained each section as presented to them. He told them all the forts along the Bozeman Trail except Fort Fetterman would be closed, and unceded Indian Territory would border their valley. Despite the detail of his report, most of the townspeople directed their questions to Gray, which irritated him because he was struggling with the emotion of Nellie's burial.

Quint Swain lamented over Fort Phil Kearny closing. Gray twisted in his chair as he answered the question. "You must understand many decisions came before we arrived. The Peace Commission signed the treaty. They were only waiting for a few Indian signatures. If not for Annie, this valley would belong to the Sioux."

Others wondered if the treaty would mean anything without Red Cloud signing. "I doubt it," Gray said. "But the Military and The Peace Commissioners think he'll eventually agree."

After another hour of discussion and squabbling about minor issues in the treaty, the people of High Meadows were pleased. Life would not change much besides the inconvenience of traveling further for dry goods and other supplies.

After congratulating Gray, Zach, and Jean on their mission's success, they told them to be sure to thank Annie and Millie when they got back home. Within three-quarters of an hour, all the townsfolk started to wander off toward home.

Chapter Sixty-Four

Graham gasped when Annie stepped through the doorway. More beautiful than any angel, her dress and veil shimmered as white as new snow. Tall and slender, she started down the aisle. Gray thought she was gliding above the floor.

Zach whispered as he leaned over to his friend. "You are a lucky man."

"Yes, I am."

As she walked, Annie's eyes and thoughts fixed on Graham. He was standing in a glow coming through the church's stained-glass windows, looking so handsome in his frock coat. His wavy hair brushed along his collar at the perfect length. He shaved the mustache he sported since before their Fort Laramie trip.

As soon as she came close enough, Gray reached out and took her by the hands. He strained to resist the urge to lift her veil and kiss her. He wanted to turn and say to the preacher, "let's make this as short as possible; we want to go home." But knowing Annie would cherish each moment of the wedding, he stood straight and smiled, drinking in all her beauty like a man dying in the desert would do if given water. The kindness of the pastor's words touched everyone present. Their friends clapped long and loud when he pronounced them "husband and wife."

Gray wasn't a touchy person. Being touched made his palms sweat. He kept glancing to his right, how many more people stood in this receiving line. The eating and dancing were a welcome relief to the kissing and hugging he endured with a silly smile on his face.

At home, Gray carried Annie over the threshold. She peered into his eyes with so much intensity Gray thought he could taste her gaze. "Thank you," Annie whispered as she kissed his lips.

"For what?"

"For giving me what I have wanted all my life."

www.ingramcontent.com/pod-product-compliance
Lightning Source LLC
Chambersburg PA
CBHW060625100726

47907CB00006B/1766